The Last Oracle

Book Three of the Sibylline Trilogy

To Dad & Maelyn

Love
Delia J. Co

A Novel by Delia J. Colvin

www.DeliaColvin.com

Firefly Press

The Last Oracle
Published by arrangement with the author
All rights reserved.

Fiction 1491059192
Paranormal Suspense Saga

Can love defy death itself?
The Last Oracle is the final book in The Sibylline Trilogy, weaving a conspiracy that dates back to Greek mythology, with a modern tale of eternal love.
As Alex and Valeria's wedding draws near, their secret plans are discovered
and now no one is safe!
To triumph over the dark forces that threaten their existence, they must risk returning to the underworld. Hidden in a secret chamber along the River Styx is the first oracle, Myrdd, whose jumbled mind holds the key to their survival. But Myrdd's solution forces Alex and Valeria to confront death, for a chance to change their fate!
THE SIBYLLINE TRILOGY - a love more enduring than life...than death...than destiny.

For Delia's blog, FAQ, and more of her books, go to:
www.DeliaColvin.com
Or e-mail her at DeliaJColvin@gmail.com.

To the gracious lady who was my mother,
who passed away during the writing of this novel.

To my father who loved her
and has been an amazing inspiration to me.

And to that brilliant and beautiful,
redheaded bundle of joy, Aubrey.

THE SIBYLLINE ORACLE
Voted Goodreads Best Book of June 2012
Selected as Digital Books Today "Great Read" June 2013
"A mix of the easy charm and undying love from *Twilight* but the intelligence, wit, and mystery of *The Da Vinci Code.*" Author/Blogger C.M. Albert
"I have a new favorite author!"

THE SYMBOLON
Voted Goodreads Best Books of November 2012
"Ms Colvin takes; Greek Mythology, and turns it into the most evocative, engaging, and visually arresting characters I have ever encountered." Al Hatman, Author
"One of the best books I've read in years!"

THE LAST ORACLE
Voted Goodreads Best Book of September 2013
"The thrills come a mile a minute with the creative and descriptive writing of Delia Colvin." Debbie Denney of Espacularaiesa
"The masterpiece of the trilogy."
"Amazing!"

CONTENTS

"It is love, not reason, that is stronger than death."
Thomas Mann

CHAPTER 1

"Do you ever wonder if the eons we have been on this earth have been an utter waste?" The man's voice echoed, and despite the words, he seemed to have more strength than typical, as of late.

The woman peered up from her tome and considered his comment for a moment. She would have been beautiful—she had been beautiful—until envy and insanity permanently ravaged her once angelic face. Some level of truth began to carve its way past the confusion and rage, and then she rejected it.

"I should have been with him," she said resolutely. "He was promised to me."

From the other room, there was a roar of laughter that echoed through the dark stone halls, followed by a rage of hacking.

"Why do you laugh?" she asked in a moment of clarity. She listened to his raspy attempts to breathe, which quieted after a moment.

"You hear and see what you wish. When the gods saw your inability to control your temper, and your susceptibility to Envy's bite, you were written off from history." Instantly, he knew this was the wrong thing to say to the woman who now had no control over her sanity or rage.

"After all I have done for you, why do you speak to me this way?" Kristiana asked. Aegemon relaxed, he had not invoked her wrath. She continued, not particularly interested in the conversation, her mind absorbed with the tome. "If not for me, you would have never seen Apollo's oracles. You would have been obscure in all of history and you would have been dust eons ago."

Now his voice took on a bitterness she had not heard in some time. "If not for you, I might have been walking the gentle slopes of the Elysian Fields for an eternity. I was happy until you came. I felt fortunate to have been chosen as Apollo's most trusted. If not for you, I might have had the love of a woman and a family. Instead, I lie here in this tomb that you call home.

"I saved you," she said calmly, flipping a page in the tome. Suddenly, her voice took on an evil thrill. "Here it is—I knew it was still possible!" Her eyes looked up as her mind became engrossed in wild machinations. She smiled and nodded. "I know just who can help me with this!" She tapped her finger on the page and then rose, the previous discussion forgotten. "I need something of his...a personal possession. Something...Oh! Yes! Yes!" She paced from room to room. "Where could it be?" Losing patience, she raised her voice in accusation, "Did *you* take it?"

He didn't respond. When she was like this, it was better to hide.

"I had it. I kept it. I know..." She located an ancient chest and pushed it open. Her once beautiful curls, now unkempt and knotted, fell on the jewels in the chest. She tossed the items behind her and they clanked loudly and echoed throughout the halls. "Someone must have taken it...perhaps it is..." Suddenly, she released a loud, frightening shriek as she held up the locket and chain. *"I have it!"* She walked back to her perch at the tome and stared at the page.

"I have only one remaining vision of the future. The Fates selfishly refuse to assist me anymore...after all I have given them!" Her fingers flexed nervously as she tried to calm herself. Then, delicately, she opened the locket, pulled out the lock of hair it concealed and kissed it tenderly. She breathed deeply and whispered to the lock of hair, "It is only with the greatest of love that I use this, so that our lives will not have been a waste! With this, I shall see through your eyes."

CHAPTER 2

Still in a state of sleep, Valeria brushed her hand over the sheets next to her, somehow instinctively sensing the distance between her and Alex. She reached out for him briefly, before succumbing to the dream.

Mist rose and enveloped the base of the woman's sandaled feet. Even with her steel helmet, and the bronze hair that spilled from the sides and back, she was beautiful. In front of her, she boldly displayed a weapon with a long, wavy blade whose reflection was so bright that it would blind any opponent. Her eyes were clear blue and there was strength in them.

She sang a song that sounded like a lullaby that had been transformed into a battle march, "Kame nana na kimithis...Kame nana na kimithis..."

Behind her trailed her other weapon, the hideous creature known as Envy.

The she-warrior approached the temple and bravely stepped inside. There was a spinning wheel surrounded by three sisters. One wove the cloth. One bound the cloth. And one held her shears and coldly awaited the moment when she would end a life. They were the Fates.

Valeria breathed deeply; something about this dream troubled her. Her hand brushed across Alex's chest and, in his sleep, he rolled toward her, eliminating the distance that had been between them the previous month since their arrival in Africa. She luxuriated in the feeling of his touch and sensed the curling of the corners of his mouth in that beautiful, sensual smile. He sighed happily, still asleep, as his hand moved under her shirt and onto the flesh of her back, pulling her into him…confirming to Valeria, that he was, indeed, asleep. Within seconds, she was back to her dream.

Lightening struck the mountain top as the three white-robed women climbed the steep path in near darkness toward Zeus's home on Mt. Olympus. There was a green tinge to their formerly ivory skin. Behind them, Envy perched with a smile.

A lightning bolt struck with a nearly deafening clap of thunder. Instantly they were back in their own room with the spinning wheel and their business with Zeus was complete.

The oldest sister, with her hand on the spinning wheel, shook her head in anger. "I have seen the vision of the mortal woman and the child."

The youngest, whose complexion had turned even greener than her sisters, snipped her shears in the air and attempted to hide her private smile.

Holding a ball of yarn, the middle sister's anger quickly escalated to rage and she began to pace. "Apollo knows that we, alone, determine the destiny of mortals. How could he grant immortality? How could Zeus permit this?"

"Zeus is too busy with his mistresses to be concerned about his off-spring. Apollo obviously has no respect for our position," said the sister with the scissors.

Attempting to calm the situation, the sister at the spinning wheel said, "Perhaps there has been a misunderstanding."

Turning coyly, the sister with the shears asked, "Sister, Apollo has created immortals! Immortals who were not born gods?"

"If that is the case, we must end this! How many of these immortal oracles are there now?" the sister at the spinning wheel asked.

"So far, one hundred have been created."

"One hundred? Well, let me assure you sisters, there will be no more! The one hundredth is the last of the oracles!" The eldest said. "We shall call the green-eyed one to do our bidding."

"How is Envy to destroy one hundred oracles with her venom?" the youngest asked, while slamming the shears closed.

"She need only plant the seed and then focus on the most powerful. The first oracle is half-mortal...his human weaknesses will be his downfall. Envy must focus on the last oracle. Handle her, and the rest will fall."

There was a knock at the door and, immediately, Valeria reached across the feather bed and searched for Alex in the darkness. All she found was the cool sheets and empty pillow where he had been hours before. She didn't need to look at the clock—the knock meant that it was 4:30 a.m.

"Mrs. Morgan?" Toma's deep voice rumbled. He knew she wasn't "Mrs. Morgan," at least, not yet. It was a bit of a sore subject for Valeria at this point.

"Yes, thank you, Toma." She rolled her legs toward the floor as her feet searched the cold tile until she located her slippers; then she flipped on the lamp. Valeria stood while pulling on her robe and glanced at the coat rack, noticing that Alex's coat was missing. She frowned as she pulled her long brown hair back from her face and opened the door.

A tiny Zulu woman stood in front of Toma with a tray of coffee, a beautiful china cup and saucer—that Valeria would never use—a ceramic travel mug—that she preferred, and a plate of still steaming biscuits. The woman placed the tray on a table, exiting without a word. Valeria thanked her and then glanced at the giant who was her bodyguard.

"What time did he leave, Toma?"

"I couldn't say for certain. Shall I interrupt Mr. Morgan?"

She knew Toma was aware of the exact minute that Alex had left, but refused to divulge anything that could cause trouble.

"No, thank you." She frowned.

Closing the door, she went to the dresser and pulled out a pair of jeans, a T-shirt, and a hoodie. It was July in Africa—winter in the southern hemisphere. During the day, temperatures were wonderful. But the morning game drive, which was conducted in the dark in order to see the nocturnal members of the "Big Five," could be cold.

Alex, Valeria, and Caleb had been in South Africa for a month, staying in a luxury camp near Kruger National Park. The huts were fantastic with their feather beds, spotless tile floors, and baths—but they were also without heat.

It had been thrilling to be in Africa with Alex, the love of her life, the man who had waited 3,000 years to have a life with her. And she loved that Caleb was with them, too; her perpetual twelve-year-old superhero with an electrical shock that barred him from most human contact, except for Valeria.

After the four painful months they had been separated by order of The Council of Delos, the month of togetherness had been greatly needed; at their reunion a month prior, they had vowed to marry as soon as they could find someone to perform the ceremony.

Since then, Alex hadn't mentioned it again. Truly, the only reason it concerned her was that he was adamant that they wait to consummate their love until they were married. Valeria had lived long enough with distance from the man she desired more than anyone.

As she laced her boots, the door swung open and her beautiful Alex stepped into the room. She immediately noticed the dark circles under his brilliant blue eyes. He was just coming back to sleep, she surmised. He brushed the scruff on his chin, and then she caught a spark in his eyes as he pulled her into his arms and kissed her gently.

"Working?" she asked.

A glint of mischief entered his eyes for a moment, and he nodded. "Mm-hmm."

She wrapped her arms around his neck. "I don't really need to go on another game drive. I could stay here."

He sighed deeply and kissed her neck. It was more romance than she had experienced with him since their arrival in Africa.

"I think you had better go."

"Are you sure?" she asked in her sexiest voice.

Drawing a deep breath, Alex pulled back. "I believe this is Caleb's girlfriend's last drive. What's her name?" He reached over and lifted a biscuit from the tray on the table, and took a bite. The moment was over.

There was no way around it; Caleb wouldn't go if Valeria didn't go. He had saved their lives twice now. And for the first time in his

2,000 years, he had a friend his age—well, the age he had been for over 2,000 years.

The young girl giggled furiously whenever she saw Caleb. Thanks to a rubberized suit, the boy could actually sit next to her at dinner. And if she touched him—as long as she didn't touch his head or neck—she wouldn't get shocked.

"Her name is Amy Smythe, and her family is leaving tomorrow. You're right, I should go." Alex pulled off his sweater and she watched him admiring his well-carved frame. He ran his fingers through his thick blond hair. "You know, it would be nice if you actually slept *with me*," she said with mock severity.

Truthfully, she was hurt by his seeming indifference to her. It made her feel as if she was over-sexed and unattractive to him. Every night he held her, but he always kept his distance. She was ready to eliminate the distance and felt frustrated that he had yet to find someone to perform their wedding ceremony.

There was another knock at the door. "Mrs. Morgan?"

It was time to go. She glanced at Alex. "Can we talk about this later?"

Alex stepped toward her and touched her face, his eyes filling with so much love that she felt ashamed for doubting him.

"Absolutely," he said, and kissed her lightly.

She smiled and then grabbed her coat and her coffee mug. Outside in the dark, she nodded to Toma, who had a large semi-automatic weapon slung over his shoulder. Toma, Caleb, or Alex were constantly watching over Valeria. She had hoped Alex would be the one watching her most of the time, but business had distracted him.

The stars were brilliant as she stepped off their porch and onto the trail. The camp had just come to life and she could smell the coffee brewing from the main lodge.

Toma followed her to their Land Rover. A guide would normally sit at the wheel and describe what was occurring, telling the guests about what they were seeing, while the tracker sat in a wire mesh chair that was attached to the hood. In her vehicle, by special arrangement with the camp, her bodyguard, Toma, drove.

Every morning, after returning from the game drive and breakfast, Valeria would ask the tracker, followed by Toma and Caleb, of course, to walk with her to the entrance of the camp. Animals scavenged the camp at night and she was fascinated by the various footprints that she identified with the tracker's assistance. She was proud to have become quite good at recognizing the prints.

Toma offered Valeria a hand as she climbed into the elevated back seat of the vehicle, and then he sat behind the wheel. Mick, their English guide, was already sitting on the passenger side; and Zamy, the Zulu tracker, buckled himself into the wire mesh seat. Valeria glanced toward Caleb who was standing with Amy's family at their Land Rover.

"Let's go, buddy!" Valeria said.

"Oh…okay." Caleb pouted as he headed toward her. Alex had stopped going with them on the game drives a few weeks before, after he had confirmed her safety. He seemed to be working so often that it caused Valeria to believe that he must be having some financial concerns. She wasn't worried. From the time she was sixteen years old, she had lived on her own with nothing more than her daily income from selling her floral creations near Central Park to feed, clothe, and shelter herself. If need be, she could do it again.

But Alex always had money at his disposal, until the day they left all of their worldly possessions to escape the beheading promised by the Council of Delos. Now, he was unable to access those resources. She wished he didn't have to worry so much.

"We have room. Can't Raiden—I mean Caleb—ride with us?" Amy begged.

"We would love for you to join us. We have plenty of room," Amy's mother added in her clipped British accent.

Well not "plenty" Valeria noted. There was no room for Toma, and Alex had insisted that Toma accompany her. But seeing the hope in Caleb's eyes, she jumped from the back of her Land Rover.

"Mrs. Morgan, I don't think that's wise," Toma said from behind her.

"It'll be fine," she said, glancing to him from over her shoulder. Of course, he was already following her.

Toma scrambled around to meet her. "Mrs. Morgan, I assured Mr. Morgan that—"

Valeria raised a hand to brush off his comments. "I'll tell Alex. We don't need to trouble him with this."

With that, she swung up into the back seat of the Smythe's Land Rover, while Caleb, with an excited grin, slid into the front seat beside Amy. The tracker and guide were pros. They knew how to handle an aggressive animal, and it certainly didn't require a *bodyguard!*

As they pulled out, Valeria saw Toma making a call on his radio. Alex had never been cross with her, but he certainly would not be happy about this.

"Tattletale," she muttered to herself.

She shook off the thought and enjoyed feeling like a fairly normal person...although, since she fell in love with Alex, life was too extraordinary to be considered normal.

The guide to this vehicle passed Valeria a blanket for her legs and then pulled into the blackness of the African bush. The Land Rover's headlights briefly illuminated the dust flying up from the road as the vehicle began to move, He was driving faster than typical. She realized that the guide was concerned about an additional delay, risking that there would be fewer animal sightings, which determined his tips.

Ganya, their Zulu tracker, turned on his flashlight and began shining it into the brush rapidly, left and right, as they drove. When they had first arrived, Valeria questioned the tracker about a set of glowing eyes that she had spotted.

"Rodents," the tracker said without delay, or sometimes, "birds." As rapidly as he had glanced at the glowing eyes, she couldn't imagine that he'd actually identified the creatures. But the guide would always patiently stop the vehicle and back it up. The tracker would illuminate the creature with his flashlight and, to her surprise, he was always correct.

Valeria marveled as the sun began to rise, lighting up the enormous African sky. It was nearly black to the west and the palest of blues to the east, with light pink-feathered clouds brushing the blue of the sky, as the yellow and orange orb rose above the horizon, touching the rounded top of an acacia tree.

Mrs. Smythe leaned around her husband and asked Valeria, "Have you seen the hippos yet? They took us to the river yesterday and it was the most marvelous experience!"

"Oh, I would've loved to have seen them!" Valeria wondered why her guide hadn't taken them to see the hippos.

"It really was fantastic!" Mr. Smythe said. "Of course, it is a bit of a jaunt to the river by foot. But you really must see them."

Now Valeria understood why her guide hadn't taken her to see the hippos. Leaving the vehicle was against Alex's rules. Just then, some static sounded on the radio and Alan, the Smythe's guide, picked up the mic and spoke into it.

"Sorry, mate, can't understand a word you're saying," Alan said into the hand-held microphone. Valeria felt relieved, as she was certain that Toma was setting the rules of the drive and that would certainly not include seeing the hippos. A few minutes later, she thought she saw dust rising in the distance.

"Would you like to see the hippos, Mrs. Morgan?" Alan asked, bringing the vehicle to a stop.

Glancing to Caleb, who was still heavily engaged in conversation, she hesitated for no more than a millisecond before responding, "Yes, I would!"

Jumping out of the vehicle, she saw that Caleb was holding hands with Amy. Getting out of the vehicle would mean he would have to release her hand, and he might not get his nerve up again. The boy lowered his brow, clearly torn, as he glanced from Amy to Valeria.

"Caleb, why don't you stay here? We won't be long." She smiled at him.

He offered her a guilty nod. Alex would not be happy about any of this—particularly that she had left the Land Rover. The first lesson of safari was that as long as you didn't stand or separate yourself from the vehicle, the animals perceived the 4x4 and its occupants as a single, large animal. By leaving the vehicle, the danger mounted exponentially.

Also, hippos were known as the most dangerous animals in Africa, killing more than lions, crocodiles, or even the unpredictable and foul-tempered Cape buffalo. The hippos, with their enormous canines and incisors, were known for being extremely aggressive and unpredictable, and worst of all, unafraid of humans. In the mornings, when the hippos would graze outside the river, unprovoked, they could suddenly charge at up to 18 mph and snap anything from canoes to people in half, without missing a step in their lope toward the safety of the river.

But Valeria justified that the guides wouldn't take her to see them if it was truly dangerous. Besides, other guests had gone down to the river and all had been fine.

The trail of dust on the road behind them climbed higher, no doubt with Toma's increased speed. She was certain that Toma wouldn't hesitate to physically stop her if he had the opportunity. Alan threw a rifle over his arm as they headed toward the brush that surrounded the river. Suddenly, she glanced down and froze as she lowered her brows.

"Alan, umm, I have a question."

"Yes?"

She pointed to a paw print, in the tan dust, that was larger than her hand. Based on the sharp ridges, it was very recent.

"Isn't that a lion? That's huge. It must be a male," she said.

Alan glanced down. "Yes," he said as he grasped her elbow, rapidly moving her back toward the vehicle.

Toma was now fifty feet from them. He was typically expressionless, but even from this distance, she could see that he was angry. She saw Caleb's sudden awareness that he had left his post of protecting her in a dangerous environment, and then guilt for having been so distracted.

"Caleb, it's fine." She smiled at him.

Just then, a loud roar sounded from not so far away.

Alan turned his head toward the source of the sound as he lifted Valeria back into her seat.

"Let's go!"

Picking up the radio, Alan alerted the others to the location of the lions. Lion sightings always thrilled their guests.

They drove off in the direction of the roar. Down a trail, they spotted a family of hyenas. That was always a good indicator that lions were near. In Kruger, the hyenas scavenged the lion's leftovers— bones; due to that, their droppings were white. Their guide had told them that in other parts of Africa, the hyenas did the killing and the lions were the scavengers.

The family of hyenas turned slowly to mosey on, leaving one lone baby hyena that was half the size of its parents. As they drew near the creature, Valeria was stunned to realize that the "small baby" was the size of a giant Labrador retriever. This suggested that the parents easily stood at least four feet tall and were possibly two hundred pounds or more. Caleb, sitting in the front passenger side, was thrilled as he looked at the hyena with great affection. Immediately, the hyena hung its tongue out of its mouth and panted, as if anxious for a belly scratch.

Caleb glanced back at Valeria and she responded instantly, "No! We cannot take him home!" Alan and the Smythes broke into laughter.

Toma pulled up directly behind them as they turned to cross a deep ravine, and then drove alongside the savannah of tall golden grass.

The peacefulness was suddenly purged by a lioness that burst through the grass no more than five feet away from them. She let out a deafening roar, which was not the least bit suppressed by the bloody shank of an animal that hung from her mouth. The lioness shook her head violently from side to side.

"She's telling the others in the pride that the rest of the kill is hers. It's a sign of dominance. The others must be near," the guide said, excitedly.

As they pulled forward, there were four giant cats sprawled around a bloody spot in the middle where the kill had been. Valeria was staggered to see how close they were to them. Toma's Land Rover almost bumped up against theirs.

"Looks like they got a bok," Alan said. She had already heard that "bok" was Africaans for antelope. She had seen them in all sizes, from the enormous wildebeest, which were considered an antelope, to the tiny twenty-pound dik-diks.

"The females do the hunting at night. If that kill had been large enough, they would have taken it back to the pride. The females need this bit of food so that they have the energy for the next chase."

One of the cats began playing kitty games with Valeria. The lioness got closer and, suddenly, Valeria thought about how the mouse typically ended up as dinner in kitty games.

"Is this normal?" she asked as her fingers pulled the blanket up higher on her legs.

"Don't worry, mum. They do this…sometimes," Ganya, the Zulu tracker, said calmly.

The cat's eyes were enormous amber orbs that never moved from Valeria. The lioness did pretend lunges toward her several times.

"Cool!" Caleb shouted in an excited voice and Amy giggled.

"Look at that creature! Magnificent!" Mrs. Smythe said as she adjusted her camera.

"Are we all right here?" Valeria asked as the lioness moved closer to her.

"Driver! Move on!" Toma demanded.

Alan rolled his eyes. He was not about to permit an over-zealous bodyguard to destroy his guests' pleasure—or his tips. He knew his job better than anyone else and had never endangered a guest.

From the corner of her eyes, Valeria saw that Toma had his hand on his rifle. It would *not* be good to shoot this gorgeous creature because it got a bit too friendly. Besides, there was no telling who would die if the shot wasn't perfect. Still, Toma had been selected for not only his instincts and judgment, but for his ability to shoot accurately.

The lioness suddenly lunged and stepped onto the edge of the Land Rover toward Valeria. At that moment, despite her nervousness, she heard the clicking on Toma's rifle and knew he was now poised to shoot this magnificent creature. As the cat rubbed its face against her legs, Valeria realized how small and insignificant she was next to it, and she fought the instinctive impulse to stand and run, knowing that would be deadly. She saw Caleb's expression—a combination of extreme guilt and awe.

"Caleb, stay where you are!" she ordered with as much authority as she could muster, with the lioness stepping up toward her. It sniffed her knees and ankles.

"Mum, they do that to me often and never bite as long as you don't stand. Do you understand?" Ganya asked. Alan was too dazed to say a word. "Mum! Do you understand?" the tracker demanded again.

"Yes," Valeria said warily, trying to find her voice.

Then, with a slight growl, the lioness moved its face near Valeria's. Nearly holding her breath, Valeria was stunned with terror, and also by the beauty of it.

"Mrs. Morgan, I want you to *slowly* move your head to the right," Toma said softly, but with authority.

If she moved to the right, Toma might decide to fire. She didn't want the lioness to be shot. But she did wish it would move off the vehicle.

Continuing to snap her camera, Mrs. Smythe leaned forward around her husband.

"It *is* interesting how close the animals come and yet we are so perfectly safe."

No one else could speak. Without removing her eyes from the cat, Valeria thought about how Mrs. Smythe was on the other side of her husband and separated by two people...or as Valeria thought at the moment, two meals, perhaps having already had a snack. Mrs. Smythe would be brought back for the rest of the pride; add Mr. Smythe's ample gut to the mix, and they would have a full meal. From the corner of her eyes, Valeria could see that Mr. Smythe's face had lost all hint of its ruddiness and his eyes were as large as saucers. Obviously, he was thinking the same thing.

Finally, the creature stepped off the vehicle, and the driver pulled forward as the lioness lunged toward them again. Valeria worried that Toma was about to fire; then the lioness stepped back and permitted them to leave. She drew a deep sigh of relief, especially when she saw Toma replacing his rifle into its cradle along the dash.

In a mixture of the shout that travelled between Land Rovers and the crackle that came over the radio, she heard, "This drive is over! Return to camp, *immediately!*"

As the Land Rover headed off through the dust, Mrs. Smythe was the only one to speak. "That was just thrilling! I shall share it with all of our friends and I am certain they will all wish to partake in this extraordinary experience! It is amazing how safe I felt; as if the animal was in a zoo."

Sitting next to Valeria, Mr. Smythe was pale and his voice was breathy. "My dear, I have no idea what you are talking about! I was certain that this young woman was cat food!"

∞

Arriving back at the camp, Valeria glanced at Caleb who bowed his head in shame as he headed toward the lodge headquarters—the only location with Wi-Fi and telephones—where Alex had established his office.

"Caleb, let's get breakfast and then why don't you and Amy play a computer game."

He looked uncertain.

"Come on. Alex will hear about it soon enough," she said, placing her arm on his shoulder. "It was my responsibility to do what he asked." The boy shook his head and she saw tears brimming his eyes. "You're still my superhero…and I'm still whole. Superheroes only come to the rescue when they are needed. Obviously, you weren't needed right then."

Caleb drew a deep breath and hugged Valeria. She could tell he was about to break down so she muffled his hair and tried to lighten the mood.

"So, Amy, huh?"

Caleb blushed. "She's okay…for a girl." He glanced up at Valeria. "But not as good as you."

She raised her eyebrows and sighed. "Yes, well, she's a sweet girl."

He nodded, relieved that he could delay telling Alex that he'd failed to protect Valeria. Sitting at their elegant outdoor table, they feasted on scrambled eggs and bacon. Alex typically joined them for breakfast. She wondered if he was still asleep—although after Toma woke him, which he most certainly did, Alex would not have gone back to sleep. Frankly, she had expected to see Alex in the Land Rover with Toma. Now she was glad Alex hadn't been there.

She glanced toward their hut just as the maid stepped out, leaving the door open as she shook out a rug. No, Alex wasn't sleeping. Valeria glanced toward the lodge office and saw that the doors were closed, for once. Then she noticed that Toma, the Smythe's guide, Alan, and both of their trackers were all missing from breakfast. The trackers and guides typically joined the guests for meals, to share their adventures and answer questions. Valeria hoped their absence didn't have anything to do with the occurrences on the drive, but she was certain it did.

She was tempted to go directly to the office and take full responsibility for her actions. Then, in a moment of cowardice, she changed her mind; she would let things cool down a bit first. She needed to go for a walk, but that was forbidden without Toma; instead, she headed back to the hut, opened her Kindle, and read Hemmingway.

After several hours, she realized that even Hemmingway couldn't hold her attention today. Her mind kept wandering back to her dream the previous evening and the lioness's response to her that morning. She took a nap and when she awoke, she realized it was dark again. No one had knocked for the evening game drive. She suspected Alex had called a halt to her participation in the drives. But it was her only opportunity to get out.

She was surprised that she hadn't seen Alex at all today, except for a few brief minutes before the morning's game drive. She had expected him to come by and gently remind her of the rules. She was certain that not seeing him was a bad sign. He had never gotten upset with her, but she had an inkling that this was going to be a first.

Rising, she went to shower and decided that she would face the situation head-on. As the water ran over her, she fought her insecurities, assuring herself that Alex loved her. Still, something was going on. His prolonged absences were getting even longer. And now, evidently, his work was calling him late at night.

After drying her hair, she pulled on her underwear and a blouse and, without buttoning it, stepped out of the bathroom. To her surprise, Alex was there sorting through some things on the bureau. He immediately turned to her and his grin expanded into a dazzling smile. She felt immediate relief.

Then she realized, a minute too late, that her shirt hung open and, although she was covered, it was more revealing than she had ever been with him before. He drew a deep breath as he reached for her and pulled her into him.

"Love the outfit," he murmured into her neck, as his arms went around her waist.

Suddenly, she was pleased with the decision.

They were interrupted by a knock and a woman's voice, "Dinner, mum, sir."

She briefly wondered why Toma hadn't knocked, but at the moment, she was entirely too distracted to care.

"Let's stay here," she whispered into his chest.

Alex pulled her in tighter and then released a tense laugh. "You know it's Caleb's friend's last dinner with us."

"Caleb is 2,000 years old. He doesn't really need us watching him 24/7." She kissed his neck and brushed her hands down his chest.

Alex stepped away from her, but the glow was still in his eyes.

"So, no game drive tonight, huh?" she asked, keeping the flirtation in her voice as a bulwark against any possible upset.

Alex grabbed the open edges of her shirt for a moment, eyeing the uncovered skin across her stomach hungrily; biting his lip, he began to button it as he cocked an eyebrow. "It seems that my presence is required if you are to attend the game drives."

"Toma! I knew it! I told him that there was no need to trouble you with it."

She was fully aware that her lapse in his "rules" had very nearly cost them her life. In fact, if she hadn't been so thrilled, she would have been terrified.

"Oh, Toma was only once source. It seems you are the talk of the camp," he said, as his eyes focused with amusement on the buttons; finally, he hooked the one above her breasts to cover the temptation. He brushed the side of her face and then shook his head, pushing aside his thoughts of her and their closeness. His eyes became suddenly serious. "Beautiful, you do know that there is a lot of danger here…and not just from the council."

"Yes, I'm sorry, Alex, but nothing happened and I wanted Caleb to have a chance to spend more time with Amy. She is such a sweet girl."

"*And,* his interest in Amy keeps him from falling too far for you." The single corner of his mouth turned up.

Yes, Valeria had thought of that. She was the only person in the world that Caleb could touch without wearing his gloves. Mani believed that because Caleb had revived her with his electrical force, something happened so that she was no longer affected by it. Since then, Caleb had developed a major crush on her.

"By the way, where is Toma?" Valeria asked as she slid on her jeans. Alex continued to watch her as he leaned against the bed.

"Toma is fine," he said, distracted by her. "He wanted to go back home to his family in the South."

Valeria's jaw dropped. "Alex, you fired him!"

Shaking his head, Alex glanced back to her. "No. He quit. Well, actually, it was by mutual agreement whereby Toma accused the guide of placing you in danger and the guide and tracker accused Toma of almost shooting them. I decided it was best if Toma left, and the camp managers agreed…and so did Toma."

"I'm sorry," she said, feeling incredibly guilty and suddenly understanding the closed doors at the main lodge.

"Don't worry, I gave him a year's wages. He left happy…and told me never to call him again." Alex picked up a cracker from a tray and bit down. "I think you seriously took ten years off the man's life."

Valeria laughed as they walked to the door. But she wondered how Alex could pay all that money to Toma when they were obviously in financial straits.

The bonfire in the near distance lit the outdoor dining area. Caleb was already there with Amy and the Smythes. She also noticed a new couple who was sitting at their table.

Alex stopped, suddenly wary. "Beautiful, why don't we sit at a different table tonight? I thought we would give Caleb a bit of privacy with Amy on their last night together."

"Okay." She shrugged, and he led her to a table near the entrance of the dining area. They feasted on wonderful South African wines, delicious wild game, and fantastically seasoned vegetables prepared al dente.

One of the guides told a story in front of the campfire about a pregnant woman's harrowing escape from her neighboring country and giving birth in a tree while the lions prowled below. As soon as the guide uttered the last syllable of the story, Alex stood.

"Would you mind terribly if we called it a night? I still have quite a lot of work to do. But I'd like to make certain you get back to the room in one piece," he said and hooked her arm. Just then, Valeria saw that the new couple, who had been sitting with Caleb and the Smythes, were walking toward them. Alex picked up his step and Valeria sensed the other couple picking up theirs as well.

"Professor Morgan, so this must be your lovely fiancée," the man said, loudly enough so that Alex couldn't pretend that he hadn't heard.

Instead of stopping, Alex increased his pace even more, while turning his head slightly. He said over his shoulder, "Yes, Tom, I apologize but we are in a bit of a hurry."

Glancing at Alex, Valeria wondered what had come over him. So as to not be rude, she stopped and turned. Alex's face fell slightly.

"Hello. I guess you know, Alex. I'm Valeria." She held out her hand to the man.

"Yeah, I'm Tom and this is my wife, Liv."

Valeria glanced at Alex again. There was something odd about his reaction. She was certain the couple felt it, too.

"You're from the states," she said, feeling the necessity to overcompensate for what seemed like rude behavior from her typically gracious fiancé.

"Yes, Wheaton, Illinois, near Chicago," Tom said.

"Nice to meet you!" Liv gushed. "We're so excited. This is our first safari."

"Wonderful. I'm sure you'll enjoy it here," Valeria said.

"We never thought we would be coming to Africa. Then our daughter decided to marry our former youth pastor. He's just taken a position in an orphanage here is South Africa and asked my husband to perform the ceremony in the wilderness."

"Tom, you…you're a pastor?" Valeria's eyes lit with excitement. She squeezed Alex's hand, but she sensed him tense even more.

"Valeria, Alex told us that you would be busy tomorrow, but I do hope you change your mind and join us. I'm certain Dave and Donna would love to have you there," Liv said.

With this discovery, Valeria's heart sank as Alex's jaw tightened. Opportunity had knocked and Alex had not only backed down, he was avoiding it. She noticed his frozen expression as the words sprang from his lips lacking his typical cordiality, "Thank you."

Liv went on, unaware of Alex and Valeria's internal battles.

"I'm certain you both have planned something better than getting married here in the wilderness, but for Donna, it is the wedding of her dreams."

"Yes. Thanks for the offer, Liv, Tom. I'm certain we will see you around the camp. Now, if you don't mind, we really must be going," Alex said as he grabbed Valeria's hand and tugged her toward their hut.

"Goodnight," Valeria mumbled, still stunned. Although it was dark, she could now sense that she was being watched by several guards.

The discovery that Alex was actually trying to keep her from meeting the pastor hurt. But she needed to put her hurt feelings aside and just ask Alex what was going on. It was a given that they would be married far away from their friends and family. Truly, she could do that. Even the previous year, when the plan had been to marry at the beautiful home in Greece, all she wanted was her family and friends from Morgana.

But she was prepared—and totally accepted—that they would be married in front of a herd of wildebeest at sunset, instead of her family and friends; wearing jeans, instead of the beautiful gown that they had selected. She accepted the idea that they would spend their wedding night in this luxury hut, instead of the comfort of their beautiful cottage where she had always imagined their first night of intimacy would take place...exactly as Alex had envisioned it 3,000 years before.

The troubling part was that she might never see her friends who, over the course of only a few months, had become the only family she had ever known. Now Valeria, Alex, and Caleb were fugitives from a council who believed in removing heads before discovering facts. And seeing their family again was a risk they couldn't take.

Still, their previous wedding plans—the dreams they had of that ceremony and of their wedding night—were merely extravagances. The only thing she really wanted, and desperately needed in life, was Alex.

As they entered the hut, Valeria took his hand.

"Does your reluctance to marry have to do with Kristiana?"

"Kristiana?" Alex was taken back. "No. Is she an issue for you?"

"No, not really. I guess I wonder if the reason you've been hesitant to marry me has anything to do with the fact that the council still considers you married to her. Please tell me the truth. Or is there something else?"

Alex switched on the light in their hut. It was already cool in the room. He brushed his fingers through his hair.

"Val, it isn't an issue for me. I guess the question is, is it an issue for you?"

She was aware that he had once again turned the discussion around to focus on her needs. "I've accepted that it isn't going to be resolved."

"You do understand that my marriage to Kristiana was ended, as it was begun, by verbal consent, a very long time ago."

"Yes, I do understand. But I know that something is going on with you. I think we need to talk."

"Yes, you are right. We should talk." Her eyes filled with dread, and seeing this, he took her face in his hands. "You are my dream. You are my happily ever after. And that, my love, will *never* change!" He kissed her gently. She realized that all there has been since arriving to Africa were gentle kisses. Alex lowered his brow and said, "Unfortunately, right now, I really do have to go. I have an emergency conference call on the other side of the world." He started out of the room. "I love you!" he said again, with emphasis and left.

∞

Valeria sat in the bed in her tank top and pajama bottoms. It was a bit chilly except for the down comforter and the hot water bottle near her feet that they always left in the evenings. She didn't seem to notice. She was wide-awake with her Kindle in front of her, but there was no book that could hold her attention right now. Alex opened the door and smiled softly at her, sensing her serious mood. She glanced at the clock. It was two in the morning.

"That was *some* conference call."

"Yes. Yes, it was." He went into the bathroom and came out in a T-shirt and pajama bottoms, and crawled onto the bed next to her. He pulled the Kindle from her and closed it. "I hope you understand, I just didn't feel that Tom was the right person to perform the ceremony."

"Will anyone be right? Alex, we've been here for a month. Are you certain there isn't something else?"

"There is nothing else, I promise you. I just want it to be right."

"And is there anything that needs to be *right*...with us?"

Alex looked up and laughed, and then seeing the hurt in her eyes, his expression softened. "You and I are," he pulled her into his arms and kissed her tenderly for the first time since they had arrived in

Africa, "perfect," he whispered seductively. "Well, except for the marriage part."

"Please, let's ask Tom to marry us. Let's wake him up. He's a romantic, I could tell. He would do it! It wouldn't be…maybe what we imagined, but we would have each other."

Alex drew a deep breath. "Val, we can't wake them up. It's the middle of the night."

She bit his lip playfully and kissed his chin. Then, in her sexiest voice, she said, "Make love to me tonight."

Wrapping himself around her, he secretly glanced toward Caleb's room. Pulling his T-shirt up, she pressed her chest closely against his. "You'll see…everything will be all right." She brushed her lips against his neck and Alex shot another, more intense, glance toward the wall that divided their room from Caleb's.

"I know you want to," she said, as she ran her hands down his chest. He sucked in a deep breath as her fingers skimmed the top of his pajama bottoms, snapping them playfully.

Then Valeria heard a movement in Caleb's room and a knock at their door.

"Can I come in?" Caleb opened the connecting door and stepped in, wearing his pajamas and looking much younger than his twelve years. He looked like he had been sleeping hard.

"Sure, Caleb," Alex said as he moved Valeria off his lap and pulled down his T-shirt.

Covering her chest with the sheet, Valeria said, "Uh, Caleb…it's just that, Alex and I were…well…"

"Caleb, you must have had a nightmare?" Alex said, with a hint of suggestion.

"Nightmare?" Caleb laughed his loud, boyish laugh and then, seeing Alex's insistent expression, he sighed in irritation. "Yeah, something like that. It was more like…" Caleb looked up at the ceiling as if thinking, and then glanced woefully at Valeria. "It was like there was a voice inside my head." Alex shook his head, but Caleb ignored him and continued speaking. "It was this angry voice that kept saying, '*Get up! Now!*' It was a nagging, annoying kind of voice. And there was something—I don't know—just, so familiar about it. It gave me the shivers." Caleb now glared at Alex, who rolled his eyes.

Valeria looked back and forth between Caleb and Alex wondering what was going on with them. They seemed at odds with each other and it was rare for either of them to be ill-tempered with the other.

"What's going on between you two?" she asked.

Caleb looked down at the floor, unwilling to respond. Alex drew a deep breath. "Val, I think what Caleb doesn't want to say is that he's scared." Alex narrowed his eyes for a fraction of a second as he stared at Caleb. "Isn't that what happened?" Then, in a near-whisper, Alex admitted to Valeria, "Boys don't like to admit it when they're afraid."

"Ah, buddy, is that it?" she asked sympathetically. "It's okay to be afraid. We're all afraid sometimes." She held out her arms to him. "Come here."

It was definitely not Caleb's idea of fun to be woken up by Alex yelling in his head to get up and leave the comfort of his own bed to sleep on their couch. He had complied several times with various excuses since they had arrived in Africa. But tonight, Caleb was tired of the game. He was pretty sure it had something to do with grown-up stuff…sex and all.

Suddenly, Caleb had an idea to end the late night wake-up calls once and for all. He glanced with mock shyness toward Valeria. "Yeah, I guess I am afraid. But guys like me, we don't like to admit it. I mean…I don't have a mom, like other kids. I guess I just…" Walking to the bed, Caleb's eyes lit with mischief. Alex rose from the bed and went to the closet to get a pillow and blanket, knowing that Caleb would play his role.

"No problem, I'll make up the couch for you," Alex said, relaxing.

Caleb climbed onto the bed and snuggled his head against Valeria's chest as Alex went to the couch with the pillow and blanket.

"Umm…well, it's just..." Caleb glanced up at Valeria and gave her his saddest expression.

"What Caleb?" She had never seen him like this.

"After that…scary dream, I just kinda feel safer right here. I guess I just need some time…like this." Valeria wrapped her arms around him tighter and Caleb glanced toward Alex with a sly smile.

Shaking his head, Alex said, "Caleb, I am *certain* you will be just fine here on the couch." As long as Caleb was in the bed, Alex couldn't be there.

Caleb continued to glare at Alex. "Val, I don't want to make Alex sleep on the couch. But ever since I saved your lives and all, I *have* been having nightmares."

"Oh, Caleb," Valeria brushed his hair back. Caleb gave her his most pitiful look. "Alex, he can stay here for just a little while, can't he?" Alex's jaw tightened before he nodded. "I mean, Caleb did save our lives, after all!"

Nodding unsympathetically, Alex punched the pillow a bit heavily and then sighed as he threw himself down on the couch.

CHAPTER 3

A monkey worked his way onto the breakfast table on the patio by the main lodge. Valeria watched as Caleb held out his hand with a piece of apple.

"Caleb, they're wild animals." Caleb was wearing his thin rubber prosthesis so that he wouldn't shock others...or the monkey. Still, Valeria felt like she needed to warn the boy, even though, in reality, he was 2,000 years older than she was—his exact age was unknown since he had no memory except for his search for Alex.

"Val, am I ever going to get to be the best man?"

Glancing into the distance, she said flatly, "Sure, buddy."

He laid out a pattern of apple pieces on the table to lure the monkey to him. "Well, when?"

Glancing down into her Kindle, she clenched her jaw and then shrugged as if it were unimportant.

"You guys are sure taking long enough!" he said with an exasperated sigh.

"Caleb, what was that name that Amy called you?" she said in an attempt to change the subject.

"Oh, uh, Raiden. Some kids call me that."

Valeria shook her head. "Raiden? I thought I heard her call you *Lord* Raiden. You didn't tell her that was your name did you?"

Pushing a piece of apple toward the monkey, Caleb answered with his attention still on the monkey. "No. She figured it out." The monkey grabbed the piece of apple and ran to the rail to eat it.

"Figured it out?"

"Yeah." Caleb grabbed another slice of apple to lure the monkey back. "That's the name I use—you know, kind of like a pretend name—when I'm playing on-line games against other kids."

"Why Lord Raiden?"

"Oh, he's a dude in another game. He's immortal and he can throw cool thunderbolts and stuff."

"I see. Yes, that does seem appropriate. So, why did Amy call you that?"

"She was watching me play and figured it out."

Hearing footsteps, she turned to see Alex walking toward them from the main lodge. There seemed to be more of a bounce in his step than in days earlier. Something must have gone well. Suddenly, Valeria heard a zap, and the monkey screeched loudly and ran away. Valeria looked at Caleb accusatorily and shook her head.

He let out a boisterous laugh. "He bit me!"

"Let me see your finger. Did he break the skin? You might need rabies shots." Caleb held up his finger and moved the layer of rubber aside. Valeria examined it, but it didn't look like it had broken his skin. "Better wash it and put some antiseptic on it. Okay?" He rolled his eyes as if she was being overly protective.

Alex glanced toward Caleb and said, "And while you're at it, pack your bags."

Narrowing her eyes, she wondered if only Caleb was leaving, and why. But there was definitely something…different in his mood. Maybe he had changed his mind about having that pastor perform the ceremony and he wanted to give them some privacy. Or maybe it was just good news on his investments. Alex leaned down and kissed Valeria. She loved seeing him happy.

"What's happened?" she asked.

"Why?" he asked coolly, but his face betrayed him and he pulled her into his arms and gave her a lingering kiss.

"Hmm…so, what's going on? Why is Caleb packing?"

"It's a rather interesting business meeting I have to attend. Thought you might want to get out of here for a while."

"Where? Johannesburg?" she asked.

"Innsbruck."

Valeria's jaw dropped. "*Austria?* Is that wise?"

"I can go alone if you prefer," he teased.

"Not on your life! You promised never to leave me again—remember?" Then she realized that there was no possibility that he would be leaving her alone, especially now that Toma wasn't here to protect her.

"That's what I thought." Alex winked. "We're flying out of here this afternoon and then catching a flight in Joburg. We'll arrive in Innsbruck late tonight, but I thought you would appreciate a bit of time near our part of the world."

∞

Innsbruck, Austria was only two hours from their home, Morgana, in northern Italy. Alex had said that, to be safe, it would be many years before they could risk being in Europe. Yet after only just over a month, they were flying not only to Europe, but they would be only two hours away from their home. Valeria was ecstatic. She knew they wouldn't be able to see anyone, or even drive down the mountain. But to be that close—and to be in the mountains in the summertime. Alex had told her stories about how beautiful the spring and summer were at Morgana, with the fantastic smells of everything in bloom.

It took her only minutes to pack her bags—not that she had that many clothes with her. Alex took his time, occasionally smiling as he saw the thrill in her eye. Then they put on the brown contact lenses that Paolo had supplied them. Their brilliant blue eye color would alert any other immortals that they were in the vicinity. Not that there were that many, but it was better to be safe than sorry.

Alex restated their safety rules: If there was any trouble, Caleb was to grab Valeria and the two of them were to get as far away as they could. Alex assured her that if they got separated, he would find them. He was immortal. Valeria was not. Still, he didn't seem too concerned.

They arrived in Johannesburg and Valeria was surprised when Alex escorted them to a private full-sized jet. Caleb was thrilled and asked if he could ride up front in the jump seat, a fold-down seat, so that he could watch the pilots.

"After take-off."

Caleb shrugged and pulled out his laptop.

In all the time that she had known Alex, he had always avoided the ostentatious flaunting of his wealth. To see him paying Toma a huge severance pay and then *this*, was beyond her reality. Something big must have occurred in his investments. Valeria and Alex sat next to each other on comfortable tan leather seats as a woman in a navy blue uniform served them champagne.

As soon as they were airborne, Alex pulled out his laptop. "You might want to rest. This is a long flight and we probably won't get much rest in Innsbruck.

"Oh, you have meetings tonight?" she asked, disappointed.

"Just a few."

"A few? So are we going to check in at a hotel first?"

The corners of his mouth turned up slightly. "No. I have…other plans." Then he cleared his throat and lowered his brow in concentration as he focused on his computer screen.

"What's going on there?" she asked.

"Just some business that requires my personal attention."

She shrugged, pulled out her Kindle, removed her contacts, and read. A short while later, a dinner of stuffed sea bass and tossed salad was served—along with her strawberry kale shake.

Caleb was busily working on his laptop.

"Alex, did you know that Caleb goes by the name of Lord Raiden?"

Glancing up from his laptop, Alex smiled. "So you've discovered his alter-ego." Caleb kept his head buried. "You know he's quite famous online, or perhaps I should say, infamous."

"Our Caleb?"

"Yes, he's probably the best in the world."

"So, Lord Raiden, what game are you mastering now?" Valeria asked.

"Ahhh, you don't have to call me Lord. That's just to make me sound kinda spooky, like in a scary movie. But I decided that playing games is pretty boring now."

"Boring?" Valeria lifted a delicate brow.

"Yeah, once you find all the glitches they're really easy. Besides, if I'm gonna be a best *man*, I probably shouldn't be playing so many kids' games."

Inside, she felt the inkling of a new pain. Then she thought about how a parent might feel, witnessing their child growing up. For the external world, she put on a smile.

"I think that's a good idea, buddy. There's a lot of life to live, and I think it would be better for you to find something more fulfilling than keeping your head buried in that computer."

"Well...I decided to make my own game."

"What kind of game?"

Caleb's eyes lit with enthusiasm. "A game that has real stuff—like when we went down to the cave and swam out. I think other kids would like to do cool things like that."

"What would you call it?" she asked, her interest piqued.

"I haven't decided yet. You wanna see what I put together?"

"Sure."

The sun was beginning to set over Africa and, below, they could see hundreds of bonfires.

"Think I'm going to want to see this, too!" Alex shut his laptop and followed Valeria over to the other side of the cabin. She folded her legs underneath her on the leather seat next to Caleb as Alex stood behind them.

"This is just the prototype and I still have to fix some stuff," Caleb said. "The goal is to get to the third triumvirate."

"Triumvirate?" Alex asked.

"Yeah. I thought that would be cool." Caleb's fingers danced on the keys as he entered code that meant nothing to her.

"What's a triumvirate?" she asked.

Leaning between seats, Alex said, "It's three people who make up a power group. So, Caleb, are you referring to the Roman triumvirate? Caesar, Pompey, and Crassus?"

"Well, yeah, kind of. Only from, like, the Greek underworld, instead," he said, as he continued to type furiously. "I was thinking it would be cool to start from the beginning."

"Chaos?"

"No. I was thinking of the first triumvirate—what do you call them?" He looked up from the keyboard, thinking, and then nodded. "Oh, yeah, the Moira?"

"The Moira—you mean the Fates?"

"Yeah. That sounds cool, huh! Guys like to play games with lots of chicks. I had to kind of soup them up—you know, to make it interesting."

"Okay, and you said there was a third triumvirate?" Alex asked.

Caleb sat back excitedly. "I got it! Okay, watch!"

As the game came up, a thunderbolt flashed and then morphed into a staff. A snake crawled up the staff and blinked with another crash of thunder. Then, the name flashed across the screen, "A Thunderbolt Production." Caleb turned to Valeria. "I thought that would be cool." On the screen, there was a boy who looked very much like Caleb in a kayak on a moonlit night. The sound effects kicked in and you could hear the surf hitting against the cliffs. Cartoon Caleb blinked and a message appeared as if someone were typing it: *Your mission, should you choose to accept it, is to rescue the damsel and her loyal guard from the cave of no return.*

Caleb glanced sideways. "Cave of no return—pretty cool name, huh."

"So, now I'm just a lowly guard?" Alex muttered with a hint of amusement.

"Well, this is just pretend," Caleb said seriously, as he typed wildly.

Valeria laughed and shook her head as she glanced up at Alex.

Cartoon Caleb paddled furiously toward the cave. Suddenly, the background music and sound effects stopped just as Caleb reached the wall of rocks that hides the entrance cave into Delos.

"Watch this!" Caleb's face lit with excitement. Cartoon Caleb looked at the wall and blinked twice, complete with sound effects, and then ran straight into the wall.

Valeria couldn't help but cover her mouth.

"It's cool!" Then seeing Valeria's concern, he said, "Don't worry, it's just a game."

The decapitated cartoon head spun several times and froze momentarily, as it looked down to see its body and the water below, reminiscent of Wile E. Coyote discovering himself as he flew off a cliff. Then, he made a sound as his head dropped rapidly into the water.

Caleb let out a rollicking laugh as the head plunged underwater with a look of irritation as it sunk past fish and other sea life. A caption appeared on the screen with a deep voice that sounded suspiciously like Tavish, saying, "You lose! You've lost your head!"

Valeria giggled.

The boy turned toward her for an instant and said, "I just wanted to show you that part. That part's easy…well, for me, anyway. Let me back it up."

This time, cartoon Caleb paddled toward the cave wall with a look of fierce determination. As he approached the stone, Caleb made a movement on the mouse pad and cartoon Caleb rolled the kayak.

"Cool, huh!"

"Mm-hmm," she responded.

The screen went dark, but Caleb's fingers flew over the keyboard and then there was the sound of a match. Cartoon Caleb held a match and looked around the cave. He stashed bags of supplies along the way.

"If you don't hitch these supplies just right, you can't make it out of the cave," he said.

Then, cartoon Caleb jumped out of the boat at the island of Delos. The frightening white faces of the dribs lurched toward him, but he zapped them just in time. Caleb's rollicking laughter drowned out most of the games' sound effects.

"I made it so you have to release an electrical charge." Caleb's face lit with exuberance with each zap.

Then a giant of a man wearing a green silk toga stepped out from the shadows carrying an ancient, double-sided axe. Obviously, Erebos, cartoon Caleb's next opponent.

Erebos swung the double-sided axe at cartoon Caleb's neck repeatedly, and each time, cartoon Caleb jumped or ducked, just missing it. Having out-maneuvered Erebos, cartoon Caleb ran to the prison cell to free a damsel in a white Greek goddess gown that bore an uncanny resemblance to Valeria with a very enhanced bust line.

"Nice likeness," Alex said with amusement.

Valeria glanced at Alex and rolled her eyes. "A bit 'souped-up' if you ask me."

Caleb blushed and shrugged. "Yeah…I…well, that's just how kids draw chicks."

"Hmm," Valeria sighed.

The heroine gratefully pulled cartoon Caleb into her well-endowed breasts as cartoon Caleb's face lit with a smile.

Then, a silly woman's voice said, "Oh, Caleb, you saved me! Thank you!" She kissed his cheeks leaving behind bright red lipstick. Then, she pressed him to her ample breasts again and kissed him repeatedly, with sound effects, until cartoon Caleb's face was covered with red lip marks.

"That's an awful lot of gratitude when they're still in danger," Alex said, still smiling. "So, was your plan to run off with the damsel and ditch the loyal, but lowly, guard?"

"Nah, I was just getting to that part," Caleb said, but he didn't type on the keyboard and the damsel just kept kissing cartoon Caleb, who every now and again would look out, blink, and shrug as if to say, "Aw shucks, 't weren't nothin' ma'am."

Valeria bit her lip to keep from laughing.

As cartoon Caleb ran his sleeve over his face, the lipstick immediately disappeared. Then he grabbed the hem of the damsel's dress and yanked, and she was left in a sexy white bikini. He took her hand, they plugged their noses, and together, they jumped into the water.

"I thought you said the loyal guard is saved," Alex complained with a smirk.

"Yeah, I'm getting to that." A character that looked like Alex jumped into the water and began fighting and gurgling in the water for help. The damsel covered her mouth in fear as cartoon Caleb rescued the loyal guard.

"Oh, I see," Alex said, raising an eyebrow.

"Well, this is all about the hero getting everyone safe. Kids wouldn't like it if someone else was taking all the credit."

"Mm-hmm." Alex nodded knowingly. Then they went underwater with the damsel clinging tightly to cartoon Caleb's neck, while his hand clung to the collar of the loyal guard.

"This is the coolest part!" They come up on an underwater cell with the arms of a headless skeleton wrapped around bars.

"Okay, that's enough," Alex said, suddenly closing Caleb's laptop.

"But I was just getting to—"

"Yes, I know." Alex rolled his eyes at Caleb. "Why don't you go up to the cockpit?"

"Cool!" Caleb exclaimed as he dropped the laptop onto the table in front of him and ran up to the front of the plane.

"Do you think this game is going to cause an issue?"

Alex shook his head. "We'll deal with it once he's ready, and decide if it's safe. For now, I think you should rest."

With her stomach full, and the gentle hum of the plane, Valeria wholeheartedly agreed. She reclined her seat and the flight attendant brought her a blanket, pillow and a lavender-scented eye mask.

When she awoke, they were preparing for approach at Innsbruck. It was near eleven p.m.

Valeria replaced her contacts, and after deplaning, they went through customs. There was a limo waiting for them outside and she recalled her last trip in a limo with Alex. It was the first time she had met Paolo. She shook that thought off and allowed herself to enjoy the feel of Europe. The limo took them through the countryside and eventually pulled into a large country estate, stopping at a guard shack. The gate opened and she noticed the electric wire running over the tall stone wall that surrounded the estate. Seeing the two-story stone mansion, Valeria suddenly understood the meaning of "old wealth."

They stepped out onto a cobblestone driveway and walked to the front door.

"Are we staying here?" Valeria asked.

The corners of his mouth turned up and he shook his head as he raised the large brass knocker and dropped it. Then he turned to her abruptly and said, "Oh! I should probably warn you—"

When the door flew open, Valeria was completely startled to see the tiny figure with a sprite of white hair and oracle blue eyes—Shinsu!

For a moment, Valeria wondered if this was a trick and the council was inside. Then she saw the expression on Alex's face.

"You are right on time!" Shinsu said, with a twinkle in her eye.

"Alex, what's going on?" Valeria asked.

"Come in and find out."

Shinsu hugged Valeria. "Well, it has been quite a long day I would expect. Did you manage to get any sleep on the flight, dear?"

Valeria nodded as Shinsu turned to Caleb and he stuck out his hand, with his glove on. Shinsu's smile brightened. "Young man, I have been waiting to meet you! You are really something else! Smart, courageous, and very clever! " She winked at him.

Caleb smiled shyly. "Cool."

Shinsu led them past the grand entry with its cream décor and massive moldings and past the overstuffed furniture with subtle complements of pastels and gold.

"There are some people who have been very anxious to see you all."

Valeria noticed that they had left their luggage in the limo; it must be a short meeting. She wondered why this couldn't be conducted over the phone, rather than at the risk and expense of a private jet and a meeting in the middle of the night. She glanced at Alex as she pushed her brows together in question. Alex widened his smile as he winked at her.

Leading them through a corridor, Shinsu headed into what appeared to be a large family room. Alex was ahead of Valeria when she heard the voices. Her eyes filled with tears as she saw her adopted family. Lars and Mani were closest and they hugged Valeria first.

"Mani," she wiped a tear from her eye. "I haven't seen you since…since New York." She remembered that horrible time that was now four months and a reality away. Then she spotted Camille, with her long, straight black hair, and her beautiful Kewpie doll eyes of brilliant blue. They hugged and cried for several minutes.

"I thought the last time I saw you was going to be the last!" Camille sobbed. "I should know Alex better than that by now."

Ava joined them and threw her athletic arms around Valeria and Camille. "So great to see you, sweetie! The Three Musketeers, reunited."

Valeria, Camille, and Ava hugged again and then Valeria glanced over and saw Daphne, the beautiful redhead who thought Alex belonged to her, standing with her arms crossed, nearly fidgeting in her discomfort of their emotion.

"Good to see you both survived," she said, in her clipped British accent, bordering on embarrassment.

"Thanks, Daph."

Valeria felt awkward not hugging Daphne, so she reached toward her. Daphne pulled back and rolled her green eyes, complements of Bausch and Lomb, tossed her long red hair over her shoulder, and then gave Valeria a light almost-hug. Camille and Valeria were talking excitedly when Alex kissed Valeria's neck.

His eyes sparkled happily. "Glad you came, beautiful?"

Afraid of the emotion in her voice, she wrapped her arms tightly around his waist and kissed his chest. Then she heard Tavish clearing his throat. She turned and hugged her favorite Scotsman with his dark gray beard, wearing his kilt and a sneer that substituted for a smile.

As she worked her way around the room, she suddenly felt the air sucked out of her lungs—Paolo was there. She couldn't help but narrow her eyes at him in disdain. He still looked Hollywood handsome with his black hair and olive complexion. She couldn't help but remember that the last time she had seen him, they had been engaged. That seemed an eternity ago...before his second betrayal that had almost cost Alex and Valeria their lives. She had to remind herself that it had all been part of Alex's plan and that Paolo had just been playing his role.

"Why are you here?" she asked, with a hint of accusation.

"I'm sorry, bella, I was invited," he said quietly, almost as an apology.

Paolo turned his face to the side, his expression unreadable.

There was no avoiding the fact that Paolo had been the cause of so much pain in her life, even if he had—as he claimed—done it all for his version of love. Valeria knew that, for Paolo, it was more about besting Alex and getting retribution for Kristiana, Paolo's sister—despite the fact that Kristiana and Alex *were truly* ancient history!

Valeria nodded at him coolly. He nodded back, but stayed in his seat, laying his arm over his crossed legs. She noticed that Alex was by her side as soon as she neared Paolo. Still, Paolo had saved their lives, at great risk to his own. But Valeria wasn't ready to put it all aside. She wondered why Alex invited Paolo to this reunion, or why Shinsu—a member of the council who had sentenced her and Alex to death—was here, in what appeared to be her home. Valeria found this home to be more Shinsu's style than the tiny flat in Florence where Valeria had stayed just a month before.

Lars brushed Valeria's shoulder. "Why don't you both take a seat and we'll get started with our business." Alex took her hand and led her to a loveseat, pulling her down next to him as Lars began speaking.

"Valeria and Caleb, I'm going to update you on what has happened in the past month. Alex is already aware of the details." Alex winked at Valeria.

"The Council of Delos was not created to be a judicial force, except where immortals were causing major world problems. Even at that, execution was never a right or responsibility of the council.

"Every member of the council in this room except, officially, the two of you, Paolo, Daphne, and Shinsu, has withdrawn their allegiance with the Council of Delos. We have now formed our own council. Shinsu has created our code of honor. Shinsu?"

Shinsu rose and opened a tan scroll, reading, "We of this council share these common and basic beliefs:

"We believe that mortals and immortals, regardless of their race, creed, or color, are created equal and have the rights of equals.

"We believe that all mortals and immortals have an inalienable right to live their own lives and to defend themselves against attack.

"We believe that all mortals and immortals have the right to think freely, to talk freely, to write their own opinions freely, and to counter or speak those opinions, without fear of punishment.

"Those who would like to join this new council are invited to sign this declaration."

Alex and Valeria rose and went to the coffee table by Shinsu and signed the scroll.

Shinsu glanced at Caleb. "Would you like to sign, young man?"

Caleb shrugged and smiled. "Sure!" He rose and then took the pen from Valeria. But then he stopped and looked up at Shinsu. "I don't want to mess up your nice paper but I'm not really sure I'm supposed to. I don't know if I'm an immortal and well…I'm just a kid."

Shinsu smiled. "Caleb, do you believe those are important rights to believe in, to support, and to fight for?"

"Hmm, I guess. I mostly don't want anyone to hurt my family."

"Well then, young man, you are most welcome to sign!" Shinsu said.

Caleb smiled, took the pen, signed the form, and then raised his fist. "Sweet!"

Valeria smiled happily and kissed Alex's cheek.

Lars cleared his throat. "We have a council member who we would like to recognize for acts of valor. Caleb, will you stand please?"

Caleb looked around, embarrassed. Lars approached him with a military ribbon. "This was presented to me by the great Roman Emperor, Marcus Aurelius in 163 AD." Lars handed the ribbon to the boy and he studied the Latin inscription. "It's yours now, Caleb. You are hereby awarded the Council's Medal of Honor, for acts of valor performed last June in Paxos, Greece. Your actions saved the lives of at least three immortals, and this council is grateful to you."

"Wow! Cool!" Caleb stared at the medal in awe.

Lars went back to the front of the room. "On to other business. Paolo, I believe you asked to address this council."

"Yes," Paolo said softly as he rose and turned to face Lars, avoiding Valeria's gaze.

Valeria shivered and looked away, remembering how Paolo's last statements at the council meetings had affected her. Alex tightened the grip on her hand, smiled, and winked, evidently unconcerned.

"I would like to apologize for my previous petition and any pain it caused." He drew a swift breath, "I wish to withdraw that petition."

Paolo stared at the ground. "Also, as you know, my sister, Kristiana, has been in hiding for 2,500 years and, by her actions, has ended her marriage to Alex." Paolo turned and looked into Valeria's eyes. "On behalf of my family, I agree to officially dissolve the marriage of Alex and Kristiana."

"Alex, do you agree to this dissolution?" Lars asked.

"Absolutely!"

Lars looked around the room and asked, "Any objections?" He winked at Valeria who, by now, had tears in her eyes.

The room was silent. Lars continued, "Before we adjourn, any other business?"

Sudden understanding flooded Valeria's heart.

Alex looked at Valeria with love. "Yes. I wish to marry this beautiful woman sitting next to me."

"Val, do you wish to marry Alex?" Lars asked.

Valeria could barely speak as she replied, "With all of my heart!"

"It is not this council's duty to approve or disapprove matters of the heart. But, as a matter of consideration, this council unanimously and enthusiastically applauds this union! This meeting has come to a close."

Alex kissed Valeria and held her. When she looked up, she saw Camille standing next to her beaming. Camille wiped her own tears and then handed a box of tissue to Valeria. Ava sniffed, "I need one, too!"

Camille cleared her throat. "All right, people! Can I have your attention please?" Everyone quieted.

"As some of you know, we have been busily preparing for our bride and groom these past few weeks." Alex brushed away Valeria's tears and she kissed him, wondering how all of this could have been in progress for weeks without her knowledge. "Thanks to Lars and Tav, we have a plan that will permit us to move the celebration to its proper location."

Suddenly overwhelmed with joy, Valeria let out a loud sob. Camille stopped and turned to Valeria. "Oh, I guess I should make sure it's all right with you. We, that is, Alex and I, thought you should be married tomorrow in the garden at Morgana. Is that all right with you?"

By now, Valeria was so happy that all she could do was cling to Alex and sob, occasionally whispering, "I love you!"

Alex glowed with pleasure. He pulled her around to face him. "Beautiful, I didn't want to tell you what I was working on until I knew we could pull it off for sure." She clung to him tightly. "I hope you are all right with all of this!"

Valeria laughed through her tears. "All right with this? I have never been so happy in all of my life!"

"All right, people!" Camille proceeded. "We have a limo for the bridal party."

Lars interjected, "Everyone is going the back route except Tav, Daph, and Paolo. Remember, there are guards around the entire camp. They may stop you. Please allow them to do their job!"

Camille lifted her arms. "Time is a wasting; Mani, Lars, Ava, and of course, the bride and groom—in the limo!" Then Camille turned to Caleb. "As best man, you can ride in the limo with us. We'll wait for you if you want to put on your full suit. Otherwise, you can ride in the front."

"Hmm," Caleb's brow furrowed for a moment. "That's cool, but I would really like to talk to Tav. Can I ride with him?"

Camille nodded. Valeria and Alex walked out to the limo and loaded in. Lars popped a bottle of champagne and poured it into crystal flutes.

"To the bride and groom!"

Valeria took her glass, as tears continued to stream down her face, and clinked it against the other's flutes. Then she turned to Alex and Camille and choked, "Thank you!"

Alex's expression left little doubt that he was as pleased to give this to her as she was to receive this special gift. Camille brought out a platter of hors d'oeuvres and Ava immediately grabbed four finger sandwiches before passing the tray around. The engine started up and there was a knock on the window. It was Paolo. Camille lowered the window.

Paolo brushed back his jet black hair and then looked away for a moment, clearing his throat, and said, "May I speak to Valeria a moment?"

Camille shrugged. "It's up to her."

Valeria refused to make eye contact with Paolo. "You can say whatever you have to say to me in front of my fiancé and my family." Alex squeezed her leg.

"I would like to…" Paolo glanced at Alex. "I would like to attend your wedding, if possible." Paolo swallowed and glanced down. "I understand if you prefer that I do not."

Valeria looked at Alex, who shrugged. "I don't care," she said nonchalantly, still not meeting his gaze.

Paolo continued, "Thank you. Also, I hope you will permit me to give you a wedding gift. Camille has seen it. I hope you will permit me to offer this gift to you." Paolo looked at Camille and she smiled, nodding at Paolo.

Camille spoke, "Val, I think you'll want to keep this gift!"

Valeria shrugged again.

Alex nodded at Paolo and said, "Thanks pal."

Paolo stepped back, the window went up, and the limo pulled away with Paolo looking very alone.

Camille waved her arms dramatically. "All right, we need to discuss details now…" Camille talked the whole way, providing Valeria with every detail of the wedding…*her wedding!* Valeria heard parts of it, but she was so thrilled, most of it went past her.

It seemed like minutes, instead of hours, when the limo pulled onto a dark road that looked more like a lane and a half, surrounded by heavy forest. After thirty minutes, the limo pulled over, and Lars and Mani jumped out and pulled a couple of artificial trees aside that were evidently camouflage, revealing a gate. Lars opened the gate while Mani directed the limo, and Shinsu's Mercedes, onto the narrow dirt road. Lars replaced the trees and closed the gate, and then Mani and Lars jumped back into the limo.

"What is this all about?" Valeria asked.

Alex patted her leg. "We wanted you to have your wedding here at Morgana. But there is still a lot of danger in this, beautiful."

Lars spoke. "We've tracked Jeremiah through southern Italy and back to Abatao. According to Shinsu, Jeremiah is distracted with his marriage to a sixteen-year-old virgin back in Abatao. That should keep him occupied for at least a few weeks. Then, thanks to Lars and Ava, plus a rented child, we had decoys lead the council to the orient. The major search has been called off. The rumor is that you all chose hell over beheading. We've installed an electric fence and infrared sensors, as well as a team of guards. We believe we can pull this off."

"Beautiful, we have an escape plan, and this is vital—if anything happens, you must leave immediately. Do I have your agreement on that?"

"Alex, I am so very grateful for this! But if there is a risk of anything happening…I just could never forgive myself if anything happened to anyone."

Ava rolled her eyes. "Did you forget? We're immortal!"

Camille nodded. "Besides, evidently, you're safer here than in Africa!" There was a light snickering amongst the oracles and, finally, Valeria realized that they all knew.

As they drove down the dark path surrounded by low hanging trees, Valeria saw lights as they approached the main house, with its massive shape. Valeria saw hints of preparation for the next day; tables and chairs had been set out, and lights were strung throughout the bushes and trees.

When the limo stopped, the rest of the oracles hopped out except for Alex and Valeria. Alex took Valeria's hand in his. "I would like a little bit of private time with you—if you don't object."

"Never!"

She heard Camille say something about Valeria needing her "beauty rest" and she smiled and nodded. She didn't want to miss a moment of her time here. She wanted to appreciate being with her family, but at the moment, she was lost in the dream of her and Alex and their wedding at Morgana.

The limo continued down to their beloved cottage. As expected, there was a fire in the hearth. Alex took Valeria's hand and they walked up the porch, surrounded by hydrangea, to the double doors that she had left abruptly almost four months prior. The cottage was as magical to her tonight as it was the first time she had seen it. Alex had constructed it for her, with her belongings that he had purchased or rebuilt for 2,500 years. It was a home truly built of love.

Inside, she brushed her fingers along the leather volumes that ran along the back wall. She stopped and smiled when she saw *Walden* and *Sense and Sensibility,* their two favorite books, next to each other.

She glanced at the door to Alex's studio and pulled him in there, past his supplies and then to the amazing paintings, bronzes, and stone sculptures of her that Alex had created over the centuries. She loved the knowledge that the room was there, although she rarely entered it as it seemed a touch narcissistic. Then he took her hand and led her back into the great room. She sat down on the couch reveling in the luxury and familiarity of the home she adored. She snuck a glance at the archway to the bedroom where they would make love the next night. Valeria loved everything about the cottage. It was the outward expression of his love for her.

She especially loved that Alex was here with her again. "Are we really going to be married tomorrow?"

Alex nodded. "Are you all right with that?" She threw her arms around his neck. "I guess that's a yes," he said.

He went into the kitchen and pulled out a bottle of 2002 Ladera Cabernet and held it up for her approval. She hadn't tasted it since…she cast off the memory of packing their cottage that awful day the previous February. Instead, she remembered the first time they had shared a bottle of it in front of the fire.

"You know, I would have been fine with Tom marrying us at two a.m. in the African outback."

Alex returned with a glass and she cozied into him as they stared into the fire's blaze of orange, yellow, and blue. She swirled the glass slowly, admiring the rich color and smell of the wine. She lifted it to her lips and took it into her mouth, savoring the extraordinary flavor. She realized her eyes were closed and when she opened them, Alex was staring at her, his mouth turned up in a sensual smile of admiration.

"I've been hoping that this would all be worth the delay. Just now, your face, as you sipped the Ladera here in our cottage, made it all worth it for me." His eyes glowed with pleasure as he took a sip of his wine, too.

Her heart pounded as much from his closeness as from the thrill of what was to come. Alex lifted his hand to the side of her face and pulled her mouth to his. For the first time in a month, she felt heat behind his kiss. Her arms went around his neck and she pressed into him, relishing the thrill of his mouth on hers. He moved his mouth a millimeter away from hers, and breathed.

"They'll be here in a few minutes," he murmured.

She leaned closer to him and then playfully took his lower lip into her mouth as she brushed her teeth lightly over it. "Tell them to come back later," she whispered.

Alex kissed her for just a moment. "Already tried. Camille's not having any of that. Probably just as well." He drew a deep breath and stood. "Give me a moment," he said with a hint of excitement.

With the warmth of the fire, and the taste of Alex's mouth on hers co-mingled with the Ladera, she couldn't help but imagine the next night; she felt the heat of desire run throughout her entire body. Alex returned a moment later. She immediately noticed that he was wearing the watch she had given him. In his hand, he had the sterling silver box, intricately designed, that she immediately recognized was the box for her engagement ring. She had been forced to leave it here four long months ago.

He smiled at her with an intensity that made her heart pound.

"Beautiful, there are some modern traditions that we have forgone for various reasons. But I would like to do this right." He kneeled in front of her and flipped the box open. He removed the note she had left for him.

She remembered the simple words she had written, "Until we meet again."

He opened the note and pressed it to his lips, as if it had been a lifeline. Then he set it on the coffee table. She saw the exquisite engagement ring he had given her the previous October. It was a brilliant blue stone, one of a kind, the same color as their eyes, a color now described as oracle blue. Alex had named it the "Cassandra Crystal." The stone was entwined with delicate platinum grapevines that ran around the edge of it.

Alex took her hand in his. "Valeria, will you do me the extraordinary honor of being my wife?"

"There is nothing I want more."

Alex bit his lip, attempting to restrain a smile. "Nothing else?"

Valeria blushed and laughed. "All right, perhaps a few more things."

"Well, I'm very pleased to hear that because I've been dreaming of making love to my wife for a very long time."

With his words, the electricity between them nearly sizzled. After all the months of feeling that she was being held at bay, now she knew—she could actually see the raw desire in his eyes and feel the heat growing between them.

"May I keep your ring until tomorrow? There's a wedding band that goes with it." He winked.

"Can I wear it until you have to go?" Alex nodded and slid it onto Valeria's hand. As she glanced at her hand in his, with the ring adorning her finger, she felt a bubble of pure joy rising inside. Her arms broke out in goose bumps and she could not longer contain her emotions as they overflowed from her eyes. "And what is that?" She pointed to the other box he held in his hand.

He sipped his wine. "This?" He raised his brows as he picked up the box. "This is a wedding gift." She opened the box. It was a double strand of perfect pearls with a pendant of diamonds surrounding another Cassandra Crystal, and matching earrings with a single pearl and a small teardrop Cassandra Crystal. Valeria couldn't speak for several moments.

Finally, her voice came back to her. "Oh, my God, Alex! They are…they are breathtaking!"

"They are no more breathtaking than the woman whom they were designed for."

She threw her arms around his neck and kissed him; then, suddenly, she pulled back, looking slightly disappointed. Alex raised his eyebrow. "What's the matter, beautiful?"

"I didn't get you anything. Not a gift, not even a wedding band."

He smiled. "Marrying you is my life's greatest gift. I don't need anything else." Alex saw that she was still concerned, and added, "If you feel the need, you can get me something on our honeymoon." She felt the heat run through her…*she did love that word!*

"How on earth did you plan all of this?"

"I'll tell you everything…later," he said huskily. His eyes were intense on hers and they were both in a spell.

There was a knock at the front door and Alex pulled away and then kissed her hand. "Our time is up for tonight."

It was Camille and Ava, followed by Lars and Tavish. "Okay, groom, it's time for you to let your bride get some girl time followed by plenty of beauty rest!"

Alex pressed his lips to Valeria's in a kiss full of promise. "I'll see you tomorrow afternoon, around three p.m.—out by your favorite ginkgo tree."

She smiled softly and stroked his face. "I will count the minutes!" Alex slid the ring off her hand and placed it back into its case. He kissed her one last time before leaving with Lars and Tavish.

Before Alex got out the door, he turned around and, with a hint of amusement, raised an eyebrow at Ava. "I trust I will not find my bride in the same condition tomorrow as she was the last time I left her with you, Ava."

Ava was already headed to the wine cabinet below the kitchen island. She turned and raised her arms innocently. "What? Don't we get some quality time with our BFF?"

"Help yourself to the wine…just not too much. I want her to be in good shape tomorrow." Alex turned to leave.

"And tomorrow night," Ava added, with mischief.

"Yes...*and* tomorrow night," Alex said as he turned back to Valeria, offering her a sensual wink. At that, Lars patted Alex's back and he turned, closing the door behind them. But the look of longing in Alex's eyes was emblazoned in Valeria's memory.

Ava got down to business, and lifted the half bottle of Ladera. "Is this any good?"

Valeria, still staring at the door, felt incredibly distracted. She nodded and then sighed dreamily. "Yeah…yeah, it's very good."

Ava laughed. "Well then…" She poured herself and Camille each a glass full and topped off Valeria's half-full glass, when Camille interrupted.

"Val, I think you will enjoy tomorrow better if you switch to Chamomile tea after this glass."

"Yes, I agree," Valeria said, still lost in her dreams about her special day for tomorrow. She glanced at Ava. "What were Lars and Tav doing? Escorting you?"

Ava shrugged casually. "Nah, guard duty. They are taking the first shift." Valeria noticed that Camille and Ava had blankets and pillows.

"And you both are staying?" Valeria smiled.

Ava put her arm around Camille and said, "Yep. I wanted to bring the popcorn and pizza, and then drink Alex's wine. But Camille won't let us."

Camille nodded. "As I said before, the bride needs her beauty rest. We have appointments for you all day tomorrow up until the actual wedding. So drink up your one glass, and then you need to get to get some sleep! You'll find everything you need in the bedroom."

"But I've been away for so long and so much has happened. I want to spend more time with both of you!"

"This weekend is about you and Alex. When all this mess with the council finally gets sorted out, we'll have plenty of time to spend together."

Ava raised her glass. "To the Three Musketeers!"

They clinked their glasses together and chatted for nearly thirty minutes until Camille glanced at her watch and told Ava and Valeria that it was time for the bride to go to bed.

Valeria went into the bedroom. It had been so long since she had been here with Alex. It was the place where Alex had proposed to her. It was the bed where she would make love to him for the first time. If home was where your heart was—hers was with Alex. The memories of his love were here, in this beautiful cottage. She brushed her fingers over her lips...and realized that yes, his kisses *still* lingered.

Out the window, next to the bed, she noticed a shadow that formed the perfect outline of her beautiful ginkgo tree, set against the backdrop of a billion brilliant stars...her tree...where they would be married tomorrow. Perfect, she thought. Then she brushed her teeth and washed her face and went into the walk-in closet. The room lit gently as she entered. She noticed a few items on her side of the closet—no doubt added by Camille, because months before, she had packed all of her clothes and left it empty. There was a cotton nightgown and soft robe. Instead, she pulled one of Alex's T-shirts from a hanger and changed into it. Pulling the robe around her, she went back to the archway between the bedroom and great room.

"Where are you two sleeping?"

Camille smiled. "We tossed a coin and Ava's sleeping on the floor. I get the couch."

Valeria furrowed her brow. "You don't have to do that! You can sleep in your own beds."

Camille shook her head. "That wasn't part of the deal."

"What deal?"

Ava popped her head up. "We knew you would want to be here in the cottage and not up at the main house. But Alex didn't want you down here alone—and there was no way that Camille was going to permit that." Camille shook her head sternly. "Alex said that someone had to be in here with you and we both wanted to come. He was going to sleep in his sleeping bag out back. But Camille told the guys that they needed to make sure Alex got some sleep, too."

"Don't you think this is a bit of overkill—the guards at the entrance, an electrical fence, and the infrared? And now you two feel like you have to sleep in here with me, and the guys are sleeping outside?"

"This has been in the works for a month. We want you safe! And our bride and groom need to be in good shape tomorrow…and especially, tomorrow night!" Camille added. Going to the kitchen, she filled a teapot with filtered water. "I'm going to fix you some Chamomile tea."

Ava plopped her feet up on the ottoman. "So you're stuck with us tonight! Besides, I'm used to being on the catamaran for months at a time. So I've missed my air mattress," Ava said.

"I'm so glad you could be here, Ava! When did you fly in?"

Ava's face became suddenly guarded as she glanced toward Camille. Ava had been searching for years for Camille's husband Jonah, who had disappeared almost 300 years before.

Without glancing up, Camille answered matter-of-factly, as she adjusted the flame under the red teapot. "No reason to avoid talking about it. We decided it was time to stop the search."

"Stop! Why?" Valeria asked, going to her friend in the kitchen.

Camille drew a deep breath. "I realized I was putting Ava and Lars in the same position I was in. Ava's been away from him for almost thirty years."

"Hey, I told you that was probably what keeps our marriage so hot."

Camille steeled herself against the kitchen island. "It isn't fair."

Ava shrugged nonchalantly as Camille continued, "Anyway, if we haven't found him by now…" her voice trailed off and she busied herself by grabbing a mug and pouring herself some tea. Valeria patted Camille's back sympathetically.

"I'm sorry."

Shaking her head, Camille pushed the grief aside. "I'm not allowing anything to lessen your happiness. So no more talk of that!"

"Well, I am so glad that both of you are here! Thank you!" Valeria hugged Camille and Ava and took her tea in to sit with them for a few more minutes. They spoke of a recent battle between Daphne and Tavish that had them all in hysterics. When her tea was gone, she rose and hugged them both before heading off to bed, although she was far too excited to think about sleep. But as soon as the lights were out, Valeria was so comfortable, she drifted off.

CHAPTER 4

The morning sun filtered through the forest's old growth, leaving beams of interrupted sunlight in the bedroom Valeria so loved. She immediately felt the thrill of what the day meant. Within minutes, Camille and Ava came in and jumped on the bed with her, laughing joyfully as they sang, "You're getting married today!"

Camille opened the windows to the cottage and a fresh breeze moved through, bringing the scent of jasmine and the trilling of birds from the trees outside. It looked like the perfect day for a wedding.

"Ava's going to run your bath. I'll make your coffee."

Ava added, "It's better that way. Nobody likes my coffee."

"I remember!" Valeria laughed joyfully.

She went into the walk-in closet and looked at the items that were hanging on her side of the closet. Valeria pulled out turquoise sweat pants and a matching hoodie that zipped down the front, and saw the matching flip-flops.

The bath began to run and she wondered how much time they would have at their beloved cottage, or if they were immediately returning to Africa. Although, after the lion episode—followed by the bodyguard episode—she doubted they would. But it didn't matter because, after today, she would be married to the man she loved with all of her heart. And she would always hold this special gift—the gift of a wedding at their home, with the people who she loved the most—as a dream come true.

Camille came up and handed Valeria her coffee in her favorite mug. Valeria sipped it, relishing its perfect blend of cream, coffee, and hazelnut. Then Camille slung her arm over Valeria's shoulder. "Don't worry. We've taken care of your trousseau."

"Trousseau?" Valeria hadn't thought about a trousseau, or even a wedding gown! She looked at Camille in sudden horror. "I just realized I left my wedding gown—"

Ava came out of the bathroom and interrupted Val's moment of panic. "Yeah, well, it was pretty well trashed anyway."

Camille raised a calming hand as Valeria began to hyperventilate. "Well, don't worry about that. It's all handled. You don't have to worry about a thing today!"

Ava didn't get upset about clothes. She ordered sportswear online from REI or L.L Bean. But this was the wedding gown that Valeria and Alex had picked out for their wedding over four months ago. Valeria didn't want Camille to know that she was upset—especially with all of the wonderful things that were happening today. There certainly was no time to travel into Trento and pick up some silky, lacy thing. Attempting to calm herself, she remembered that even if she didn't have an appropriate dress, this wedding was a far cry from what she had been willing to accept just a few days before.

"I did bring a few sundresses—Oh! I have my navy blue pencil skirt and a white cotton blouse. It isn't really a wedding gown, but it's better than my blue jeans."

"I said I handled *everything*!" Camille said as she rolled her eyes. "You will have a gorgeous wedding gown. Don't worry! Now get in the tub."

Luxuriating in the bath, Valeria took her time, dreaming of her long-awaited wedding, with her beautiful Alex—now only hours away—and then the wedding night...here, with her husband. After her bath, she threw her sweat suit back on and sipped a fresh cup of coffee. Today, she would absolutely hold to her two-cup rule.

Camille made Valeria scrambled eggs with finely chopped vegetables and bacon, and then ensured that she ate every bite. That didn't take much convincing—Valeria was hungry and it tasted wonderful. A knock came at the door and Caleb handed Valeria a bottle filled with a thick olive green liquid.

"What, in God's name, is that?" Camille said with disgust.

"I knew you would love it!" Ava piped in from the couch as she casually flipped through L.L. Bean's catalog.

"Ahh! Caleb, Tell Alex, thank you and that I love him and I can't wait to see him in a few hours!"

Caleb laughed. "He said to tell you that last night was the last night he's spending away from you. Now, I have to go get ready to be the best man!" He turned and started to run down the stairs, and then spun around and rolled his eyes. "Oh, yeah, and he said to tell you he loves you, too."

The sun caught the edge of Valeria's face; she moved to enjoy its warmth as she sipped her strawberry kale concoction. Then a car pulled up in front of the cottage.

"Right on time! Paolo's wedding gift," Camille said.

Valeria nodded, suspiciously. Still, if it was all right with Camille, it was probably an acceptable gift.

"Ava and I were in a panic about your wedding gown!"

Without glancing up, Ava flipped a page in her magazine and said, "You were in a panic. I'm not that picky."

Camille ignored Ava and continued, "Then Paolo called and said that he had seen your wedding gown in Paxos at our home there. He had intended to re-create it for you. But when Alex called and said you were ready to be married by a preacher on safari—we all decided it was time to move on this now and there was simply not enough time to have that exact dress remade. So, Paolo picked one out that is absolutely beautiful, and I know you will love it. And, just as importantly, I know Alex will, too!"

"*Paolo* picked out my..." Valeria questioned in horror.

Seeing her friends face go pale, Camille patted her shoulder and, attempting to sound calm, said, "If you don't love it, I have several other options to choose from. Don't worry."

The person at the door carried a long white garment bag. He hung it up on the door jam. Valeria stared at it, frozen. Camille unzipped the bag slowly, removed the dress, and held it up, turning it so that Valeria could see the back as well.

It was very similar to the gown that she and Alex had selected— but with the richness of an antique gown from the 1930s. It was made

51

of heavy silk satin. The gown was sleeveless and had a cowl front neckline, as well as a deep cowl in the back, with a body hugging bias cut and wrapping seams. She glanced at the A-line skirt and noticed how the back flared to an elegant train.

Valeria's eyes filled with tears and she lifted her fingers to her mouth. "Oh, my God," she gasped staring at the gown.

Camille's eyes widened in concern and she clasped her hands nervously. "Don't worry, okay? I know I have her number here. I'll have them bring up the others." Camille tried to calm her inner hysteria. She had guessed wrong. Now they needed the other gowns— none of which, in Camille's estimation, were even near the beauty of this one.

Valeria shook her head without taking her eyes off the gown.

Ava grabbed Camille's phone. "Hold on, I think she's coming around."

"It's the most beautiful dress I've ever seen!" Valeria whispered softly, taking in every exquisite detail.

Camille and Ava both let out a long sigh of relief.

"Oh, thank God! I was about to have a stroke!" Camille said putting her hand on her chest to calm her pounding heart.

A woman answered the phone on the other line but Camille was too relieved to even notice and hung up without a word.

Ava turned to Valeria with her hands on her hips. "You know, you could have said it was the most beautiful gown you had ever seen *before* the 'Oh, my God.'"

The seamstress remained to make any adjustments but none were needed, the dress fit perfectly. Valeria didn't know how Paolo did it, but he had exquisite taste and seemed to know her exact measurements, better than she knew her own.

The girls heard another knock and Ava rose from the sofa and held open the door, bored with all of the hubbub.

Camille glanced at Valeria. "I told them they had to come in one car. We don't need the attention of four vehicles coming in and out of Morgana."

It was a crew from Elizabeth Arden for the full-bridal treatment, which included a massage, a manicure, pedicure, and a facial.

"Camille, I hope Alex is getting the royal treatment, too," Valeria said, removing the cucumbers from her eyes as the white mask dried. She lifted her lemon water and sipped it, as a woman kneaded her calves. The woman doing the facials glanced at Ava, in irritation. Ava had eaten the cucumber slices that had covered her eyes.

Camille rolled her eyes at Ava and then said apologetically to the technician, "Yes, I know."

"Hey, these are good. I'm still hungry. Is there anymore of the eggs from breakfast?"

"No. You ate five of them, plus a half a pack of bacon!" Camille accused.

Ava shrugged. "I'm a hungry girl!"

Camille returned her attention to Valeria. "Alex is being pampered—well, not quite to this extent. But he's not the bride," Camille tried to smile but from under the clay masque it looked comedic.

Later, a makeup artist expertly worked her magic on Valeria's face. As the woman packed up her cosmetics, Camille stared intensely at the bride, causing Valeria to take in her reflection in the mirror. Finally, Camille frowned.

"It's too heavy. You'll have to redo it."

The makeup artist turned to Valeria, and in a heavy Italian accent said, "Ze bride likes it. Does she not?" Evidently, the question was for Valeria.

"Camille, I think it's…fine—"

Raising her hand, Camille interrupted Valeria without even looking at her and continued speaking to the artist, "She says it is *fine*. Do you want to know how *fine* translates? It means she hates it. We need a fresher look. She is a bride!"

"But for ze pictures—"

"Don't argue with me on this one or I'll phone your manager and insist they send up someone who can do the job right!"

"But I am the premier artiste at Eliz—"

"You won't be an artiste anywhere if you don't fix this!"

Wondering if it was that bad, Valeria looked in the mirror. She thought it looked all right. Although, heavier than she would like.

But with Camille's direction, and another forty-five minutes, Valeria had to admit, the makeup made her look like her, only much better. Her face had a glow that she liked and her eyes and lips definitely stood out.

A stylist pulled Valeria's long brown curls into a loose French roll, and hooked it with a platinum and diamond hair comb that Camille said would be Valeria's "something borrowed."

As the woman pulled out her hairspray, Camille stopped her. "Don't use that lacquer on her!" Camille glanced through her own handbag and pulled out a "light hold" hairspray. "Use this one. And don't triple-coat her hair with it—just once lightly."

"We cannot have the bride's hair falling out at the reception!" the stylist argued.

"If it falls out, it falls out!" Camille snapped. The stylist gasped in horror at that idea. But Camille continued, "She has gorgeous hair! But she doesn't want to keep her husband waiting while she shampoos and dries her hair tonight, does she? She has to be able to comb it out."

"Tonight!" Valeria thought, as a warm shiver ran down her spine and tears formed in her eyes.

At last, with Camille completely satisfied, the crew left and Valeria's friends went up to the main house to dress.

The smell and warmth of the day, with a hint of coolness from the mountains, was intoxicating. Valeria had changed into the undergarments that Camille had left for her—even they were exquisite—and then she pulled on a white silk robe. A small orchestra warmed up outside, and the chatter of guests increased.

Alone at the vanity in the bathroom, Valeria admired the necklace and earrings that Alex had given her. She sipped her mimosa and rose to peek out the curtain again hoping to catch a glimpse of Alex. She was surprised to realize that she didn't feel an ounce of nervousness—which she thought was normal for a bride.

Finally, Camille arrived looking gorgeous; she had her hair pulled up and was wearing a deep-blue gown with lace across the neck and arms. Valeria glanced out the window again, now *needing* to see Alex. Suddenly, she noticed that there were rows and rows of white covered chairs. Obviously, more than the family would be there.

"Camille, how many people are coming?"

"Oh, we're keeping it small. There are about sixty guests."

Valeria rolled her eyes. "*Sixty!* Where did you find sixty people who we know who aren't immortals?"

"New York."

∞

Taking her time and appreciating Camille's assistance, Valeria stepped into her wedding gown. Camille zipped it and instructed her not to eat, drink, or sit down until the reception.

Her heart raced with excitement and she wondered what Alex was feeling. Ava returned with Camille's and Valeria's bouquets. The bouquet held gardenias tipped with a pearl and deep blue belladonna, surrounded by greens and a deep bluish-purple ribbon; it was truly a work of art. As she looked at her bouquet, her eyes flooded with tears once more.

"Camille—it's all so beautiful! Thank you!" Valeria hugged her friend, and then said, "Oh, and now I'm going to ruin all this makeup!"

Carefully wiping a tear from her own eye, Camille said, "The woman swore to me that you are completely waterproof. I've left the makeup remover on the sink for tonight and you'll need it." She smiled. "But you look absolutely stunning!"

There was a knock and Camille opened the front door and smiled at Mani.

He was wearing a tuxedo with a boutonnière of belladonna and lily. Mani was one of Valeria's favorite people in the world. She went to hug him and felt the amazing luxuriousness of the silk on her skin. It was the first time she had seen Mani in a tux. She smiled at how handsome he looked.

"I was hoping to walk you down the aisle, if you'd like."

The emotion welled up inside of her. Mani would be at their wedding! He had been forced to avoid their previously planned wedding due to the council. Now, not only was Alex's closest friend here, he was going to walk her down the aisle.

"I would love that!" she gushed.

Mani held a special place in her heart; the man who lived in Alex's original family home, who'd lost his own symbolon, his wife, nearly 500 years before. Yet he still spoke to her every day of his life. Valeria hoped he would again know love. He had so much to offer.

Camille brushed Valeria's cheek as the music began.

"Val, you look gorgeous! Mani, make sure you pace her to the music. When you hear the next song, count to ten, then you're on!" Camille said before carefully going down the stairs and then disappearing behind the blue hydrangea.

Mani smiled. "You look stunning."

"You look very dashing yourself." She hugged Mani with excitement as the music changed to her cue, a stirring instrumental.

"I believe it's time I take you to your husband."

Stepping out the front door, Valeria and Mani walked down the steps, around the corner to the side of the house, and under the ginkgo tree that originally made her fall in love with Morgana. She couldn't keep the smile off her face. Everyone was standing already and she saw friends from New York and Trento but, at that moment, she was looking for only one face.

They turned up the aisle and, at last, she found his eyes—glowing with love and joy, looking so very handsome. The rest of the walk she floated on the dream that was now a reality. She was almost aware of Caleb standing next to Alex. She saw Alex's hand reach out for her and she took it—finally with him. She was aware that Lars was conducting the ceremony, but she didn't hear a word of it. All she truly saw was the face of the man she loved more than life, looking at her with adoration, his eyes rimmed with tears, as were hers, his face glowing with love. Alex began their vows:

"In your eyes, I have found my home.

In your heart, I have found my love.

In your soul, I have found my own."

It was only a breath later when Lars pronounced them husband and wife. Alex pulled her into his arms. As his hand brushed her face, he lowered his mouth to hers and kissed his wife tenderly and lovingly...and a bit longer than reasonable in public.

Alex and Valeria Morgan walked down the aisle. There was an open horse carriage in the driveway and an absence of vehicles—which Valeria didn't notice—and they rode up the magical, wooded path to the main house. Camille rode behind them with the wedding party and, as they arrived at the main house, she led the newlyweds into a private room off from the kitchen. She handed them both glasses of champagne with strawberries, which they almost acknowledged.

"All right, you two have five minutes and then a couple shots with the photographer before the reception. Okay?" Neither Alex nor Valeria responded. They gazed into each other's eyes with so much love, Camille felt uncomfortable. "*Well...okay?*" she asked impatiently.

Alex nodded. "Okay," he said, softly, his attention never leaving his bride. "Camille, will you please close the door?"

The door closed and they were alone as husband and wife. Alex pulled Valeria into his arms. "I have never seen anyone so beautiful in all of my existence." His eyes lit with emotion and his mouth came down on hers with more love and passion than ever before.

She felt her knees weaken as her heart rose to her throat, and Alex drew her in even closer. "Ohhh!" she said breathlessly, in little more than a whisper. Her fingers traced the side of his face. "Where have you been hiding that kiss?"

Alex's eyes sparkled with amusement. "I've been saving that for my wife." His lips moved along her jaw line and an intense flash of heat moved straight to her stomach. Suddenly, she felt a sizzle of energy between them and she wondered how she would make it through the reception. His face filled with emotion and he stared at her in utter amazement. "*You are finally my wife!*" he said.

Valeria stroked his face. "And *you* are my husband...any chance we can skip the reception?"

They both laughed, and shook their heads. Then a knock came at the door and their private moment ended.

The bride and groom joined the crowd to cheers and applause. They sat at their table as the caterers served Steak Diane prepared tableside, with Caesar salad, grilled asparagus, and potatoes. Valeria honestly couldn't eat more than a few bites.

"Were you gonna ignore me all night?" She heard the heavy New York accent that was unmistakably Weege! Ken stood with her, his large hands in the pockets of his ill-fitting baby blue suit.

Weege and Valeria hugged. When Alex started to shake her hand, Weege grabbed him and gave him a bear hug.

"What a surprise!" Weege gushed to Valeria. "You disappear a month ago after going off with Paolo...*who I intend* to have a few words with tonight. I've been calling him and couldn't get a return call. I thought he'd kidnapped you or something. I was ready to call the FBI!"

"She was! She was calling 'em. But I said, 'Hon, they're just having a good old time—let 'em be!' Ain't that what I told you, Weege?" Kenny said.

Weege nodded in annoyance. "And then, only two days ago, Alex called and the next thing I know, we're flying on a *private* jet to an unknown destination!" Weege turned to Alex. "I do typically need more than two days notice with my busy social calendar."

Alex nodded. "My apologies."

"Ahh, it's okay. I mean, you got the shop closed for the three days so we could be here. Mackenzie had no choice! He had to say yes!"

Valeria glanced at Alex and he winked.

"So, this is the guy you were so crazy about!" Weege gushed and then, turning to Alex, she shoved her thumb into his chest. "See, you thought you could do better? Well there is none better than Val!" Weege admonished.

Alex smiled. "Agreed!"

Valeria rolled her eyes at Weege, who made the assumption that Alex had dumped her a few months before, rather than what had actually occurred—they were torn apart by the law of immortals and had their lives threatened.

"Thanks for letting us keep Charlie for now!"

"Charlie! How is he?" Charlie was Valeria's sweet King Charles spaniel that Alex had given to her via Paolo during their separation.

"We was gonna bring him," Kenny said. "But your friend Camille, she said she wasn't having no fuzzy mop jumping up and ruining your day."

"Let us know when you want him back. We'd keep him in a heartbeat, but he is yours and well...well, Kenny and I decided we needed our own," Weege said.

"Your own dog?" Valeria asked.

"No, our own family," Weege said, cryptically.

Stunned, Valeria suddenly understood. "You…you are…you and Kenny?"

"Yup…she's knocked up," Kenny said proudly. "Everyone said she was too old but—"

Weege lowered her brows and elbowed Kenny.

"Heeeeyyyy!" he said, as a button popped off his ruffled shirt exposing a hairy belly. "Damn, babe—ya did it again! Looks like I need another safety pin!"

"I'm only thirty-nine," Weege said, although Valeria distinctly recalled celebrating Weege's thirty-ninth birthday several years before. "Besides, I read somewhere that it's the new twenty-five!"

"Oh, my God, Weege! Congratulations!" Valeria hugged them both.

Alex excused himself to say hello to a business associate. Weege continued, pointing toward Alex. "He must be filthy rich! And such a nice guy! Don't understand all the cloak and dagger stuff—guess he wanted to surprise you. But the bus without windows was a bit much even if he is a bazillionaire. Now I see why you bought those contact lenses. His and her eye color—must be a European thing. Wonder if it'll catch on in the states. Do you think Ken and I should try it?" Before Valeria could think of a response, Weege continued, "Nah. Neither of us has an eye color I'd duplicate. But your eyes do look real good with all that jewelry you got on."

Weege was unaware that Valeria's eyes had returned to their original color after her 'accident' the previous year. They had been close friends until she had met Alex and the family. But there was little personal information that Valeria had ever purposely exchanged with Weege. Still, she loved her friend and was pleased to see her.

The band picked up the pace and Kenny smiled. "That's our song, babe!"

"Well, I guess it is now! Keep in touch, will ya?"

"I'll try." Valeria squeezed Weege's hands. "Things are pretty crazy right now."

"Oh, yeah, with Alex's business and all…married to a billionaire…understand."

Valeria wanted to correct her, but again, there was no way she could explain what was going on without violating Weege's sense of reality.

"Go, dance with Kenny!"

The stars seemed to brighten. Lars and Ava were doing a great jitterbug. Camille was dancing with a very old man who ran a patisserie shop in Trento. Tavish had grabbed Sherry, a schoolteacher from town, and was dragging the poor girl across the dance floor. Then he did a 180 and switched to her mother, Pamela, as they began to dance an elaborate Tango. Caleb was dancing in boxes with Marling, the photographer. Even Mani was dancing and heavily engaged in conversation with her chiropractor from Manhattan, Dr. Lesli—how did Alex find *her?*

Valeria saw Pauline in a white chef's coat. She was Alex's source for leather-bound books—and evidently a great caterer. When Pauline took a few moments, at Camille's insistence, to dance with her husband, Silvio, Valeria brushed her shoulder. Pauline turned in surprise and gave her a hug.

"I'm so pleased that you're here! And by the way...fantastic food!" Valeria said.

Pauline smiled sweetly. "I wouldn't miss it!"

There were several of the previous interns whom she had worked over the years, Dawn, April, Kristin and Cindy dancing in the middle of the dance floor. At another table were Marv, Laura, Amanda and Misti, who had managed some of her larger floral accounts.

As she glanced up, she caught sight of Paolo and instinctively frowned, and then realized that was rude.

"Paolo, hello."

"Hello, Bella—though bella fails to do you justice today."

"Paolo, please," she interrupted.

"I do not wish to offend you. I witnessed your vows to Alex," his eyes drifted to the heavens and he seemed near tears. "I know that you love him. I know that I have interfered with that."

"Thank you for the gown."

He shrugged without making eye contact.

"Paolo, it was…" she swallowed and her eyes filled with tears. "It is the most beautiful wedding gown I could have ever imagined. Thank you."

Shrugging, he looked away. "It was something I could do for you." He glanced momentarily at her. "Did Alex tell you everything? About helping you? Did he tell you everything, bella?"

"Yes, Paolo. He told me everything. And thank you for what you did."

"Then why are you still angry with me? You thought you could marry me the last night I saw you. And then I did what I must to save your life, and now it seems as if you hate me."

"Paolo," she touched his shoulder, "we all did what we had to do. Yes, I would have married you to keep Alex and my family safe." She shrugged. "Perhaps we could have been reasonably happy. Yes, I think we could have been *reasonably* happy. But always there, between us, would be my deep love for Alex. And *always* there would be your violation of my need for him. There is no marriage that could survive that."

"Perhaps." Paolo hung his head. "I still—"

"No, Paolo. Not now," she interrupted.

"Yes…you are right." He turned from her and shoved his hands in his pockets. Valeria glanced over and noticed that Alex had been watching their conversation closely while dancing with Camille.

The music lowered and they heard the tapping of champagne glasses for a toast. Alex returned to her side.

"Everything all right?" he asked.

"Wonderful," she whispered in his ear.

He took her hand and led her to their seats as Caleb stood looking slightly nervous in front of the crowd; everyone quieted.

"Hi. I'm the best man and I'm supposed to say something nice. But…well, umm…I'm just a kid, and so I thought Lars or Mani should talk instead of me. But, umm, they told me that the best man is supposed to talk and that I should just talk about Alex. So, umm, sorry if this is lame." Caleb fidgeted and cleared his throat. "I've known Alex…well, a long time, and he's always been kinda like a dad to me.

"He's someone I always want to be like because, well, he can do all kinds of cool things and he never yells at me…well, hardly ever anyway." There was a chuckle of laughter from the crowd and Caleb looked down, clearing his throat again as a momentary squeal came from the speakers. Caleb looked as if he was in trouble, but Lars flashed a smile and a thumbs up to him, as if to go on.

"I used to think that I never wanted to be in love because it made Alex so sad when Val was away and—well, I just didn't think I wanted to ever feel like that.

"But then I see how different Alex is when he's with Val, and I realized that…well, it was like all that unhappiness just disappeared and you kind of forget it was ever there. Umm, well, I think that Alex's life is kind of special because...well, because of how much he loves Val." There was an emotional "ahhh" from the crowd, and with that, Caleb's courage rose as he continued. "Alex would do anything for Val—he would swim through the river of death, he would even give her up if he had to—because he loves her that much. I realized that Alex is lucky to have that kind of love. And he's especially lucky that it's with someone as special as Val. So, I guess that's all!"

He sat down abruptly and handed the microphone to Lars, who chimed in, "To Alex and Val!"

Everyone applauded and Valeria blew Caleb a kiss. Camille stood and took the microphone from Lars.

"I've never had a sister—until this year. Valeria you have become my sister and my closest friend and confidante. And now you are *officially* part of my family. You are honest and loving and the kind of woman who inspires us all to be better.

"I cannot think of a finer man for you—as Caleb so beautifully expressed. Alex is the kind of man who chases his rainbows, regardless of the difficulty, regardless of the personal hardship and pain. To see him finally have the woman of his dreams makes me believe that miracles can come true!

"I love you both! To Alex and Valeria!"

Everyone cheered and Alex and Valeria rose to embrace both Caleb and Camille.

Then the music began and it was *All the Way.*

"You know that's our song," Alex said as he pulled Valeria onto the dance floor.

A few minutes later, Caleb asked to cut in, so Alex asked Shinsu to dance. Mani danced with Camille and Tavish danced with every woman under seventy at the wedding.

As the evening progressed, Daphne sat by herself, with her chin in her hands, looking bored and depressed. The candle light from the crystal chandeliers seemed to intensify the star-studded sky. Paolo noticed that they were the only two sitting at the tables, with the exception of Tavish and Kenny who had both taken a break from the dance floor and seemed to be arguing, but you could never tell with Tavish. Paolo knew Daphne only by sight. Most of their encounters had involved an exchange of insults.

"So, bella, you aren't dancing with Tavish?"

Daphne rolled her eyes. "I'd rather shoot my foot off," she said.

Paolo sat down next to her and shrugged. "Valeria makes a beautiful bride."

Daphne glared at Paolo. "I've heard quite enough of that for tonight!"

"You are melancholy, also."

Ignoring his comment, she tried to think of an insult but was too depressed to even care.

"We must dance," he said.

Daphne glared at Paolo again and then took a good look at him and sighed. With a shrug, she took his hand.

As they slowly moved over the dance floor, Paolo touched a mark on her neck. "Have you always had that mark?"

Daphne pulled back in disgust. "Oh, dear God, please don't tell me you have one! I have heard that line before, you know."

"Well then, I shall have to show it to you…later this evening," he smirked. "Or would you prefer to search for it?"

Daphne rolled her eyes, but then after a moment, her expression softened. "Perhaps."

Tavish was back on the dance floor, with his arms and legs flailing wildly. He glanced at Valeria, who was dancing with Mani.

"Cin I cut in?" Tavish said in his heavy Scottish accent, made stronger by the ale he downed like water. Valeria opened her mouth; she knew she should say yes, but as much as she loved Tavish, she just couldn't bring herself to dance with him.

"Tavish, Valeria was just telling me that she needs to sit for a while. I suspect I may have stepped on her toes a few too many times," Mani said with a slight wink to Valeria.

"Mani, you may be a doctor but you're a bit of a clod if you ask me. And really, your lack of style in your dance is unforgiveable."

Mani bit back a smile. "Yes, well, in any case, I believe Valeria would prefer to sit for a while."

"Yes, yes, Tav, would you mind?" Valeria asked.

"Not at all, lass!"

They walked to the tables and sat down. Valeria took in the beauty of the evening with the tiny, twinkling lights that resembled fireflies and ran along the edge of the grass. Small tea light candles hung from ribbons on the tall timbers that surrounded them. A waiter walked by with champagne and Tavish grabbed two glasses, handing one to Valeria.

"I am happy to see ya married. That lad has been by himself for too long." Tavish narrowed his eyes as he continued, "And this is a bit of a delicate subject but I feel a responsibility."

"Oh?" She wasn't certain she wanted to hear it.

"Well, lass, I dislike being vain, but ya can thank me later for any successes tonight." Tavish's eyes sparkled.

"Alright," Valeria choked out.

"Well now, you probably didn't know this...though I am certain that you've suspected—old Tav, here, is quite the ladies' man!"

Valeria just nodded and took a sip of champagne to keep her snickers to herself, though Tavish was totally unaware of the effect he created.

"Oh, I've given many a lass the drum treatment." Valeria covered her mouth with her napkin as the champagne shot out. When Tavish glanced at her, she let out a bit of a cough trying to keep from laughing. "Ya all right there lass?" He patted her back a bit too heavily. "As I was saying, old Tav always leaves the ladies with a smile...in fact, they call it the Tavish glint, in my parts."

"I'm sure."

"I informed the laddie of my trick. See, you would not know about these things, but we men...oh, I was not thinking of wee men," Tavish said as he let out a roar of laughter. "I meant, us men. Well, we get in a hurry...as will probably be the case with the lad," he tossed his head back and shrugged, "being inexperienced in these things. So I shared my secret. I told him: when you feel like you cannot hold it back, grit yer teeth like so..." Tavish clamped his jaw down and opened his lips revealing his yellowed teeth. To which, Valeria lost her composure. To hide her laughter, she hugged Tavish and her body shook. Tavish patted her back. "There, there lass. I know it's a lot to behold...quite attractive, I'm told. Ah, lass, I can see you're touched!"

Seeing Valeria's expression, Alex rapidly approached her. "Tav, I believe I need to dance with my bride."

"Ahhh, she's had quite enough of you clods tromping on her toes! But she is your wife, and you have a right to abuse her if you wish."

"Thanks, Tav," Alex said with as straight of an expression as he could manage.

Tavish raised a finger toward Alex. "Remember how I've instructed you, lad!" And facing Alex, Tavish bared his teeth as he thrust his hips.

Alex's eyes widened and he bit his lip to restrain his natural response as he pulled Valeria's hand into the crowd, tears of laughter streaming down her face.

Tavish turned to a couple of New Yorkers who sat at the table. "Did you see how touched the bride was with my bit of advice?" Tavish leaned back and threw his arms over the chairs on either side of him, rocking back a bit as he looked up in thought. "I have often seen the desire in her eyes for me. But it just wasn't meant to be. Alex is like a brother to me. Ahh, well...that's her loss, I suspect." The New Yorkers broke into laughter but Tavish didn't notice. He drew a deep breath. "Time for another ale!"

Alex and Valeria danced closely and then Valeria whispered, "I want to be alone with you."

"You know, Tavish mentions a good point," Alex said, and Valeria noticed a slight flinch in his eyes.

"What's the matter?"

"It's just that I don't have the experience like—"

"Like?" She knew whom he was thinking of and it wasn't Tavish. She saw his eyes move toward Paolo. "I knew it was a mistake inviting him!"

"Paolo's been well-behaved, of late. However, there is merit to something he said to me many years ago. He suggested that you would be better satisfied with…well, you get the idea."

"Yeah, well Paolo can be a big jerk!" Valeria said, irritated.

"He is right, though. It's been 2,500 years since I've made love to a woman. I just hope you aren't expecting…" He looked away for a moment.

She reached up and took his face in her hands. "Hey, look at me," she said softly. His eyes stared into hers. "I wouldn't want it any other way. Tonight will be about us and nothing else matters."

Alex kissed her passionately as his hands moved over the uncovered small of her back; again she felt the sizzle of energy between them. They heard Camille clear her throat and they both looked up.

"You two look like you are ready for some time alone."

Valeria beamed and Alex winked at her.

"I need to take care of a few things before we leave," he said. He kissed her forehead and then stepped toward Lars and Ava who stopped dancing and turned toward him. Valeria watched as Ava kissed and hugged Alex and then the three of them began to speak in hushed tones.

"I think he's more nervous than I am," Valeria said to Camille.

"He's waited longer…and let's face it, the pressure is *all* on the guys!"

"I never thought of it that way. I guess you're right. Camille, what should I do?"

"Be yourself. Trust me, that is *all* that man wants! I've left some things for you in the cottage. Wear all of it, some of it," she gave Valeria a mischievous grin, "or none of it."

Alex returned and took her hand. She held the train of her dress as they walked through the magical forest path with its romantic trail lighting. It felt as if she had stepped through time and was now in Shakespeare's *Midsummer's Night Dream* with the fairies Oberon and Titania hiding nearby.

She saw fireflies doing their dance of love and the scent of jasmine filled her senses. Neither Alex nor Valeria could speak out of their nervousness and excitement. As they passed by her giant ginkgo tree, where they had been pronounced husband and wife hours before, Alex suddenly swooped her into his arms and carried her up the porch and through the double wooden doors. He set her on her feet in the living room in front of the fireplace.

Staring at her husband adoringly, she brushed the side of his face and whispered, "Do you know how much I want you?"

Alex chuckled, but it didn't sound like Alex. He kissed her gently. "Would you like to change first while I…well, I'll take care of a few things." He cleared his throat and when he spoke again, it sounded more like Alex.

"I…was wondering, if you would like a glass of wine…first?" His hand caressed the back of her neck for a moment and then his fingers played momentarily on each vertebra, lingering on the small of her back. Another rush of heat flashed across her skin. She was certain he could see her every emotion—a cross between passion and sudden fear.

She forced herself to look away. Obviously, he wanted to move things a little more slowly than she did. Now she wasn't certain what to do.

"Yes. Please," she said woodenly, thinking how silly that sounded. Did Alex know which question she was answering? "I meant," she said softly, "yes, to both. I'll change and I would like a glass of wine."

In the bathroom, she found a pearl-colored silk negligee with a matching robe. She wondered if she should put on the robe, but opted against it. Then she realized that Alex had a vision that he felt compelled to duplicate but it was a vision of what could be—not what was. Still, it was the vision that had kept him dreaming of her and fighting impossible odds for over thousands of years.

That vision was why they were here together, married, and so very happy. She wondered what her role was in the vision, and how did she play it when she didn't know what it was. On the other hand, Valeria didn't want to be chained to what she should do. Not tonight. Still she felt the need to honor the vision and wondered how she would do that.

After brushing her teeth and washing the makeup off, which took roughly three attempts, she bent over and, with her boar hair brush, stroked the underside of her hair repeatedly before flipping it back. The curls fell softly to below her shoulders, and she glanced at her reflection in the mirror. Immediately, her eyes drifted to the south and she noticed that the thin silk of her negligee left absolutely nothing to the imagination.

She rolled her eyes. "Oh, Camille," she muttered. She wished she had the nerve to walk out in just the gown. Instead, she pulled on the silk robe. Then she noticed a small triangle of material dangling from the hanger and pulled it down. After surveying it for several minutes, she realized with shock that it was a g-string.

With a shake of her head, Valeria recalled Camille's words, "Wear all of it…some of it," and then with a playful grin she had added, "Or none of it."

"Oh, my God!" Valeria said in terror.

Alex tapped hesitantly on the door. "Everything all right?"

Gulping, she pulled the cream silk panties from her wedding lingerie off, pulled on the g-string, and with one more glance in the mirror, she drew a deep breath.

"Yes…everything's…uh, fine…I'll be out in a minute."

Why was she suddenly so nervous? Feeling ridiculously over-dressed, she pulled the robe off. As she reached for the door she caught sight of the g-string's line under her gown as she glanced in the mirror. She reached under her nightgown and pulled it off without letting go of the door handle. The door swung open and she flipped off the bathroom light.

Alex stood frozen with his eyes locked on her. His breath hitched as he began to breathe again. He was barefoot next to the bedside table, having shed his jacket and tie, with his shirt unbuttoned. The small flame of a wooden matchstick blazed in his hand and the glow of candles cast a romantic radiance throughout the room. He had turned on soft music and lit numerous candles throughout the bedroom and living room. The fireplace blazed yellow and red and lit up the cottage in an extraordinary way.

"You…you take my breath away," he whispered, as his face flooded with a desire she hadn't seen him give into before. Then, distracted by the fire lapping at his fingers, he blew out the match, his glance quickly returning to Valeria. Even from the distance, she could see his chest pounding, nearly as hard as hers. She was certain that, in the golden glow of candlelight, there was not a trace of mystery left to her beneath her gown. Instead of shyness, that was exactly what she wanted.

"Do you…want some wine?" he asked as a courtesy that he didn't want to fulfill.

The shake of her head was nearly imperceptible as she stepped toward him, drinking him in from beneath her dark lashes. He swallowed and his nervousness touched her heart, flooding her with even more love for him.

Alex reached for her wrist and turned it up and caressed it. His lips caused a thrilling warmth that ran through her entire body. He smiled and ran his hand down to her locked fist, gently releasing her fingers. He pulled the bit of material from her hand and surveyed it. Suddenly, she realized that she still had the g-string in her hand. In that instant, he also realized what it was. They both laughed and she bit her lip.

"I'm sorry, should I be wearing that?" she asked, wondering if she was violating his vision of the evening.

The movement of his head was slight as his eyes lit in mild amusement. He set the g-string on the bedside table and glanced back at it, lowering his brow for a moment. "Perhaps…later?" he said with a trace of hope.

Then his arms went around her and he pulled her in as he kissed her deeply, but with a tenderness and heat that was new and intoxicating.

Lifting his face inches from hers, he bit his lip again. She could feel the trembling in his fingertips as he moved his hands from her waist up her sides, without his typical caution, and up to the shoulder of her gown. "This is beautiful, but I would like to…" He pushed the straps down her arms and stopped before it dropped below her breasts. "Is this all right?"

Suddenly, it was *very* all right. She nodded as tears flooded her eyes, reflecting her deep need for him. He pushed the gown off her arms and his eyes locked on hers. The gown stopped at the curve of her hips and with her eyes never leaving his, she slowly lowered it the rest of the way down, so that she was standing naked in front of him.

"You are breathtaking!" he said, overwhelmed with a desire that very nearly overtook him.

She was shocked at how comfortable she felt…and by her absolute need for him. But then, he was her Alex—her symbolon—the man she was meant to be with. He pulled her into his arms and their kiss deepened as she pressed against him. He ran his hands down her and she felt the thundering of her pulse reverberating throughout her entire body. When his fingers and mouth moved down her neck, she shuddered again and released a small moan.

"Umm…Just one thing," she said as her mouth brushed just below his ear. He raised his head and turned toward her, looking somewhat concerned.

She ran her fingers up over his bare chest and then to his shoulders pushing his shirt off.

"Oh." Alex let out a nervous chuckle. He quickly reached for the button of his pants and she put her hands over his, stopping him.

"Please, let me," she said gently, as she took his hands and kissed them. Then she took in the look and feel and taste of his chest while his hands brushed over every inch of her. She slid her fingers down his chest and over his stomach as her mouth traced its way down to his heart. She felt him shudder as she grasped the top of his slacks. Locking her eyes on his, she bit her lip again. Alex pulled her face up to his, nearly distracting her from her quest. She fumbled with his buttons, feeling a bit foolish.

"Do you want help?" he asked, his voice breathless. She shook her head no, determined.

Breaking her concentration from his face, she glanced down, and, through the soft glow of candlelight, she found the hook and then the button. She heard his breath hitch several times when her fingers slowly grazed his bare skin as she unzipped his pants and pushed them off his hips. They released and fell to the ground.

Alex and Valeria stood for the first time together with nothing between them; not silk, nor distance, nor time. His mouth came down on hers in an avalanche of emotion and, although he attempted to restrain himself, his body yearned for her with a need that had been denied for far too long. He drew a rough breath and then picked her up, gently lowering her onto their marriage bed.

Laying next to each other, luxuriating in the taste and touch and feel of each other, Alex took her face in his hands and looked at her with so much love that all she wanted in the world was him…closer, deeper, completely.

"Make love to me," she whispered.

And this time, he nodded.

It was there, in their own bed, in the cottage that he had built for her, that—as in his vision from 3,000 years before—they made love for the first time…and the second…and the third…

∞

Deep shudders of pleasure ran through both of them and then faded into wonderful ripples of memory as they clung tightly to each other. Alex kissed her again, breathlessly, and she pressed into him for a moment before he rolled onto his back, pulling her with him so that she was on her side and still wrapped around him. The flame from the candles had long since disappeared into a hollow of wax and they now basked in the glow of the full moon shining in from the window, setting the room aglow in a magical light.

She marveled at the wonderful dewiness of their bodies and how they seemed to fit together so perfectly—hip to hip, chest to chest, their legs entwined. She brushed her lips over his chest, as her hand trailed down to the dips in his midriff. They both continued to revel in the mystery of the extraordinary emotions released during their lovemaking.

He turned his face toward hers and the passion in his eyes took her by surprise. "I would have *never* believed it was possible that I could love you more," he said.

She smiled and brushed the side of his face as she pulled up on her elbow.

"Well, now, Mr. Morgan," she said with a breathy, seductive voice that she had previously not possessed, "did you mean that literally or figuratively? Because I believe that tonight we have proven that there are no limits."

He released a soft, sexy laugh. She had never heard that aspect of him before. "Oh, I believe we are probably approaching the daily limit."

She smiled and wrapped herself tightly around him.

"Alex, thank you so much for this."

"Making love to my wife?" He snickered. "Just part of the job," he said with a relaxed and joyful smile.

Her smile broadened but a tear touched her eye. "All of this!" she whispered. "The wedding of my dreams here at Morgana, our wedding night in our beautiful cottage, inviting Weege, and," she shook her head, "I don't believe I will ever be able to express to you what this has meant to me!" A tear rolled down her cheek.

"Hey, no tears. Besides, it isn't over yet." His smile grew playful. "We still have our honeymoon."

She took in the rise and fall of his chest, still a bit too fast, and her fingers played with the bit of hair over his heart. For several hours, they laid there, both feeling complete, as they learned every inch of each other.

"What time is it?" she asked completely relaxed and happily entwined with her husband.

He stroked her arm and then turned his wrist to capture the moonlight on the dial of his watch.

"Hmm, three," he said, his voice sexy with sleep.

"Three...really?" She stretched. It seemed like they had been making love all night. She couldn't seem to be awake next to him without wanting to possess him again—tasting him, touching him, taking him.

He smiled and nodded lazily, as he moved his face down to hers. "It seems that you've had other things on your mind." He kissed her nose. "Not that I've minded." His smile broadened, as he settled back against the pillow. Valeria sighed, as Alex ran his fingers down her side. It felt so natural to be this close to him—so perfect. She had always thought he was beautiful, but being with him tonight was a whole other level of appreciation.

"I guess I owe Kristiana a thank you," she said, and she noticed her voice sounded different...more confident.

Alex stretched lazily as the corners of his mouth turned up. "Yes. She was a great teacher..." He bit his lip. It was the first time he had ever spoken of his sex life with Kristiana, but Valeria could tell there was more he wanted to say.

"What?"

Alex shrugged, his eyes sparkling with a hint of amusement and the deep joy that they shared.

She rolled on top of him. "I'm waiting."

"I had some other teachers."

Valeria pulled back in surprise. "Who?"

"Oh…Vatsyayana, Cleland, Miller, Lawrence, and James, to name just a few."

"Should I be jealous?" she teased.

"Hardly!" he reached his other hand around to her leg, pulling it up on the side of him. "They're authors: *The Kama Sutra*, *Fanny Hill*, *Lady Chatterley's Lover*, *Tropic of Cancer*."

"James? What could James Joyce have taught you in this arena?"

He playfully swatted her bottom. "Not James Joyce...E.L. James." She pulled her head back, so he continued, "You know, *Fifty Shades of Grey*."

Lifting her eyebrows, she asked, "*Fifty Shades*? Hmm! Was this all a recent course of study?"

He let his finger trail over her swollen lips. Unexpectedly, she opened her mouth and pulled his finger up into her mouth, dragging her teeth across it as her tongue lightly caressed it.

"Last February, I realized that it was unfair to you that I was so…inexperienced…" He drew another deep breath, and she released his finger. "And, a little overly anxious." He ran his finger back down her neck lingering over her breasts.

"You were anxious? You could have fooled me with all the distance you were giving me in Africa!" she said. "But now, I definitely know better!"

"I ordered every book on the subject."

"When did you have time to read them…I mean, you were in phone conferences…" Sudden realization hit her. "Oh. You weren't on phone conferences." Alex chuckled and shook his head. "But when you came out from your meetings…or, I guess, from your studying, why were you always so distant?"

He leaned his nose against hers. "If I hadn't been, I can assure you that tonight would not have been our first time together. Thank God for Caleb!"

"Caleb?" She thought for a moment and then realized that Alex had been using their gift of non-verbal communication to cool things down. "I wondered what had suddenly gotten into him."

Alex shrugged innocently, and Valeria rolled her eyes. She had fallen for it hook, line, and sinker!

"Well, thank you for doing so much...research. So, *Fifty Shades*, hmm?"

Alex blushed a bit. "Yes, well...forty million women can't all be wrong."

"And so...is there something to it? I mean, it's about being tied up and all, right? I don't know if I can do that. Is that what you want to do?"

Alex's joyful laugh reverberated through her body. "Not unless you're interested. I prefer you," he thought for a minute and then smiled again, "unleashed! I did learn some interesting tips on sensory deprivation though—you know, blind folds. We can try that if you get bored."

"Oh, I'll never get bored with you!" she said resolutely. "But that sounds...interesting, and...kind of kinky. But for now," she happily leaned her nose in close to his, "I'm hungry."

During their lovemaking, Valeria had discovered her own sensuality and confidence and it had been incredibly freeing. Alex had obviously taken notice.

The corners of his mouth turned up again. "You might have to wait a bit. I'm afraid you've about worn me out tonight."

"Sorry. Well, not really...but this time, it's for food." She jumped up naked and walked into the kitchen. "Besides, I've heard that oracles recovery is legendary." They both smiled. "Do you think there's anything in here?"

Alex watched her. "My God, *you are* beautiful!" he said, his voice full of reverence.

Valeria suddenly realized it was the first time she had ever been so comfortable with her own nudity, and she loved how liberating it felt. "I think I could live with you like this!" she said.

"Yes, I've been thinking the same thing. That's why I chose a particularly private location for our honeymoon."

"We can't stay here?" She opened the refrigerator. "Well, thank you, Camille!" she said as she strolled back in with a platter full of fruit and chocolate.

As she scooted her engagement ring back on the bedside table so that she could set down the tray of food, she noticed the candlelight playing off the crystal of her ring. It was a luxury to wear it, but after nearly scratching Alex with it several times during the night, she decided it was better to remove it for sleeping...and for other things. She'd kept her wedding band on though—which was a work of art in itself! The platinum band had grape vines delicately moving around it that joined the vines on the engagement ring when they were placed together. How Alex could have designed something so perfect for her, so long before he had actually spent any time with her, was remarkable. She assumed it was the magical understanding between symbolons.

Valeria picked up the framed photograph of the two of them—her favorite—it was their first picture together and it had been a gift from Camille. She set it back down, refilled their shared wine glass, and rolled back to her previous position on top of Alex. She picked up a strawberry and tasted its sweetness, as Alex sipped the wine.

"So, the million dollar question..." She said, as she playfully gave him a bite of her strawberry; she watched Alex as he sucked the piece of fruit into his mouth and bit down, his eyes never leaving hers. Alex handed Valeria his glass of wine and she sipped it, and then used his chest as a resting place for the glass. "How long can we stay?"

Alex thought for a moment. "If there isn't any sign of trouble by tomorrow, we might be able to stay for one more night."

"You don't expect any trouble do you?" she asked, taking a bite of the decadent chocolate.

He gazed into the distance, and then shook his head. She knew better than to take his response at face value, but decided she wasn't going to force a discussion—especially not tonight.

"So, where are we going?" she asked excitedly.

He shook his head lightly, amused at her energy, and then set the wine glass on the bedside table. "I was wondering when you were going to ask. But aren't you tired yet?" he asked playfully as he rolled her over.

"I'm too excited to sleep," she said.

He smiled and evaluated the look in her eyes carefully. "Hmm, my guess is that you'll be asleep in less than five minutes." He kissed her nose and crawled out of bed. "Be right back."

Alex took the tray back to the refrigerator and then blew out the candles. When he returned, the corners of his mouth turned up—she was asleep. He raised his eyebrows. "Told you...five minutes," he said softly, not wanting to wake her.

He stood there watching her soft breaths as the moonlight bathed her perfect face and shoulders in a mystical white goddess-like sheen. He felt the thrilling and overwhelming joy as he again realized that this extraordinary woman, who he had dreamt of and desired for an eternity, was now finally, and irrevocably, his wife. He blew out the last of the candles and crawled into bed next to her. Instead of facing away from her, as had been his habit to avoid temptation, he turned and pulled her tightly into him as their legs and arms wove their bodies tightly together and they both drifted into delicious sleep.

CHAPTER 5

It was a delicious dream and Valeria curled tightly into her husband, wrapping herself in closer as she listened to the soft crackling of the fire. Alex's arms responded, even in his sleep, brushing his hands along her hips and nuzzling his nose in her hair as his lips brushed her ear.

There was a moment of disorientation when she considered that the crackling of the fire must be a part of her dream, though she had a slight awareness of danger and something urging her to wake.

As she continued to battle her consciousness about the reality of the fire, there was a loud pop that broke through her dream, and she bolted straight up. Immediately, Alex jumped out of bed and quickly took in the situation. Flames crawled along the ceiling from the artist's studio, next to the fireplace, filling the great room with smoke.

They sensed a new source of air that fanned the flames and watched as they quickly spread toward the entrance. Then they heard Mani's frantic voice coming from the front door as he shouted, "Alex! Valeria!"

It took Alex no more than an instant to pull on his pants and lift a dazed Valeria from the bed and onto her feet. Reaching down, he grabbed the first bit of clothing he found—his shirt—and slid it over her. He buttoned a few of the buttons as she stared at the flames.

"All of your work!" she cried, as he pulled her into the great room and toward the front door. Then she saw the leather-bound books. As she reached to grab *Walden,* she saw her left hand and her lone wedding band.

"My ring!" she said, pulling free from Alex's grip.

Suddenly, it began to rain flaming cinders in the great room as the blaze gleefully danced toward the bedroom and front door, devouring the ceiling behind it. From the bedside table, she reached for her engagement ring and the picture of the two of them that she loved.

"We have to go," Alex said.

A loud hissing began, like a boiling teakettle. It evolved to a whistling whine that grew more intense by the second. Their eyes searched behind them and into the great room for the source of the sound...that seemed to lead to the door of Alex's studio. A rumbling, combined with the whine, made Alex's eyes grow wide with realization.

He wrapped his arms around her waist and quickly rolled them both over the bed, away from the direct line of the flammable art supplies in his studio. The whining had become a wail as they reached the floor; he covered her protectively as a deafening explosion shook her to the core.

When she opened her eyes, she looked up to discover a surreal world with missing walls and pages of books that had, moments before, been on the other side of a wall. Now they were floating...billowing down endlessly. She breathed in and began to choke. Alex took her face in his hands and examined it for a moment.

"Are you all right?" he asked.

She stared at him completely dazed. Everything had happened so fast—one minute she was asleep in his arms, and then there were explosions and fire and she couldn't quite grasp it all. But she knew they needed to get out of their beautiful cottage...their enflamed cottage. She glanced at her hand and saw only the picture frame. The ring was gone. As her eyes followed a route, over the mess that had been their bed—now covered in debris—she caught site of the glistening blue stone sitting on top of a pile of fluffy down that had once been part of Alex's pillow.

She saw Alex glance toward the window at the front porch and nod as in a non-verbal communication. Most of the glass was already blown out, but the panes remained. Then she saw movement from outside, although the state of her mind and the smoke made it difficult to think clearly.

"Stand back!" Mani shouted, and Alex pulled her face down into his chest and barred her again.

She heard a loud crash and the tinkling of glass. In an instant, Alex swept her up in his arms and, without a second thought, stepped barefoot over the broken glass to the window, passing her into Mani's arms. Immediately, she noticed that she could breathe, and she could feel the cool wood of the porch under her feet. Mani continued to support her, sensing her lack of balance.

"Mani, please help Alex!" she said and struggled to stand on her own as she leaned on the outside of the window sill to stabilize herself, suddenly aware that she was shaking.

Alex leaned out the window and gave her a quick kiss. "Be right back," he said.

Before she could object, he turned and shot chest first over their bed, reaching for the ring. Now, the ceiling in the bedroom was ablaze.

She stood voiceless in her terror and was suddenly aware that she was clutching their picture to her chest. The smoke parted and she saw that the other side of the room had crumbled, blocking the other window. Then she saw the blood and glass that gaped from the soles of Alex's feet and she felt the air being sucked from her lungs. As he turned back toward the window, the roof of the cottage seemed to groan, and then released a fiery beam. Alex jumped back so that the beam missed him, but now he was trapped inside.

"Oh, Alex…come out, please come out," she said to herself over and over again.

"Val, it's all right!" he shouted, attempting to calm her. She thought he was saying something else to her but she couldn't hear it. Then, as the flames increased, he disappeared for a moment and then returned, shrugging at Mani as he tossed out Valeria's engagement ring and his watch.

"She needs to leave," Alex yelled over the crackling of the fire.

"No!" Valeria screamed, reaching for Alex through the window. Mani grabbed her and pulled her back.

Leaning near the gaps between the beam and the window, Alex shouted out to her, "Val, you have to leave now! Do you understand me? You have to leave! I'll meet you there," Alex said.

"I'm not leaving you!" She heard him coughing and then he pulled back and disappeared in the smoke.

"Valeria…Alex is all right," Mani said.

She kicked and tried to push Mani's hands off from her. Just then, Alex returned to the window and she saw he had something in his hands and was trying to move the flaming beam. The material instantly went ablaze and his hands burned. Surrendering that location, she thought she saw him at the other window.

"We have to help him, Mani!" she cried, but Mani just held her.

Alex held up his hands and shrugged. Suddenly, there was a loud hissing sound—much louder than before. Alex stared toward the studio and then at Valeria in alarm and yelled, "Propane! Get her out of here!"

Mani lifted her off her feet and ran toward the woods as she kicked and struggled to get back to the cottage.

The ground rumbled angrily in an ear-shattering explosion and she felt as if she were airborne. The next thing she was aware of was the cool earth under her body and face. Suddenly, she was transitioned into a silent world with no loud fire and no shouting, only the shrill ringing in her head. It was a few seconds before she turned her face—stunned—and brushed the dirt from her mouth. She felt the rumble of Mani's chest. Did he say something? Then she was lying on her back and Mani was kneeling next to her. She couldn't quite focus but he seemed to be surveying her as his mouth moved…still, there was only the ringing.

In a daze, she reached her hand first to her hair, and felt that it was now tangled and entwined with pieces of pine and debris; then she moved her hand over her lower lip. When she moved her hand away, she saw the brilliant red of blood.

Rolling onto her side, she sat up and saw hundreds of tiny flames that blazed on the ground near them. Her eyes rose with horror to where her husband had been moments before. The porch was still there but there was a huge hole in the roof where the stone fireplace stood.

She tried to stand up but she was shaking so badly that she couldn't find the strength. Instead, she began to scramble on all fours toward the cottage. She felt strong arms around her. Turning, she recognized Tavish. There was a loud crackling that broke through her wall of silence as a part of the roof caved in on their bedroom.

Her left ear did an angry pop and she could hear the roar of the fire—although it was dimmed by the still intense and shrill ringing—and another high-pitched sound. Then she realized, it was the sound of her own screaming.

Tavish clung tightly to her. He was saying something, but she was unable to make anything out. She fought him and cried out as the rest of the family arrived.

Everyone seemed to be more concerned that she was upset than the fact that her husband was burning to death inside of their home. It was an incongruity to her. No one was going to get Alex out except her. She continued to struggle to get free of Tavish's grip. Her ears popped again and she heard Tavish. "He's all right, Lass."

"Why aren't you getting him? He's your friend! We have to get him out of there," she sobbed.

She saw Caleb and heard him say over the ringing, "I'll get him, Val, I know where he is!"

By then, Camille had arrived and, seeing Caleb running toward the inferno, she grabbed him by the shirttail so that he had to turn around. "Caleb! No! Your job is to stay by Val!"

Valeria screamed Alex's name over and over in a voice that she could barely hear over the ringing in her head as she fought against Tavish's grip. She knew she was hysterical—but no amount of reason could make her understand why their friends wouldn't let her get him. Camille moved her face inches from hers.

"Val! Val!" Camille said calmly, her voice rising above the ringing. "Listen to me! You have to listen to me!" she commanded.

"Why aren't the fire trucks here? Why isn't somebody doing something?" Valeria screamed.

"Val!" Camille said, holding Valeria's face for emphasis. "The cottage will be in ashes before the trucks can get here and we can't let anyone on the property right now." Valeria cried and continued to struggle. Camille raised her voice as she continued, "Valeria, listen to me! Listen! Alex is immortal! He will be fine! But *you* are in danger and we have to get you out of here *now*!"

"I'm not leaving without him!"

"Lass, you must do what Camille says. We have sworn an oath."

Mani walked back to Valeria and spoke calmly. "Valeria, an enemy has somehow broached our security. It is extremely dangerous for you to be here now. Alex will survive and will join you later."

She shook her head vehemently; if she left without him, she was terrified that she would never see him again—and that was a risk that she simply could not take!

Pulling all her wits about her, she stopped struggling and forced herself to relax. Finding every bit of strength within her, she said, "*No one* is taking me out of here without my husband!" Her chest heaved heavily with emotion. "Do you hear me? Do you all understand me? I'm not leaving! Not without Alex."

Tavish said sadly, "We will force you if we must."

She had to calm herself so that they would listen to her. She drew several slow breathes.

"Yes, Tav, you could," she said as she nodded repeatedly for emphasis, and then drew another deep breath. "But how long will you hold me prisoner? Because *I will* come back here as soon as I can get away." Tavish nodded. "So, I want all of you to listen to me now! Are you listening?" she said, trying to keep the tears out of her voice. "I am not leaving here without Alex. So let's figure out how to save my husband from this fire! Alright?" She looked around and bit her lip, and even through her fog, she grimaced as her teeth braised the cuts on her mouth.

Camille glanced at Lars who nodded, and with a resigned expression, he ran around to the back of the house and disappeared. There was movement through the flames and she knew Lars was inside. Valeria put her hand over her mouth and held her breath. A few moments later, Lars emerged carrying Alex over his shoulder.

Mani said softly, "I'll get my bag." Then he headed toward his home.

Lars coughed before laying Alex down on the ground. Valeria rushed to her husband and saw that his skin was covered in black soot and he was barely conscious. She touched the side of his face and gently brushed her lips over his; with relief, she felt that the air was still moving through his lungs, although it was weak.

"You're going to be fine now." She kissed him again.

His mouth began to move in unspoken words and his eyes fluttered, as if he was trying to open them.

"Relax. Doc will be here in a minute," she said, as calmly as she could.

Lars issued rapid-fire orders, "Let's revamp the escape plan. Mani can't be a decoy—I want him to stay with Alex and Val." Lars looked at the burns on his arms and hands. "I'm in no shape to drive for at least a few hours. Tavish, you'll need to shave your beard—quickly. Where's Daph?"

Valeria paid no attention. She was watching Alex struggling to breathe and obviously in pain. Mani returned and started to place a mask over his face and, again, Alex moved his mouth and fluttered his eyes. Mani glanced at Valeria from head to foot and then responded aloud to Alex's non-verbal question. "No serious injuries that I can see. A few minor abrasions. Nothing that will not heal soon."

Alex sighed and nodded, and then moved his mouth again. Mani answered, "Yes, my friend, we will keep her safe...as agreed." Then, Mani placed the oxygen mask over Alex's mouth.

Camille said, "Caleb needs to stay with Val. I'll drive."

"You'll need additional protection," Lars said. "I'd feel better if Tavish and Caleb went with you. I'll be the decoy and Ava can drive."

"I think I need to stay with Val," Camille said.

Ava nodded. "I agree with Camille. And no one would believe that Alex would have Valeria driving in this situation."

"What do you suggest?" Lars asked.

Just then, Daphne and Paolo emerged from the woods, running toward the blazing cottage. Paolo glanced at the fire and the color drained from his face as he cried out, "Is she..."

Relief flooded Paolo's face when he saw Valeria on the ground near Alex. Paolo went to her and touched her shoulder. "Bella! Thank God, you are safe!"

For a moment, she seemed unaware of his touch and then she slowly turned her head and followed the arm up to see Paolo's face. In an instant, she was standing, suddenly enraged as her fists pounded on his chest and she cried, "You did this, didn't you? You couldn't allow us even..." she huffed, as tears escaped her eyes. "You couldn't allow us one night of happiness!"

Confused, Paolo bit back the pain of her rage and tried to pull her into him to comfort her. Instead, she screamed at his touch. Paolo winced as if he had been physically hurt by her actions, and he backed away from her. Daphne put her hand on Paolo's shoulder and stared at Alex for a moment. Then she swallowed, and said to Valeria, "Paolo didn't do this." Daphne turned to Lars. "I was with him the whole time. I swear it!"

Lars nodded to Daphne. "We need a decoy. Can you and Paolo do that?"

"Yes," Paolo said, resolutely, and then glanced at Daphne in confirmation.

"Absolutely," Daphne added.

Lars went to reach in his pockets and then shook his head, frustrated that his hands were too badly burned. Ava reached into his pocket and then tossed the keys to Paolo.

"Those are Alex's keys. Drive to Rome," Lars said. "That'll give us enough time to get them where they need to go. Don't stop anywhere. There are baseball caps and Alex and Val's jackets in the back seat. Put the sunglasses on as soon as the sun comes up. The windows are dark enough that it should work," Lars ordered. He glanced at his hands. "Damn this hurts."

Paolo and Daphne ran to the side of the house, where Alex's car was parked. Within minutes, they were tearing down the road at breakneck speeds.

Camille squealed a Mercedes SUV to the front of the cottage. She looked to Ava. "We need your car for Alex."

"Of course." Ava nodded, holding on to Lars as he sat on the ground looking at his burns.

Valeria couldn't seem to grasp her new reality. She felt a hand on her shoulder and, this time, she turned to see Camille. The ringing lowered and then dissipated.

She felt a blanket covering her shoulders and she was suddenly aware that she was shaking violently. She brushed Alex's singed hair from his soot-covered face and his eyes fluttered for a moment.

"It's all right, Alex. I'm here. I'm not leaving you."

"Val, there's a duffle bag with your clothes in the van. Why don't you change? Put these on." Camille set the turquoise flip-flops on the ground.

Kissing his forehead, Valeria said, "I'll be right back."

With that, she slipped her feet into the flip-flops and tightened the blanket around her. She stopped and turned. "Alex needs this more than I do." She laid the blanket over him and a quiver of sobs came over her. She shoved them back and walked to the van.

The seats in the back of the SUV had been laid down making room for Alex. In the front passenger side, she saw two black duffle bags, one of which had a pink band. She unzipped it and located a pair of jeans and underwear. Then, she walked to the other side of the SUV and pulled them on.

The hatch opened and Camille tossed in Mani's leather medical bag. Valeria saw Ava, Tavish, Caleb, and Mani as they carried Alex on the blanket toward the SUV.

Lars continued to issue orders. "Tavish, once Alex is set, you'll follow Camille in your car out the back gate."

"Right."

Lars added, "If there's any trouble en route to the safe house, do whatever you have to do, but I want Val out of there—regardless of what she says! Understand?" Tavish nodded. Lars looked at Caleb who seemed particularly upset by all that had transpired. "Caleb, do you understand?"

The boy nodded somberly.

Camille crawled into the back of the vehicle and signaled to Valeria. "Come here. We're going to pull Alex in on the blanket."

Mani and Ava arrived at the hatch with Alex. Camille and Valeria grabbed the blanket and pulled. Alex moaned and Valeria stopped, releasing a sob.

"We're hurting him!" she said.

"Val, we have to do this quickly. Lift and pull on three. Ready?"

Wiping her face with her sleeve, she nodded.

"One, two, three," Camille counted and nodded at Valeria; they pulled quickly. Alex cried out, causing Valeria to release another sob; he was unconscious, but inside the vehicle. Tavish drew a deep, shaky breath and then nodded to Camille as he shut the hatch. Mani climbed in the door opposite Valeria and tried to fit his long limbs into the cramped quarters in the back of the vehicle.

"Please let me stay back here with him. I won't get in the way," Valeria said softly, and Mani nodded.

Lars called to Tavish. "Tav, run up to the house and get your car. Camille will meet you there. Whatever happens, Caleb stays with Val! Alright?"

Tavish nodded. "Yes," he said, as he took off on the foot trail.

Mani re-strapped the oxygen mask on to Alex's face as Camille put the car in gear and they sped up to the main house. The tables and chairs were still where they'd been just hours ago, when they had danced so happily. The sky was soft blue and pink with a hint of sunrise kissing the hills.

The memories were still so fresh in her mind that it made the current events seem as though they must be a nightmare. She kept imagining that she would wake next to Alex in their beautiful cottage and he would assure her that it had all been a bad dream. Then they would make love again.

"Caleb, Val needs a jacket. There's one in either of the duffle bags there by your feet," Camille said.

With Tavish's car behind them, they raced off to the back gate as Caleb tossed a tan trench coat to Valeria, who took it and wrapped it around herself.

Mani opened his leather bag and then glanced at Alex, who was moving his jaw but no sound was coming out. "Yes, I am aware of the symptoms of shock," Mani said matter-of-factly.

"Shock?" Valeria asked.

Mani pulled out a small flashlight from his shirt pocket. "Yes. Alex is concerned that I will be distracted with his injuries and fail to care for you."

"Follow the light," he said, and she looked from left to right with some irritation. Alex was the one who needed the care. Mani touched her face and neck. "Are you still cold?"

"No," she said, although she was still shivering. He pulled the jacket tightly around her.

"Caleb is there any water?"

"Check the center console," Camille said to Caleb, who dutifully pulled out a bottle and handed it to Mani.

"I want you to drink this. Stay warm and I believe you will be fine."

"Yes," she whispered, as her voice was nearly gone from all of her screaming. Despite the fact that Alex clearly had third-degree burns over his hands and arms, he would be unhappy if she argued.

Mani pulled on some rubber gloves, and then removed several packages of sterile gauze pads and a liquid. Pouring the liquid onto a gauze pad, he turned Valeria's face toward his and looked at her lip.

"This will sting for a moment."

She cringed and saw the cloth come off her lip with just a trace of blood. She would have fought him, but she was certain that any argument would only delay Alex's care.

Then he turned to Alex and lifted his arm.

"Mani, shouldn't we wrap the blanket around Alex? He is probably in shock."

Nodding in a way that seemed more as if he had only acquiesced, Mani said, "Caleb, is there another blanket?"

"Caleb, there are two sweaters in Alex's bag. One is for Val to put on. The other is for Alex."

As Mani lifted Alex's arm, Valeria got a closer look at the charred skin, blood, and soot.

Glancing at Valeria critically, he asked, "Would you like to help?" She nodded.

"Hold the gauze in place while I tape it, please."

She held the bandage on Alex's hand as Mani began to tape it to an unburned portion of Alex's arm. Alex's fingers curled a fraction on hers. The love that she felt in that subtlest of movements overwhelmed her, and a few tears escaped. She would have wiped them away except she would have had to release his arm.

"Umm, shouldn't we clean the burns first?"

"Later will be better," he said, glancing at her. "He *will* heal, Valeria."

As Mani opened another package of gauze, Alex's eyes flickered almost open for a moment. He moved his finger as if he wanted to say something. Mani nodded again. "Are you certain?"

"What?" Valeria asked.

Mani drew in a deep breath. "I will do as you wish."

"What did he say, Doc?"

As Mani finished wrapping the gauze around Alex's forearm and elbow, he reached into his bag. "He wants Morphine." Mani glanced up. "And he wants me to tell you that he will be all right."

"It didn't look like he said that much."

"He asked for morphine." Mani pulled out a vial and switched on the overhead light. "He is getting weaker. But he has been asking us to assure you that he will be all right."

Valeria forgot that they were able to use thoughts instead of words. "He doesn't look all right," she said quietly, as she brushed Alex's hair from his forehead.

Rifling through his bag again, Mani said, "I can assure you that he will be all right...but it will take time."

Pulling out a hypodermic needle from the bag, he inserted it into the vial and held it up toward the light as he drew the plunger. Valeria touched Alex's unburned fingers, and they again curled slightly on hers. Another tear escaped and rolled down her chin.

"I thought immortals recovered quickly."

"Yes, but these are serious injuries. They will take more time."

Valeria eyed the third-degree burns on his arm. "His burns?"

Mani shook his head, then tapped the hypo and squirted the air with a small amount of liquid that came from the needle. "It is the smoke inhalation that will kill—" he stopped abruptly as Valeria choked back a sob before it completely surfaced. Mani glanced at her and restated, "His body cannot survive this much damage."

She felt herself going into hysterics and felt Alex's fingers move again on hers. "You said he would be all right!" she said, hyperventilating.

Mani shook his head, irritated with himself. He looked at Alex. "I am sorry, my friend. I will do better."

He wiped the inside of Alex's arm with an alcohol pad. For some reason, the smell of the alcohol made her head start to spin.

Camille shouted back from the front, "Val, why don't you come up here. Caleb can get in the back." Valeria shook her head. "Alex wants you to come up here. He doesn't want you to watch this."

Brushing his face, Valeria said, "I'm not leaving you."

Mani withdrew the hypodermic needle, replaced the cap over the needle and tossed it into his medical bag, and then pulled off the oxygen mask. The mask left a white mark around Alex's mouth and nose where the soot had been. His eyes fluttered and then opened for a moment. He moved his mouth and she could hear that he was trying to talk to her. She leaned down and his eyes looked at hers for a moment. He whispered, "Be back…" His eyes began to roll, and then closed. "Can't...miss..." he murmured.

He mouthed another word and she played it over in her head and then realized it was, "Honeymoon."

"Don't you die on me, Alex Morgan!" she said.

"Alex will survive this. But not right now. I had hoped that we might be able to keep his body alive, so that the recovery would be easier, but there was too much damage. Still, he will recover."

Valeria fought back the tears. "I don't understand this. You said it was from…from…"

"From smoke inhalation. Yes."

Valeria felt the need to argue the point. "But Mani, he was breathing when he came out. Shouldn't we put the mask back on? Maybe it's not too late."

As he returned the supplies to his bag, Mani said, "Smoke inhalation can kill in several ways." The vehicle turned and a streetlight briefly lit up the back of the car. "The smoke from the cottage contained enflamed particles and they damaged the walls of the lungs. Also, he may have breathed in toxins from the chemicals, from the art supplies." Setting his hand on Valeria's arm, Mani said calmly, "Valeria, Alex will die...but he will also recover."

A cry escaped her throat. She looked down and tried to understand the reason to all of this. "Okay…okay…you said that immortals come back within twenty-four hours?" She swallowed, wondering how she could stand to see Alex die—even if it was for only a short while.

Mani nodded as they passed a car on the road. "Yes, but the healing process is not easy."

"That's why he needs the morphine—for the pain?" Valeria asked.

"The morphine was for your benefit," Mani said as he shifted and began to wrap Alex's other arm.

"I don't understand."

"For some reason, the morphine," Mani looked up from the bandages for a moment, searching for the right words, "seems to *quiet* the healing process." He returned to his work and Valeria waited for him to continue.

"When oracles return from death, their bodies seem to go through some agony. They cry out and writhe, though having personally been through that process numerous times, I don't recall it being particularly uncomfortable. The morphine remains in the body through the death and rebirth and quiets the process. The disadvantage is that the drug is another injury, so to speak, that we must recover from. So it will take Alex a little longer to recover."

"How much longer, Mani?" Valeria said with a gulp. The thought of more than twenty-four hours of seeing Alex like this—or worse—seemed incomprehensible.

Mani finished working on Alex's hands and chest, and crawled to the back of the vehicle to look at Alex's feet. He pulled a large shard of glass from Alex's foot and Alex made a slight sound. "This must wait until later. The car is moving too much and there is not enough light."

Alex's eyes were slightly open and wandered until they finally found Valeria's for just a moment.

"I love you, Alex," she whispered, as she brushed her hand over his face.

Alex blinked his eyes, weakly. She leaned down to kiss him and, for a moment, his mouth moved toward hers; then he drew a deep breath as his eyes rolled up into his head and back to hers, releasing a long and final exhale as his head lay lifelessly on her lap.

"MANI!" she choked.

"Yes, I know," he said softly, and then moved back toward her.

Suddenly, she released a long, agonized cry as she clung to Alex. She couldn't breathe, and felt an intense pain as if her heart had been ripped in two. She grasped her chest and struggled to breathe.

"This may help." Mani pressed the oxygen mask to her face. "The pain will pass in a moment. Try to breathe."

It was several minutes before the agonizing physical pain passed; then all Valeria felt was the extraordinary loss of her beloved husband. Mani soothed her, but underneath his calm, Valeria felt the pain of someone who also loved Alex, and that of a man who could sympathize with losing his symbolon. Once she was breathing again, Mani pulled the sweater off from Alex's chest and wrapped it around Valeria.

Leaning down to Alex, she kissed him again, and whispered through her tears, "Hurry back to me—okay?"

Mani was quiet for a moment. "He requested a lethal dose of morphine. He did not wish for you to witness his slow death nor the painful healing. Once the body of an oracle has sustained what it considers a terminal injury, it will continue until that process is complete before the spirit will rejuvenate it."

Leaning against the back of the driver's seat, Valeria pulled Alex into her, knowing she wouldn't hurt him now. She could feel his body cooling and ached at the silence in his chest. She pulled his jacket around both of them and closed her eyes, trying to believe that perhaps, when she awoke, he would be whole again.

The sun had just crossed the horizon as Camille pulled into Shinsu's estate. It would have been a beautiful morning. She should have been waking in his arms in their bed, in their cottage…which was now gone, along with all the pictures and belongings that Alex had collected over centuries. Another round of tears arose as several guards took Alex from her and carried him on the blanket and into the house. Valeria was consumed with a loneliness she could never have imagined. The world was foreign and cold in a way that it had never felt before.

"Take him to the main guest room," Shinsu said softly, and then hugged Valeria after she exited the SUV. "It was such a beautiful wedding, dear." Shinsu smiled, but it lacked her characteristic spark.

Following Shinsu inside the house and up the stairs, Valeria felt heavy with exhaustion. The guards entered the room and laid the blanket, which held her husband, on the center of a white fluffy feather bed. She brushed her hand over his forehead and then saw the soot on her hands.

"I suggest you shower and then sleep. It will help the time to go by quicker," Mani said.

Nodding, she took the black duffle bag into the bathroom. She stared at herself in the mirror. Her hair was a mess of debris. Her face was covered with almost as much soot as Alex's. In the duffle, she found toiletries. She brushed her teeth and then turned on the shower.

It took several times of washing and conditioning her hair before she felt the debris and knots clear from it. Then she leaned against the wall of the shower and released all the sobs that she had held tightly inside, as the hot water poured over her neck and back. Still, she moved as quickly as her body would allow, fearing that Alex would wake up and she wouldn't be there.

Then the unbidden thought struck her—what if he didn't wake up? What if they were wrong? She wondered how she could ever bury him as he had buried her. How could she live with this pain and emptiness?

She shook her head violently. She couldn't permit herself to think that way—it allowed it to be a possibility and that was unthinkable! She forced her mind to other thoughts; he would wake up in hours— only hours, now. Then they would be on their honeymoon.

Drying herself, she found a lotion that Camille had packed for her. She sniffed it and nodded. Alex would like the smell. She dried her hair and put on a pair of yoga pants and a T-shirt. When she picked up her clothes from the floor, she realized that they reeked of smoke.

As soon as she opened the bathroom door, the overwhelming smell of smoke, singed hair, and death hit her. She choked at the vision of Alex on top of the blanket, his hands and feet bandaged, wearing only the slacks from the night before, with no movement of his beautiful chest.

Mani and Camille sat in matching overstuffed chairs that they had moved near the bed.

"You look better," Camille said. "Is there anything you need?"

"I need some help."

"Anything! What?" Camille asked.

"I don't want him to wake up like this," she choked, as she gestured toward his face covered in soot.

"It would be easier to wait until he is healed," Mani said softly.

Drawing a rough breath, Valeria went into the bathroom and turned on the faucet, adjusting the water's temperature. She pulled a hand towel from a stack of rolled towels under the counter. She held the towel under the faucet until it was soaked, and then wrung most of the excess water out of it. She picked up two large bath towels and went back to the bedroom. Mani and Camille glanced at each other and Camille rose to leave.

The sun had just risen, but there were a few clouds and it left an eerie glow in the room. Valeria sat on the edge of the bed and lovingly wiped it across her husband's face. The towel was immediately covered with a dark, intense hue, a blend of blood red and black from the soot. She thought of the line from *Les Miserables*, "Red, the color of desire! Black, the color of despair!"

She turned the towel again as Camille returned with a washbasin filled with warm soapy water. "Do you want help?" she asked.

Valeria offered a slight shake of her head. Camille was leaving when Valeria remembered her manners and said, "Thank you, Camille."

"All right, I'm going to give you some privacy." She turned at the door. "Do try to get some sleep! You really are going to be honeymooning soon, and this part will all be only an awful memory. But Val, as Alex will tell you soon, he was willing to pay this price."

"I wasn't willing to pay *this* price…" A sob interrupted her. She was in no shape to argue. Her husband was dead. He had been in extreme pain, and perhaps he would heal—she had to hang on to that piece of hope. But their beloved home was destroyed, along with memories of eons. Still, if Alex was recovering, nothing else truly mattered except that the people whom she loved were safe.

The water in the pitcher had a wonderful warmth with a hint of lemon scent as she wrung out a fresh cloth and stroked it across his neck and chest, where hours before she had tasted the sweetness of his skin. She realized that, although it could be easy to get over-emotional about the cottage, the only thing that mattered was seeing her husband alive again.

"I'll be back in a little while. You really should try to sleep," Camille said, patting Valeria's shoulder before she closed the door and left

It was difficult to get her thoughts around the idea that he wasn't dead. Death was not a complete stranger to her. She remembered giving her father the obligatory final kiss goodbye. People had expected it. But he was a man who had been cold and distant to her, long before his death. Still, he had been her father and she always felt that she should have felt more—despite his inadequacies as a father.

With her father, it had been no more emotional than kissing a doll. There was nothing that had been *him* there. Although, the only time she had ever kissed her father was on Christmas, in front of the crowds when he had insisted, while he played Santa. Otherwise, their relationship had been impervious to emotion.

But this was very different. Touching Alex, though it was a shock to feel the coolness of his body, it also soothed her knowing that, soon, it would be warm again. She closed her eyes, praying that her husband would soon be alive and smiling at her. *That dream* was only a day away. She could close her eyes and try to make the day disappear.

Suddenly, Valeria was exhausted. She crawled under the sheets next to him and cried herself to sleep.

When she awoke, the sun was nearly to the horizon. Early evening—twelve hours left. She rolled away from Alex and sat up. In the rocker next to the bed, she saw Mani. "Have you been here all day?"

"I rested after you fell asleep this morning. I replaced Camille a few hours ago," Mani said, as he stretched his long frame. "I still need to attend to his feet, but I did not wish to wake you." He rose and pulled several instruments from his bag, and then, with a trash container next to him, he began pulling shards of glass from Alex's feet.

"How did he do this with me?"

Narrowing his eyes, Mani paused in thought.

"I have often wondered. I believe hope has carried him through the difficulties." He thought for a moment, and then continued examining Alex's feet under a bright light. "He sometimes waited centuries for you, many times finding you too late. There have been countless times that he has watched others hold you as you took your last breath; each time wondering if he would ever see you again." Mani narrowed his eyes. "I do not know how he has survived. As you now know, losing your symbolon is very painful. Camille says that it takes a piece of your heart and I believe that to be true."

Realizing that Mani had been alone for so long, she felt ashamed of her reaction. "I'm sorry Mani. I know you have faced more with your wife, than I have with Alex."

After pulling a final shard of glass from Alex's foot, Mani began bandaging it.

"Even now, centuries later, I wonder when Lita will return to me—knowing it is not possible." Mani drew a breath and then changed the subject back to Alex. "Somehow, Alex has always been very patient with you. He feels an urgency, due to what has been your very fragile mortality; knowing the torturous pain that lies just on the other side of it. Yet he is always concerned about stifling your exuberance. He forces himself to allow you the opportunity to live and experience life, as on the safari, while he pushes his fears aside. It is really quite noble."

Valeria nodded and they were quiet for some time. Finally, Mani finished working on Alex and sat back down.

"I still smell like smoke," she said. "I think I'll take another shower." The truth was that she felt the tears welling in her again and she was too ashamed to cry in front of Mani.

She turned the knobs on the faucet until the water was steaming and stepped under the showerhead. This time, she let the hot water run down her shoulders and neck for almost thirty minutes while she attempted to wash away the sobs. Despite the fact that she had slept all day, she was exhausted. Thinking it through, she realized that although the night before…before the fire, had held an extraordinary luxury, it had been days since she had slept well. Excitement and stress was now taking its toll. She was comforted by the warmth and softness of the towel. Then she dried her hair, and changed into a tank top and a pair of flannel pajama bottoms, pulling on a robe over it. She padded back to the bed and lay down next to Alex; pulling his lifeless arm under her neck, she curled against the silent hollow of his chest.

"I wish you would come back to me," she said, kissing the place over his heart as quiet tears blurred her vision and she fell back asleep.

Her mouth was parched when she woke. She turned to the nightstand and felt for the glass that was always by her bedside. It wasn't there. Then she remembered where she was and what had happened. Something was different and she couldn't put her finger on it. She turned back to him and touched his chest, his face. He seemed to feel warmer, and she felt a thrill. Leaning toward him, she brushed his face and then leaned her ear to his chest. It was quiet, but she heard the weak beating of his heart. Ripples of gratitude rushed through her.

"Thank you."

Pulling her cotton robe on, she went to Mani's room—although she hated to wake him. When there was no response to her tapping, she went to the staircase. From the living room, she could hear voices and quickly discerned that they were having a family meeting.

She didn't want to pry, but on the other hand, this most certainly was now her business. Down the turn of the staircase, she could see the entry; to the left was the living room.

Lars said, "We need to convince Alex that it is in all of our best interests to go after them now. It's obvious that…" His voice faded out. Ashamed of herself for eavesdropping, she started to turn, but then justified that it was her business. She wondered about what Lars had said, it was obvious that…what?

Without permitting herself to listen further, she headed down the stairs and cleared her throat. All eyes went to her on the staircase as if they were concerned about what she had heard.

"I'm sorry. I don't mean to interrupt…it's just…Mani, I just…" Mani immediately rose.

"What is it, Valeria?"

"It's Alex—he's…he's back," she said, surprised that she choked when she said it.

Mani was already walking toward the staircase. She glanced down and saw that all of the family, except Daphne and Paolo, were in the formal living area.

As they returned to the room, Mani checked Alex's vitals.

"This is a very good sign." Mani glanced at Valeria. "Have you slept?"

"Yes."

He narrowed his eyes. "You still have circles under your eyes. I suggest you sleep in the other guest room. It will be a few hours before he is alert."

"Thanks, Mani, but I'm not leaving him."

Mani hooked up an IV above the bandages in Alex's elbow. "This will assist the healing process."

"What's he going through?" Valeria asked.

After tapping the IV line several times, Mani sat down next to her on the bed. "Bodies take a very long time to die—even mortal bodies. Cells continue to live some time after the vital organs have stopped. With an oracle, our soul sometimes steps away in extreme conditions. These bodies require a very narrow parameter of conditions to survive.

"For oracles, the difference appears to be what our souls do with these bodies. The DNA of an immortal oracle is different from that of mortals.

"Alex is struggling to repair this body. I do not know if the morphine actually eases the healing process. But he does seem calm— does he not?"

Valeria nodded.

"It has only been eighteen hours and he is already breathing. That is a good sign. But Alex has suffered several severe injuries that require healing. Then he will require recovery from the morphine."

As Mani was leaving, Camille entered with a tray of food including eggs, bacon, toast, and croissants.

"You haven't eaten much in days."

It was near midnight, but Camille was right, it had been days since Valeria had eaten more than a few bites of a meal. Sinking into the rocker, she took a few bites of egg to appease Camille, and then nibbled on the toast. Camille nodded and then left, closing the door behind her. Valeria reached for her Kindle and began reading—attempting, unsuccessfully, to ignore the discussion that she was certain was continuing downstairs.

CHAPTER 6

As the light began seeping through the window, she moved her head and opened her eyes. She craned her neck left and right, attempting to release the tension. As her blurry eyes wandered across the room, she saw the door still closed, Alex's bandaged feet and the frame of his body under the sheet, his chest, and then the strong chin and his brilliant blue eyes as he watched her. It took her a moment to recognize, with surprise, that he was awake and she let out a cry as she leapt into his arms.

"Good morning, beautiful," he said as a weak smile crossed his face.

Alex wrapped his arms around her and held her close. She noticed that he was warmer than usual and she suspected he had a fever.

"I've missed you," she said, attempting to hold back the tears.

"Some honeymoon, huh," he murmured as he tried to wake up. "I'm sorr—"

She placed a finger over his mouth and shook her head. "Let me get Mani."

Moments later, Mani arrived and she could see the relief on his face.

"Sorry for the sleepless night, buddy," Alex said to Mani, his voice hoarse as he tried to sit up. Failing, Alex looked at his bandaged hands in irritation.

"Nights," Valeria said. "Mani was on guard duty the night of the fire. I don't think he's had much sleep in days."

"Thanks, Doc." Alex rubbed the side of his face with the back of his bandaged hand. Then he said, as if it were an effort, "Beautiful, would you mind making me one of your kale concoctions." She watched as he pushed a smile to his eyes. "I think I'm going to need all the help I can get...for the honeymoon." He winked and then coughed.

She took his bandaged hands in hers and kissed them.

"Alex...I'm your wife now, and ever since I've known you, you've had this need to protect me. But this is no longer just on your shoulders." She stroked the side of his face. "I'm tougher than you think and I can handle it all—as long as you're with me." Alex nodded as Lars and Ava walked in the room.

"You're right, beautiful. Lars, let's make sure Val's included in any significant conversations."

Lars smiled. "Glad to see you back with the living."

"Lars saved you in the fire," Val said.

Alex frowned. "Why would you do that?" Then Lars and Alex exchanged a look. "Oh. Well, thanks, Lars. I owe you one." Then Alex glanced at his wife. "Love, you have to do as Lars says. As you can see, I've recovered."

Steeling her glance she said, "You can ask anything of me, except to leave you. That, I will never do again."

"Fair enough," Alex said, struggling to maintain strength in his voice. "Lars, what do we know about the fire?"

Lars brushed his fingers over his eyes. "The fire began over your studio and spread rapidly to the front of the cottage. We checked infrared and it was traced back to one of our guards."

"I assume you interviewed him," Alex said, with a raspy voice.

"Yes. Ava and I conducted the first interview ourselves. Yesterday, Tav interviewed him as well."

"And?" Alex had the control, but his voice was so weak Valeria was concerned that this was more than he should be doing.

Tavish entered as if on cue and waved a hand. "The man was a patsy. He was extremely low intelligence; easily hypnotized. I think it was *her*—I think she has the evil eye."

"The evil eye?" Valeria asked. "I thought that was jealousy,"

"It's a might more than that!" Tavish added. "For some, at least."

Lars narrowed his eyes and said, "Alex, we may have our suspicions, but *there is* one person who can help us find the answers we need."

"I suggest that we have this discussion after Alex has had more rest," Mani interjected

"Yes, yes, of course," Lars said.

"That particular discussion is going to be delayed for some time," Alex said, his eyes already closing from exhaustion.

The family rose and started to leave when Alex added sleepily, "Doc?"

Mani stayed behind, although Alex's eyes were already half closed. "Doc, you know I can't think about that now." Mani nodded and dropped his gaze to the floor as if some painful memory had been brought up. Alex continued, "Not forever—just not now."

Again, Mani nodded. "We can discuss this after you've slept. I do understand that now is the time for you and your bride."

"Yes…" Then Valeria saw a hint of a twinkle in his eyes, even though they were half closed and he was nearly asleep. "And, Doc, I am a newlywed. And I desperately need..." Valeria saw the corners of Alex's mouth pull up in his sensual smile and it caused her to blush. Then he chuckled softly, his voice past exhaustion. "I need...a shower and a shave. I need to clean up."

"Yes, well, your *'needs'* will have to wait until you are healed," Mani said raising a single brow. "You can shower in a few hours. But you still have the morphine to deal with, so I might suggest you wait a few days for your...other *needs*."

"*A few days?*" Alex said, as his eyes closed completely.

"Yes. You are still recovering."

By then, Alex's jaw had gone slack.

Valeria sat down in the chair as Mani left.

Once the door closed, Alex's eyes opened slightly and he swallowed. "Oh no, you don't—come here," he said groggily. She smiled and crawled into bed with him, and laid her head on his shoulder. She kissed his chest and pulled up the blankets around him.

"I'll be all right soon," he whispered.

"I know," she said, and closed her eyes and drifted to sleep again.

∞

There was a knock on the door. When Valeria opened her eyes, Alex was again watching her with a smile, and the spark was back in his eyes. She felt his hand brush the side of her face, and then he turned toward the door. "Come on in, Doc."

Standing in the entrance, Mani observed Alex and said, "You look much better!"

Valeria got up and moved so that Mani could get to Alex, who swung his legs over the side of the bed. "I'm feeling much better!" He turned a flirtatious smile toward Valeria. "Don't go too far." He winked and she sat in the rocking chair by the bed.

"You know there are things that must be done, in regards to this incident," Mani said, as he tapped on Alex's palm and watched for a response.

"Feels fine," Alex said. Mani picked up Alex's other palm and tapped with no response from Alex. "Doc, I am aware that there is a…*situation.* But really, that isn't new information. It will just have to wait until after our honeymoon." Mani lifted Alex's arm and ripped off the tape.

Alex yelped, "Hey!"

Mani smirked. "It's better if I do it quickly." Then Mani ripped the rest of the tape from Alex's arm.

"Easy there, Doc!"

The gauze was black and red, but when Mani removed it, the skin underneath was completely healed—except for the red strips of hairless skin where Mani had removed the tape.

"You know, sometimes your bedside manner leaves something to be desired," Alex muttered.

A slight glint crossed Mani's eyes. "Let that be a lesson about deserting your beautiful bride on your wedding night." Mani ripped the tape off the next bandage and Alex yelped again.

Mani touched the bottom of Alex's foot and Mani noticed a slight flinch. "A few more hours on your feet."

Alex hopped out of the bed. "I'm fine." But Valeria could tell he was still in pain.

"You should be gentle with your body. I have not seen you go through withdrawal from the morphine."

Alex nodded as he leaned on the bed, looking at Valeria. "But as I said earlier, I have gone far too long without," his face lit in a mischievous smile and she caught the spark in his eyes, "a toothbrush and a shower." He brushed his fingers over his chin. "And a shave."

Mani shook his head at Alex's attempt at humor. "My friend, you are still recovering! I've done all I can do, but you must give your body a chance!" Alex shrugged him off, with a smile. Mani packed up his supplies and, with another warning glare, left Alex and Valeria alone.

"Do I have any clean clothes here?"

Valeria nodded. "Yes, Camille packed a bag for you. It's in the closet, but Mani says you need to rest a little longer."

Alex's eyes sparkled. "Beautiful, I know Mani will baby me, if I allow it. That's the way he's wired. But I would like to clean up." He brushed her hair back from her face and kissed her nose, taking a deep breath in. "I smell like smoke!"

Hobbling into the bathroom, Alex sorted through the toiletries and pulled out a change of clothes.

"You know, you were right...earlier," she said. He drew a deep breath trying to remember their discussion. "You do need a kale smoothie and so do I!" She heard Alex's groan. "You'll like it. We do have a honeymoon, and based on our first night...we're both going to need all of the energy we can get!" She offered a wicked smile and then left Alex speechless—and smiling.

By the time Alex headed downstairs, he had only a slight limp. The family stood and cheered as he took a bow.

Valeria handed him the green drink, while she sipped hers. Alex shook his head in acquiescence, clinked glasses with Valeria and said, "Bottoms up!" He took a drink and then nodded, in analysis. "All right, I can live with that."

As Alex sat down, Caleb approached him looking upset. "I think I just got too caught up in being a best man to be a superhero."

Valeria messed with Caleb's hair and said, "You did fine, buddy! This wasn't your fault and everyone's all right now."

Caleb nodded his head then narrowed his eyes in thought before responding, "Cool." Then he took a seat.

"I hope this seemingly impromptu meeting is about how to get us out of here," Alex said.

Lars shrugged. "If you insist, but there are some things we need to discuss first."

Raising his hand, Alex said, "I'm sorry, Lars, we're not going to have that discussion right now." Then he glanced at Shinsu and toward Mani. "I apologize specifically to both of you. I know you have a vested interest in this discussion, but it is just not going to happen right now." His voice didn't carry his typical strength, but his intention was shining through. "Right now, I only want to know two things: Is it safe for Val and I to leave on our honeymoon, and how are we going to ensure my wife's safety outside of here."

Valeria blushed when she heard Alex call her his wife.

Mani stood. "Alex, Valeria, I don't think you understand the seriousness—"

"Doc, you know I love you like a brother, and normally I would do anything...anything for you. But I want this clear to everyone." Alex glanced around the room to ensure they were all listening. "The *only* thing I am going to do right now, and the *only* thing I am going to discuss with all of you, is how I am going to take this beautiful woman, my bride, on our desperately needed honeymoon." Alex looked into Valeria's eyes and she saw the bright light of love shining through him. Alex kissed her and then rolled his head heavily to the couch and closed his eyes for a moment. When he reopened them, he looked weary. "Lars, can we get out of here safely?"

"We will...figure it out," Lars said, as he looked away; a clear indication to the others that the discussion was over. "I guess."

Alex nodded. "Can I keep her safe?"

Lars thought for a moment, and then nodded, resigned. "Probably. You were safe in Africa—well, reasonably safe in Africa," he said, glancing at Valeria. "But then, nobody knew where you were. It appears that the less people who know where you are, the better your chances."

Valeria narrowed her eyes. "You suspect Paolo!"

"Not directly," Lars said, and changed the subject. "All right, so when do you intend to leave?"

Alex glanced around the room. "I'd leave now if you told me we were safe."

Tavish spoke, "Laddie, can't you see that she's out there? Don't you understand all of this could be resolved?"

"She? Who is out there?" Valeria asked. Alex closed his eyes and shook his head as if he didn't want to discuss it. "Kristiana? Or do you think it was someone from the council?"

"At this time, we have no evidence of Kristiana's involvement," Alex said, now weary. "Until we have some hard evidence, I don't want to begin throwing around blind accusations."

"Couldn't the fire have been an accident? We had candles burning earlier," Valeria offered.

Mani shook his head. "No, Valeria. I was on guard duty. The fire did not begin inside the cottage." Mani looked at Alex. "I'm afraid I must agree with Tavish."

"Trust me on this—it's exactly as the old evil eye!" Tavish said.

Alex looked at them all and nodded. "I understand, and I appreciate your viewpoint, really I do. I don't mean to disregard all that you have done for us." He patted Valeria's leg. "But we need this time. We all knew the wedding was a big risk. And thanks to all of you, my bride is still in one piece."

Ava frowned. "Alex, it isn't that we don't want you to have a honeymoon. Lars just thinks that there is a timeline and it's rolling."

Valeria noticed that Lars was wearing a polo shirt with no sign of the injuries from a few nights ago.

Camille stood and brushed her hair back. "I have to say that I agree with Alex. I've seen all the data. I know there are things to handle. But this particular situation existed long before the wedding and I assure you those opportunities will still exist in a few months, after their honeymoon."

Valeria felt a thrill—they would be honeymooning *for months!* She felt her face redden and then noticed the corner of Alex's mouth curve up in that delicious smile. He rubbed his hand along her lower thigh—a movement he would have never done before—and then noticed the speckled beginnings of a full blush rising to her cheeks and neck. She smiled and brushed her hand along the back of his hair.

Camille continued, "Alex is right, they have both been through so much, and they need this time to celebrate and enjoy each other *alone!*" Camille glanced around and, without waiting for anyone else to acknowledge her statement, she took it as the winning final statement in a court case. With a warm smile, she ended the conversation.

"I'll take your silence as agreement," Camille pushed. Lars and Mani looked away. "Good!" She turned to Valeria. "I have already sent out a personal shopper to replace your trousseau. She and I will be tied up all day. It will take Lars, Tav, and Alex most of the day to make the travel arrangements. Depending on what they work out, I intend for you to be out of here tonight."

Lars paced across the room with his arms folded, as if trying to find a reasonable counter argument. Unable to dissuade Alex, he turned and shrugged. "All right. I'll arrange for transportation to the location we discussed."

Finally pleased, Alex smiled and took a sip of his green smoothie.

CHAPTER 7

By eight o'clock that night, they were on their way to a secret location. The limo wove along the mountains toward Switzerland. Mani had warned Valeria that Alex might still go through withdrawal, and she could already see that he was not feeling well, but she hoped that it would all be over soon.

"We're catching a flight out of Zurich," Alex explained, and she noticed a bit of sweat on his brow. As he wiped it away, she noticed that his eyes looked glassy, as if he were feverish.

"Are you feeling all right?"

"Fine," he said abruptly.

Valeria bit her lip and checked his forehead. "You have a fever. Should we turn around?"

He shook his head. "No. This will be over shortly."

They arrived at the Zurich airport. Alex wore his brown contacts, and by the time they were checking in, he had the chills.

Valeria purchased a blanket and wrapped it around him to try to calm the shivers while they waited for their flight to Newark, New Jersey. She found a bench and wrapped her arms around him.

After a few minutes, she said, "Alex, I'm going to get you a cold bottle of water. That may help."

"Hmm," he said, as if he was just too weak to speak.

At the shop, she grabbed a bottle of water and looked at a travel-sized bottle of aspirin, wondering if he could take it. An exceptionally skinny woman wearing high platinum shoes and over-bleached hair tapped her on the shoulder. "You American?"

"Yes," Valeria responded.

"Well then, I have a word of advice for your friend over there," she said in a heavy New Jersey accent.

"He's my husband." It was the first time Valeria had called Alex her "husband" and it felt wonderful.

"Well, okay, for your husband then. These Swiss hospitals are fine to dry him out, but—"

"It's the flu," Valeria interrupted defensively, as she pulled the aspirin bottle to her chest.

The woman raised an eyebrow as if she knew better. "Yeah, honey. I've seen this before." She pointed a bright red fingernail at Alex. "Get him hooked on cigarettes and coffee...that's my advice. He's gonna need to transfer his addiction."

"My husband has the flu."

"Right. I spent time in rehab here." The woman narrowed her eyes at Alex. "Fine looking man—what a pity."

Tossing some money on the counter for the water, Valeria moved to block the woman's view of Alex and said, "I have to go."

"I'm just saying," the woman said. "Try aspirin or Motrin?"

When Valeria returned to Alex, she noticed he was shivering furiously, so Valeria wrapped her arms around him and whispered, "Do you want some aspirin?"

After a few violent shivers, Alex said through gritted teeth, "No...let's just let it run its course."

They boarded and located their first class seats. His hands were shaking as he tried to fasten his seat belt, and he noticed Valeria's look of concern.

With his eyes set at half-mast, he pulled the blanket around him.

"No worries," he said, attempting a smile. "I just need to sleep a while." He patted her leg as he leaned into the seat awaiting take-off. The plane rolled out and, within a few minutes, they turned off the seatbelt sign. Alex pulled the blanket around his neck and rolled onto his side as he drifted into a restless sleep.

A few hours later, the sky had become a purplish-blue ahead of them, with a golden hue bronzing the sky from behind. Most of the travelers had closed their window shades, and the lights were dim. Valeria watched Alex continue to tremble as he battled the demons left behind in the wake of the morphine. When the shaking stopped, she took his hand and fell asleep. It seemed only a short time later that the captain announced that they were on approach to Newark and the sun had risen.

Valeria tapped Alex on the shoulder, and his eyes opened wide and clear as the corners of his mouth turned up playfully, as if the previous forty-eight hours had been only a nightmare.

"Good morning." He pulled her mouth to his. "I believe it's time for a honeymoon!" he announced, and then kissed her as he shed the blanket. "I thought Newark might be less conspicuous as a destination. I'm going to clean up," he said, as he stood and opened the overhead bin. He headed to the restroom with his toiletries bag and a clean shirt.

Ten minutes later, he returned, looking like a model on a billboard.

"We have a brief stop before we continue on to our destination." His eyes brightened as he raised an eyebrow. "And then, we officially begin our honeymoon."

She smiled as the thrilling heat moved through her—the word *honeymoon* had an even more powerful effect on her now, with the memory of their wedding night still fresh and again her face turned a flaming red.

Seeing her blush, Alex burst into joyful laugh as he brushed his hand over her face and then pressed his lips to hers in a kiss full of promise.

As they exited customs, a uniformed limo driver held a sign that read, "Morgan."

"I don't want you to get your hopes up, love. We can't stay in Manhattan. Too many people would expect that. But I thought we could spend a few hours here before we head off."

"That sounds wonderful!"

They drove into Manhattan. She felt a thrill at being in the location she had considered home, until she met Alex and discovered their cottage—the cottage that was now a pile of ashes. Then they hit the stopped line of yellow cabs.

"Perfect time to be here; there are so many cars that no one would notice one more," he said.

They drove up Columbus and then turned on 95th—her street. Valeria longed to be walking the streets with him. She remembered how uncertain she felt the last time they had been here. She had been completely mesmerized with him, and felt like a silly schoolgirl. He still mesmerized her—and she *still* felt like a silly schoolgirl. But now, she knew him and she knew *them*...and now they were married forever.

She stared with longing at the steps where she had stood with Alex nearly a year before. He had seemed so confident when he followed her into her brownstone. Now she knew how difficult that must have been for him. Other men might do that—Alex didn't. She sighed happily.

"Sorry, beautiful, we can't risk getting out here."

"That's alright."

She did love New York, and she missed her brownstone, although it was considerably smaller than she remembered, and a world less romantic than their cottage. She shook her head. The cottage was replaceable, even if Alex had filled it with mementos that he had collected over the eons just for her. Alex's centuries of artwork, the collection of leather-bound classics, and the family pictures were gone. But her husband was here, with her, and very much alive! She had always hoped to come back to New York with Alex—and here she was, no longer living an obscure life that offered her so little. Now, she was Valeria Morgan—Alex Morgan's wife. What a different world it had become!

They pulled into Central Park and the limo pulled over. Alex thanked the driver and tipped him and then he took her hand as they strolled through the southern half of the park under its deep green branches, passing children playing, and listening to musicians strumming their instruments next to the Bowman Bridge. They stopped to watch couples in rowboats on the lily-covered lagoon. Then Alex lifted his wrist and glanced at his watch.

"Are you hungry?"

She thought for a moment and then with some surprise said, "You know, actually, I am famished!"

"Good! I believe it's time for breakfast then."

As they walked along the trails, she remembered the only time they had been to New York together and how they had gone to breakfast less than a mile from here. They crossed out of the park and entered an exclusive apartment complex.

"I wanted to take you for breakfast at Tiffany's—not coffee and a doughnut from a street vendor—but an actual breakfast on the top floor. However, it seems that I could not gain access to a private and unobstructed view of Central Park."

They passed the doorman, and a uniformed attendant held the elevator for them. As they stepped onto the elevator, the attendant pressed the "P" at the top of the buttons.

"To the top," Alex said with a gleam in his eyes.

The doorman smiled. "Yes, Mr. and Mrs. Morgan. We've been expecting you."

The elevator opened to a luxurious entryway. A woman stood at the only door on the floor, wearing a white chef's uniform, with her long, dark gray hair tied back.

"Mr. and Mrs. Morgan! I'm Sarabeth Levine."

Valeria's jaw dropped. "As in, our favorite restaurant Sarabeth's? As in, Oprah's 'favorite things,' Sarabeth's?"

The woman nodded and Valeria entered the suite.

"We have you set up out here." Sarabeth led them through a fantastic apartment with a glassed wall and elegantly furnished terrace that looked out over Central Park and the city.

"Mrs. Morgan, I understand that you have a preference for our frittatas. And then to drink, coffee with cream and can I bring you both a mimosas?"

"Just one mimosa for my wife," Alex said, as he took Valeria's hand in his and kissed it.

"How did you arrange all of this?" Valeria asked in shock.

"We are actually right on schedule. I was afraid we might miss it. We do need to catch another flight in a few hours."

Moments later, a fruit salad was served with coffee and a mimosa for Valeria, and freshly squeezed orange juice for Alex. The sky was a glorious shade of blue with a few thin pink clouds that seemed suspended. The smell from the apartment was of freshly baked goods, bacon, and coffee. On the terrace, the air was still cool with morning and promised to be an extraordinary day.

Reaching across to him, she took his hand in hers. "You look better."

"I feel better!"

"You didn't need to do the morphine for me."

"It wasn't completely selfless. The sooner I was gone—the sooner I would be whole and with you on our honeymoon." The corner of his mouth turned up and his eyes sparkled.

Seeing him whole again, she could begin to think about their future. And while she was enjoying herself here with Alex, the shadow of the past few days hadn't completely lifted. But she allowed herself to anticipate their time alone and wondered if they would go to Bermuda, the Hamptons, or maybe even Maine.

Alex's smile broadened. "I can see your mind going a million miles a minute and I should warn you now that I have no intention of telling you until we arrive." He winked at her and then pointed to the east side of Central Park a few blocks from their location. "That's where I met you."

It seemed to be only chance that had led her there and into Alex's arms…and her destiny.

"Where you rescued me," she said. "I still remember the moment when your arms came around me—"

"You mean just as we were both hit by the kid with too much testosterone and way too much car!" He laughed.

She sighed. "Yes...when you saved me." She looked up in thought. "It felt as if the world shifted at that moment and was finally...right."

He took her hand in his and kissed it as their eyes filled with love, but they were interrupted as breakfast was served.

A server placed a plate in front of her with a beautiful frittata, fried potatoes, and Sarabeth's own English muffin. "Alex told me that you like my English muffins."

"They are fantastic! Thank you!" She had only dined there once, the day she had met him, and he remembered everything. The waitress served Alex Eggs Benedict with a tossed salad. It was the same meal they had eaten on their first meeting.

After the dishes were cleared, and Sarabeth and the staff left, Valeria glanced inside the apartment toward a door which promised to be the bedroom. She rose and went to Alex and put her arm around his neck. "Can't we stay here?" Her eyes focused on his. "We could order in," she whispered, and kissed the side of his face as she ran her fingers under the collar of his shirt to his chest.

He pulled her around and onto his lap. "Oh, you could so easily convince me to stay," he said softly, and then drew a deep breath as he brushed the hair back from her face. "But I don't want to worry another day about your safety—especially after the fire. Whoever lit it is obviously…" He turned his head as if to end that sentence. Alex rarely slipped, and he had not intended to discuss danger or the fire. She realized, then and there, that he was still recovering. His eyes brightened. "I have other plans for us. I hope you'll humor me." Alex glanced at his watch. "As a matter of fact, our ride should be here any moment."

"Our ride?" Valeria heard a hum.

"Yes, sounds like he's here. Come with me."

He took her hand and led her back inside the apartment and out the front door toward the elevators, where she spotted another hallway. He opened a door and went up some granite steps to another door. When he opened the second door, they were flooded with a cacophony of sound as a helicopter landed a few feet from them.

They loaded through the open entry of the chopper and the door was closed by the co-pilot. Alex picked up a headset with a microphone attached and pulled it on his head, handing another to Valeria. Then she saw Alex's mouth move and heard with a slight lag through her headset, "Beautiful, the mic is voice activated. Up front is Captain George." Alex signaled to the pilot with dark sunglasses and deep tan.

"Good morning, ma'am!"

"Hello, George!" She heard her voice over her headset.

Alex offered George a thumbs up, and they lifted off.

They crossed Central Park and flew over the Hudson continuing south toward Battery Park and the Statue of Liberty. It was a magnificent day and, sitting next to Alex, she reveled in being back in New York with him—even if it was for just a few hours.

They circled Lady Liberty, which was thrilling, and then headed east toward the Hamptons. She thought how wonderful it would be to spend time with Alex in the Hamptons. The flight along the coast was beautiful, and then they turned inland. Alex said, "East Hampton," and they circled a small airport and landed.

After removing their headsets, Alex patted George on the shoulder and then helped Valeria out of the chopper. As soon as they were clear of the blades, Alex wrapped his arms around her. Again, she saw the gleam of joy in his eyes.

"Are we staying here in the Hamptons?"

He shook his head. "No…" He brushed the side of her face and kissed her tenderly, and then drew a deep breath. "No. Unfortunately, we have several more hours until we reach our destination. There were more direct routes, but Lars and I agreed that this was better."

He led her to a small jet.

"What about our suitcases?"

He lowered his brow. "Mrs. Morgan, it seems that we have an issue with trust!" he said, and then his mouth turned up in his sexy smile.

Valeria hated surprises—but this one, she was willing to accept.

After a few hours of flying in the small jet, Valeria heard the captain say something about Puerto Rico. She hoped they weren't staying in Puerto Rico—her memory of it was loud and obnoxious. She was certain a lot of that had to do with her frame of mind, having just found out that Paolo had lied to her, combined with too much rum and Paolo…and the hangover…and to top it off, seeing Alex for such a short time and believing it was the last time she ever would.

Still, they were on their honeymoon and anywhere they were alone for an extended period of time would satisfy her needs. But no matter how much she tried to convince herself, she just did not want to be in Puerto Rico. The plane landed and Alex retrieved their luggage himself. They hopped in a cab and transferred to a small airport a few miles away. The cab pulled into the hangar area and dropped them off near a shack that said, "Avgas."

Alex carried their bags through a sea of single engine planes and then stopped as if to present a surprise. There, in front of her, was a single-propeller aircraft with a high wing that looked as if it had seen better days. After all the luxury, this was a bit of a shock. Alex's grin continued to widen as he loaded their bags into the back of the plane.

The seats were heavily worn red and black leather. Valeria looked at Alex confused.

"What's the matter? You don't like my plane?"

"This…this is yours?"

Alex nodded appreciatively at the old gray aircraft. "Yep...well, more appropriately *ours.*"

"Ours," she said hesitantly. "We're going to…fly in this?" Her concerns were numerous.

He gazed at the extended nose in the front and ran his hands over the wing with affection, as if it were a miracle of the sky.

"She's got a lot of miles on her. But she's perfect for what we need!"

"It's a 'she'?" Valeria asked in a teasing tone.

"Come on!" he said excitedly, as he opened the door and helped her into the passenger side. The plane had the smell of old leather. Then he walked around to the front of the plane and opened the door, grabbing a plastic coated sheet of paper from an area on the center console. Valeria watched as Alex walked around the plane checking several things before crawling in next to her.

He seemed to be checking several gauges, and then he started the engine. Alex put on his headphones and placed a pair of voice-activated headphones on Valeria's head.

"You ready?" he asked excitedly.

"Not sure," she said hesitantly.

He laughed and patted her leg. "You'll be fine." He cranked a knob on a two-way radio and she heard voices; then she made out Alex's voice in the mix.

"Tower, Helio one two eight one two, V-F-R to the east. Taxi for take-off, I have Bravo," Alex said.

A voice answered, "Helio one two eight one two, Isla Grande Tower, taxi runway niner," the tower controller said, and then in a friendly voice added, "Good to see you back, buddy! I expected it would be a while after the last trip."

Alex had a thrill in his eyes that Valeria had never seen before—it appeared there were a lot of things she had yet to discover about her husband.

"Helio eight one two, taxi runway niner. Thanks tower!" he said.

They taxied down a piece of pavement, parallel to a single runway. As he prepared to turn onto the runway, Alex stopped and his grin widened. "I've imagined this for a while. So forgive me for reveling in pleasure," she heard his voice through her headset. "By the way, you are now my official co-pilot, so you'll need to read this off please."

"What does the co-pilot do?" she asked, as she took the list from him.

The corner of his mouth turned up seductively and his eyes gleamed, and then he closed his eyes, shook his head as if releasing the thought, and said, "I have to admit that I've had a few fantasies about what that job might entail...but, *for now*, the co-pilot reads off the checklist. We'll figure out the rest later."

"Well, what did your other co-pilots do?" Then thoughts ran through her head. "Never mind, I don't think I really want to know."

"I've never had another co-pilot," he said, adjusting a few knobs.

"No! Really?" Valeria asked incredulously.

"Not a one!" He winked. "I've held that position open until you could fill it."

She read off part of the checklist as Alex looked at various gauges and said, "Check."

"Good. We're all set." He glanced at her from behind his dark glasses. "Are you okay with this?"

How could she tell him she was terrified? She decided that she couldn't.

"No. I think it's fine."

"Fine?" Alex smirked.

"Yes." She scooted back in her seat and looked straight ahead. It wasn't that she didn't trust Alex—it was the old rusted plane that gave her doubts.

"Well, all right then. I'll take that. It's probably the best I'm going to get right this minute." He rotated a knob on the radio and said, "Tower, Helio eight one two, ready at runway niner." Alex looked down the runway and then said, "Your job is to watch for other aircraft. See any?"

She looked out the window and shook her head. "No."

"Good!" she heard, as his voice came in over her headphones.

The only thing she heard next was the tower saying, "Cleared for take-off."

"Here we go." Alex glanced at Valeria. "Ready?" She shrugged, nervously.

The aircraft rolled down the runway and, within a few seconds, they were airborne. Alex cranked the plane hard to the left and they were immediately over the turquoise sea. Valeria saw the cruise ships not far from them and she was amazed at how quickly she went from fear to thrill. It felt as though the plane was weightless. Alex did a quick sideways glance and, as if it were possible, his smile widened even further as they headed out over the coastline to the east.

"Will you tell me where are we going now?"

"You'll know in about an hour. See that aircraft ahead of us?" Alex pointed off to the north. Valeria looked and saw nothing. Then a plane appeared out of nowhere and seemed to shoot right past them at a slightly higher altitude.

"Wow!" she said with awe in her voice.

Below was a cove with the most perfect white beach surrounded by extraordinary turquoise waters. Ahead of them, the sky was the deepest blue, marked with clouds that looked like cotton balls.

She occasionally heard Alex talking to the air traffic controllers but she couldn't understand all that they were saying. It seemed as if they had only been airborne for minutes when she heard Alex through her headphones. "We're making a pit stop."

They banked sharply over the water in front of a much larger jet. She felt Alex pull up on the nose of the plane as he conversed with the tower. Then she realized the jet was going to the same runway right behind them.

"Alex, you said that my job was to tell you about other planes?"

"I saw him," he said, and tilted his head for a moment. "Don't worry."

She attempted to look casual and heard the slight delay as her voice came over the headset, saying, "I'm not worried."

Behind Alex's sunglasses, she could see his eyes dancing with amusement as he released a joyful laugh.

Then the tower came on again, "Helio eight one two, confirm you *can* make that first taxiway. Or do you need to go around?"

A pilot with a slow southern drawl and the control of an airline pilot interrupted Alex's response, "Tower, that boy could sit that bird down on the threshold and make an immediate 180. You're dealing with greatness here. Watch and be amazed."

Valeria noticed Alex's slight chuckle. "Tower, we can make the first taxiway. Don't want to alarm my passenger or she'll never fly with me again. And thanks, Jack!"

"Good to see you, Alex," the airliner said.

The plane touched down smoothly not far from the exit and, with no jolting whatsoever, exited the required taxiway. Valeria heard, "Welcome to St. Thomas, taxi to the ramp." Immediately, the jet shot by behind them and Alex waved.

They taxied past the main terminal and pulled up in front of a tired brown building with several rough looking planes in the lot. The prop stopped spinning and Alex jumped out. "Wait here. I'll be just a few minutes."

She saw him walk around the plane carrying blocks, evidently for the tires. A moment later, he walked toward the drab building and disappeared inside.

In less than a minute, he came back out swinging a set of keys around his forefinger. He helped her out and wrapped an arm around her waist as they strolled toward the front of the drab building.

"Almost there," Alex said as he walked toward a rusty 1980 Ford Escort. Valeria hated to be a snob, but the car looked filthy. "I hope you don't mind," he said with a wink.

"Uh, no. It's…"

Before she could answer, Alex opened the door. The interior was coated with a heavy layer of dust and wreaked of cigarette smoke. Then he tried to close her door and the hinges were rusted so badly that he had to put all of his weight into closing her door.

He climbed into the driver's side and cranked the engine. After sputtering several times, the car eventually started.

"Ahh, they just don't make 'em like they used to," he said with a hint of humor.

"Yes, and thank God for that," Valeria muttered.

They drove two miles along the coast and pulled off onto a dirt road that wove through a steep narrow path and ended at a shack with chickens, goats, and trash.

"We're here," Alex said, popping out of the car and then coming around to open her door.

The structure was made of tin and had over twenty chickens on the roof. Trees surrounded the shack but she could see light under the branches and assumed it to be the coast. A young black man came out of the shack, excited to see Alex. She prayed they weren't staying here for long. Suddenly, she felt a nudge at her hip and saw a goat that was butting its head against her. She tried to move and so did the goat. Several chickens cackled as she tried to step out of the goat's way.

"Alex?"

"Oh, sorry, beautiful," he said as he led her toward a shirtless man with deep black skin and dreads. "This is Jimmy."

"Ah, hallo, ma'am! You da missus? Good to meet you!" Jimmy said cheerfully with his strong island accent.

"Hello," Valeria said, a bit unnerved that the goat was following her.

"Take a stroll through the store. The boy is taking a bit longer than usual. Might be something you need—take a stroll," he encouraged. "You never know."

Alex glanced at the goat and then said, "You never know."

He led Valeria into the shack that had only a single row of shelves. There was a clear plastic case with a few week-old doughnuts. Alex pointed at them. "Hungry?"

Valeria shook her head and was certain her husband had been possessed by another man.

Around the corner was a rack with a hundred different types of rum and a few bottles of wine. He brushed his fingers along the dusty bottles as if looking for something specific. His fingers lighted for a moment on a three-dollar bottle of Boone's Farm strawberry wine. Then he turned, and she thought she heard him snicker as he continued down the aisle.

She remembered Weege's words at the wedding, "Men...they all change after they get that piece of paper!"

Still, this couldn't be the same guy who brought in a jumbo jet to fly them alone from Africa to Europe; the guy who asked her if she wanted him to buy her a fleet of yachts. Not that any of that was particularly appealing to her. She didn't need or want much, except for Alex—which she realized was a very far cry from her purported minor needs.

She heard an exchange between a young boy and Jimmy outside.

"Looks like our starters have arrived!" Alex said as he headed for the door.

Valeria nodded as if she understood. It must be something they could use to start that heap of rust they were driving, in case they needed to; although, she was certain she would prefer to walk. She followed Alex back out to where the goat was waiting and, of course, it nudged her as soon as she walked out the door. A shirtless boy of about six, wearing a wet pair of cut-off jeans, came from a trail in the woods carrying two lobsters.

"Lobsters!" Valeria said.

"Yes. What were you expecting?" Alex asked playfully.

Jimmy held a bag and the boy dropped the lobsters in. "You need some chickens, maybe?" he said to Valeria, as he waved at the scroungy looking birds that were hovering everywhere.

"No. Thanks, Jimmy!" Alex handed him some money and then held out a few bills. "This is for Linc."

"You spoil da boy." Jimmy's grin broadened. "I give you a separate bag for da hens…"

"No, thanks," Alex said.

They loaded back into the Ford and, to Valeria's relief, drove back to the airport. Alex loaded the "starters" in the back of the plane and they took off again.

This time, they flew only a short distance back to the west. Alex circled over the peak of a lush green mountain and dove into a valley. The plane circled down and then she saw a small patch of dirt that could have been a landing strip—a very small landing strip on a steep incline. She held her breath as Alex placed the plane down perfectly and taxied just off the end of the runway where there was only room to turn around and park an old red Jeep.

The smile was still on his face as he helped her into the doorless Jeep. The floorboards were covered with sand, but it did appear to be in better condition than the Ford.

"I'll come back for the rest," he said.

"Alex, where are we?"

"St. John."

He turned the key and the Jeep roughly kicked a billow of black smoke from the tail pipe. It lurched and then moved smoothly up the steep incline, and then around the steepest and sharpest hairpin turn that she had ever encountered. She held her breath but the Jeep made the turn and, at the top of the mountain, there was a sandy lot that led to a house—well, almost a house. It was an open-walled home with tile floors and magnificent views down a lush green valley to the Caribbean.

"What is this place?"

"It's one of our homes." Alex jumped out of the Jeep and came around to the passenger side to lift her out of the seat; he carried her into the main area of the house. "And, *this*—is as close to a threshold as I have here," he said, setting her down in front of a mahogany four-poster feather bed. She brushed her fingers along the soft netting tied to the post.

There was a sofa and two chairs inside along with a small table. The patio area had a fire pit with two Adirondacks and a small table on either side. There was only one solid wall on the mountain-facing side of the cabin. The large red tiles extended beyond the corner supports—which were really the only thing resembling a wall—to what might be considered two decks, each with their own spectacular view.

On the forward deck was a doublewide lounge chair with cushions in soft blues. The other deck was home to a claw foot tub. Along the back wall was an area that served as a kitchen, with a two-burner gas stove and oven, what appeared to be a new coffee maker, and a brand new blender. A bookcase, covered in paperbacks, extended along the majority of the back wall. He noticed her eyeing them.

"Books don't do well here," he said, suddenly unsure of his plans to bring her here. He evaluated the look in her eyes. "Is this okay?" He continued nervously, "I always wanted to bring you here but, for our honeymoon, I had intended something a bit more elaborate. After the fire, Lars and I agreed that we needed some place where no one could find us."

"This is where you were!" she said, suddenly confident.

"What?"

"You were here. When I was in St. Croix, you were here." She turned to him and her eyes widened. "Of course, that's why I didn't see you at the airport when I left." She looked at the place with new eyes. "Oh! And you left early so that you could catch the afternoon flight back to Europe. A commercial flight wouldn't have gotten you back to Puerto Rico on time and we would have been at the hotel in Puerto Rico...together."

She brushed her hands over the soft pastel cotton of the down comforter. The luxury was in the extraordinary detail, and Alex knew luxury.

"I wondered where you were and what you were doing. It all makes sense now," she continued.

"If you wanted to know, why didn't you ask me?"

She shrugged as she continued to take in every detail of the home. "I guess...well, this may sound silly, but I was afraid you had gone someplace with," she glanced down and then her eyes darted briefly to him, "Daphne." She bit her lip. "Weege says 'don't ask what you don't want to know.'"

He chuckled and raised his brows. "Are you jealous?"

"No," she replied too quickly. "Maybe." Valeria examined the fabric of the sofa and could picture Alex relaxing there.

"Don't be. This is definitely not Daphne's style," he said softly, as he approached her. "But, regardless of *her* style, Daphne is definitely not my style!" His eyes softened as they filled with love. "There is only one person who is my style—one woman whom I have *ever* desired." He brushed the side of her arm. "And only one person I have ever brought here." Alex's eyes narrowed, evaluating her response. "Is this place all right?"

"This is..." Valeria swallowed as tears came into her eyes. "Absolutely perfect!"

Alex sat down on the bed and pulled her into his arms. "Good, because Mrs. Morgan, I want to spend as much time alone with you as I can get!" His eyes filled with desire and he kissed her mouth as his fingers brushed along her collarbone.

Valeria felt the familiar rush of heat. She brushed the side of his face; then, with a short kiss, she said, "Do you think it would be possible for me to shower and change?"

Putting his passion on hold, he drew a deep breath and released her. "Of course! I should have…I'm sorry, love!" He took her hand and led her back out to the porch where a showerhead was mounted on a steel hose.

Valeria pulled at the white silk that served as a shower curtain and asked, "Is this…"

"It's a parachute."

"Really?"

As he bit his lip, he said, "You can hop in and I'll bring you a towel. I'll shower when you're done."

Their wedding night seemed like such a long time ago, and she was anxious to be on their honeymoon. But it felt like the first time again, and she wanted it to be as wonderful as their wedding night. She wished that the silk negligee had survived the fire, although, she was certain that Camille had replaced it with something just as beautiful. Here, there was no place to rummage through a suitcase, nor to change in private—except a small bathroom without a mirror. Alex saw visions of them married and comfortable with each other. The getting there...well, that was another story. Suddenly, she could see the embarrassment on Alex's face that he had not thought of that for her.

"I'm sorry, Val. Of course, you need some privacy." His face reddened and he shook his head briefly. "Why don't I get the suitcases while you shower? I'll leave your bags here for you and then I'll go take care of...a few things." He drew a deep breath. "I'll be back in about thirty minutes. Is that enough time?"

She suddenly felt silly, but she did want the time to clean up. She turned away from him and cleared her throat wishing she had the courage to say that he didn't need to go through all of that. "Yes. Thank you," she responded, a bit more formally than she intended. Alex nodded and headed down the hill.

Behind the steel pole and showerhead was a bench. She pulled the curtain closed around the bench and turned on the water. Then she stripped down and felt the water run down her body, cooling her and washing away the travel and the worries of the past few days. In a moment, she heard Alex outside of the curtain and could see his hand through a small opening as he set a towel down on the bench for her. His fingers hesitated on the towel—there was something so sensuous about his long fingers. Suddenly, she felt the aching urgency of days ago and, without thinking, she reached for his hand, needing to feel his fingers on her again. With her other hand, she pushed open the parachute.

"Come here," she said.

Alex froze, staring at her as the water ran down her. She stepped toward him and pulled at his shirt. He kicked off his shoes and, in a moment, his clothes were off and they were together under the cool water, wrapped in each other as his mouth brushed hers first lightly, and then with the passion that they had discovered only a few nights before.

CHAPTER 8

That evening, they sat under billions of stars by the fire pit, sipping the most extraordinary wine that Valeria had ever tasted, stuffing themselves with lobster, salad, and baked potato.

She discovered that this home had storage, including a fantastic wine cellar under the house.

Alex glanced away from the fire to Valeria, and smiled lazily as he lifted a finger toward her face. "What is that expression?" he asked, completely content.

She looked up at the stars for a moment, and then her smile broadened. "I'm...happy," she sighed, as she ran her fingers through his tousled hair. After the shower, they didn't take time to brush their hair, and had made love while the sun set in brilliant hues over the Caribbean.

Alex beamed and kissed his bride, and then smiled mischievously.

"What?" she asked.

He was someone who had made a practice over eons to never say what he was thinking, and to release it all now made him feel like a fish out of water. Finally, he said, "You know everything was so serious yesterday with...well, you know. I thought it was time for some...fun." He laughed. "You should have seen your face when we got into that beat-up, old Ford in St. Thomas!" Alex laughed and shook his head. "It was everything I could do to keep a straight face."

"And I thought I was hiding it so well!" she said, dipping a strip of lobster into the butter, and then stuffing it into her mouth.

"When we got off the flight and took a taxi to change airports in Puerto Rico…" Alex shook his head, obviously amused. He lowered his brows. "You don't like San Juan."

"How did you know?"

"It is pretty easy to tell when you don't like something." He brushed her nose. "You crinkle your nose and then you bite the side of your lip," he said, running his finger along the curve of her mouth. He sighed again. "I guess I should have told you that we weren't staying there, but I was having considerably too much fun." He smiled again. "Puerto Rico can be a lot of fun. I'll have to show it to you sometime—actually, I was thinking we could go there for your birthday."

She scrunched her nose. "Isn't it customary for people to celebrate their birthdays in their favorite locations? I know we can't go back to Morgana, but why not here?" Considering Alex's desire to please her, she added, "Really, the only thing that matters to me is that we are together."

"It'll be fun." He pulled her in and kissed the top of her head. "Mani has a place there overlooking a cliff, and the family plans to meet us there."

She pulled back from him and stared in surprise. "The family is meeting us in Puerto Rico for my birthday?"

"It'll be fun."

At that moment, she understood. The purpose of the "celebration" was so that Mani could ensure that she was no longer affected by the curse. Still, she wouldn't concern herself with it. Alex seemed happy and content and she would not break the mood to discuss anything so dark or serious.

She cocked her head. "So, what is a 'starter' anyway?"

"A starter...well, I typically snorkel for my own lobsters, but when I first arrive, I pick up one from Jimmy. I've been getting starters from Jimmy's family for over fifty years."

"Oh! Yeah! A starter...okay."

"When that goat started nudging you and then Jimmy suggested that we go into his store, it was everything I could do to keep from laughing."

She giggled softly and, hearing his carefree laughter, she felt the joy fill her soul as she curled into him. "Tell me about this place."

Alex lifted his glass of wine and took a sip as he stared at the fire. "This place is my escape. Nobody knows where it is—except for you now." He kissed the top of her head. Valeria brushed her hand down his open shirt thinking it was quite a luxury. "The landing strip isn't published. Hardly anyone can land on it, and I can hear anyone who comes up the mountain from quite a distance. It was the only place I could think of that I wouldn't worry about your safety."

Valeria moved her knees up so that her toes curled against Alex's. She loved his khaki shorts and admired his tanned, muscular legs...and even his feet were beautiful. Hesitantly, she said, "When I was in St. Croix, I prayed, regardless of the cost, that you would be on the flight out of Puerto Rico with me. When I didn't see you, I wondered how you had hidden yourself so completely."

He took her face in his hands. "Do you know how close I was to picking you up, loading you into my plane, and heading up here?" He looked back at the fire. "But that's not the life I want for you. I want to take you anywhere you want to go. I would love to spend a few months a year in Manhattan with you. Have you ever been to Paris?"

Valeria shook her head no. "I don't really care where we are—as long as we are together and married! I could spend a lifetime here making love to you."

Alex sighed happily. "Well, except for Puerto Rico."

She picked up a stick and began playing with the fire. "I would like to spend my birthday with you in New York. Do you ever think there will ever be a day when we can do that?"

"I don't know. There are some things that need to happen, but until we get bored with our life here, I'm feeling quite selfish about my time with you."

"Well then, we will be here a very, very long time," she said sleepily.

∞

They awoke with the sunrise and the soft Caribbean breeze blowing across them. The sky was the most amazing color, dotted with small white clouds. It was one of the most perfect mornings she had ever experienced, wrapped around Alex.

Kissing his chest, she noticed his boyish grin.

"What are you smiling about?" she asked, brushing her hand along his face.

Alex sighed, happily. "It's really our first morning of married life!" He leaned on his arm. "Well, I mean—with both of us alive and all." She kissed his chest and luxuriated in running her hands along it, then trailed them down to his hips. "I thought I would make us breakfast and then we could do whatever you would like." He smiled suggestively. "Although, we really should go snorkeling today."

Valeria crinkled her nose and bit the corner of her lip.

He rubbed his finger over her lip and shook his head. "All right, snorkeling tomorrow. If you would like, perhaps we could go for a hike. There's a particular view I've been fantasizing about sharing with you for years."

She curled into him. "I would love to see that view...later." Just then, she saw something in a corner of the room and leaned forward. "Alex? What is that?"

Alex rolled his eyes happily. "It's called a guitar. You know, strings, neck, you pluck it or strum it."

Valeria laughed under her breath. "And what do *you* do with it?"

Alex shrugged. "Depends on what I'm in the mood for."

"Will you play it for me?"

"I'll tell you what. You humor me with the snorkeling tomorrow, and I'll humor you by playing the guitar tonight." He kissed her nose. "But you may be sorry you asked."

"So...you've been fantasizing about a hike?" she asked, with a sensual smile full of promise.

He nodded and then rolled out of bed. She pouted...until she took in the view of him. He turned back toward her and lifted a brow. "Unless marriage has changed you, I believe it's time for your coffee."

A smile sprang to her face as she watched him pull on a pair of shorts and head to the coffee maker. He pressed a button and, in a moment, Alex presented her with the perfect cup of coffee.

"Hmm," Valeria sighed as she clutched her cup of coffee.

"How about breakfast in bed?"

"Only if you're joining me," she said.

She watched the way he smiled and was instantly glad she asked.

∞

The hike was through a deep green, tropical forest. They wound their way from the cabin, along a steep, rocky trail. There were places where the trail was almost missing, though parts of it were repaired by Alex— she guessed. They reached a giant boulder and he steered her down a secret path that she would have missed if he hadn't shown it to her. They crossed a creek several times, stepping on stones.

Alex carried a pack with their lunch so that they could enjoy their meal with an ultimate view from the top.

The hike was a feast for the senses, with all of the herbs that grew wild. Ferns and orange and red blooms seemed to sprout up everywhere. The coolness of the forest, and the wonderful and various scents that sprung up around every corner—as well as her husband beside her—made Valeria want to pinch herself to be certain it was real. Alex was obviously thrilled to be sharing this special place with her and her enthusiasm over the mountain was apparent.

They reached a point where the trail seemed to end. There was a vertical climb that was too steep to walk.

"We climb from here," Alex said, grabbing on to a root. Valeria's eyes widened in excitement as she took hold of a thick tree root and began scrambling up the vertical. Hanging on to the roots, they scrambled for almost twenty minutes, until the trail again appeared to end. Valeria turned around, but trees blocked the potential view.

"Is this the top?" she asked, quizzically.

Alex shook his head no, and then pushed aside a bush, showing the edge of a boulder.

"We're going to walk along this ledge, but it's safer if you take off your shoes."

Stepping onto the ledge, Valeria saw that below was a series of drop-offs ending with a pile of boulders.

"Val, lean against the stone," he said, as he kept his arm on her back.

When the boulder that they had been leaning on ended, Valeria's eyes widened as she looked up to see a fifty-foot waterfall that descended into stone bowls next to them.

Alex said, "That's not the best part." He turned her around and, from the edge of the bowls, there was a 200-foot drop-off that looked out through the valley to the sea.

They sat with their legs dangling from the cliff and ate their sandwiches and fruit.

"Did you hike here every day when you were alone?"

"No, not every day." Alex thought for a moment. "There are always improvements that are needed...on the trails, at the cabin. I restock supplies." His eyes narrowed as he stared off to the sea. "When you were in St. Croix with Paolo, I focused on being here with you. I kept telling myself it would be very soon, so I kept myself busy with...remodeling and improvements."

"What kind of improvements? I did notice the coffee maker and the blender."

"The tub was a necessity. I brought in a bed instead of a cot," he said, and then the corner of his mouth turned up. "You know, I do have a few traditions."

"Such as?"

"I was hoping you would ask." His smile broadened, and then he took Valeria's face in his hands. "Just so you know, I can hear anyone within a mile of here. And in over fifty-three years, I've only seen others here once."

He hopped to his feet, stripped off his clothes, and stepped into the bowls and under the waterfall. Valeria stared in awe. He was the most beautiful man she had ever seen, and the site of him under the waterfall was incredibly erotic.

He stepped out from the waterfall and, seeing her expression, he smiled and lifted his index finger, signaling for her to join him.

"There is something about you and water that is just irresistible!" he said.

The electricity between them sizzled and caused her to completely abandon her insecurities. She stripped off her shorts and T-shirt without a moment's hesitation, and took his hand as she stepped into the warm pool. He pulled her into his arms and they made love there, in the stone pools under the waterfall, with the warmth of the Caribbean sun.

As they napped on the stones, Alex rolled to his side and faced her, a spark in his eye. "Do you want to try something truly adventurous?"

"Do I want to say 'yes' to this one?" she said, crinkling her nose.

Alex laughed. "Well, since it is July, there isn't a lot of water right now. I thought you might like to scramble down the creek. It's quite an adventure and I can help you."

Valeria couldn't say no when he looked so joyful about the whole thing. Besides, it did sound like a fun adventure. Valeria sat with her knees pulled up to her chest by the edge of the eight-foot drop. Alex lowered his legs and then clung to the rocks; shirtless, he lowered himself down. Immediately, he raised himself back up in a chin-up and saw her staring with wide-eyed amazement at the ripples in his arms and chest.

"I think I'm definitely going to like this!" she said. He winked and then lowered himself.

"I'll help you on this drop. Most of the others are four feet or less so you'll be able to do them on your own," he said, as she lay down on the granite and rolled her legs over the edge, feeling Alex's hands on her hips.

"I have you!"

"Okay," she said with a hint of hesitation.

"Put your hands in the small indentation on the stone and lower yourself. I won't let you fall...I have you. Now, drop."

She let go and landed flat on her feet and felt a thrill.

"That was fun!"

Alex laughed again and she was excited to know that she enjoyed something that brought him so much pleasure.

They worked their way down dropping down from shallow cliffs, forging deep ravines, hanging on to branches and trees, and scrambling over boulders until, at last, they reached the base of the trail near their cabin. Outside their pleasure of each other, it was the most fun Valeria had experienced in a long time. Once she saw the back of the cabin, they held hands.

She glanced up at Alex and began to laugh. "You should see your face!"

Alex glanced down at his still bare chest, and started laughing, raising a brow. "I'm not the only one!"

They laughed for a few minutes and then he grabbed her by the belt loops and led her into the shower with him, clothes and all.

They slept for hours in the late afternoon heat, with the cool breezes blowing across their bodies. Alex propped himself up on his elbows next to her, running a finger over her sun-kissed shoulders.

"Not bad for the first full day of our honeymoon!" he said.

"Not bad at all," she said, with her eyes aglow with love. "I think besides our wedding day—and night—that this is the most fun I've ever had."

"It's only the beginning," he whispered, and then he kissed her shoulder. "By the way, did you remember that those lobsters were only 'starters'?"

"Are you going to tell me what that means?" she asked.

"It means that we need to either go snorkeling for fish or lobster—or we could run down to Jamaica Joe's."

"After that hike, these legs aren't running anywhere tonight."

Alex nuzzled her neck. "Just the hike?" he whispered.

"No. Not just the hike," she said with a giggle.

"And by the way, I meant running figuratively," he grinned. It was so unusual to hear Alex make jokes, and she loved seeing him in such a light mood. "I thought we could take the boat. Jamaica Joe's is a small island café. I thought we could take in a little dinner and dancing."

"Is it safe?"

"I think it might be smart for you to wear your contacts as a precaution, but they all suspect that I live on St. Thomas. Jimmy is there to assist with the illusion. His ancestors have worked for me for a hundred years. Jimmy has let the place go, but I can trust him. His grandmother told him so many stories about ancestors who betrayed sacred oaths that he'll never say a word. Linc will probably leave the islands but he can always manage it from a distance."

∞

The outing gave Valeria a chance to wear a sexy little sundress that Camille had packed for her. They drove down the mountain winding down the steep hairpin turn, past the plane, and all the way to the base of the mountain. There, Alex parked under a tree and pulled out a small sailboat. He dusted it out and pulled a cushion from the back of the Jeep and set it down on the bench on the back of the boat; he helped Valeria onto it and then pushed them off.

With an almost nonexistent wind, he skillfully wove along the shoreline staying close enough for her to feel safe. The moon glowed silver and perfect on the smooth water and she was finally feeling relaxed.

"There it is!" Alex said. There was a shack built on a dock. Alex stopped in front of a ladder. He tied up the boat and then climbed up the three steps and onto the dock. Then he reached down and helped pull Valeria up.

Immediately, a giant of a man approached them looking almost like Brutus from Popeye. His face was unshaved and he wore a colorful shirt.

"Alex, hearts are gonna be breaking—for once you got company!" Then the man looked Valeria up and down and pulled his fist to his heart. "And my heart is breaking! Who is this goddess?" Joe said, still eyeing Valeria.

"Joe, this is my wife, Val."

"Wife? You been holding out for this one—now I understand! Nice to meet ya, Val. You newlyweds? Tell me he ain't been leaving you home alone at night!"

"We're on our honeymoon," Valeria said shyly.

"Well, last time I saw Al, here, a few months back, I thought maybe he might be doing himself in. I told Deano, the bartender, I was afraid of that. You leave him back then?" Joe asked.

Valeria opened her mouth but couldn't find the appropriate words. It didn't matter, Joe didn't require two people for a conversation. "Well, next time you decide to dump the guy, give old Joe a call, will ya?"

"Thank you, but I could never replace my husband and he has promised me that I'll never need to."

"I'm just sayin'," Joe said, and then immediately busied himself with a table.

They had a casual dinner looking down on the sea turtles and other marine life moving through the Caribbean. Their dinner tasted even more delicious because of the exertion of the day's hike. Someone began to play the steel drums, and Alex took Valeria's hand and led her to the dance floor; they danced under the starlight, joyfully ending another day in paradise.

It took Alex almost a week of encouragement to get Valeria into the warm Caribbean waters. He began by taking her out with him on his dinghy, while he speared fish or gathered lobsters.

She was amazed at his skill as he maneuvered the boat around coves and rocks as if it had wheels under it. Then Alex would put on his snorkel gear and dive down, finding the perfect lobsters or fish and returning to an always-tense Valeria.

One afternoon, he pulled the boat into a sandy cove and they both got out. Alex built a fire and played the guitar while Valeria built a sand castle. When it was time to sail back, she realized that she was covered with sand and didn't want to get back into the boat. Alex dipped under the water to clean off. She stepped in nervously and then, realizing how comfortable and beautiful it was, stepped in a bit further. Once she rinsed off, she climbed back into the boat and waited.

"Did you notice this beach is deserted?" Alex said, surfacing behind her.

"Yes."

"Well, I was thinking…"

She sat in the boat hanging on to the edges, although it was still beached.

"Alex?" she said, suddenly frightened.

A moment later, something sprang out the water and immediately she recognized it as his swimming trunks. They landed in the front of the boat with a splat.

"Alex, that's not funny," she said.

She heard him on the other side of the boat. "It was kind of funny."

"Okay, maybe just a little, but I'm still not getting in," she said.

"Come swimming with me," he said, as he swam along in a few feet of water.

"Now?" She looked around.

"Yeah..." She saw the sensual turn of his smile.

Within seconds, she had stripped and was, for the first time, enjoying herself in a large body of water.

It took over a month until Valeria was snorkeling and loving it. Alex promised to take her to some of the other islands as she progressed. At night, they sat by their fire pit and ate lobster, while Alex played the guitar. Everything he played sounded so sweet and romantic. In his music, she could hear the sad yearning of his life before; she knew that this had been a place where he would come to think about her over the years. Now, they were living the most beautiful life she could imagine.

She brushed her finger along the body of his guitar where there was pearl inlay that read, *Orpheus*. "Why does that say Orpheus? That's not the brand is it?"

Alex smiled and said, "Well, actually...I made this guitar. I named it Orpheus."

"Orpheus? Why?"

He shrugged. "I guess, for many years, I felt a sort of kinship with Orpheus. Not in talent...but in love lost." He narrowed his eyes and looked away. "I should probably rename it now."

She kissed his neck and took a sip from her cold beer. "I think I've heard of Orpheus."

"Hmm. Do you want to hear the story? You do realize, by now, that most stories from mythology don't have happy endings."

"I have my very own happy ending," she said, as she smiled and pulled his arms around her. He nodded and looked out to sea.

"Orpheus was a legendary musician and poet from ancient Greece. On their wedding day, his bride, Eurydice, was walking amongst her people, in tall grass when she was attacked by a satyr—"

"A satyr?" Valeria interrupted.

"Yes, companions of Pan with goat-like features, including a goat-tail, goat-like ears, and sometimes a goat-like phallus."

"Oh, dear! Were they real?"

Alex shrugged. "I've never seen one, but I imagine so. You will have to ask some of the immortals. Perhaps Paolo knows, but I don't believe that he is that old—Myrdd would know, if he were still around to ask," he said.

"In any case, the story goes that Eurydice struggled with the satyr and fell into a nest of vipers where she suffered a fatal bite on her heel. Her body was discovered by Orpheus who, overcome with grief, played such sad and mournful songs that all the nymphs and gods wept.

"On their advice, Orpheus travelled to the underworld and, with his mournful music, he softened the hearts of Hades—he was, by all accounts the only one ever to do so. Hades' only condition was that Orpheus must walk in front of Eurydice and not look back until both had reached the upper world. Orpheus knew that Eurydice would be in spirit form until they exited the underworld and took solace in feeling her presence as they began their trek.

"But there were other challenges: Orpheus had to get by Cerberus, the three headed, flesh-eating dog that is the guardian of Hades. So he took out his lute and sang and played and, eventually, Cerberus was lulled to sleep.

"As Orpheus continued his trek, he began to recall stories of Hades' trickery and, soon, he doubted that his beloved was still with him. Just as he reached the portal of Hades and daylight, he needed to know, so he turned around to gaze upon her face. But because Eurydice had not yet crossed the threshold—"

"What happened?" Valeria asked, certain she didn't want to hear the end.

Alex drew a deep breath, "She was immediately pulled back into the underworld...and this time, forever."

"This story needs a new ending," she said curling into him. "What happened to Orpheus?"

"He was inconsolable. He refused any company and was one day attacked and beheaded."

"I thought he was a god!"

"He was...perhaps that's the secret that Jeremiah discovered. How to end the life of an immortal." Shaking off the thought, Alex added, "On a happier note, the story goes that he was at last reunited with his beloved Eurydice in the Elysian Fields...what Dante called, Paradiso."

Alex looked distant and, seeing his seriousness, she said, "I think you need to rename your guitar. Something that reflects our happy ending."

"I agree. And perhaps we had better stick with Jane Austin and Shakespeare's Sonnets," he said.

∞

The tropical rain poured down over the lush green hills as Valeria leaned her back into Alex's chest in the claw foot tub. Despite the rain, shards of sunlight broke through the cumulus clouds and lit the Caribbean in various shades of turquoise and azure.

She rolled her head against his chest, as the steam rolled off the tub. He lifted his arm and lovingly brushed her brown curls back, and then wrapped an arm around her as he kissed the nape of her neck and in her ticklish spot behind her ear. With his free arm, he reached down to the table next to the tub, and handed her their shared glass of wine; she took a sip and savored the cool taste of the rich flavors of prune and oak. She savored it for a moment before swallowing. Then, she turned and kissed Alex deeply, letting him sample the wine from her lips.

Yes, she thought, he saved the "good wine" for them, and she liked sharing it with him so much better! She remembered his comments from her first girls' night with Ava and Camille, before she realized that he was saving a special bottle for the two of them. She smiled. That night, almost a year before, was the first time it really clicked that he might be interested in her, despite the numerous hints. Sometimes, she was a little blind to the obvious.

She handed him the glass and he took a slow sip himself, then set the glass back down and moved his arms around her again, brushing his fingertips across her in an incredibly erotic way, causing her to arch back into him. As she looked down at his hands covering her body, she was in awe that there were no signs of the severe burns from just a few months before.

As if he was reading her mind, he said softly, "I'm as good as new, Mrs. Morgan." Then he kissed her neck again, taking his time on her bare shoulders. She sighed, as a tear rolled suddenly from her eye. He caught the tear with his finger and turned her face toward his.

"Hey—I'm all right," Alex said softly.

Her breath caught. "It is just...so...amazing."

She stopped the sob, but it wasn't pain that caused it. It was the overwhelming joy she felt from having her husband, her symbolon, by her side—whole, healthy, and head over heels in love with her. It was amazing how much she could love someone. She never knew that she had that level of love within her. And here he was, this beautiful man who adored her. And they had a lifetime together...or more. His hand brushed her wet hair away from her neck.

"On another note, I was thinking...you might like to try something new?"

Valeria's face lit in an amused smile as she leaned back and kissed his hand.

"What did you have in mind? Blindfolds already?" she asked, lowering her voice with a playful hint of seduction.

"Actually, I *was* thinking about," he kissed her neck again, "perhaps, a few new experiences," he said suggestively.

She raised her eyebrows. "Like what?" Her insecurity kicked in, and she suddenly wished she had been more knowledgeable about the art of seduction before they married. Blindfolds were one thing, but there was a whole other world of seduction out there that she'd yet to experience, and felt suddenly shy and inadequate.

Alex laughed and raised a brow. "Nothing like *that*. I think we do pretty well in that arena."

"You would tell me if we weren't, right?"

Releasing a long, carefree laugh, he wrapped his arms around her adoringly and soon she found herself smiling. "Yes, I think we do more than just *very* nicely!" he said, his lower lip barely brushing her neck, in exquisite torture.

"So, you said you wanted to try something new?" She trusted Alex and, whatever he wanted to try, she would be a good sport.

"No, I said I thought *you* might like to try something new," he corrected, with a hint of amusement. "Like a trip off the island for a few weeks before we meet our family in Puerto Rico."

Valeria yawned sleepily. Baths did that to her, despite the lingering desire she felt just from being within the folds of Alex's arms. Although they seemed to spend an inordinate amount of time in bed making love and then napping, they were also hiking and snorkeling daily. Sometimes, she had a pull in her gut and she wondered if they were supposed to be doing something more important. She wondered if that was what Lars and the others had suggested.

She pushed that thought to the back of her mind. They were on their honeymoon, and what were honeymoons for but making love and spending as much time as possible in each other's arms? Life would require other things of them later. Now was their time. Besides, Alex had spent 3,000 years waiting for this, and she was certain she could spend a lifetime, or more, living this wonderful misty life in the forest…as long as she didn't think of their lost cottage.

"Puerto Rico? That's months off yet," she said.

Alex laughed again. "No, love, it's weeks away."

She narrowed her eyes. The trip to Puerto Rico was for her birthday, which was near the end of October. They were married in July.

"Isn't it August?"

He laughed again, but this time, she noticed just a hint of tension in him. "It's mid-October."

"No—it can't possibly be!" She went through the weeks in her mind. It seemed like only a few weeks and she couldn't possibly imagine that months had passed. She felt the tug of time passing and the knowledge of a secret darkness that they would soon have to explore. She wasn't ready to think of any of that and so she pushed it aside.

"I am sorry to tell you that time has gone by entirely too fast here with you." He brushed his mouth along her lower lip and, seeing her concern, he added, "Don't worry. The honeymoon is definitely not over! I just thought we could try a few new experiences. I would like to take you scuba diving…" He waited, and when she didn't object, he continued, "And then I thought we would go to St. Lucia for a week of luxury and room service alone, before heading up to meet the family."

The part about diving was the last of what she heard and she turned around to face him.

"I thought to dive you had to go through a certification course."

"Yes, well, you can do a resort course where a dive master guides you through a trial."

"Who would do that?"

"Me."

"You? Alex, I thought you were afraid of water and then I see you snorkeling every day and now I discover that you can teach scuba diving."

"We all handle our fears differently. I'm not a fan of the open sea, but here in the bathwater of the Caribbean is a completely different story. I know you'll love it. I did get my certification specifically so that I could share this experience with you."

"When did you learn to dive?"

"Last spring," he said, avoiding the fact that it was when she was with another man. Maybe he needed a challenge like that to keep his attention from the loss.

"Oh, while we were apart."

"Yes, well, after our experience last fall when we both almost drowned again—and would have, if not for Caleb—I realized that it might be a valuable skill for us both to learn. Besides, we hadn't completely ruled out scuba for a rescue if it came to it in Delos."

Valeria's brows pulled down and she analyzed his face for a moment. She tilted her head. "I just realized something about you, my beautiful husband..." She bit her lip and held up his left hand as evidence. "Who, by the way, still does not have a wedding ring," she teased, weaving her fingers with his as her tone became more serious. "You never lie to me, but you often withhold the full truth." She kissed his hand.

He narrowed an eye and looked at her for a moment, and then, seeing her certainty, he lifted a shoulder and tilted his head in slight acquiescence.

"You should tell me," she said softly.

He looked away and shook his head. "Not now. Maybe later."

"Later then," she acquiesced. "Let's see...you said something about another island?"

"St. Lucia," he said, glad that the subject had changed.

"Why St. Lucia?"

"It's one of the most beautiful islands in the Caribbean."

She kissed his fingertips. "And what makes one lush paradise in the sea different from any other?"

He moved the fingers of his other hand along the edge of her face and then pulled her in for a kiss. He stared into her eyes, lost in his love for her. There was something different about her, he was certain of that. Something more confident—more knowing. He couldn't quite put his finger on it.

"Alex?"

"Yes?"

"St. Lucia?"

"I'm sorry, beautiful!" He drew a deep breath. "Apart from being your run-of-the-mill paradise with an artists' colony, the Pitons are breathtaking!"

"The Pitons?" she asked.

"Yes. The Pitons are twin volcanoes that surge up almost a half mile out of the Caribbean. Actually, they are volcanic plugs—a landform created by hardened magma within an active volcano."

"All right," she said hesitantly. "But do you really want to leave here?" she asked reluctantly.

The corners of his mouth curved upward as he brushed her hair back from her face. "I thought we could go diving tomorrow, and then the next day we'll fly out to St. Lucia. It's near the end of the long chain of islands, and I think we can risk a luxury hotel there, which will offer us all the privacy we'll need. I just thought it would be nice to have a change of scenery."

"Hmm. Well, let me just tell you..." Valeria's eyes followed her fingers as they trailed from Alex's face, down his chest, and then disappeared beneath the water, causing him to gasp at her new boldness. She said, "I've got all the scenery I need right here!"

Alex moaned, as he leaned in to kiss her. "I guess a few more hours here wouldn't hurt."

CHAPTER 9

The next morning, she ate breakfast in bed, reading, while Alex—who had eaten hours before—lay next to her wearing faded jeans, a gray T-shirt, and black-rimmed glasses, mulling over financials on his laptop. She glanced over, appreciating the view.

"Why do you wear glasses?" she asked.

He smiled. "I don't need them. I have perfect vision, but they magnify the screen so that I have a bigger picture. With the glasses, I get three screens on one. Then I allow my intuition to guide me."

"Interesting!" she said, as she took a bite of her frittata and looked back down at her book. She lowered her brows as she read, "I come from there, where I would gladly return. And now, love has moved me and compels me to speak."

Alex smiled, adding, "Beatrice's words to Dante. I didn't know you were reading *The Divine Comedy*."

"I've read everything else here!" Then Valeria shook her head. "If Beatrice really loved Dante why would she gladly return to Paradiso without him? It wouldn't be Paradiso without you! I would have written it, 'I come from there, where I would gladly return—if not for your absence.'"

At that, Alex laughed joyfully, put down his computer, and pulled her into his arms.

Later, they drove down the hill and then sailed around the island. They stopped at a beach and Valeria immediately noticed it was not nearly as nice as where they typically snorkeled. The sand was darker and the water was choppier.

"Why don't you snorkel for a bit while I set out the gear?"

She nodded and stuck her toes into the light surf, wearing a paisley blue bikini and a deep tan. She tied her hair in a ponytail, stepped further into the water, and pulled on her fins, snorkel, and mask. There were reefs, but the snorkeling was not nearly as impressive as at other parts of the island. The water was choppy and all she saw were tiny clown fish. After about twenty minutes, she swam back to the shore.

"I'm guessing this will be about right," he said, as he fastened a weighted belt around her and lifted a single tank onto her back. She shivered as she pushed her arms through the straps, remembering their dangerous swim out of Delos. Her breathing had been too heavy and she had run out of air. She had fought Alex to surface, risking being caught in the current and taken deep into the cave, never to escape. If not for Alex's quick reflexes, they would both be dead. She shuddered and Alex held her for a moment, knowing why her fears were surfacing.

"Beautiful, I wouldn't suggest this if I didn't honestly believe you would enjoy it," he said, but she could sense his hesitation. She decided that he was merely responding to her apprehension, and so she nodded again, but said nothing.

Alex continued, "Let's sit in the water so that we can go over a few things." He walked into the water a few yards and they knelt, while her face was still above the surface. "All right, well, I know you know how to clear your mask and your snorkel. Clearing your mouthpiece is similar to clearing a snorkel—except simpler. Just blow out and it clears."

Then he ran through the rest of the basics, including the hand signals that she needed to know.

"Alright," she said, wondering what she had really gotten herself into.

"We'll stay fairly close to shore. Ready?"

"Yes," she said spitting out the rough water that had splashed her. She was already shivering.

"Remember to control your breathing. But if your air runs low, we can always snorkel back, so it's no big deal, okay?"

"Alright."

She pulled down her mask, put the mouthpiece in, and followed Alex. Within seconds, they were in another world—a calm, but vibrant, world—that resembled a well-lit aquarium that was abundant in sea life that she hadn't seen while snorkeling. The water didn't seem to be deep at all. In fact, she felt like she could almost stand up and reach the surface. Although she was certain, due to her earlier snorkeling, that the water was at least twenty feet deep.

The white sand beneath them was marbled with sunlight, and the colors of the fish, the coral—everything—was brilliant. Alex turned and pointed to Valeria's right, where a sea turtle swam by; she couldn't help but feel thrilled at the sighting. They continued over the gentle waves of white sand and between two giant pieces of coral, easily ten feet tall and almost as wide. Alex gave her the hand sign that indicated danger and pointed to a yellow and white striped fish with numerous spine-like appendages, well camouflaged by the coral.

They swam along a sand path between the coral. Although Valeria felt calm, she could hear her own breathing and knew it was entirely too fast. Alex lifted a finger indicating that she should wait, and he went to the coral and came back. He took her hand and opened her fingers, and then, from a few inches above, he dropped a tiny creature that resembled a thorny octopus. It drifted the few inches into her hand.

The creature felt so delicate and was so beautiful that Valeria immediately fell in love with it—and diving. Alex returned the creature to the coral and they swam for another twenty minutes before Alex signaled that it was time to return. Valeria was surprised that she was disappointed.

As they crawled up onto the beach, the weight of the tank and belt made it so that she didn't have the strength to get out of the water. The mild tide pulled her back in, and then the next wave brought her back onto the sand and she began crawling again, only to be washed back out a few feet. Alex was quick to pull her to the sand and remove the near-empty tank from her back. She stood, with her legs feeling like rubber, and stepped through the sand like a drunk.

The experience hadn't felt tiring, but now she was exhausted. Alex went to the sailboat and pulled out a beach chair and a towel, and then built a fire to warm her.

"I'll be right back," he said, as he took a spear gun and went back into the surf. Within five minutes, he returned with a large purple fish. They sat by the fire and roasted fish on skewers and drank cold beer.

That night, back at their cabin, they lay on the hammock under the stars. The nerves, and the exertion of the day, had caused her to sleep several hours when they returned. Now, she felt the enormous joy of being exactly where she wanted to be, with exactly whom she wanted to be with.

"Alex, Mani said something when you were—well, out of it after the fire." Valeria glanced at Alex. "He talked about how difficult it was for you to live with my deaths so often."

He nodded, quickly pushing those images away. "It was the dream of this life that made it possible for me to survive." He kissed her hair and said softly, "Still, the reality is far more fulfilling than I ever dreamed it could be."

"I can't imagine what you must have gone through." She swallowed. "But I guess I'm wondering about something else Mani said. He said that he couldn't imagine you were so patient with me when all the time you felt the pressure of my impending mortality." Alex didn't respond. "I wouldn't want you worrying about me, if there was something that we needed to do so that you could feel the same way I do."

He turned and kissed her. "And how do you feel here?"

She leaned into Alex's shoulder. "I feel safe…and loved."

He stroked her hair. "That's my intention." He smiled, pleased. "Really, I don't think we have anything to worry about. I mean, even with the fire, all indications are that you are immortal. Your recovery from the plague and pneumonia—and hypothermia—were all extraordinary, indicating the type of recovery we would expect from an immortal." He sighed lightly. "Not to mention your eye color and, if that isn't enough, you've swam in the River Styx without even a heel exposed—Achilles has nothing on you!"

Valeria thought for a moment. "Then why were you so concerned about me at the wedding?"

It was Alex's turn to think. "I guess you are a new genus of us, and we aren't quite certain how your body will respond to health challenges." They watched as a shooting star moved across the sky. "I'm confident that you can survive anything."

Valeria secretly made a wish on the star that everything would stay as beautiful and safe with Alex as it was now. "Tell me about your family."

"The family?"

"No. *Your* family. I'll never get to meet them, but I want to feel like I know them," she said.

He pulled her in closer and they stared at the stars.

"My father was an adventurer. He was an extraordinary worker and a dreamer. Mother was his perfect mate—his symbolon. Mother had the most beautiful auburn hair. Father said she had the face of an angel. Certainly to me she did," he paused in his reverie.

"Antonia was two years younger than me. We never seemed to have the sibling rivalry that most children have."

"Did she look like you?" Valeria asked in a sleepy voice.

"No. At least, I don't think so. She was a tiny thing with a face that could be one minute filled with mischievousness, and the next completely angelic." He sighed. "She was a feisty thing...always wanting to wrestle—which I did inform her was completely inappropriate for a girl," he said in a teasing tone that made Valeria giggle. He sighed. "She was my closest friend...until Mani."

"What happened to them?" she asked, unsure if she wanted to ruin the mood, but needing to know.

"We knew there were troops coming for me, so we hid in the forest. I was terrified for my family's safety and determined that I would give myself up to Aegemon's troops to save them. Father insisted that if one of us left, it would be the end of our family forever. Finally, I lied to him. I told him that I had seen a vision, and that I would go and we would all be reunited. When the troops came, I left. Father came out, ready to fight, but mother convinced him that I would be back. As fate would have it, father was right—I never saw them again."

"I'm sorry," she said.

"It was a long time ago," he said casually. "Father was quite an amazing man. He was passionate about what he was passionate about…and that was his family, especially my mother. She was most definitely his symbolon."

"You had visions of the troops? I thought—"

He stopped and pulled back in surprise. "No, it wasn't my vision."

She brushed her hand lovingly over his chest. "Whose vision was it then?"

"I actually don't recall. It could have been any of them—maybe even all of them."

"I don't follow."

"Mother, Father, and Antonia were all oracles."

Valeria rolled up on an elbow, her eyes growing wide. "*You were a family of oracles?*" She pulled her brows down in confusion.

"Yes. Didn't I tell you that?"

She shook her head. "No. Never."

"Well, it doesn't really matter anymore because they're all gone."

"Alex, I remember you told me that your family feared for your sanity, due to your visions." She glanced up at him. "I guess that made me believe that they were mortal."

"Their visions were more like," he pursed his lips in thought, "intuition. They didn't think of it as odd. Whereas, my visions gave me a violent physical response. Also, my visions were," he shrugged, "much more...precise and vivid."

He hadn't been completely honest. It was only his visions of her in danger that gave him the violent reactions. And the other concern was that, since she had been with him during this lifetime and she had survived her twenty-seventh birthday, he had not had another vision. Most of the time, he allowed himself to believe that it was because she was no longer in danger. But after the very real danger with Aegemon almost a year before, then with her collapse in New York, and even their threat in Delos—not to mention the incident with the fire at the cottage—Alex was concerned that he would no longer have visions of her safety. Perhaps he was too distracted. Or, perhaps, none of those events would have been fatal.

"So, what happened to your family?" She turned to face him. "Do you know?"

He shook his head. "No. I assume that Aegemon's troops came back for them eventually. I heard that Father took an arrow to the heart on Morgana. I also assume that he had been trying to defend Mother and Antonia. But everything was so grown over by the time I returned, that I've never discovered where he was buried." Alex looked into the distance attempting to disguise an old ache with a casual tone.

Valeria brushed the side of his face. "I'm sorry, Alex." She changed the subject. "You said there were some things that needed to be done so that we can live without hiding. Can I ask what they are?"

"We need to discover who is responsible for the fire. And there's an old friend who can help us. The only problem is we will need to...bring him back into the picture."

"Myrdd?" she asked.

This time, it was Alex's eyes that widened in surprise. "Yes, exactly!"

CHAPTER 10

For the first time since their arrival, they took the red Jeep down the steep, deeply-rutted road to the hidden air strip and Alex's beloved Helio. Valeria discovered that departing in the Helio was more frightening than landing, but within seconds, they were airborne and just brushing some of the treetops.

As they flew over the chain of islands across the Caribbean, and toward their destination, Valeria realized that being inside the sun-baked cabin of the Helio all day was getting to her. She quickly hopped out at the fuel stops, but the strong smell of gasoline made it worse. She tried drinking more water, determined to enjoy this trip. Finally, she decided that it must've been from all of the exertion and nerves from the previous day while scuba diving.

The Pitons loomed high on the horizon of St. Lucia, grand and beckoning. Alex circled the volcanoes to give Valeria a better view. As they pulled out of the second circle, Valeria looked at Alex in near terror.

"I'm going to be sick!"

Grabbing a bag stashed in the dash, Alex handed it to her, and Valeria spent the next five minutes vomiting in the bag—and to her relief, not all over the plane. They landed and Valeria got sick again. This time, she ran to the bathroom and was grateful for the privacy.

They arrived early and so she had a few minutes. In the lobby of the open building, a small television left over from the '70s blared.

The announcer of the talk show sat with his two guests on cheap folding chairs.

He looked at the notes in his lap and then into the camera. "We would like to thank you for your responses to last week's topic, 'The harmful effects of alien blue rays on humans.'

"This week, we have Melanie Martin with us, author of *Just Call Me Cassandra: The Reincarnation of Cassandra of Troy*. Also with us, is Professor Tracy Lowe, Ancient History expert from Duke University in North Carolina."

"Reincarnation—oh, please!" Valeria quipped as she rolled her eyes and smiled at Alex.

"Farfetched to say the least." Alex winked.

The camera panned their faces, and Alex narrowed his eyes as he leaned forward.

"Professor Lowe, you have some questions for Melanie?" A neat woman, with her hair tightly bound in a bun, brushed an imagined stray hair back into place before nodding and leaning slightly forward.

"Yes, thank you for inviting me, Mr. Devries." The professor turned to the woman sitting next to her. "Ms. Martin, I've read your account of events in Cassandra's life. And it reads like a modernized Epic poem. But were you aware that there was extensive editing of the Epic poems, from approximately 560 to 528 BC? It's believed that the story that you share—that Apollo cursed you by spitting into your mouth—was added by Aeschylus, who was sending a message to the colonies of the Empire that to move against Athens—and by association, Apollo—would incur the wrath of the god, just as Cassandra suffered the wrath of Apollo when she deceived him."

Valeria lowered her eyebrows and smiled at Alex who was watching intently with a smirk on his face.

Professor Lowe tilted her head to the side and asked, "Are you familiar with historical methods of investigation?" Ms. Martin shook her head as if disinterested. "It does apply here."

Alex's smile widened. "Oh, Ms. Lowe, you learned well!"

"You know her?"

A loud voice boomed in the lobby of the airport, "Mr. and Mrs. Morgan?" They both turned to the door where a black man in a white shirt and blue slacks stood.

"Yes, that's us," Alex said, standing. They both walked toward the man and then Alex turned back toward Valeria. "Miss Lowe was a student of mine. She was originally interested in law."

"Hmm…and I'll bet Ms. Lowe was quite fascinated by her ancient history professor as well."

"Hmm?" Alex asked, pretending not to understand Valeria's insinuation. But Valeria saw the slight smirk of his upturned mouth and couldn't help but giggle herself.

"Oh, nothing," she said.

They went to lunch and toured several artists' studios. They fit in quite well with the other wealthy tourists, as they wandered through the streets, taking in the local shops, and purchasing gifts for Weege and the family. They came upon an elegant jewelry store. Alex was looking at a gold ankle bracelet for Valeria when, suddenly, a ring caught her eye.

"Alex, look!"

In the case was a man's ring with a large stone that resembled the Cassandra Crystal. Gold and platinum surrounded the stone in an artistic rendition of the triquetra.

"What is that stone?" Valeria asked.

"That is a three carat tanzanite. Your missus has excellent taste, sir."

"Yes, she does," Alex responded.

"Do you like it?" Valeria asked.

The clerk held the box toward Alex and he removed the ring, placing it onto his left hand.

"I think we just found my wedding band!" He smiled at the band on his left ring finger and kissed Valeria.

The limo wound through the tropical rain forest en route to their hotel. Valeria was exhausted, but relieved that her stomach handled it well. In the lobby, there were a myriad of stairways.

"Each room has its own unique bridge. Of course, you don't have a room—we have you in an infinity pool sanctuary," the woman said, as she checked them in.

Valeria turned to Alex and her eyes got big as she said, "Sanctuary? Sounds like we're a near-extinct breed."

"We are," he whispered in her ear.

The woman escorted them into their room. "They say that the cleanest air in the world is here on St. Lucia," she said. "Each infinity pool sanctuary at Jade Mountain is a carefully designed, individual work of art and architecture. All of the sanctuaries celebrate an unparalleled view of the Pitons and the Caribbean Sea. In all of our sanctuaries, the fourth wall is open to the views while, at the same time, allowing for complete privacy."

Their sanctuary was exactly that, offering a view of the lushly covered Pitons and calm inlet of the Caribbean. They had an infinity pool in their room. It was the most extraordinary hotel room she had ever seen, let alone stayed in.

As exquisite as the view was, Valeria had gotten used to their afternoon naps during their honeymoon. So she rolled into bed while Alex worked. That evening, they sat in the infinity pool with glasses of champagne and watched the sun set behind the Pitons. Then they dressed for dinner at a five-star restaurant. Fortunately, Valeria still had a dress she hadn't worn. She had gotten used to casual skirts and swimsuits. It was fun to see Alex in his dress slacks and white linen shirt; he looked so incredibly handsome, especially with his deep tan that made his eyes significantly brighter than they already were.

As they sat at dinner, Alex said, "The first time I saw St. Lucia, I thought I would build a home for us between the Pitons, but they're volcanoes. Also, I thought there might be too much shade there. So I built our home on St. John, instead."

"I love our home there. Not quite as much as…" She stopped speaking, unwilling to spoil the mood. "Actually, I guess St. John's is your getaway," she said nervously.

"You were right the first time—it is *our* home now. Everything I have is yours—including my heart." Alex kissed her hand. "But you've had that for a very long time."

∞

They woke the next morning in their king-sized bed, to the luxury of room service. Alex took the tray from the server and tipped him well.

Then he set it down on the bed and poured Valeria a cup of coffee with the perfect amount of cream.

"Just the way you like it," he said, stirring in the cream.

As she sipped it, she thought it wasn't the coffee she liked. It tasted *off*—maybe the cream was bad. Still, she didn't want to say anything to Alex. Then she smelled the eggs and bacon and, suddenly, she worried that she was going to be sick again. She set her coffee down and took a few deep breaths, trying to control the nausea. It was disappointing to have the flu when they were really on their last days of their honeymoon.

What a great memory for Alex, she thought. She glanced out at the view of the Pitons with the rising sun shining on them, and then at the tiny sailboats below. She wished she could appreciate it more. Then, suddenly, the nausea swept over her and she bolted for the bathroom— not even taking the time to close the door all the way.

Alex paced back and forth a few times, feeling awkward and helpless; then he went to the door that was slightly ajar. He pushed it open as she vomited in the toilet again and he went to pull her hair back.

"Don't watch me! Please, Alex! Please, just leave!" she said between violent, empty heaves.

He tried to argue, but then acquiesced for her sense of dignity and backed out, reluctantly sitting on the bed.

A few minutes later, Valeria came out of the bathroom, having brushed her teeth. She glanced at Alex who was looking down at the tile floor.

"I'm sorry, Alex. I haven't had the flu since I was a kid," she said, as she curled onto his lap. Seeing his hurt feelings, she brushed his face with her hand. "I feel better now. I'm sorry for yelling at you and pushing you away. I'm just so embarrassed."

He wrapped his arms around her but he couldn't look her in the face. Finally, he glanced up and tried to smile.

"Val..." he began, tentatively.

"Alex, I'm sorry that I've ruined the end of our honeymoon," she blurted, as her eyes filled with tears. Then she realized how ridiculous that statement was and that she had just told the love of her life that all of his efforts had been ruined. "I don't know what I'm saying—our honeymoon wasn't ruined! And it still isn't over...maybe this is just a twenty-four hour bug or something." Still, he didn't say a word. He just sat with his face locked in some expression that she couldn't quite grasp. She drew a deep breath in an attempt to withhold the tears that rimmed her eyes. He patted her leg without looking at her, obviously deep in thought. "What's the matter, Alex? I'm sorry...it's just that we're on our honeymoon and no woman wants her husband to see her like that."

Again, he attempted a smile.

Finally, he spoke, but there was a strange tone to his voice. "You didn't do anything wrong." He glanced up at her and brushed her face. "Val, I don't mean to be overly personal...but do you have..." He shook his head. "I mean, have you had..." He looked up in frustration, expecting that she would not force him to finish his question.

She would have answered if she had any clue of what he was asking. *Had she had a flu shot?* Or did she have food allergies? She wished they could just ignore this and get back to their honeymoon.

Something must have been wrong with the eggs they had the morning before. Or perhaps something about scuba diving just disagreed with her—maybe someone who was sick had used her mouthpiece—that thought made her gag, but she managed to push it from her mind.

"Have I had what?" she asked, as his face reddened and he turned away.

"Val," he said with a nervous gulp. "I don't really know about these things." His face flushed again.

"About what?" she said, beginning to feel just a bit frustrated.

His voice seemed higher than in his normal range when he asked, "Could you be..."

Sudden understanding flooded her consciousness, and she almost laughed—and then she realized that he was serious.

"Oh! You're...asking about my cycle?"

No one had ever asked her about her menstrual cycles, except the social worker who wanted to ensure that she wasn't pregnant...yet.

"Oh!" she said, embarrassed.

Suddenly, her mind reeled back to the awkward conversation with her caseworker. The woman who Valeria always imagined had been conned one too many times.

"Listen to me, Valeria. Birth control is your responsibility! Don't you think for an instant that you can trick some boy into marrying you and giving you a happily-ever-after because you allowed yourself to get knocked-up. I've seen that far too often. Do you know what they do, Valeria? They leave you—do you understand me?" she said, waving a small foil-wrapped package.

That little conference had occurred a month after Valeria had turned fourteen and she had prayed that the woman wouldn't demonstrate the use of the condom on a banana again. She had seen little boys naked and she couldn't imagine that they could grow into something that would fit into a condom.

"Here—take these and remember what I said, Valeria! Birth control is your responsibility!"

Suddenly, she understood Alex's question all too clearly.

"Alex, no...*No!* I'm not." She started to laugh when she heard her voice, realizing that she sounded nearly hysterical. This was silly because Alex was her husband and they needed to be able to talk about these things. "I'm sorry, I didn't even think about," she gulped, "birth control. But I'm sure I'm not..." She couldn't even say it. "I haven't ever had a regular cycle and, last year, after the plague, I haven't had one at all."

Alex wasn't her first lover. But he was the first man to *make love* to her. She had been engaged to David and they had slept together, occasionally, for years. And, although she had offered to get some form of birth control, David had preferred to use condoms. It always made her feel as if he felt that she was diseased. He had seen the blood test she'd taken for him, and he knew she had a clean bill of health. But somehow, her background as a foster child lent itself, in David's warped way of thinking, to promiscuity.

Somehow, she had believed that the high fever had destroyed her ability to have children. But, frankly, she didn't believe that oracles had children. None of them did—except Alex's parents, she remembered. It had been her responsibility to think of these things—Alex would have never thought of it. She again remembered the social workers words and cringed.

"Men leave when they are trapped."

Her stomach was flat. She had gained some weight, but during the honeymoon, that was to be expected. Besides, she wasn't running like she used to do. Certainly, she would know if she was carrying a child in her belly.

He patted her leg calmly. "Val, let's call Mani."

She shook her head, embarrassed. "No, Alex! I'm not...I would know if I was. Please don't call Mani," she begged.

"I can call the doctor at the resort, but frankly, I would prefer that Mani examine you," he said flatly. He was upset, Valeria assessed. She did not want anyone asking her what type of birth control she had used, and was horrified to have to admit that she had failed to plan. They would give her that look—as if she was trying to get something past them. She imagined the patient look of concern on Mani's face suddenly filled with suspicion when he discovered her error.

"I'm certain I'm not...but if you are going to insist on this, you can buy tests in a store."

"In a store?" Alex asked. She bit her lip and nodded.

"Alright, I'm going to have them drive me to the store and see if I can find a test. Maybe they have a pharmacist here who can get one for me. I'll be back within the hour."

He sat her on the bed next to him and absently brushed his lips over her forehead. Then she watched as he dressed without showering or shaving—something he never did—and headed out the door without another word to her.

She glanced at her belly again. For some reason, she never even thought of the possibility of having children, and—by his reaction—she suspected that Alex hadn't either. Valeria had to admit, there was a piece of her that was excited by the thought; and then she felt ashamed of herself for the seeming deception.

Shaking her head, she wondered, what was she thinking? She wasn't pregnant. She was just—it was probably all those gas fumes from yesterday. She lay back down on the bed. Still, what if she was pregnant, and what if Alex wasn't just stunned? What if he didn't want children?

All her fears continued to build until he walked back in the door, looking incredibly solemn, and handed her a brown paper bag. She stared at it for a moment.

"Val, would you ease my mind and take the test now?"

Taking in his words, she realized that he wanted her to "ease his mind." That certainly told her how he felt about it all. He did feel trapped by her irresponsible actions. A wave of insecurity engulfed her and she fought back her tears again.

At least, in the bathroom, she could hide her tears if they came. Then when she came out, she could reassure Alex that she wasn't pregnant, that it was just the flu as she suspected. Then they could plan on...birth control. She should have asked him to pick up a box of condoms while he was at the market. Of course the results would be negative, and the sooner she got this test over with, the sooner they could get back to the joy of their honeymoon.

But now, it would be a while until they enjoyed spontaneous lovemaking without the prerequisite condom—despite the fact that she was still certain she wasn't able to have children. Perhaps Mani would be able to confirm that on their trip to Puerto Rico.

Valeria vowed that she would never again do anything that would make Alex feel as though he were tricked into parenthood—even though it was impossible. Something special between them felt as if it had evaporated, and she worried that it was gone forever.

No, she couldn't believe that. Things would be normal as soon as she showed him that she wasn't pregnant. Next week, Mani would confirm that she couldn't bear children and that would be that. It wasn't necessarily what she wanted, it was just the way it was.

She scooted off the bed, feeling wooden as she carried the little brown bag into the bathroom and shut the door without saying a word—not out of anger, but confusion. There had been too many changes in their relationship and expectations in the past hour.

∞

The two red lines on the white stick were clear enough. According to the test she had taken twenty minutes before—and the instructions she had read and re-read five times—that meant she was, indeed, pregnant.

Her emotions were a mishmash of excitement buried in the shame of having done this to her husband—who clearly did not want children. She couldn't bring herself to leave the bathroom, instead opting to read the instructions once again, believing that perhaps she had missed something and this was all a mistake. How could she tell him?

She fidgeted as she heard his footsteps approach the door and linger for a moment. Then he knocked softly.

"Val? Is everything all right?"

Unable to trust her voice, she refused to answer him. She knew she couldn't stay in the bathroom forever. She rose from the edge of the bathtub and walked to the door. By the time she opened it, she was sobbing. She held up the stick that bore the proof of her irresponsibility, and fell into his body to hide her shame. His arms slowly folded around her, as he whispered in her ear, "It's going to be all right. Everything's going to be all right."

He held her on the bed for an hour while she sobbed and then fell asleep. Alex ran his thumb over the dark circles under her eyes. Then he rose; he couldn't think about this in the same room. Somehow, he felt that she would sense his thoughts and he didn't want that now. He walked out the front door and down the green hillside until he could see the Pitons. He dropped to the ground and pulled up his knees as the terrifying memory flooded his vision.

CHAPTER 11
Florence, 1573

"I could never take her youth," Alex said from the ancient room in the Medici castle that served as their classroom.

Mani stepped forward and took the book that Alex was staring at.

"Love Poems," Mani said, raising his brows as if the book was evidence of Alex's feelings, and then he dropped it into Alex's satchel. "Lita tells me that Isabella speaks of you with great affection. You could easily pay her dowry."

"She is a child, Mani. I want her to choose me when she has the wisdom to make that decision."

"In the state's eyes, she is a woman. She will be married to this other man unless you step forward."

"It's too late for that now," Alex muttered, tossing another book in his bag. "Whomever she marries will age while she remains young and beautiful. That's why you and Melitta must remain here at the palace. When the time is right, you can bring her to me. I will tell her the truth about her mortality, and then—and only then—if she chooses me, we will be together for eternity."

∞

He intended to be gone before Isabella left the feast, in order to avoid the inevitable goodbye. It was something he simply could not bear to say to his beloved. Isabella had sensed that, and was waiting for him in the stables.

"Was I such a terrible student that you could not delay your leave until such a time as I might properly wish my dearest tutor well?"

Alex's smile was wistful. Even at fifteen, she had a radiant beauty and he knew that he must be cautious with his glances toward her.

"Hardly!" he said, tossing a bag onto his saddle and then fastening it. Staying busy was his best defense. "I am certain, Isabella, that you have far more on your mind than the comings and goings of your tutor."

She brushed her hand along the neck of the horse as Alex continued fastening his saddlebags.

"Since I first met you, I used to dream that you were a prince who someday might carry me off."

Alex's expression became a subtle cross between a smile and a wince. He stopped his activity and turned to her.

"And now you are betrothed to a prince—Signore Carrara, isn't that correct?"

"Yes, but he isn't a prince—not a real one. Father says that he is handsome and powerful. He says it will be a good union."

"I'm certain your father chose wisely," he said returning to his activity.

"Yes. If only a certain tutor saw a match with me as a good union."

She did love him! He drew in a deep breath and tried to keep his joy from betraying his feelings.

"Although that tutor would be *quite* honored," he forced himself to breathe out, "your father would *never* consider that a good union!" He could sense that she was embarrassed. To ease the tension, he smiled softly. "My hope for you, my beautiful Isabella, is a joyful life."

The moment had passed and now they were left with the awkwardness of her confession.

"May I ask, tutor...what will you do now?"

"Thanks to your father, I have references that will assure me a post with any royal family." His eyes narrowed. "However, I don't believe that there would be another child so bright as you to hold my interests."

"You could stay on. Perhaps in the not-so-distant future you could tutor our children."

"Yes," he said, clipping his response. He wasn't certain he could watch another man treat her like property again. He wasn't certain he could bear to watch her love another man. But the reality was that she would not age beyond twenty-seven, only blossom, and it would only be a matter of years until her husband would be dead and gone. Alex would stay here and be a part of her life; and now, knowing that she cared for him, it would be easier to wait for her. Only twenty years—fifty at the most—and he would have his eternity with her, if she still chose him.

"You will return for my wedding, won't you?"

"Unfortunately, I've made other arrangements that I do not believe I will be able to reschedule," he said, a near lie. Seeing the hurt expression on her face, he said, "Remember, Isabella, you may always visit me at my humble estate."

"Morgana."

"You remembered." He smiled.

"Of course! I shall remember everything about you." Her eyes glowed intently and he knew he had to leave.

∞

The horse seemed to resent the trip back to Morgana and away from Isabella, almost as much as Alex did. His lazy clip-clop was beginning to annoy Alex. Then he realized where his annoyance truly was coming from. It was evening, and Isabella, his Cassandra, was married to another man...again.

It was right that he left. If he had seen her walking down the aisle, he wasn't certain he could restrain himself from confessing his love for her—or worse, kidnapping her. As much as Isabella's father admired Alex, it would be treated as an act of war. And she would feel frightened instead of loved. They would be in hiding, instead of her living the life she was destined for.

He returned to Morgana and busied himself with the cottage that he had built for the girl—not the princess. The large estate up the hill might be more to her liking. He had to think only of the future—he had to stay busy with preparations of Morgana for the day when she would finally be here with him. He would work on the larger home.

After weeks of hard work, he received a letter.

My dearest tutor,

I received your message and your very generous wedding gift...too generous. Thank you, we shall treasure them always.

Soon we will be travelling to Venice and then north. My husband was disappointed to not have met the tutor who I ramble on about. As my father insisted that you be retained as a tutor for our children, my husband wishes to meet you in person.

My dear husband tells me that he is familiar with your "Morgana" and believes that you have a home large enough to accommodate two weary travelers.

I hope it is not too presumptuous of me to ask. We shall arrive next Thursday at noon. If it is not possible, we shall stay at the nearby inn in Trento.

Your former pupil, now all grown up,
Isabella

Alex stared at the letter as he awaited Isabella's arrival. His heart pounded and he longed to see her. Secretly, he hoped that her husband was a buffoon, but he knew her father too well. He adored his daughter and would not have permitted a buffoon into the family.

He heard the carriage and exited the cottage. He would be cordial to her husband and offer them a room in the main house. He would retreat to his cottage where he could dream of his life someday with Isabella.

The door of the carriage flew open in what was deemed a most unfashionable manner, but Isabella's exuberance defied the rules of the day. The coachman rushed to help her out of the carriage, but Alex beat him to it and lifted her by the waist, lowering her to the ground as he had done many times. This time, her arms squeezed around his neck and her eyes sparkled.

"You look well, Isabella. Married life agrees with you."

"It does!" she said with a spark that took the wind out of Alex. "I am anxious for you to meet my new husband!" she whispered.

Alex explored the changes on her face. She was flush with excitement and, this time, it was not because of him—it was because of her husband. His heart sank. Still, in fifty years, at the most, this husband would be gone.

The man stepped out of the carriage and Alex saw him from the corner of his eye; he was stylishly dressed, tall and slim, olive-complexioned, and had jet-black hair. Then, Alex heard the all too familiar voice. "Bella, so I finally meet the man who shall tutor our children."

Alex felt his heart sink. He glanced over to confirm his suspicion, barely concealing his surprise or his anger—it was Paolo. Alex wondered how Paolo could have known where Isabella was. Why would he have married the one woman who belonged with Alex? Paolo knew she was Alex's symbolon.

The last time he had seen Paolo, 2,000 years before, Alex had refused to fight him in a dual. It was a ridiculous idea—what good was a duel with immortals? Once Paolo and Alex realized that Cassandra reincarnated, and they found her body in the river, Paolo expected that Alex would return to his sister, Kristiana, and again be the dutiful husband.

Alex, in his deepest grief—having just lost Cassandra again—told Paolo that he could no longer be with Kristiana, that the marriage was a mistake. Paolo had drawn his sword, prepared to run Alex through and defend his sister. When Alex did nothing to defend himself, Paolo opted to release his rage in a more satisfying way—with his fists.

Paolo beat Alex to a pulp—with Alex never once raising a hand to block a punch. After more than twenty minutes, Paolo stood looking down on a nearly dead Alex with disgust, wiping the sweat from his face. Tears brimmed Paolo's eyes when he said, "You are no longer my brother."

Now, here Paolo stood; the smirk on his face revealed that he had won this battle. There would be no marriage to Isabella in 50 years or 1,000—this husband of hers would never die.

Isabella touched his arm. "Alex, are you all right?"

Paolo pulled Isabella away from Alex. "Careful, Bella, men are not immune to your charms...not even servants."

Isabella's face flushed as she pulled her hand back from Alex's arm and looked down. "I apologize if I was..." she drew an embarrassed breath. "Permit me to introduce you. Alex Morgan, this is my husband, Paolo Carrara."

Alex narrowed his eyes slightly, through his nausea. Of course, Paolo had taken on the name of his home town of Carrara.

"Paolo," Alex said, attempting to disguise his disgust. It did not get by Paolo, whose glee was also evident.

"Alex, I believe that good manners require your wishes for our successful marriage. Although, I do understand that you are not of the same...breeding as our kind," Paolo said.

"Of course..." Alex forced himself to try to breathe normally, but his jaw was clenched and he was afraid of what would come from his mouth. "Felicitations on your marriage."

"I was waiting for you to wish us a long and happy life!" Paolo gloated.

Alex sucked in a long breath.

Paolo continued, "Incidentally, my bride and I do intend to have a...*very long*, happy life together." He leaned forward. "I must confess that our wedding chamber held a myriad of delights," Paolo said lasciviously. Isabella pulled back in horror as Paolo shrugged. "He is a man, Bella. Men speak of these things, do they not?"

"Yes, Isabella, *some men* do speak of such things," Alex choked out.

Paolo cleared his throat. "I do not wish to seem unappreciative to you as our host, but Isabella is no longer your student. I must insist that you address my wife properly."

"*Paolo!*" Isabella replied in embarrassment. "We are guests of Signore Alex."

"I apologize, my love, but servants must not get too familiar. I have learned this the difficult way."

Alex couldn't bear one more minute of Isabella's embarrassment. He sought to end the discussion.

"Signora Carrara, as I stated in my letter, my humble home is certainly not up to your standards."

"You are far too modest, Signore Morgan. Please permit me to be the judge of that," Paolo said, pointing to the cottage. "What is this? The stables?"

Isabella shook her head. "Dearest! Signore Alex is a tutor without the wealth that we have both been blessed with. Still, this cottage appears quite charming and *quite* to my liking! Though I would never wish to intrude, may I see the interior?"

Inside, there were numerous artworks all bearing Isabella Carrara's face. Alex shook his head. "It is a simple bachelor's home. Please allow me to show you to the main house. I am certain that would be more to your liking and expectations. However, as I stated in my letter, the Inn in Trento is far superior to my meager offerings."

"I think I should like to see this—what did you call this shack—a cottage?"

"It would not suit your tastes," Alex restated, attempting to restrain the anger in his voice. Paolo's wealth, the money that placed him so far above Alex's station in life, had been created by Alex.

Paolo smirked again and squeezed Isabella around the waist. "Please allow me to be the judge of that." With that, Paolo brushed his lips sensuously along Isabella's neck, causing a physical reaction in her, followed by her obvious embarrassment.

As Paolo stepped up the porch, Isabella smiled softly at Alex. "I would never have agreed to intrude on you if I had known that my husband could be so..." She shook her head. "He has always been so kind and charming. Please forgive him. I shall insist that we leave immediately." Then she lowered her eyes. "I believe this is all my doing. He must have sensed that I had...an obvious schoolgirl crush on my tutor. My father tells me that it is not uncommon when a girl is tutored by a man. He says that is why most fathers forbid it."

Alex smiled. It was so like her to take responsibility for Paolo's bad behavior. "Most fathers are not presented with such bright children, male or female. And please, I do not wish you to be embarrassed."

Inside the cottage, Alex could hear things being moved around and doors slamming.

"What is he doing in your home?"

"It is all right, Signora."

Paolo emerged moments later and his eyes narrowed at Alex.

"Bella, I believe this will suit our needs for just a few nights. I saw no indications of bedbugs or rodents. Come, see for yourself."

Isabella glanced at Alex who was nearly shaking. He couldn't stand the idea of another man making love to his symbolon in the bedroom he created for the two of them.

She lifted her hand. "My husband, on this occasion, I must disagree with you. I will not take my tutor's home. He is a dear friend, and that is over-stepping the bounds of that friendship. Please, Signore Alex, show us where you would like us to stay."

Alex led them up the path and Isabella seemed delighted with the wooded trail.

"I was most pleased by your wonderful gift," Isabella said.

"What was it? A tree? I do not know what we shall do with another tree. Boboli Gardens is tended to by the finest gardeners and they have informed me that they have no place for it," Paolo said with a nearly innocent shrug.

Isabella's face twisted. "I shall find a place for it! It has special meaning for me. Signore Alex told me a story when I was a child about a magical tree with ointments that healed. You may not know this, but he saved my life as a child with a magical ointment from the ginkgo tree. Did you know that they also bring good fortune? That is why it is such a special gift and has such great meaning in my heart."

"Wild trees belong here in this untamed land. Not in manicured gardens," Paolo said.

Isabella smiled at Alex. "Yes, at this we do agree. Signore Alex, I think I should like to think of my tree here—perhaps on the side of the cottage for some shade." She continued up the trail. "Of course, then it will give us an excuse to come and see my favorite tutor and my favorite tree."

"Alright," Alex said, still battling his pain from the discovery.

"And when you see it, you will think of me?"

Alex flinched and then whispered to Isabella, "Always."

∞

It was only a few months later when Alex had another vision and he knew then that his Isabella would die in childbirth. As soon as he recovered from the vomiting and the shakes, he headed to Florence and the Palazzo Pitto, praying he was not too late.

Alex's prayers were answered, and Isabella was not yet with child! But Paolo took Alex's warnings as a ruse to keep him from his marital bed. Alex offered Paolo a transference, which he refused. Even Mani had attempted to talk reason to Paolo.

A year later, Alex received a letter from Lita, who served as Isabella's nurse. When he entered the castle, everyone appeared in mourning. He could barely breathe and dared not utter the question that plagued him. He headed up the stairs and found Mani.

"She does not have much time left. Lita believes that Isabella has been waiting to see you once more," he said.

Over the course of the year, Alex had written Paolo and asked to please include Mani in any medical decisions. According to Mani, Paolo had ignored his warnings.

Running up the stone steps, Alex passed Paolo and worked to suppress his anger. Isabella's father was outside of her room and said, "She has been asking for you."

Alex entered the chamber. It was a grand room, but entirely too ornate for his liking. In the bed, he saw her, and although his heart demanded speed, he stepped cautiously toward her.

"Tutor!" she said weakly.

"Yes," he responded, heartbroken.

Isabella waved a thin arm to him and he approached. She was pale, and it was obvious that these were her last moments. Alex felt his jaw tremble and he turned away.

"Come," she said and patted the bed next to her and then glanced at her nurse, Melitta, Mani's wife. "Please, leave us for a moment," she said.

Alex sat down next to Isabella feeling the pain of loss for her, for himself, and even for Paolo. She stroked her hand along his face.

"Dearest…dearest…Alex." He blinked as she continued, "I prayed that you would come."

"For you I would do anything, Isabella," he whispered, holding back his tears.

She licked her lips and looked down at her stomach as she stroked her belly. "I do know that she is…gone." Isabella's eyes flooded with tears. "I can feel it." She bit her lip and closed her eyes as another tear escaped. Her face seemed even paler and it only enhanced her beauty. "I have something that I must tell you. But please do not judge me harshly for this."

"As always, I would only ever think the very best of you. And you should know that I will never betray your confidences."

"My husband...he is a good man. But sometimes," her tiny hand reached over to his and she pulled it to her lips. Unable to stop himself he squeezed her hand and she pressed it to her belly and whispered so softly that he could barely hear her, "sometimes, I dream that she is yours."

The room grew darker. He longed to tell her that he loved her, too—that he had always loved only her. Instead, battling his tears, he nodded, squeezed her hand, and said nothing. She closed her eyes and her tiny hand released his just as Paolo entered. Alex pulled his hand from her belly and rose, unable to face Paolo.

As Alex exited her chamber, he heard Paolo cry out. And the physical pain ripped through his own heart with a vengeance as he fell to his knees, mirroring Paolo's cries.

CHAPTER 12

Valeria woke for the first time in months without her husband beside her. The sun was about to sink behind the Pitons; she had slept almost all day. *Where was Alex?* She remembered the revelation that had changed their future, and put her hand to her stomach. Then she rose and moved to the door and down a hill until she found him sitting with his face in his hands. She approached him and heard him saying, "No, I could never have taken your youth."

She touched his shoulder, and he spun his head and pulled her into him with such grief that all she could do was hold him.

Finally, she brushed the side of his face and asked, "Are you all right?"

"Yes."

"It will all be all right," she said as a statement, without any of the earlier insecurity.

"Yes," he replied.

"Alex, you're doing it again."

He lowered his brow.

"You're hiding something."

He shook his head—not so much to disagree, but to end the conversation. He kissed her forehead but his eyes were still lost in the memory.

"Please talk to me," she urged.

He knew he needed to respond, and he didn't want to lie to her. "It…it doesn't really matter anymore."

"A vision?"

"No—no, nothing like that. Really," he said with a cry in his voice.

Normally, she would have let it drop. Alex could paint on a smile and she was usually satisfied. Except now, everything was different. She sat without saying a word.

Finally, he saw the expectation of a response. Yet she didn't force him. Instead, she smiled softly. It overwhelmed him sometimes how much he could love her. Something was very different about her—yet so very familiar. He kissed her forehead and swallowed.

"I've lived a very long time and I've seen...things."

She brushed her hand along his face and he tried to smile.

"Things from the future?" she asked gently.

He shook his head. "If they were from the future at least I would know what to expect. Instead, I battle...memories. One can never win a battle against memories."

"You can tell me."

"No," he said with finality.

She knew that his insistence was due to the pain, and she brushed her hand through his hair.

"All right then." She hesitated a moment, hurt, but she understood. "I'm going to take a shower and dress for dinner. Why don't you call Doc?"

"Yes, I should have called Doc earlier. Perhaps he can meet us here," Alex said.

"Alex?" He glanced to her. "If I truly am pregnant, a week won't make a difference. We can see Mani at his home in Puerto Rico. I'm certain he intends to run some tests," she said, leaving out the comment that it was the year anniversary of the curse, and now there were two lives to be concerned about.

Alex nodded absentmindedly, as if he only half heard what she was saying. She brushed her hand along his cheek and turned him to face her. She could see the near tears in his eyes. She spoke soothingly, "*I meant* that you should call Mani and talk to him about all of the things that you are thinking about. The things that you feel you can't share with me. You need someone to talk to. Call him."

Then she took his cell phone from his pocket, opened it, and dialed Mani's number. She heard Mani answer immediately, concerned when the call came in.

"Hello, Mani. Yes, we are all healthy. I believe Alex would like to speak to you." She handed the phone to Alex and rose. "I'll be in the shower and I won't listen. Please talk to him."

As she was walking back up the hill, she heard Alex say, "Hi, Doc. Yes, we have…some news." She turned and watched as he moved his fingers to the brim of his nose and nodded. "Yes." He waited a moment. "Val is—I mean—*we* are expecting."

∞

They spent the week enjoying the room and rarely leaving it. Room service became their friend and they ate in most nights. Alex's mood had lightened a degree. She only had a few more episodes of morning sickness and the last time she allowed Alex to hold her while she vomited—knowing that he needed to feel useful. It had taken all of her nerves to permit that because she was afraid it would disgust him.

His dark mood, she also realized, was probably coming even before the pregnancy due to the anniversary of the curse—also known as her birthday. She didn't think that oracles could even have children, until Alex told her about his family. Still, she wondered if he was worried that the pregnancy added doubt to her immortality. At least now, he was talking to Doc every day and that seemed to be helping.

At last, they were leaving for Puerto Rico, and Alex seemed relieved. Valeria had hoped the honeymoon truly would go on forever. She thought of the last golden days on St. John and the scuba diving. She forced herself to eat some dry toast and brought some soda crackers for the trip. They took off from St. Lucia, this time avoiding any circling. In fact, the Helio was capable of lifting off almost immediately, but Valeria noticed that Alex used significantly more runway than necessary. She also noticed that his boyish grin was missing, and he hardly spoke the entire trip.

"That's Puerto Rico," she heard Alex's voice say over the headphones. "There's a landing strip right over there for Mani's."

Within minutes, they had landed on a private dirt strip. Lars stood next to a golf cart as they taxied to the end of the runway. Alex hopped out and tied down the plane, and then helped Valeria out.

"Glad to see you both!" Lars said, extending a hand to Alex and throwing his arms around Valeria. "Camille wanted to come down but there wasn't room for everyone and your luggage."

They drove over a dusty hill to an adobe red hacienda with a large wooden gate. The gate opened electronically. Alex sat in the back of the golf cart with Valeria and patted her leg. It was good to see their friends!

Inside the gate was a courtyard of matching red tiles and large planters overflowing with flowers and greenery. In the center was a fountain. The walls of Mani's home were mostly glass. From the courtyard entrance, Valeria could see all the way through the home and out over the cliffs, with the view of the back porch and the ocean below.

Camille was waiting in the courtyard and said, "Aw, I'm sorry your honeymoon had to end with you feeling ill. But I'm sure the rest of it was fun!"

Jumping out of the slowing cart, Valeria ran to her friend. To her shock and humiliation, she found herself battling tears. Camille sensed it and whispered, "Everything all right?"

Repressing the sob, Valeria struggled and then was finally able to paste on a smile. She pushed back from Camille just as Ava and Tavish came out to greet them.

"We had a wonderful time at St. John," Valeria said.

"And I hope you are up for the birthday celebration we have planned for you next week."

"Next week? Oh…" She glanced down and then, without hesitation, she said mechanically, "That sounds wonderful! Thanks, Camille."

Caleb bound out of the house with Charlie the dog in tow.

"Caleb! Oh, my little Charlie!"

Caleb stopped just short of Valeria and looked a bit oddly at her. Charlie wiggled his back end excitedly and seemed to be begging her to welcome him. She bent down and pet the pup—reminding her of the awful time when Alex was away from her. Valeria began to reach out for Caleb, but he stepped out of reach.

"Mani says I need to stay away from you for a while," he said, as if hurt by the idea that he could ever hurt her.

"Mani said that?"

"Yeah. He said it was just to be careful. But look!" Caleb pointed to Charlie. "Your friend sent Charlie back! Shinsu said I could keep him,"

"I'm glad you have Charlie!" she said without considering it. "Caleb, did Doc say that you need to stay away from me even if you have your suit on?"

"He said it would be best if I keep my distance for now." Caleb looked down. "I would never want to do anything that would...well you know...hurt you."

Valeria smiled at him. "I know, Caleb. And I don't believe for a second that you would, but let's wait and see what Doc says, okay?" She so wanted to reach over and muff his hair.

He gulped. "Yeah, okay. Are you sick?"

She shook her head. "No, not really. Doc just wants to run some tests."

They greeted Ava and Tavish. Mani was noticeably absent. They sat in the living room and chattered about the honeymoon.

Although things were better with Alex, she noticed that his mind was a million miles away. She would often catch him just staring out at the sea. Perhaps he was just exhausted. He didn't really seem to sleep much lately. A few times during the night, she thought he was sleeping, only to realize that he had closed his eyes but she could tell that his mind was still racing.

Valeria felt the tears forming, and again tried to gulp them back. When she looked back up, she saw Camille glance back and forth between Alex and Valeria and then said, "Val, let me help you unpack."

As soon as they headed up the stairs, Valeria's tears began to fall.

Coming from the kitchen, Ava said, "Hey, girl time! I'll get the food." Valeria couldn't turn to acknowledge Ava. But Camille came to the rescue and offered Ava a subtle shake of the head and a non-verbal, *Not now.*

"Trouble in paradise," Ava muttered before disappearing.

Once they were alone in the bedroom, Camille closed the door and then said, "Okay! What is going on with you and Alex?"

Suddenly—and to Valeria's horror—the tears turned into full-out sobs. Camille held her and patted her back, but Valeria didn't seem to have any control of it.

Finally able to speak, Valeria said, "I think he's...angry with me. I got sick and Alex asked me to take a pregnancy test—"

"A PREGNANCY TEST?" Camille interrupted in a voice two octaves higher than her normal range.

With Camille's response, Valeria felt even more ashamed. She looked down and sobbed and finally said in a small voice, "It was...positive."

"Oh," Camille said. Obviously, this was knew news to her. "Pregnant! I had no idea that was even...possible." She thought for a moment. "Well, that explains all the new equipment Mani brought in. So what's the issue?"

Valeria continued to sob. "I don't think Alex wants it. And…" her voice trailed off.

"And?" Camille demanded.

"And I'm afraid that he thinks I tricked him into getting pregnant. I didn't even think about birth control! I don't know how I could have forgotten that. I just…"

Having actually said the words aloud, the sobs increased. After a few minutes, Camille got up and came back with some tissues. As Valeria wiped her eyes and blew her nose, Camille said, "Val, I can absolutely assure you that Alex would never think that of you! I'm sure he is just in shock at the idea of being a parent—as well as the obvious implication."

"Implication?"

"It…well, it suggests that you are still…mortal," she said softly. "I am absolutely certain he is just afraid."

"I don't understand. Alex's parents were immortal and they had two children. I would have thought he would have been a bit excited."

Camille dipped her brows in surprise. "I can imagine how that made you feel. You and Alex need to talk." She glanced toward the door with a glaring fire in her eyes, in what Valeria was certain was a non-verbal command.

"Please, I don't want Alex to see I'm upset," Valeria sobbed. A moment later, she heard Alex's rapid pace up the steps to the bedroom door.

Lifting her arms in an attempt to calm the situation, Camille said, "Val, I can assure you that this is all a misunderstanding, and Alex needs to talk to you! You need to ask him about Ian and Morgana."

"Val?" Alex knocked on the door hesitantly and then opened it. Alex stood looking incredibly sheepish. He shoved his hands into his pockets, suddenly not certain that his wife wished to see him, and upset with himself that he didn't even sense that she was upset.

Camille stood between the two of them, glaring at Alex with her hands on her hips.

"What have you been saying to your wife? Do you know what she thinks?"

Alex looked completely baffled by Camille's silent communication, and Valeria could see that there was a *lot* of communication going on between them.

"Will you please talk to your bride? You two talk and then let's all meet downstairs later."

Alex was obviously stunned by Camille's communication. After they were alone, and behind closed doors, he went to his wife and wrapped his arms around her as his mask fell from his face leaving only love and concern.

"Val, beautiful, I am so sorry! I have been such a...jerk, as Camille so aptly reminded me. But she was right to do so! I've been thinking about the situation and completely forgot how...vulnerable you must feel."

He pulled her chin up to look at him and she could see the dark circles under his eyes from his lack of sleep. She could also see how disappointed he was in himself. He continued, "I *never* thought about anything other than how to keep you safe. *Never*. And I would have never thought that you...*tricked me*," he said, as if the idea were the furthest thing from his mind.

The words, and the look on his face, caused her to feel ashamed of herself, and she couldn't even look him in the eye. He lifted her chin up again. "I am so very sorry for leaving you with your thoughts. I should have known that by not talking to you, your very vivid imagination would take hold."

He took her face in his hands as his eyes filled with love. "You must know that I think only the *very best* of you. You must know that I...*adore you.*" He swallowed. "For 3,000 years, I've had one dream—to be with you. To be honest, I never dreamed of children, but only because I didn't believe it was possible," he said softly.

"I don't understand why it would be so...surprising to you. Your parents had two children."

Sudden understanding flooded his face. "Oh—Ian and Morgana." He rolled his eyes and said to himself, "That explains a lot!"

"After you told me that story, I should have thought about birth control. I should have. I was lectured about my responsibility for years and I...I just didn't think about it," she admitted.

He knitted his brows, clearly upset by her words.

"Val, I need to explain a few things. Ian and Morgana are my *adopted* parents. They were oracles and they rescued us. They found me rocking Antonia in the burnt ruins of our war-torn village. I was little more than two years old. Antonia was only a few months old. They are the only parents I remember."

"Oh, Alex—how awful!"

He shook his head. "I don't remember much of it."

"Are there any oracles who have had children?"

Alex thought for a moment and then drew a deep breath. "No."

The reality was sinking in.

"So...I'm not immortal," she said flatly, thinking of the repercussions.

Slowly, Alex shook his head, unable to say the words.

Finally, finding his voice, Alex said, "That has been my concern. I'm sorry that I didn't share it with you." He pulled her up onto his lap and kissed her neck. "As far as birth control—it would have been my responsibility, too." She glanced up at him and he wiped a tear from her face. "Val, I've never considered children, but that doesn't mean I wouldn't want them." He gulped again and let out a long sigh.

He rocked her in his arms as he swallowed back his emotion. "There are some things that are frightening about this. I have seen the frailty of the mortal body—of your mortal body. I want to believe that you will be all right. I need to believe it. I just…" He choked. "I can't lose you again."

Valeria pressed her lips to his neck and whispered, "You won't lose me again. And if you do, I'll come and find you. You'll see—we'll be fine."

They lay back on the bed, wrapped in each other's arms until the stress of the past two days caught up with them and they both drifted off to sleep.

CHAPTER 13

"Hey, beautiful." Alex woke Valeria gently. "Doc is ready for you—if you're up for it."

"Yes. Might as well get it over with," she said.

He led her by the hand down the stairs and into an office that had been turned into a physician's office. Mani hugged both of them.

"I'm going to perform an ultrasound. Home pregnancy tests can provide a false positive or be misread. Come and lie down on the table."

She lay down as Alex stood by holding her hand. Mani scooted her yoga pants down, revealing her lower abdomen and then squeezed a tube of cold gel over the area.

"I apologize. I should have heated the bottle."

"It's not too cold," she said, despite the shiver that ran down her spine.

Mani pressed the wand to her lower abdomen and moved it around while Alex and Valeria stared at the monitor. Mani zeroed the monitor in on something and Valeria and Alex stared, trying to determine what they were looking at. Mani leaned toward the monitor and pointed with a pen.

"That is the baby's heart." Mani nodded toward the monitor. "Congratulations." Mani turned the speakers on so that they could both hear the heartbeat.

Valeria felt overwhelmed and watched as Alex's eyes had a moment when he allowed himself to dream, before they shifted to fear—followed by the replacement of a pleasant mask and a kiss to Valeria's forehead.

Mani went on, "Valeria, since you don't recall your last cycle, we will monitor the baby's progress by ultrasound."

He moved the wand again and suddenly there was a profile of a baby.

"See here? Mani said, as he brushed a capped pen along the screen. "You can see the face and nose here. Here are the hands. See, it is sucking its thumb."

"Mani, I had no idea that babies grew that fast! I'm probably only a week or two along, right?"

"The fetus is considerably more than a couple of weeks along. See its fingers and toes? By the size and development of the fetus, I would guess you are about fourteen weeks."

"That's nearly four months!" Alex said. "Doc is that possible? Val just began feeling sick last week. Besides, we've been drinking wine and hiking." His words all ran together in a nervous train of thought. "Oh, and I took her scuba diving!" he said with sudden dread.

Mani turned off the Doppler and removed his gloves. "The fetus looks fine."

"Do you know…what it is?" Valeria asked.

"I'm sorry, Valeria, I don't have the expertise to tell at this stage. In a few more weeks it should be evident." He pushed back the Doppler, and said, "I'll give you both a minute alone. We can talk more outside."

Valeria wiped the slimy clear liquid from her belly. Alex helped her sit up and they went outside and sat in the Adirondack chairs in the courtyard overlooking the Caribbean.

Mani smiled. "Do you have any questions for me?"

Valeria wanted to laugh and cry and she wanted Alex to feel like she did. But right now, she would have to be satisfied that he was here with her and loving her—not drowning in potential loss.

"I have a lot of questions," she began. "I understand that oracles don't have children. But Alex is an oracle. So how can this be?"

Mani thought for a moment, and then leaned forward as he clasped his hands. "You bring up a very good point, Valeria. One that I have no answers for. I don't believe that we can discount your immortality without input from…others." His gaze shifted to Alex. "But, it does no one any good to worry about this. We must remain hopeful and we will all do our best to safeguard the health of both you and the child."

"Will the baby be an oracle or a mortal?"

"I cannot believe that oracular visions would pass genetically. There were only a hundred oracles and I believe we would have heard of offspring. But when the child is born, we will test its DNA."

"Why is it that oracles don't usually reproduce?" she asked.

"I can only believe that when the body is not concerned about death, or populating an environment, that it no longer reproduces."

He continued, "Of course, in your case, it is very interesting. Your DNA appears as an oracle and your eye color matches ours. But the fact that you are pregnant is an indication that there is some other force at work in your body. I cannot explain it, but at this point, both mother and child appear to be healthy."

Valeria sighed happily, and squeezed Alex's hand.

"Do immortals reproduce?" she asked.

Mani's eyes narrowed in thought. "The first few generation of gods could reproduce fully, even with other creatures. After that, there was a declining incidence of mixed specie reproductions.

"Of those immortals who were changed by the River Styx, I personally know of none, except for you, Alex, and Caleb. However, it has been said that Achilles fathered mortal children."

"I wonder if because we swam in the River Styx, if it changed our physical make-up?" Valeria asked.

"I don't know." Alex said.

"Paolo's eyes are darker than yours." She thought for a moment. "So are Caleb's."

Alex nodded.

"Paolo is the son of a god?" Valeria asked

"Evidently," Alex said.

She wanted to know how she could have been pregnant with Paolo. She would ask this question when she was alone with Mani.

"Alex, you said that because I swam through the River Styx, that I would be immortal, even if the oracle DNA didn't kick in. So, it looks like—despite the evidence—I am still…mortal?"

"Val, we have been trying to answer the riddle of your immortality for some time. What we do know is that you are an oracle, but for some reason, your body is still not behaving as a typical oracle. It also takes two to make a child and so, for that matter, neither is mine," Alex said.

"Looks like we're just in time," Lars interrupted, as he and Ava entered through the screen door and pulled up two chairs. "It's time we talked about answers," he said as he stared at Alex for a moment, who hesitantly nodded. Ava stroked Valeria's arm and winked. Tavish entered behind them and pulled up a chair backwards; sitting down, he nodded to Valeria.

From upstairs, they heard Camille holler down, "Lars, don't start without me! I told you I would be ready at four o'clock. The rest of you are early—for once!" Camille teased.

Lars smiled. "I've heard that before."

"This is a family meeting?" Valeria asked, as Caleb lumbered in and sat down with Charlie next to him.

Camille entered and excitedly hugged Valeria. "I'm so excited that you're pregnant! I hope it's a girl!" she said, as she sat down on the other side of Valeria.

Lars, as usual, got right down to business. "Val, we need to get some answers. Part of Alex's concern has been about your health, and the health of your child. And if you aren't immortal yet, we need to fix that. There is only one person we know who may be able to shed some light on this situation. His name is Myrdd."

Valeria looked at Alex. "Yes, he was the first oracle."

Alex nodded. "That's right."

"I thought he had been executed in Delos." she drew in a deep breath remembering how she'd almost been beheaded.

Suddenly, things got very quiet. Valeria glanced at Lars and saw his intense focus on Alex, as if their non-verbal communication was taking place. Immediately, she realized that this was the discussion Alex had said would need to wait until after the honeymoon—evidently the honeymoon was over. She felt the tears well up inside her again and she pushed them back.

"What's going on?" she asked.

Mani responded, "Valeria, do you recall our discussion about the council when you were in the hospital?"

Valeria thought for a moment, and then she remembered. She had been in the hospital in Manhattan recovering from dehydration when Doc had told her the story of his symbolon, Lita, and also about Myrdd.

"Valeria, this council, with Jeremiah, was not always the way it is. At one time, the council, led by Myrdd, was one who sought to expand understanding and reduce the prejudice between the immortals and the oracles, and to improve the world with our gifts, as Apollo had intended. Jeremiah was able to gain power with accusations that Myrdd had violated sacred agreements. As a result, he was executed."

"Melitta began a petition to remove Jeremiah as the council head. I was away when it was presented at the next council meeting, 500 years later. She was executed, along with all of the other petitioners. My name was on that list."

"I don't understand how they...I mean, they are—were— immortal. How did they..."

Mani looked away for a moment, and she could see that he didn't want to discuss it with her. Then he turned and looked her straight in the eye. "They were beheaded."

Valeria looked at Alex. "Alex, what did Myrdd do?"

"He was accused of bringing a mortal into Delos. He didn't challenge the accusation so it is likely true."

Trying to make sense of this, Valeria asked, "How would Jeremiah know about these rules of oracles when you don't?"

Lars sighed and lifted a hand. "There are those that weren't pleased with the creation of oracles. Of course, there is Aegemon, but there are others. Some of the gods were upset, as were the Fates. It's also possible that Jeremiah has a link to Hecate—a goddess of the underworld with secret powers. Or possibly he is linked to the Fates— maybe a combination."

"But if beheading was not Myrdd's Prima Mortis, he should've recovered in twenty-four hours, as you did."

A cloud moved over them blocking the warmth momentarily, and Valeria shivered lightly. Alex brushed his hand along her arm and then said, "Val, we don't know where or how Jeremiah got this information, or how he managed to discover these charges against Myrdd. As far as why Myrdd and the others haven't been recovered—the predominant theory is that, besides their Prima Mortis, there is one other condition where oracles don't recover, and that is when the event that created the 'death' continues. It has long been believed that Jeremiah stores the head and the body apart so that the 'condition of death' continues."

"But you're right, Val. You have to wonder how a mental giant like Jeremiah put that together," Ava said sarcastically. "That guy isn't bright enough to tie his own shoes."

"We hypothesized that the deaths—or rather, lack of recoveries—of the others, may have something to do with Erebos' involvement or perhaps his double-sided axe. But recently, we acquired some evidence that the bodies and heads are stored separately—which supports Mani's hypothesis," Lars added.

"So, you plan to conduct a search in order to reunite Myrdd's head and body," Valeria asked.

"Yes," Lars answered, and Valeria noticed everyone was staring at her.

"How are you going to do that? Don't you need to have an idea where the bodies…and heads are stored?"

Alex bit his lip, and Caleb leaned forward and smiled. "Can I tell her?"

Both Lars and Alex glared at Caleb and said, "No!"

Charlie hid his head as if they were upset with him. Lars raised his eyebrows in question at Alex, who reluctantly nodded. Lars said, "Alex and Caleb made a discovery when you were swimming out of Delos." He paused for effect. "Two underwater depositories. They spotted skulls in one of them and Alex is certain he saw bones that resembled leg bones in the other."

Valeria turned toward Alex. "Why didn't you tell me?"

"I wanted to tell you but everyone said no," Caleb added.

"I…I'm sorry." Alex brushed his fingers through his hair. "I knew we would need to…to do something with it, and I felt that you had been through so much." He bit his lip and grabbed her hand.

She tightened her grip on Alex's hand as sudden understanding came through. "You want to go back there!" she accused.

"Val, I—" Alex started.

"Alex, please tell me you aren't possibly thinking about swimming in there again." She felt her throat tighten and, the next thing she knew, tears were flowing down her face. She didn't want to cry, but these days, she didn't seem to have much choice in the matter. "No! You are not going to make this child an orphan before she can even…"

Alex looked away and Mani pulled his chair directly in front of hers.

"Valeria," Mani said, as he squeezed her hand gently. When she looked up he continued, "I would go alone—the rest of us would go alone—but without Alex's knowledge of the exact position, the dangers increase exponentially. All of us owe a debt to those who are gone. My wife is one of them, and so I do have an ulterior motive. But I do believe it is in all of our best interests to recover these oracles."

She didn't want to make sense of this situation. Lars added, "Besides possible information from Myrdd, we also know that there were at least ten executions. Those ten would help provide a small army to battle Jeremiah, if it comes to that."

Finally, Alex said, "Beautiful, I've known since I saw the depositories that we needed to go back. At the time, the political situation was far too hot to make the attempt." He sighed. "Now it's different. I believe that this must be done so that all of us can be safe again. So that, perhaps, we can raise our child in the safety of our home...or anywhere else we wish."

She shook her head and then looked into Mani's eyes, and her face softened.

"Your Lita is there." Then, with a sinking feeling in her chest, she said, "Who…who would go on this expedition?" she asked.

"Val, this would be a whole other ball game than when we escaped with you. This time, Mani and I would scuba in with a vacuum and bring the contents back to Morgana. And now we know that we can get in and out of there undetected."

"You have known for months that you were going to do this. You even have a plan in place," she turned to Alex accusatorily. "You should have told me. Please don't do this!" she pleaded.

"I…I have to." Alex swallowed. "It'll be all right."

Valeria glanced angrily at Lars and then at Camille. "Camille, please talk sense into them!" Suddenly, she started to cry again. "I need you!" she said to Alex, and then turned to the rest of them and swallowed. "I need all of you!"

After a moment, Camille said, "Val, I'm afraid I agree with Alex and Lars. We have to do this. Not just for you." Camille looked to Mani. "But for our friends who have been taken."

"Well then, I can scuba! I'm going in with you!" she said.

Lars, Mani, Camille, and Alex unanimously responded, *"No!"*

Alex took Valeria's arm. "You can't. There are risks to swimming into Delos. If you won't think about yourself, then think about the child."

Lars nodded. "And how much attention do you think Alex will have on the chore if you are there?"

Valeria put her face in her hands. "I can't believe this is happening."

Camille rubbed Valeria's back. "It'll be all right. Lars, Ava, Mani, and Alex will be there together and the sooner we get some answers, the sooner you and Alex won't have to hide anymore. You don't want that life for you and your new family, do you?"

Valeria attempted to nod but she just couldn't agree to this. Suddenly, she saw the purpose of Alex's insistence that she learn to snorkel and scuba. He wanted her to know how expert he was with it all. Also, if she knew how, it would help reduce her anxiety.

Alex brushed Valeria's hair back. "We'll be careful. If I didn't feel like it was critical to your safety–I would never agree to this. But, beautiful, we have to do this."

Fighting back the sobs Valeria asked, "And when is this happening?"

"The plan is to fly out tonight." Valeria released a cry. Lars continued, "We have a house across the Ionian from Delos, in Italy. With the time difference, we'll head out as soon as we land."

"What about…I thought you couldn't fly and dive the same day," Valeria asked grasping at straws.

"That's decompression sickness. Really not a factor for us," Ava said.

"All right…and then?"

"We'll transport the remains back to Morgana. That will give us a few days to revive Myrdd. I know we're cutting it close, but Alex wanted to wait."

Valeria looked at Alex, upset. "I wish I would have known that we wouldn't be going back to St. John."

Alex closed his eyes. "I'm sorry."

"Val, let's be straight about this," Lars said. "Your birthday is in a few days. If we're going to do this, it would be better to do it before your birthday. The hope is that if there is still an issue with…the curse, Myrdd will be able direct us."

"The curse…" Tears spilled from her eyes. "Alex, are you in agreement with this?"

His eyes filled with love and concern. "Yes, beautiful, I am," he said softly.

"Well, I'm not." She glanced at Lars and Mani. "I love you all. I hope you know that. But I'm not ending my honeymoon like this. Alex, please give me one more night with you on St. John."

Alex looked at Lars and Mani, and then back to Valeria, and nodded. "You're right. You deserve that."

She pulled at his hand and said. "We deserve that."

Landing just before sunset, they drove up the familiar drive.

"Do you want to go to Jamaica Joe's?" he asked.

"No. I just want to be here with you...alone."

He nodded, and then brought in the supplies for dinner that they had brought from Mani's. He wasn't back to the joyful man from before the life-changing discovery, but his love and affection weren't as guarded by his fears.

Valeria showered while Alex boiled the crabs and prepared a salad. They both sat silently by the fire.

Alex rose and went to the hammock, and her heart stirred when she saw him lift a finger and signal for her to join him. They curled together staring at the Milky Way, relishing the last night of their honeymoon. She was glad for the feeling of his arms around her, and the way his fingers brushed along her ribs as his feet played against hers in the hammock; but what she really longed for was a sense of normalcy.

Valeria was lying against Alex's chest, and he moved her hair back, lovingly. "I'll never get tired of seeing that," he said softly.

"What?"

"Our mark. The mark that shows that we belong together."

"So, I'm branded," she teased. "I wish I could see it," she said, as she ran her fingers along the triquetra on his hand and then laced her fingers with his.

Alex laughed as he looked up at the sky. "I guess we're both branded."

"Tell me about Myrdd," Valeria said softly.

Stroking her hair he said, "Hmm, well, there's a lot to say about Myrdd. He's one of the most interesting characters I've ever met. When I knew him, he was strong and powerful—my guess is that he was that way even before he was an oracle. He just...knew things. Of course, that was before."

"Before?"

"Yes, before he lost his sanity."

"What happened to him?"

Alex narrowed his eyes. "I'm not sure of the details. Remember how we told you that Aegemon had the oracular temples built where there were ethylene vapors? In those days, we knew so little. In any case, he lost his sanity years after we parted ways. From what I've gathered, he was lured into one of Aegemon's temples by a woman. Part of my hesitancy in going in after him was that we just didn't know how much of the real 'him' was left—if anything." He smiled. "I'm feeling romantic tonight...I think I'd rather tell you the story of Myrdd and his symbolon."

"Myrdd's symbolon?"

"Hmm-hmm. Although, I have to warn you that, as with most of mythology, the ending is a bit unsatisfying." She nodded, resisting his glass of wine.

"Myrdd was Jeremiah's first execution—for that matter, it was the first time the council had ever exercised their 'right' to execute anyone. Myrdd could have, and should have, defended himself, except that he was shocked into silence."

He kissed the top of her head before staring back up into the stars. "Myrdd was born mortal and had lost his beloved wife many years before he became immortal. He used to tell me that the world lost its brightness the day that she left this world. I know how he feels."

Valeria brushed her hand over his chest.

"When Apollo made Myrdd immortal, he also promised Myrdd that, one day, he would bring his wife back from the Elysian Fields."

"That's like...heaven, right?"

"Yes." Alex thought for a moment. "When I first lost you, I prayed to Apollo to accept me into the Elysian Fields, as I was certain that you would be there. But then Daphne convinced me to wait. She suggested that I could go there and wait for you for an eternity without ever seeing you. So, I chose to wait."

"Daphne, huh? Are you certain that her motivation was selfless?" Valeria smirked.

Alex laughed lightly. "Well...not completely. Still, her reasoning was sound."

"Even if you had gone to the Elysian Fields, I would have found you eventually!"

"Yes. You would have." He patted her leg. "But if we had been in different worlds it becomes complicated. Remember, as with the story of Orpheus, Hades does not release any souls easily. Given the opportunity, he would most certainly deceive you or up the ante on any exchange.

"So, Apollo made the promise to Myrdd that, one day, he would bring back his wife. He knew that it would require an exchange, and then opportunity knocked.

"The god had fallen in love with a mortal woman, Coronis. Although Zeus was famous for his flings, he did not approve of mixed marriages. So Apollo kept his marriage to Coronis a secret. He intended to make her immortal, but that would have tipped off Zeus. Soon, Coronis was expecting—by the way, the mythological accounts of this story are quite different from the facts as I remember them.

"Apollo's visions of his son became legendary—so much so, that Asclepius was seen as an actual living, breathing god. There are even statues of the god known as 'the healer' when, in fact, he was never even born. Interestingly, the rod of Asclepius, a snake-entwined staff, is the symbol of medicine today."

"How can that be?" Valeria asked.

"Another case where belief creates reality." He kissed the top of her head, feeling very fortunate about his own reality. Then he sighed. "Envy's bite was rampant in those days—I guess it still is. There was a story of Asclepius bringing the dead back to life with his healing powers. This angered not only Zeus, but the Fates," Alex continued. "The Fates were upset that Asclepius might usurp their power because, previously, they were the only ones who would determine when the thread of life was to be cut. Even Hades worried that with Asclepius's healing skills, there would be no more deaths, which would limit his power in the underworld. Lastly, Zeus was enraged by Apollo's defiance, and of his secret mixed-marriage."

Alex looked up and his jaw tightened. "This may not be the best story to tell you right now."

Shaking her head, she tapped on his chest affectionately. "It's all right! I want to hear it."

"Well," Alex said hesitantly. "The story goes that when Coronis went into labor, Zeus struck her and the child with a thunderbolt." Valeria's gut tightened, and she pulled her hand to her stomach as Alex laced his fingers with hers there. "There are stories that Apollo removed the child with a blade. Some say Asclepius was resurrected by Zeus in an effort to make amends with Apollo."

"Coronis, of course, died and was sent to the Elysian Fields. Having lost his wife and only child, Apollo spoke to Hades of an exchange. But to extract Coronis from the underworld would require another being of equal magnitude and importance to Apollo, and there was no other mortal who could fulfill Hades' demands. Also, Apollo was concerned that Zeus and the Fates would continue plotting against Coronis.

"What happened?"

"Apollo allowed time to pass, and then approached Hades with a trade. Myrdd's wife, whom he knew was in the Elysian Fields, for a god. Hades greedily accepted the offer—believing that Apollo was going to send a poor, unsuspecting god to the underworld. When Hades saw Charon's boat arrive—"

"Charon?"

"Yes, the ferry man of Hades who carries the deceased down the River Styx, from the world of the living into the underworld. One must have a coin to pay Charon; if not, it's said that they will wander the underworld for a hundred years."

"The dribs," Valeria said, as she cringed and Alex nodded.

"In any case, Hades was shocked to see Apollo arrive on Charon's boat. He accused Apollo of trickery. But their bargain had already been struck." He patted her leg. "And that...my love, is how Apollo was reunited with his wife, Coronis, and Myrdd was—very briefly—reunited with his symbolon—Shinsu."

"Shinsu? You mean Shinsu was...*mortal?*" Her jaw dropped as Alex nodded.

"Apollo made Shinsu an oracle. She was transformed while still in the underworld. I've always appreciated her wisdom that transcends Apollo's gifts."

"Does Shinsu have a mark?"

"Probably. She's the reason that Apollo created symbolons. Apollo had seen the sadness in Myrdd's eyes and Myrdd told Apollo of the pain of living beyond all of those whom he loved. At that time, Apollo was still chasing young nymphs and goddesses. Still, Apollo had the wisdom to understand.

"He decided that the world would be better with more oracles. The story is that he blew into the heavens and loosened some of the stars; and as they fell to the four corners of the earth, Apollo gave one more breath and split them in two. He told Myrdd that we would know each other by our marks."

He brushed his lips along the side of Valeria's face. "It must be true, because I fell in love with you long before I saw the mark."

"What about those who don't seem to have mates—like Tav?"

"I don't really know. Just like with Paolo and Daph. They certainly aren't made for each other like we are. But they do seem to be a good match."

Valeria nodded, and they were quiet for a moment.

"Do you ever worry that I'll never be all that I was...before?"

Alex stroked her hair. "You mean more to me now than ever before!"

"I sometimes worry that you see who I was...who I used to be."

Alex turned Valeria around to face him, his face filled with love. "Beautiful, I love you!" He leaned in toward her. "Do you understand? I love...*you!*" He kissed her tenderly.

"Well, you haven't made love to me since...the test." She swallowed. "Do you still want me...like before?"

"Of course!" he said. "I will always desire you! I just don't want to hurt you or the...the baby."

"No. That's not how we're doing this," she said.

"No?" he asked, and then laughed for the first time all week, the corners of his mouth turning up in the way that she loved.

Valeria shook her head. "No," she said, and then kissed his chest. "I'm not so fragile, and if I'm nearly four months along, that means that...all of our honeymoon activity...hasn't hurt the baby at all." She brought her face to his. "Alex, I want to," she said, as she brushed her hand over his chest and then stared into his eyes, "I need to make love to you."

He stared at her for a moment and then pulled her into him, pressing his mouth to hers, first gently, and then with all of the fear and anxiety suddenly removed. With a deep need, he pulled her into him and they made love.

∞

She must have drifted off because, when she opened her eyes, it was early morning and she was in their bed. She looked around, but Alex was nowhere to be found. She jumped up and then nausea overtook her, causing her to run into the bathroom. In an instant, Alex was there.

"It's all right," he said, rubbing her back. "It's all right," he soothed as she wretched. Then she rocked back onto his lap as he carried her back to bed.

"You need to eat something. Maybe a strawberry kale shake?" She nearly gagged at the thought. Alex measured her expression. "Toast?"

"Where were you?"

"I've been storing everything. We probably won't be back here for a while." He studied her face and realized that she was upset. He sat down on the bed next to her and looked into her eyes.

"Val, I am a very selfish man. I simply cannot bear to see anything but joy on your beautiful face. But more than that, I wouldn't want to live in a world without you. So if there is anything that can be done to protect you...I have to try."

"I'm not going anywhere," she said softly, still battling nausea. "Not if I can help it."

CHAPTER 14

The dark cloud seemed to have lifted as Alex made breakfast for them. Valeria pouted when Alex suggested that she nix the coffee. Finally, he gave in and poured her a small cup.

"But we'll have to find some natural decaf once we get settled," he said.

Then they finished packing up their honeymoon home and took off for Puerto Rico, where they would transfer planes and head to Italy.

With their brown contacts, and Valeria's darkly tanned skin, she easily fit in with the locals. Instead of transferring to the large international airport, as they had four months before, they were shuttled in the beat-up Ford Escort to a mid-sized jet.

Camille, Lars, and Mani were already aboard. Lars reported that the rest of them had headed out the day before to prepare the equipment.

Daphne was keeping Paolo distracted, although Camille and Lars insisted that no one believed that Paolo was a danger. But he was still a member of the council, and would certainly be interrogated. The less he knew the better. Valeria felt there was more to the story, but she was weary and slept almost the whole flight, curled up with her head on Alex's lap.

The flight landed on the southeast side of Italy in the coastal city of Brindisi. A limo was waiting for them and drove them a short distance to a large home that looked a bit dated.

"We needed to find something quickly in this location that wouldn't attract a lot of attention," Alex explained apologetically.

"Besides, we won't be staying long," Camille added.

It was a single story home about 3,000 square feet with plain brown wood siding and tan bricks. There was dirt instead of grass that led down to a dock. There Caleb, Ava, and Tavish were working on an impressive-looking yacht and what looked like a pontoon boat.

Ava jumped off the yacht and approached them.

"Storm's coming in. It looks like it'll clear up by tomorrow," she said.

"We're already a day behind," Alex said nervously.

Valeria hooked her arm through his. "It'll all work out. You'll see."

Caleb ran up to see them and stopped short again. "Are you guys really having a baby?"

Valeria nodded and Caleb continued, "If I'm very careful can I hold it?"

"Of course, buddy! But it has to be born first—and you'll have to wear your suit."

Lifting his fist, he pulled down and said, "*Sweet!*"

Valeria noticed that Alex couldn't quite get into the spirit of the congratulations. It would take him some time to get used to the idea, and he was still trying to get past his fears.

They walked down to the boat dock and Valeria saw that what looked like a pontoon boat from the distance, was actually a boat with two large vents covered with gauze. Tavish had a wood saw and a large piece of plywood that he was cutting.

They walked inside the house and it was actually quite nice. There were dark wood floors and earth tones throughout.

Camille evaluated Valeria's face and said, "I think you need to sleep."

"I slept on the plane," Valeria said.

"You never really sleep on planes," Alex added. "We're just going over the details."

"Then I'll stay up," Valeria said rubbing her hand over her eyes.

As Tavish brought in the whiteboard with their plan, Lars began to explain. Ava's boat would tow a specially designed barge out that was made to look like a pontoon. Caleb would continue to kayak as the divers kayaked into the cave offshore from Paxos, towing the flexible, triple-insulated, lightweight tubing.

Shinsu would provide the entrance past the adamantine gate and into Delos and the River Styx. The wall remained closed when the council was not in progress, and always during the day—except while Shinsu was there.

Once in the caves, Ava, Lars, Alex, and Mani would use night vision goggles. As they reached the door to Delos, they would tie the kayaks off and Ava and Alex would swim the River Styx, pulling two hoses, with the divers secured to a rope to prevent them from drifting down the river of death.

Shinsu would work on "official business," in case any of the dribs or other council members were in Delos. She would be in direct communication with Tavish via hidden microphone—who would communicate with the divers to begin or cease excavation of the underwater depositories.

Hose A would bring in the water and sediment vacuumed from the first depositories back to the pontoon—that was actually a barge. It would be deposited into bin A, that would act as a filter and keep all the sediment while draining the water. Alex and Ava would lead the diving portion. Lars and Mani would swim the length of the lines to eliminate kinks or problems of any sort. Caleb would continue to kayak between the boat and the cave and assist anywhere needed. Tavish would stay on the barge once they were stationary, and handle any issues or corrections with either boat until all the crew returned.

Once the first depository was empty, they would seal off the first bin on the barge and then use the second hose, hose B, and bin B. Ava and Alex would close the end of the hoses and swim back to the kayaks, and Tavish would notify Shinsu. Once the swimmers were out of Delos they would kayak back to the yacht and then they would all return to the house at Brindisi.

The debris would be loaded into a truck and driven back to Morgana. Alex and Valeria would head toward Rome and a flight to parts unknown.

The debris would be mixed with sand and deposited on the grounds of Morgana. As winter was approaching, huts had already been constructed for the potential new inhabitants. They would need to be taught modern languages and history before leaving Morgana. It was with some regret that their best teacher, Alex, could not be there.

Lars went on to explain that, from the count of known executions, there could be as many as ten oracles recovered. These oracles would require food, clothes, some kind of housing, bathing and toilet facilities, and some kind of orientation. Lars had arranged for three outdoor showers and two porta-potties to be brought to Morgana via the back road. With any luck, they would have Myrdd back with them within a few days and he would provide the answers they needed.

Valeria's birthday was now only four days away.

Caleb was excited about the expedition and laughed gleefully at the thought of another adventure. He had been in hiding at Shinsu's since the fire.

The next morning came and, as promised, Alex had secured Valeria her favorite coffee in water-processed decaf. It had been several days and, although she missed the wonderful jolt of caffeine, she was happy to have the taste.

Camille, who had insisted on coming with them, and also insisted that she would *not* be in the water, would stay with Valeria on the yacht. The two of them would play the part of sunbathing tourists and serve as a distraction if needed to onlookers.

They both wore their bikinis, although Valeria felt somewhat self-conscious of her changing body. Alex wore his swim trunks and a T-shirt. They curled up in the back of the yacht while it sped out toward Delos, with Ava at the helm. Valeria vomited off the back of the deck—and this time, she felt no shame when Alex held her and pulled back her hair. Camille brought out soda crackers and Valeria felt better.

Just the act of moving toward Paxos and Delos brought on such negative emotions in Valeria that she wondered if there would be a time when she could be here and not feel anxious. Then she realized that, at least this time, Alex was her husband.

Alex, Mani, Lars, and Ava put on their wet suits, minus the hood, and loaded their tanks and masks. With his fins in one hand, Alex pulled her into his arms as his lips moved to hers. Without looking back, he went to the ladder, she brushed her lips with her fingers...and, yes, his kisses still lingered.

"Don't worry—I'll be safe! I promise." He lifted a finger to his lips and blew her one last kiss and said, "I'll be back before you know it!" Alex glanced at Caleb. "I'm counting on you to protect her, okay?" Caleb nodded.

They loaded into their kayaks. Then Ava said, "Remember guys, roll the kayak in and out at the cave entrance. Otherwise, we may need to search for *your* head!" The guys nodded, and Alex and Mani towed the hose, between their kayaks.

As soon as Valeria couldn't see them anymore, Camille took her arm. "Come on, let's be sunbathers."

Fortunately, it was a gloriously warm day. Although most of the tourists had left, the warmth was drawing out some of the locals. Camille and Valeria sat on the back deck of the yacht and both coated their skin in sun protection. Camille gave Valeria a large container with lemonade in it as Caleb paddled around them.

Camille said, "Don't watch the entrance. If anyone is watching us they'll know something is up."

Valeria put on her sunglasses, so she could glance toward the caves without being spotted. "Camille?" Valeria asked and Camille lifted up on her elbows. Valeria thought for a moment and then said, "Do you think they'll be all right?"

"I do. If Alex felt that there was any risk, I assure you, he wouldn't have permitted you to be here!"

"You think it will work?"

"I don't know, but I hope so."

"I...I couldn't take..." Valeria gulped, and Camille sat up and raised her sunglasses.

"It will all be fine in just a few hours. You'll see." She slid her glasses back down and took a sip of her lemonade.

"I don't want to intrude, but can I ask you about Jonah?"

"Sure, what do you want to know?" she said, settling into her lounge and closing her eyes.

"What happened to him and why did you decide to stop the search"

Camille got thoughtful for a moment, then she rolled over onto her stomach so that she could face Valeria.

"When Alex found you last year, and Ava came home to help, it was the first time that Ava and Lars had been together for an extended time in over thirty years. I saw how much fun they had together and I realized that it was just selfish of me to keep them apart. Of course, I had to balance that with my feeling that I was abandoning Jonah—but I think, for now, it is the right thing to do," Camille said.

"That must have been a difficult decision for you—and for them."

"They tried to tell me that they could keep the search going. They said how Ava likes her independence. I think Lars does, too." Camille looked dreamy. "But I could see the look in their eyes. They want to be together and Lars doesn't want to live on the boat."

"Well, I guess that makes them perfect for each other. When I was with David, I always thought we were independent people—then I met Alex."

"Exactly! Being with your symbolon is a whole different ball game," Camille said, as she adjusted the shade over her.

"What—are you saying that Lars and Ava aren't…" Valeria said.

"They don't seem to have marks like the rest of us. The mark you and Alex share is the most distinctive that I've ever seen. Still, Lars and Ava love and enjoy each other." Camille added, "Val, you're staring at the caves again."

"Sorry," Valeria said as she took in the vision of Caleb on his kayak. It was fortunate that it was such a gorgeous day—unlike the day before, or the day she and Alex had escaped from Delos. She would never forget how violent that current could get against the cliffs.

It was the last week of October and the tourists were gone. This allowed Shinsu to access the cave during the day so that she could open the adamantine gate, allowing the divers access to Delos. Tavish appeared to be napping on the pontoon with his hands behind his head. Valeria had watched the occasional bubbles that rose to the surface and was glad the water was calm.

She needed to keep her mind occupied. "What happened with Jonah?"

"I've told you this, haven't I?"

Even with her deep tan, Valeria saw that she was already turning pink. She sat up and adjusted the shade so that it would cover her face, and then lathered more sunscreen on her shoulders and chest. "I'm burning all ready."

From behind them, Tavish yelled, "I never worry about sunscreen!"

"He heard us?" Valeria asked.

"I have excellent hearing!" Tavish shouted back.

"He's been listening to us," Valeria whispered.

"You'll have to do better than that if you want to keep your secrets."

Valeria rolled her eyes but she really couldn't stay mad at Tavish.

"It doesn't matter, Tavish has heard the story."

"That I have! But don't let me interrupt you lasses."

Camille sat up and said with irritation, "We won't, if you stop interrupting us!"

Tavish shrugged and seemed asleep again.

"Jonah and I were living on the west coast of Africa. I had always been able to avoid Aegemon's attacks because my visions were typically early enough that we had time to move. But one day, Jonah had to make a day trip down the coast to do some trading. He was gone over four hours when the vision came. I packed us up and tried to reach him before he could return home. I was almost half way there when I had another vision of someone abducting him." Camille swallowed. "I...ran up and down the beach ten miles there and back for days." Camille looked down. "I was never certain who took him. It could have been Aegemon, or he could have been captured by the slave trade."

"How awful! Camille, I can't imagine the...not knowing. If it was the slave trade, do you have any leads?"

"From the sounds of it, I believe it was the Boston slave ships."

"*Boston* slave ships?"

"Yes, they sent rum from Boston to Africa and exchanged it for slaves. The slaves were taken to the West Indies and traded for sugar cane, and the sugar cane was brought back to Boston to make rum. But what's interesting is that not one of the Boston ships ever completed the slave triangle. So we checked all available manifests.

"Ava found a ship's manifest that listed a blue-eyed slave with a similar name. That ship went down off the coast of Puerto Rico, but in over sixty years, we've found nothing. This is all I have left of him." She pulled up the medallion from around her neck with a symbol on it, faded by time.

"I'm sorry." Valeria put her hand on Camille's arm. "I know I shouldn't give you…well…I don't want you to think I have any inside knowledge or visions," Valeria said, speaking as if suddenly compelled. "I have to tell you that I think you are going to find each other. And I want to tell you to please don't give up." Valeria wondered what had possessed her to say such a thing when, clearly, Camille was just starting to accept that Jonah was gone.

A light breeze cooled them and Valeria pulled her long hair into a ponytail and rolled over. Suddenly, Tavish popped up from his position and spoke into a microphone hooked around his ear, "I'm ready for you here and Shinsu says you're clear there."

Then he nodded to an unheard voice and started the noisy generator. Camille went below deck and pulled out a stereo; she cranked it with loud rock and roll, hoping the generator would blend in, and just sound like music from a distance. Tavish pulled on earphones to block out the sound of the generator.

The muddy mix began dumping into the barge and, occasionally, a bone would shoot out of the hose. A large pile built quite quickly.

From a distance, Camille saw a boat approaching. She rolled her eyes and yelled to Valeria over the noise of the generator, "If we didn't have bad luck…" Tavish and Caleb both glanced in the direction Camille was looking—obviously, they had picked up her concern from Camille's unspoken communication.

As the generator cranked down, Valeria heard Tavish cursing, and then he spoke into the microphone, "You'll never guess who's come for a social visit!"

Camille turned down the music.

Valeria asked with alarm, "Jeremiah?"

The boat drew nearer and Valeria saw the jet-black hair and movie star good looks of Paolo.

"We forgot to tell Daph to take Paolo anywhere but here!"

Instantly, Valeria grabbed for her shorts and Camille's hand stopped her.

"Don't! Your shorts don't cover your belly—besides, it will draw his attention there."

The speedboat pulled up with Paolo behind the wheel and Daph lounging in the back. Suddenly, Daphne seemed to have received Camille's communication. Behind her dark glasses, there was a sudden look of terror as she looked at Valeria and then down to her stomach. Then, just as quickly, she replaced the look with bored disinterest. Paolo's mind quickly went to assessing the situation as he glanced at Valeria and then to Camille and then to the barge and Caleb.

"Valeria, you have returned from your honeymoon so soon?" Paolo said with a smirk.

"Who says the honeymoon's over?" Valeria said, as she lifted her glasses and glared at him in disdain.

Paolo tied off his boat and jumped on board the yacht. Valeria rose and noticed his eyes instantly evaluating her body. She grabbed her shorts and held them over her stomach.

Then he cocked his head to the side. "Why would Alex bring you here, bella?" He pressed his lips together in thought as Valeria fidgeted.

"I guess he didn't know you were in town," Valeria said, and then instantly regretted it. "I'm sorry, Paolo. I didn't mean to be cruel."

"You know, bella, it isn't safe for you to be here." He glanced down into the galley to see if Alex was there, and then added, "If your husband loves you so much then he should not leave you alone here—I would never leave you in danger."

Valeria was about to add that Paolo was the one who put her in this danger in the first place, when Camille piped in, "Well, what am I? Chopped liver? And are you completely blind or did you not see Caleb and Tav?"

Paolo nodded, still looking at Valeria critically. "I believe your birthday is this week. We could join you in the celebration."

"Another time," Valeria said, as Daphne offered Camille a desperate glance behind Paolo's back.

Paolo stared at Valeria's body, evaluating, and Valeria continued to fidget nervously.

"For crying out loud, Paolo!" Camille said and glanced at Daphne.

Then Paolo turned his eyes to Tavish. "There is something…something is not right," he announced.

Daphne jumped onto the boat and took Paolo's hand. "Baby, I forgot to tell you that they were coming down here." Paolo looked at Daphne as if he knew better. Daphne pulled on Paolo's hand. "Come on. Let's leave them alone. It's clear we're not wanted here."

Paolo pulled away and began walking toward the pontoon. Suddenly, Camille spotted a long bone protruding from the mess and glared at Tavish who moved his foot in time to bury it while looking a little too innocent.

"What is that?" Paolo asked.

Tavish sneered at Paolo. "I've often suspected that you weren't all that bright. What does it look like? It's mud—as if it's any of your business."

Paolo walked back over to Valeria and took her hand, raising it from her stomach, and she sucked it in. She couldn't see much weight on her—how could he? He stared at her belly, and Valeria quickly pulled her hands away from his and moved them back to her stomach. Paolo lifted his glasses and looked at her critically. "Bella?" he said slowly. "Either you have put on some weight on your honeymoon," his eyes narrowed, "or you are…"

Camille stepped in. "Oh, my God Paolo, you are such a jerk! You don't say that sort of thing to a woman! Daphne—get him out of here. Valeria might not slap him, but I'll probably slug him if he doesn't leave!"

Daphne was glancing quickly between Tavish and Camille. "Come on, Paolo! Let's go. Tav is right; this is none of our business!"

Paolo ignored the insults and continued to speak to Valeria, "I am right, am I not, bella?" His confident glare suddenly transitioned to concern. "You are…" His eyebrows lowered and he put his hand on Valeria's arm. "You are with child," he said softly. "Despite the color of your eyes." Paolo seemed upset. "Valeria, is Mani watching you carefully?"

Valeria gave Paolo a half-nod. She didn't really want to acknowledge his comments. "I'm fine."

Paolo looked over toward the cave and then at the mud and to Valeria again. "You will need to find Kristiana. I can help—perhaps more than this project."

Tavish's eyes narrowed with his face frozen in mock cordiality. "Well now, if we wanted your help, we would have certainly asked for it."

Camille stepped forward. "Thank you, Paolo. Perhaps we can discuss that later, but right now, it would be best if you both left."

"I will be in touch," Paolo said, and then he brushed Valeria's arm. "Please believe me that I only want to help you." Valeria half acknowledged Paolo and went below.

Paolo and Daphne jumped back into their boat and untied it; before Paolo's boat was beyond visual range, Tavish announced into the microphone, "Might as well re-start. He knows."

Tavish paused as his finger was on the generator switch, and a communication came in. He glanced at Valeria who was coming back up from below. "She seems alright—starting up."

The generator came back on and for the next hour, there was a brief break when mud stopped coming in.

"Let's seal this up. Don't want any bodies coming out of the mud while we're on the highway!" He released a long, exuberant laugh. Caleb climbed up on the pontoon and helped tie the tarp around the mud. Valeria was getting tense about the time.

"Aren't they about to run out of air?" she asked.

"No need to worry lass, they have back-ups. Ava's done this many a time. She's quite the expert!"

Then Tavish yelled into the mic, "Ready to go!"

Valeria was baking in the sun, feeling slightly nauseous and finally decided to go below to lie down. The cool air from the cabin felt good, but she wouldn't be able to sleep or relax until she saw that Alex was safe again.

Finally, the generator turned off. Valeria went back up top and held her breath watching for signs of the kayaks. Her breathing constricted as she stared at the entrance, unable to look anywhere else.

It was twenty minutes before she saw movement near the rocks and, a moment later, she saw Alex. Valeria tried to wait, but with her experience in the Caribbean, she surprised everyone by diving into the water and swimming after him. He pulled her onto his kayak and she discovered she couldn't let him go. He laughed softly as he held her. Then he scooted her around to behind him and paddled the rest of the way to the boat.

Tavish cranked the hose back onto the pontoon and finally Lars and Ava appeared in the kayaks bringing up the rear.

Alex attached his kayak to the pontoon and then crawled up the ladder and lifted Valeria back onboard and into his arms.

He smiled and winked. "I told you I would be safe!"

She kissed him and ran her finger along the red marks around Alex's eyes from the mask. They loaded the kayaks back onto the boat, secured the tarps, and headed back to Brindisi.

Alex removed the wet suit and sat in the back of the boat with his arms around Valeria. He was obviously exhausted, as was she. "We were going to wait to leave Brindisi until morning, but after seeing Paolo, I think it's best that we leave tonight."

Valeria nodded and fell asleep on the deck while wrapped in Alex's arms.

CHAPTER 15

Valeria watched as Alex walked away from her, down a grassy knoll, arm in arm with a woman with long bronze hair. The woman began to sing a Greek lullaby and leaned her head against Alex's shoulder as they walked; her voice, syrupy with a heavy Italian accent, said, "You won't ever look back?"

Alex's eyes lit with passion. "Never!"

Valeria saw the woman turn, and then the nearly angelic face glared at Valeria from just inches away. "See what happens when you steal my husband?"

The angelic face turned as she again snuggled into Alex's arm. Behind them were two gravestones that read: "Valeria Morgan and baby, Died 2012."

Valeria woke startled. The dream was so real that she could still see the face so closely to her own—the face that looked so pure one moment, and so menacing the next. She stared at her location, disoriented. Then she realized that she was still on the deck of the yacht, and the sun was setting on the Italian coast ahead of them. She saw Tavish at the helm and no one else. Alex's sweatshirt had been under her head and she pulled it on. It fit like a short dress and she pushed up the sleeves. He had been wearing it and she could smell his wonderful scent all over it—a mix of soap with a hint of aftershave. She wandered to the cabin where she overheard conversation.

Alex said, "He knows. And if he knows, I believe Val is in danger. I just don't see how I can bring her back to Morgana. I think we need to go back to Mani's home in Puerto Rico."

Lars replied, "No one would guess that we would bring her back to Morgana. I think that might just be the safest place for her."

Alex stood, upset. "I don't follow, Lars. After our wedding night, I don't know how this can even be an option. I think we need to go back into hiding until we can question Myrdd."

Lars shrugged. "Sun-Tzu said 'Keep your friends close and your enemies closer.'"

Valeria interrupted, as she walked down the stairs. "You must be talking about Paolo."

Alex sat down near the steps and pulled her onto his lap, snuggling into her.

"Sorry to have left you. You looked like you were down for the count." She put her arms around him and kissed his neck, trying to absorb his warmth. He grabbed her hands and held them in his. "You're cold!"

"So, what were you talking about?" she asked

"Val, you should know that Lars interrogated Paolo after the fire and it does not appear that he intended to purposely leak any information."

"Despite that, you have your suspicions," she said with a shiver.

"I do," Alex said. "You and I have enemies. There is no question about that, and I believe that Aegemon leads the list. We have heard nothing of his death or even reports of the plague in this part of the world. So, I believe that he may still be out there.

"Then there is the Council of Delos. But an anonymous fire isn't really their style. They like public executions. And then," he hesitated, wishing he didn't have to say it, "there is Kristiana. We don't know where she is. But there is a suspicion due to the timing of her disappearance and her alliances, that she may have something to do with this. And lastly, Paolo does belong on the list of suspects. But my personal feeling is that Paolo is not directly involved. However, his communication with his sister may be a factor whether he realizes it or not."

The boat rocked gently with the passing of a larger ship.

Lars said, "No one has seen Kristiana in over a thousand years—not even Paolo. But Kristiana was known to dabble in sorcery. We don't know how she developed these skills but we believe that she may have somehow infiltrated Paolo's mind. But that is all purely supposition."

"Hecate," Valeria said.

"What?" Camille asked.

"Oh, nothing. I don't know why I said that. I don't even know who that is," Valeria said.

Camille narrowed her eyes. "Hecate is written as both a mortal and a goddess—as if no one were really sure. She was a master of witchcraft. You would have known of her when you were in Troy."

Valeria shook her head embarrassed. "I don't know, Camille. I don't remember anything about her and I'm not really sure why I said her name." Lowering her brow Valeria asked, "Did I ever meet Kristiana?"

Alex shook his head. "No, I wouldn't think so."

Valeria hesitated. "Did she…Alex, did she have bronze hair and well…was she much more…voluptuous than me?"

"Why? Did you see her?" he asked with concern.

"No. I just…" She shook it off. "It was nothing, I'm sure."

"Beautiful, you must tell me if you have seen her, do you understand?" Valeria nodded. Alex continued, "Did you have a vision?"

"No…but I did have a…a very strange dream."

"Tell me about it."

She thought for a moment. There was no way that she could tell Alex the full content of the dream. It would be too upsetting to him—and perhaps for nothing. "I think the hormones are probably affecting my dreams." She tried to smile as she rubbed her belly subconsciously.

Mani offered, "Yes, odd dreams can be the result of hormones. However, if you saw Kristiana in those dreams, it is possible that she is communicating with you. It is important that you try to recall every detail."

Valeria looked away. She hated to lie to him, but she couldn't tell Alex the contents. "I don't know. There was a grassy knoll. I don't remember seeing any trees. There were outcroppings of rocks." She hesitated and then said, "She seemed to know…about the baby."

Alex's face darkened and he looked at her. "Let's do this the easy way." He turned her to face him and reached for her hands for a transference.

"No!" she said as she pulled her hands away. "Really, let's just drop it. I'm sure it was nothing."

Alex's face became more concerned and he was about to force the issue when Camille put her hand on Alex's arm. "Alex, it's obvious that Val doesn't want to share the dream with you." Valeria let out a soft sigh of relief and glanced her thanks to Camille.

"I understand that, Camille, but I need to know if—"

"*If Kristiana is involved?*" Camille interrupted. "We all know that it's a safe bet that she is—and that Paolo is an unwilling participant in her games." She looked at Lars and Ava. "I think Alex is right—they should go back to where Val was safe, in Puerto Rico. There were no attacks there, and Mani can keep a close eye on her."

Mani lifted a hand. "I believe that may be the best plan. We can drive to Rome and fly out tonight."

"But that isn't fair to you, Doc! Melitta needs to see you as soon as she's revived," Valeria argued.

"*If…*" Mani said under his breath. And then his voice gained strength. "Right now, we must protect you and the fetus. All else must wait."

"Did everyone forget what all of this risk was about? Val's birthday is only a few days away. Myrdd is supposed to have answers that we need to save Val and her kid," Ava said. At this, Alex's eyes widened and his arms moved around Valeria protectively. "I'm sorry, Alex. I don't want to hurt you, but come on!" Ava added.

"Alex," Lars began calmly. "Due to Myrdd's known lack of mental clarity, we need to orient him as quickly as possible. He knew Val and you best. If Myrdd returns and is disoriented, it will cost us valuable time if you're not there. We can't revive these oracles without the protection of Morgana. We've already used Shinsu's home and I think we need to stay clear of it for a while. But the fact is, you and Val need to be wherever Myrdd is when he revives."

Tavish stepped downstairs. "We've docked—no thanks to any of yous. I've listened to you all blabber on and I have some thoughts meself."

Everyone nodded.

"We came up with a plan and regardless of that nyaf, we need to follow it," Tavish said

"What's a nyaf?" Valeria asked.

"Paolo," Camille said.

"Yeah—what a worthless piece of shit, that one is!" Tavish's laughter filled the room.

Lars raised a hand. "Our only hope to save Val, and this child—*if* the curse is still a factor—is to have the people Myrdd knew best there with him. That is you and Val," Lars said to Alex.

"As much as I agree with all of you, I simply cannot agree to bring Val back to Morgana right now. It is just too risky. I'm taking her back to Puerto Rico. Val? Are you okay with that?"

Valeria sighed. "I appreciate what all of you have done here. Alex, I will do whatever you believe is best."

"In that case, we'll leave tonight with the remains, as planned, and head to Morgana. Alex—you, Doc, and Val should wait a few hours at least, and then head for Rome," Lars said.

∞

The two giant bags of mud were loaded into the back of a commercial dump truck while everyone showered and changed. As they loaded up the two cars, Tavish peered up the coast.

"What is it?" Alex asked.

Tavish handed Alex the binoculars and pointed. To the north, the shoreline curved, and as Alex tried to focus the lenses, he suddenly saw binoculars staring back at him—Paolo! Alex waved and Paolo waved back. A moment later, Paolo was in his boat heading toward them.

"I guess he really does know," Alex said.

"I'll beat him to a pulp if you'll allow me," Tavish said, gnashing his teeth together.

"No. I'll handle this. Make sure Val doesn't come out, all right? No need to upset her," Alex added.

A few minutes later, Paolo had parked on the dock and was walking up toward the house when Alex stopped him.

"What do you need, pal?" Alex said coolly.

Paolo lifted a finger. "She is with child," he said, almost as an accusation.

"Stay out of it!" Alex warned.

Biting his lip, Paolo scanned the windows of the house searching for Valeria.

"Have you considered, even for an instant, how your most obvious interest in my wife may affect Daph?"

Paolo narrowed his eyes. "She knows how I feel."

With a cynical chuckle, Alex said, "Yes, I believe we all do. That's not really fair to either Val or Daph."

"You wish to lecture me on this? For thousands of years you have permitted Daphne to stay by your side like a little puppy dog. And then you impregnate Valeria. Do you not recall what happened the last time? Or must I remind you?" Paolo said, stepping toward Alex aggressively.

"I allowed you to beat me once. I won't permit it again."

"You won't *permit it?*" Paolo sneered.

"No, I won't." Alex stood his ground.

Paolo crossed his arms and then shook his head at Alex in a mix of anger and disgust. He huffed, releasing his tension and stared at the sinking sun as it moved behind a palm tree, as he tried to calm himself. "I would not hit you again."

"I know," Alex said. Paolo knew that if he attacked Alex, Valeria would never speak to him again.

"Is she...all right?" Paolo asked, still peering at the windows. "What did Mani say?"

Alex shrugged.

"I hope you have a better plan than attempting to revive that crazy old man."

Alex pressed his lips together and drew a deep breath. "I think it would be best for everyone if you pretended that you didn't see anything here and just left."

Gulping, Paolo nodded. "Yes, I am certain that is true." They were silent for a moment. "May I see her?"

"She's had enough drama today. Sorry."

Paolo nodded again, and then added, "Will you…promise to keep her safe?"

"I promise I will do everything in my power," Alex said, softening.

Through the darkness, they could see Tavish's large frame step outside. "Need any help, Alex? You know I'd be glad to get rid of any trash that's hanging around the place."

"Thanks, Tav. Paolo was just leaving."

"I hope I will see you both again soon," Paolo said as he headed down to his boat. The house he was staying in was four homes down and it took him only minutes to reach his dock. Valeria came outside as soon as he was gone.

"Paolo, huh?" she asked.

"It'll be fine," Alex said as he guided her into the house and away from Paolo's watchful eyes.

∞

Knowing that Paolo would be able to see them leaving, they decided to wait until his lights went out. It was after three a.m. when Alex and Valeria loaded into the Porsche and pulled out of the driveway with Caleb. Mani would meet them at the airport in Rome. Reaching the road, Alex turned on his lights and drew a deep breath. He wasn't certain what he expected, Kristiana and Jeremiah standing outside the house with hatchets? He laughed and shook his head.

"What?" Valeria asked, smiling and hoping there was some news that would lighten both of their moods.

"Oh, nothing. I guess I've been expecting the goblins and gremlins to be hiding behind every corner and I just realized how ridiculous that was." They both laughed—although she could sense something was not quite right. She decided it was the eerie moonlight on the country road. Still, it had felt good to laugh, even if there were goblins and gremlins waiting for them. Then she reminded herself that it would only be five hours until it would be daylight and they would be in a major city, boarding a flight with Mani and Caleb.

Alex contemplated his feelings about Kristiana. He hadn't yet been able to accept that she was the one causing so much of the pain in their lives. Yes, she had a temper. But accepting that she would murder him—or Valeria—was too much. It meant that he had brought the danger into their lives by the choices he'd made, and that was simply too much to accept.

They drove down the dark roads of eastern Italy and Valeria was exhausted—again. She realized that it must be the pregnancy making her want to sleep all the time. She glanced at Alex and saw that he looked tired as well. Perhaps driving five hours tonight wasn't the best move. Valeria rubbed Alex's shoulder and he leaned into her hand.

"Hmm—that feels good," he said.

"Let me know if you need me to drive," Valeria said. "You look like you need sleep more than I do."

Caleb leaned forward. "I'll drive! I'm not tired."

Valeria and Alex gave Caleb a smile. "Thanks buddy, but I think the authorities would have a problem with that," Alex said, and then glanced at Valeria. "Why don't you try to rest? When you wake, if you feel up to it, you can drive," he suggested.

"I will," she said as she closed her eyes and leaned her seat back just a bit. They were only a few miles down the road when Valeria put her hand to her forehead and moaned softly.

"Val? What's the matter?"

"I can't believe it—I haven't had one of these since I was a kid," she said. "The doctor told me it was somehow associated with a migraine."

"You have a migraine?" Alex said with sudden concern, and she could hear the terror behind his words. He shuddered as he remembered Mani's report of how she had died in 1907, as if she had been struck by an electrical charge in her brain.

"No." Feeling his tension, she patted his arm. "Really, it's nothing—I had these all the time when I was a kid." She closed her eyes. "It's like a circular flickering of light in one of my eyes—like a kaleidoscope."

The news hit Alex with a jolt—she was experiencing the same phenomena as he did during his visions! He slowed the car and stared at her. From his rear-view mirror, he noticed something. "What is that?" he asked.

Over the gently rolling hills, perhaps a mile behind them, he could see a car that appeared to be flashing its brights on and off.

"Maybe it's the cops in a high-speed chase! Can we follow them?" Caleb asked excitedly as he watched the lights appear and disappear over the rolling hills, quickly gaining on them.

Valeria put her face in her hands and, within a few minutes, she lifted her head, now deathly alert.

"Alex? I…"

Alex looked alarmed, "Are you all right?"

"No…no, I'm not. We're not okay,"

"Val?" Alex asked, starting to panic.

She brushed her hand over her forehead.

"Do you need me to stop? Are you sick?" he asked.

Valeria looked around. "Alex, I think we're going to be in a car accident in a few minutes." She adjusted her seatbelt. "Caleb is your seatbelt fastened?

"Yeah," he said.

"Did you have a vision?"

"I think so. Oh no!" she said, glancing at the curve ahead of them. "It's not far now."

"Is it the driver behind us? Should I pull over?"

"No, he's coming for…" She let out a cry. "He's going to hurt her."

"No one is going to hurt my family! Tell me what to do? Turn around? Pull over? What, Val?"

"I think it will be very bad if you stop and he's too close to turn around," she said, as she drew a deep breath. "He's around this bend."

Valeria put her hand on Alex's arm. "It isn't Paolo's fault—don't be angry with him. We'll need his help."

"Tell me what's going to happen," he said, and then his voice choked. "Please don't leave me, Val?"

"We'll be all right as long as…"

They saw the car behind them was only a few blocks back, and now they could hear the horn honking as well. It disappeared behind a hill. Ahead was a bend in the road, and a car was parked with its headlights on. Suddenly, the car roared to life and squealed out just as Alex's phone began to ring.

"It's Daph," Valeria said without looking.

And then the car that had been parked gunned its engine and turned directly toward them. Alex swerved hard to the left to miss it, but the other car echoed Alex's moves and caught the front right fender as Alex's front left wheel hit the dirt shoulder, barely missing the steep edge of an embankment before they skidded to a stop.

It was silent for a moment and Alex asked, "Val? Caleb? Are you..."

Suddenly, the other car backed up. Alex glanced out his window at the four-foot drop, as the other car seemed to be positioning itself for a direct hit on the front passenger door. Alex stepped on the gas and turned the wheel as the headlights aimed for Valeria. But the wheels on the Porsche just spun.

"Come on! Move!" Alex commanded but he couldn't get any traction. Valeria stared into the headlights, now inches from her, and closed her eyes. Just before the other car's headlights disappeared into Valeria's door, their car inched forward grudgingly. There was a gnarling of metal and a tinkle of glass, and then they heard the low aching of unsupported metal as the front tires lost hold of the shoulder and the car began to roll. The other car took advantage of the situation and slammed into it one more time, this time driving the Porsche into a slow roll down the embankment. All that could be heard was the thud of bodies and suitcases being thrown about and the tinkling of glass as it clinked throughout the car.

Valeria felt her head hit several places. The air bags deployed and, finally, the car lodged upside down. Except for a hissing from the Porsche, there was nothing but silence. She could see lights outside the car, and if she could have focused, she might have feared another attack. Then she saw a smaller light moving toward them. She heard a pop and then felt a pop near her face as her airbag deflated.

"Val! Val! Are you alright?" Alex asked terrified.

She heard a click, and then a thud, and worried that the car would start rolling again. She felt confused and something ached—maybe a few things ached.

She wanted to know that Alex and Caleb were all right but she couldn't seem to speak without a sharp pain in her side.

"I think...I think I busted my shoulder," Caleb said, and then Valeria heard another clink of a seatbelt and a thud in the back seat. She heard Caleb howling, "Owww! Ouch! Ouch!"

Valeria thought she heard voices. Was it her father? No, she remembered, he had been gone a long time. Someone was swearing in Italian at another man who was sobbing. She couldn't quite put it all together. Her head was spinning and the darkness wasn't helping. She couldn't focus on anything.

"Alex?" she moaned.

"Val! Val!" his voice sounded frantic. She felt something warm and wet dripping on her.

"Alex?" She didn't seem to be able to say anything else. She heard several voices that she knew she should recognize.

"We must get Valeria out of here!" the man with the Italian accent said—the one who had been cursing. It was a familiar voice to her. She knew that she should know whose voice it was.

Then she realized why she knew it. "Paolo," she said, and then cringed when she spoke his name aloud.

"Yes, bella, I am here. I am going to help you."

She wanted to say, *I want Alex to help me*, but she didn't seem to be able to speak.

A minute later, she saw lights moving and heard Mani's voice.

"I'm okay, Mani," Caleb said, almost crying. "I think Val's hurt bad."

Then she heard movement and saw lights on her, and then heard the gasps. She shut her eyes.

"I'll need two sets of hands...Doc?" Alex's voice seemed to be near her, above her—or was it beneath her? The back door opened.

"Give me your good hand, Caleb," Daphne said.

"Bella, I am here," Paolo said.

Valeria felt Alex's hand on her face. "We're going to get you out of here, love." She tried to nod but nothing seemed to move as it should. "All right, Paolo, let's make a cradle so that we are head to head and then we can release the seatbelt. I'll support her and you release the seatbelt. Then you can take her shoulders and pull her out." Alex paused. "Let me see the flashlight."

Valeria moaned and grabbed her stomach.

"It's all right, beautiful, we'll have you out of here in a minute," he said and suddenly a light was moving over her. She could smell gasoline. "Wait! I think her leg may be pinned." There was movement and she felt Alex's hands on her ankle. It felt strange and then she felt a sharp pain that ran from her ankle to her knee and she cried out, feeling suddenly faint. "I'm sorry, love! I'm sorry! But we have to get you out of here!"

"Caleb?" she whimpered.

"He's...he's okay. He's out with Doc," Alex said.

"Okay, Paolo, ready? On three—one, two...three." They lifted her at the hips and then she fell into soft arms. Immediately, there were sharp pains all over her body that she couldn't quite identify. She didn't want to let out a cry but it escaped anyway.

"It's all right, love, I have you now. I have you," Alex said over and over.

They started moving her again and she wanted them to wait—she didn't want to hurt again. But they kept going, and then she saw lights shining in her face and felt her head spin, and everything went black.

A few minutes later, Valeria woke in Alex's arms. There were bright lights all around them and she realized they were from the headlights of the cars that surrounded them. She brushed Alex's face and he suppressed a sob. He was badly bruised and cut.

"Are you," she whispered.

"I'm okay," he said.

"Caleb?" she whispered.

"Caleb's going to be fine. He dislocated his arm but it's probably already healed. It's not the first time." She felt him draw several long breaths. "I...Val, I need to lay you down so that Doc can take a look at you."

She shook her head in protest and then another car pulled up.

"Where is she?" Camille demanded.

She could hear Ava and Lars both barking orders and she could still hear the unknown man sobbing.

"Let's lay her down on the blanket," Ava said.

"I'm sorry, but this is going to be uncomfortable," Alex said, and she could tell it hurt him more than her. Still, the pain was excruciating; black spots flooded her vision and she felt nauseous.

Mani was looking down at Valeria as Alex sat by her side and Paolo was by her feet.

"May I have some room?" Mani asked Paolo.

"Of course," he said, and hurried out of the way.

"Valeria, I'm going to wrap your leg."

A plump man who Valeria had never seen was still sobbing and speaking in Italian to anyone who would listen. Daphne seemed to be comforting him. Valeria wondered who the man was. Even Lars patted the man on the back, but couldn't seem to look him in the eye.

Her head was still swimming. Mani's face moved toward hers and became distorted. He backed up until she was able to focus on him.

"Valeria, you must listen to me. Stay alert. You must stay alert." She just wanted to close her eyes and sleep; then she saw Alex's face looking so distraught and, suddenly, she was terrified. What was wrong with her that her first thoughts were of herself and everyone else except the one being who truly mattered.

"The baby?" she heard herself ask. She saw Alex choke and she reached for him, but that hurt too.

"Bella, please tell me you are alright?" Paolo said, as he moved in next to her where Mani had been.

As if for the first time, Alex realized that Paolo was there. He felt the anger well inside of him and felt a nearly uncontrollable rage building. He rose and grabbed Paolo by the back of the shirt, dragging him away from Valeria. Paolo struggled to get back to his feet.

"You! Get the hell out of here. Just get the hell out of here! Haven't you done enough—"

Camille interrupted, "No, Alex! Paolo warned us."

Paolo spoke to Alex as if the last exchange hadn't happened. "I have a helicopter that will transport her to a hospital. I must stay with her."

Alex shook his head. "My wife doesn't want you near her—and neither do I!"

"Alex...I went to sleep tonight and had a vision of this wreck; I had a vision of the fire as well."

"Don't bullshit me—you're no oracle!"

"No, Alex. I am not. There is only one explanation." Paolo gave Alex a knowing look. "You know...you know Kristiana's...skills," he managed to say.

"Go on," Alex said grudgingly.

"Kristiana once spoke of an ability to transfer the will of one to another via the eyes."

"What are you saying?"

"She wishes to harm Valeria—or you, by harming Valeria," Paolo said. "I am certain of it now."

"Your revelation is about a year too late, pal,"

"The helicopter is coming. Alex, I must ask you to allow me to accompany Valeria."

"*In your dreams!*" Alex screamed, as the hum of the helicopter grew louder.

Paolo grabbed Alex's arm, and Alex swung at him in an effort to get free, but Paolo pulled him into a hug.

"My friend, my brother, I swear to you—on Valeria's life—that I am here to help and I will never again do anything to harm you or your wife!" Paolo's voice was in pain. "Please, allow me to help."

Alex pulled free and then, hesitantly, he shrugged. He didn't want to forgive Paolo. Alex desperately wanted someone to blame...someone other than himself, for bringing Kristiana into their lives.

"Alex, I speak the truth. You must believe me."

Closing his eyes, Alex concentrated on calming his breathing...and his rage. Then, without meeting Paolo's eyes, he nodded and returned to his wife as Mani tended to her injuries. Alex kissed her forehead. "You're going to be alright, Val. We have a helicopter that's going to transport you to a hospital."

"No—we should go to Morgana," Mani said.

The wind picked up as the helicopter landed, obscuring all other sound. The medics rushed to Valeria and checked her vitals. Alex put his hand on the medics arm.

"She's...she's pregnant," he choked.

Mani introduced himself and told them that he was her doctor. They rolled her onto a stretcher and, this time, Valeria's cries were silenced by the volume of the whir of the chopper. Mani walked with her as Alex and Paolo followed.

The medic stared at the two men, both intending to board. "Only her husband and the doctor may travel with us."

Paolo stared at Alex for a moment, and then said, "I am her husband." The medic nodded and Paolo climbed on board.

Alex said, "May I speak to her for a moment?"

"Only a moment," the medic said, as Mani inserted an IV into her arm.

Alex brushed her hair back. Valeria tried to focus on his face and she reached for his hand.

"Beautiful, I'm going to leave you with Mani. I need to get another ride, but I'll be there with you again as soon as possible."

Valeria shook her head, but an oxygen mask was over her face. "Don't leave me."

Alex had tears in his eyes. "It won't be for very long. And you are in the very best hands."

He choked as he walked off the helicopter. Paolo gazed at him before turning to play the role of the dutiful husband.

Daphne glanced at Alex and saw the red stain on his polo shirt. "Alex, let me at least—" She started to wipe the blood from a scrape on his face.

Alex pulled away. "I need to get to Morgana! Someone has to get me a plane or a chopper. I need it now!"

Daphne put her hand on Alex. "Please don't be angry."

Alex glared at her. He was very close to accusing her of working with Paolo so that they both got what they wanted. But in 3,000 years, he had never been cruel to her and he didn't want to start now. "Daph...I...just..." he sighed and then walked away, but she followed.

"Paolo sent a ride for us. We aren't totally self-centered," Daphne said.

Camille was consoling the man who had hit their car. He told her that he had been cleaning Paolo's pool and then, the next thing he knew, he almost killed a pregnant lady. Alex paced nervously until he heard the second chopper.

∞

A few hours later, the second helicopter landed on the front lawn of the main house at Morgana, carrying Alex, Camille, and Caleb. Daphne had insisted that Camille take her place and that she would drive Paolo's car to Morgana.

Alex rushed up the steps and into the main house as the blades of the medical helicopter that transported Valeria began to slowly turn. His eyes darted upstairs to the bedrooms—no one was there. Then Mani—who was having a discussion with one of the medics—glanced up at Alex and nodded toward the kitchen. Alex's eyes traced the line down the hallway and stopped at the library door. It was the room where Alex and Valeria had shared their private moment after being pronounced husband and wife. He remembered their kiss and how incredibly fortunate he had felt that day. Now he prayed that she survived.

As he stepped past the medics, with his heart pounding furiously, he saw Paolo dutifully holding Valeria's hand while she lay in the hospital bed—the new addition to the room. Alex fought back his anger and fear and went to her side. Biting back his emotions, he glanced at his wife on the hospital bed that Mani must have had delivered; seeing that she was breathing, he sighed.

"Mani says she will be all right," Paolo said softly, continuing to hold Valeria's hand. Alex breathed out a sigh of relief mixed with rage that Paolo was the one telling him the news. As gently as was possible for him at that moment, Alex placed his hand under Paolo's arm. Paolo rose as if completely unaware that he had crossed the line. Then Alex led him to the door.

"You wish to speak privately?" Paolo began.

Alex forced himself to close the door gently, in Paolo's face, rather than the violent action he so wished to release. Then he fought back his tears and returned to his wife.

Even in the dim light of the room, he could see that she was not all right. She was wearing a clean, light blue hospital gown, but was still covered in blood and bruises and, now, bandages. Alex tried to hide his emotions as he went to her and kissed her and held her hand.

"Is she alright?" came Valeria's weak voice.

"Who?"

"Our daughter," she whispered.

He kissed her hand. "So, it's a 'she'?" He tried to smile, but it failed him. There was a knock at the door and Mani entered. Two men followed with several pieces of equipment.

"Doc?" Alex said, desperate to hear the official word. "How is she?"

"It appears that both the tibia and fibula are fractured just above the ankle. There is also a bruise on her right lower rib, I suspect another fracture. Her wrist may be sprained. She's badly bruised over most of her body and will likely be uncomfortable for a few days."

Mani turned to Valeria and smiled gently. "Valeria, I think it would be best to do an ultrasound."

As exhausted as she felt, Valeria had to make certain the baby was all right before she considered sleep. Alex held her hand as Mani neatly folded the sheet at the base of her abdomen and then raised her gown up. Alex cringed as he saw the deep purple bruise that ran across the lower part of her stomach from where the seatbelt had been. Mani squirted the cool liquid on her belly and then took the wand and ran it over her —not seeing any indication of a heartbeat. Alex could see the concern on his face as Mani continued to move the wand all around her belly.

"Doc?" Alex asked, suddenly frightened. Valeria's hand tightened on his as a tear ran down her cheek.

Mani lowered his brow and pressed his lips together. "Valeria, let's try another angle. If we help you, can you roll toward me?"

"Is she okay?" she whispered.

"Give me your arm. Alex can you help?"

They moved and Valeria cried out in pain. Instantly, the rapid heartbeat came over the speakers and relief flooded Alex's face. Valeria smiled wearily and relaxed into Alex's arms.

"The fetus appears to be unharmed," Mani said as he snapped off his gloves. "Still, you have some internal bleeding. Valeria you can sleep now. To protect the fetus, you will need to be on bed rest for at least two to three weeks. We will do another ultrasound then and decide how to proceed."

"Alex, you need to sleep too," she whispered.

"I'm not leaving you."

"Good, then lay down with me," she whispered sleepily.

"I don't want to hurt you," he whispered back, and kissed her ear.

"You won't. Please," she said as she patted the bed next to her.

Alex went to the other side of the bed, away from her broken bones, and lay down cautiously while Mani continued to wrap her injuries.

Mani went on, "Valeria, we will use a soft cast on your leg but you will not be able to put weight on it for at least six weeks. I'm afraid there isn't much I can do for your ribs. You may want something for the pain."

"No, I'm fine." With that, she fell into a deep sleep. Alex never left her side throughout the night—taking solace in every breath she took.

As he brushed the hair from her face, he noticed how pale she was and the numerous bruises that covered her face and arms. Then he whispered, "Please don't ever leave me."

∞

The rest of the family arrived mid-morning. They found Mani and Camille asleep on the couches in the living room; Caleb was curled up asleep on the floor, his electronic game still in one hand, and Charlie in the other. Paolo sat, brooding, in a chair facing Valeria's room.

Daphne rushed in and saw Paolo intensely focused on the closed bedroom door leading to Valeria. She approached him hesitantly, uncertain as to where they stood. She was almost next to him, and ready to turn and run, when he finally saw her. He rose and, with his face filled with desperation, embraced her as if she were his lifeline.

Lars said, "Let's all get some sleep. We can talk about this after we've slept."

When Paolo pulled back from Daphne, his eyes were filled with tears. Brushing the side of his face, Daphne said, "Alex will keep her safe while you get some rest." Taking his hand, she led him up the stairs. It was the first time Paolo had been welcomed to stay in the main house.

∞

Valeria woke at four p.m. and found her door opened and Alex gone. She tried to sit up, but was seized with pain in numerous parts of her body. Immediately, Alex was back in the room with her. "Sorry, I just went to shower and shave. Caleb was here until just a few minutes ago. How do you feel?" he asked.

"Oh...sore." She tried to smile. "Are you okay?"

Alex nodded. "Had a few minor injuries last night. But they've healed up." He sat on the edge of the bed. "Uh, I need to tell you a few things before Paolo returns, which will probably be any minute. We don't want Kristiana to know where you are and it appears that if Paolo knows—so does she. If Paolo leaves, the likelihood of another incident is high. So, Camille and Daphne came up with an idea that I think just might work."

"What?" she whispered.

"I don't have time to go into everything right now. But we're just about out of time. Please don't worry about what happens in the next few minutes. Also, I won't be able to see you right away—but I want you to know that everything will be all right."

"Where are you going," she whispered, unable to find the strength for her normal speaking volume.

"Don't worry. I'm not doing anything dangerous, I promise you that."

She wanted to ask what was going on with Paolo's constant vigilance, but she just didn't have the strength.

"Camille's going to come in so that I can be part of a discussion with Paolo. And remember, there's nothing to worry about in the next few minutes, all right?"

She lowered her brow and nodded—even that hurt!

Camille stepped in cautiously, looking more than a little stressed. "Are you alright?" She sat on the edge of the bed. Valeria nodded. "You certainly look better than last night!" Camille tried to smile and then got serious. "How are you feeling?"

"Alright, I guess," she lied.

"I guess Alex told you that we have a plan." Camille said in a near whisper, Valeria nodded. "He's afraid this plan will be too upsetting to you but I've assured him that you're stronger than he thinks. In any case, it's important that you don't...worry too much about it." Valeria nodded again, as Camille peered toward the door, nervously. "Also, I should warn you that Alex is going to ask you to do some things that you won't want to agree to. In fact, I would guess that you would completely object to some of it. But I want you to remember that there is more to this than what you will see on the surface." Camille glanced at the door again. "Just trust me on this."

Camille looked completely exhausted. "Oh, and lastly, we don't want any discussion about our project here with us recovering the oracles; and absolutely *no* mention of Myrdd." Camille nervously glanced at the door. "You'll learn more later."

Valeria nodded and was nearly asleep again.

Camille pulled a turkey baster filled with red fluid from a drawer. "Caleb smuggled this in under his sling a few hours ago." Valeria narrowed her eyes at the baster.

"It's blood," Camille said as her eyes grew large with excitement.

"Caleb's arm?" Valeria whispered.

"Oh, it's been completely healed since early this morning. But he was getting such a kick out of having an 'injury' that he kept the sling on. That's when I had the idea. If I had thought of this while Paolo was sleeping, we wouldn't have needed to sneak it in. Delayed brilliance—what can I say!"

She carefully placed the baster in Mani's medical bag.

"What..." Valeria started coughing and the pain in her rib felt as though it were ripping through her—followed by all the dull aches in her body.

Camille swallowed. "I'm sorry you're in so much pain."

"What's the..." Valeria couldn't think of the word for the baster and she couldn't point as every move was painful.

"Don't worry, it isn't real blood. Tav and Caleb made it," Camille whispered.

Alex came in again, looking a bit pensive with Paolo in tow.

"We've been talking, and I think you need to permit me to see the vision. We need to know if Kristiana is actually communicating with you or if it was just a bad dream. I am aware that it was threatening. You don't need to feel like you are protecting me," Alex said.

Paolo stood by as Alex took Valeria's hands in his. As Alex kissed her fingers tenderly, his eyes lit on her with so much love that all of her worries disappeared and she was at once, lost in   him. She felt the energy of the transference as it ran from her fingers to his. She saw a brief smile graze his face and she realized that she was recalling their wedding night and honeymoon. She grimaced—she still had no control of her transferences.

"Just relax," he said.

She drew a deep breath while the smile continued to cling to the corners of his mouth. Then his eyes got wide and the color drained from his face.

"Kristiana?" she whispered as a statement.

Alex nodded slowly. "We need to bring the family in."

By silent command, the entire family funneled into her room. Alex said, "I'm going in search of Kristiana and I believe I know where to find her."

Lars began to speak, "I agree—"

But before he could say anything else Paolo said flatly, "She will simply kill you."

Feeling the panic rising in her, Valeria cried out in a mix of anguish followed by the pain of exertion. "Please! Alex, promise me you won't do that! Please!" She needed his agreement. Alex seemed to be undecided.

"I don't want to upset you, Val, but it's the right thing to do. Kristiana and I were married and obviously we have...unfinished business." Alex glanced up at the ceiling for a moment and then to Paolo.

Suddenly, Valeria understood; that had been a communication for Kristiana. As long as Kristiana believed that Alex was coming to her, she might not try to harm her or their baby.

Lars said, "Val, while I don't necessarily agree with Alex on this, we do both agree that Paolo and Caleb should keep an eye on you."

"I'm sorry—but no."

"Do you still suspect me, bella?" Paolo said, obviously hurt.

"No," she said, and in that moment she realized she was no longer angry with him. "No, Paolo. I just can't believe that Daphne and Alex would be comfortable with that," she said in a breathy voice to avoid the pain in her ribs.

Daphne stepped forward and put her hand affectionately on Paolo's arm and drew a nervous breath. "Valeria, I know that you and I haven't been close." She shrugged and rolled her eyes. "Perhaps that's a bit of an understatement." Daphne took a deep breath, and continued, "I can tell you that the last thing I want is for Paolo to spend more time with you. I am certain that Alex feels the same way. But the fact is that you and the child are safer with Paolo near."

Lars walked toward Valeria's bed. "Daphne is right. And you know that Alex wouldn't agree to this unless he had reason."

Valeria rubbed her forehead and glanced at Alex who nodded. Then she aimed a quick glance at Camille, who also nodded, so Valeria consented by nodding in return. Alex looked relieved.

They brought in a chair and a cot for Paolo. When they brought in a four-panel screen, Paolo raised a hand.

"How do I watch Valeria with a screen blocking my vision of her?"

Daphne smiled. "We can leave it by the wall for now. But the woman does require some privacy!" she said, raising her eyebrows.

"Yes, you are right," Paolo said.

Alex looked particularly tense. Valeria wondered about Camille's communication and what was about to unfold that she should prepare herself for. As the day rolled into evening, Paolo remained on duty from his chair in the corner. He glanced up from his book and said, "Bella, I hope you know that I would never intentionally harm you."

Valeria was too exhausted to reassure Paolo. She shrugged noncommittally and she could tell by his silence that he was hurt from her response. A few minutes later, Alex returned with Daphne.

Daphne held out the crystal glass to Paolo. "I thought you might like some wine." Paolo nodded and took a sip. "It's Alex's good stock," she whispered conspiratorially.

Valeria was surprised by the exchange. She would have never expected Daphne to serve anyone—well, except Alex. Daphne sat down on the arm of Paolo's chair as he read. After an hour, when the glass was nearly empty, she picked it up, left briefly, and returned with it refilled. Paolo didn't seem to notice as he continued reading. Daphne brushed his shoulder, and he smiled up at her; even from the distance, Valeria could see that his eyes looked a bit glassy. Then Daphne offered a slight nod to Alex and, a moment later, Mani entered the room.

"How are you feeling Valeria?" Mani asked.

She started to say that she felt fine for someone who had just broken a rib and her leg...and was pregnant. But before she could say a word, it seemed as if Alex noticed something in her appearance. He asked, "Val, everything all right?" She didn't feel good, but she felt no worse.

Paolo started to lean out of his chair. Alex glared at him and Daphne pressed him back down.

"I'm sorry, Alex. We'll give you some privacy," Daphne said as she pulled the screen open, blocking Paolo's direct view of Valeria. Paolo started to object and Daphne added, "Paolo! She's with Doc!"

Mani took a small flashlight out of his pocket and held it over her eyes. Then he rose and pulled off a printout that came from the machinery that was attached to her. He studied the report for a moment and then turned to her.

"Valeria, the oxygen saturation in your bloodstream is extremely low." He turned a piece of equipment and then lifted an oxygen mask and adjusted the elastic band behind her head. "We will keep this on you for the time being." She tried to relax but Alex's face looked so full of concern that it was difficult to tell if Mani was telling her the truth or if this was the deception Camille had been suggesting to her earlier in the day. Valeria breathed deeply, now concerned for their child.

"Is she all right?" Paolo asked rising out of his chair again. Again, Daphne pressed him back down.

Mani stood as Alex continued to squeeze her hand. "Let's see if the internal bleeding is controlled."

Valeria narrowed her eyes and she looked at Alex, who winked at her with no joy in his eyes. Had she imagined that the baby was fine? Now she was concerned. Mani had said that there was some bleeding. Maybe there was more than he had wanted to say at the time. Alex squeezed her hand and gave her a comforting nod. Paolo was peeking through the breaks in the screen.

"Hey, pal, how about giving us some privacy," Alex said.

"Do you need us to leave?" Daphne asked.

"For the ultrasound the screen should be fine," Mani intervened.

Mani adjusted the sheet and then pulled Valeria's hospital gown to just above her naval. He folded it neatly and then squeezed the cold liquid onto her belly.

Turning the monitor so that only Alex and Valeria could view it, Mani moved the wand to show the babies rapidly beating heart. Valeria relaxed a bit. Then Mani moved it further and it showed a clear silhouette of the baby sucking her thumb and moving the fingers of her other hand. Valeria was momentarily overwhelmed and glanced at Alex who had tears in his eyes. Then Mani held a finger over his mouth.

"It looks like..." he changed the resolution and the vision changed. "I'm sorry, I am unable to find the heartbeat."

Valeria's eyes widened in alarm and Alex mouthed, *It's fine!* Then Alex lifted a single finger and pointed toward Mani. She noticed that Mani had the turkey baster in his hand. First, he wiped the gel from Valeria's stomach, and then he squeezed the cold red goo over her thighs. It shocked her and she let out a sound, which was a mistake because of her ribs, and caused her to moan in pain.

"What's wrong?" Alex asked and brushed her rib lightly.

"Alex!" Mani said and took a towel and soaked it with the baster. "Daphne, please ask Camille to come immediately."

Valeria lowered her brow. Mani would never ask Daphne to get Camille, as their non-verbal communication was so powerful.

Valeria expected Daphne to say, "Go get her yourself!" She was stunned when Daphne jumped up and went for the door.

"Camille, Mani needs you!" Daphne said with more urgency than Valeria thought her capable.

Paolo stood and took a few steps to the edge of the screen. He weaved a bit and then grabbed the screen for support.

"Is my Bella all right?" he asked.

He looked so pitiful that Valeria could barely stand the ruse. The hurt on Daphne's face was palpable when she stepped from the door and took him by the shoulder.

"Baby, she isn't your Bella anymore. She is Alex's Valeria." She supported him as it looked like he might fall over at any moment. Mani lifted a blood soaked towel onto a tray, leaving it in Paolo's sight.

"Yes, I know. She isn't my Bella anymore," he said sadly.

"No, she is not. Come, we have to leave now," Daphne said calmly.

Paolo staggered a bit. "What is wrong with me?"

"You drank too much wine," Daphne said, as she continued to guide him out. Once they were in the doorway, Paolo grabbed the doorframe and turned.

"I am sorry; I seem to have drunk too much wine." Mani nodded toward him and then lifted another blood soaked towel. Paolo continued, "Mani, do you promise to take good care of my...Alex's Bella, if I leave?"

Mani looked up at Paolo and his face softened.

"Yes, Paolo, I will take good care of her."

Paolo turned back around to head down the hall and Camille impatiently closed the door right behind them. All action froze as they all listened to the motion in the hallway. They heard a few steps and then Paolo said, "Once, long ago, she was *my* Isabella."

Daphne's voice sounded softer than usual. "No, it only seemed that way—it's easy to fool yourself, but they were never ours."

There was a thud followed by a drunken groan in the great room and Camille nodded.

"Beautiful, you're fine. Bear with us for a few minutes," Alex said, and then ran to the window and opened it. He pulled in a stretcher from outside the window and carried it over to the bed, laying it next to Valeria. Camille unsnapped Valeria's hospital gown and replaced it with a clean one; then she crinkled up the stained gown, and placed it blood side up in a laundry hamper. Mani snipped a container of blood and soaked the gown, then poured the remainder in a bowl and placed it on the tray with his instruments.

Alex rolled Valeria toward him to transfer her onto the stretcher, and he paled when she cried out in pain as her leg twisted.

"I'm sorry!" he said, still trying to gently adjust her legs onto the stretcher.

Valeria's head was spinning from the pain and she was certain she was going to black out. She looked up and thought she was seeing things. A woman wearing a hospital gown, with hair similar to Valeria's, stood next to her. As soon as Valeria could focus, she realized it was Ava, wearing a wig. Ava gave Valeria a quick smile. Then Alex and Mani lifted Valeria toward the window as Camille changed the sheet. Ava lay down on the hospital bed and pulled the oxygen mask over her face.

Outside, it was cold and Valeria shivered as she heard, "Easy does it, lass, we've got you."

"Lars, can you cover her feet?" Alex asked.

She felt the blanket being carefully adjusted over her feet and then she was staring up at brilliant evening stars. Alex hopped out from the window and pulled the blankets around Valeria tightly, and then he kissed her forehead.

"I'm sorry, beautiful, but I'm going to have to stay here for a while," he whispered. "It shouldn't be too much longer. I'll be down as soon as I can." Then he looked to Lars and Tavish, and said, "Please be gentle with her!"

Valeria still couldn't quite follow what was happening. She watched as Alex climbed back into the window and closed it. Then he blew her a kiss and went to Ava's side, nodded, and took her hand.

It was a painful journey through the twilight canopy along the wooded trail. Every step caused a myriad of pains shooting through her body. She hadn't realized how sore she was until she felt the jiggling and jarring of the trail. She tried not to make any sound, wondering where they were going and concentrating on the extraordinary smells of the forest in the fall.

"Are you all right, sweetheart?" Lars asked.

All she could manage was, "Uh-huh."

They passed a clearing and she glanced over to see their beloved cottage burnt to the ground. A few pieces of Alex's charred sculptures sat on the edge of the ashes. She felt the sadness well inside, until she saw the one thing that made it all right. Their ginkgo tree looked completely unmarred. She could see the golden leaves in the moonlight—no burnt branches! Her ginkgo tree had survived, and so had they!

A few minutes later, she saw Mani's home. Tavish and Lars laid her on the bed but this time she failed miserably at withholding a moan and she realized she was shaking.

There was a roaring fire in the fireplace and the warmth seemed to calm her.

"All right, Val, we need to roll you over to remove the stretcher."

"Can you give me a minute?" she whispered between the trembling. She wasn't ready to move again. But she realized that it wouldn't be easier in one minute or thirty. "Okay," she said, as she tightened her jaw and drew in a deep breath.

"It'll be easier if you breathe through it," Lars said. She kept her eyes closed and nodded. "One, two, three..." And in a single motion— and with a single cry from Valeria—Lars and Tavish removed the stretcher and she was on the bed. The whole experience had been painful and exhausting. She was certain that if she were more aware she would want to understand all that had happened. But now all she wanted to do was sleep.

What she did understand was that the baby was all right and that, now, Paolo—and Kristiana—believed that there was no baby. They also thought they knew where Valeria was when, in fact, they did not.

Lars brushed her arm. "As soon as Paolo is completely out— which shouldn't be too long— Alex will be here and we'll start mixing the mud." Lars reached over and grabbed something; in the low light of the fire, Valeria couldn't tell what it was. "This is not going to be the quietest location at Morgana, but it may very well be the safest for you now. I think it's safe to say that you will need these with all of the immortals we might bring back." Lars produced a set of earphones.

"At least we're hoping they come back," Tavish added.

"Yes...we hope," Lars said.

"How many do you expect?" Valeria whispered.

"We don't know. After Myrdd was assassinated, the oracles avoided the council for hundreds of years. There could be as many as ten."

"Tav is going to stay with you for a while," Lars said, and Tavish's mouth opened in a smile that would scare young children had she not known his heart.

"Good," she whispered.

"I'm glad you're all right sweetheart. I'll see you tomorrow," Lars said, and then he kissed her forehead and left.

Tavish was sitting in a rocking chair by the fire.

"I've been thinking…" He looked down at his hands. "I see you and the laddie and it has me thinking…perhaps it's time for old Tav to settle down."

Tavish stared into the distance and she could see his sadness.

"Have you ever been in love Tav?" she asked in a revered whisper.

He shook his head slightly.

"I highly recommend it."

He sat there without saying a word, his eyes transfixed out the window at the stars. Finally, he cleared his throat. "Achhh! Who am I trying to kid? I'm just too much man for one woman!"

Valeria's rib hurt as she tried not to laugh. Her whole body hurt from the ordeal tonight. She glanced around the room. This was the home that Alex had been raised in; she couldn't overlook the significance of the evening.

Within minutes, she felt herself drifting off. In her dreamy state, she suddenly heard the sweet, high-pitched giggle of a little girl and could see her older, more serious brother chasing her. Valeria heard the woman's gentle voice, "Antonia, those are your brother's arrows—not toys for you to tease him with. Now give them back to Alex!"

The dark-haired child turned and handed the bows to the boy with the dark blond hair.

The mother's long auburn hair flowed over her shoulders. Her complexion was creamy. But it was the kindness in her eyes that made Valeria dream of a loving mother. She wished that this was not a dream and that the child she once was and this little boy and girl could all curl upon the mother's lap by the fire. Valeria felt tears of yearning form in her heart.

"That's a good girl, Antonia. Now give your brother a hug and ask his forgiveness."

"I love you, Alex. I'm sorry for being bad." The little girl kissed the boy's cheek. He softened, and then wiped his face in mock irritation.

"That's it. Now off to bed for both of you!" the mother said.

Valeria yearned to see them more clearly. The woman's warm voice was so inviting that she mourned the loss of a woman whom she had never met.

The door swung wide open and a man stepped through. "Ahhh! My children!"

"Papa!" They both cried out in excitement. Young Alex hugged his father around the waist while Antonia clung to his leg.

"I had a sticker in my finger today, Papa," Antonia said.

The man muffed Alex's hair and then lifted the little girl into his arms. "You did?" he asked, terribly concerned, although Valeria was certain that his entire way of life was entrenched in real decisions of life or death.

Valeria liked the man, too. She felt a safety in his presence—similar to her feeling of being with Alex.

"Yes, Papa, but Alex pulled it out for me."

"Alex is a good boy!" The man hugged the young girl while he pulled the boy into him. "Such a good boy!"

Then it all went dark, although she still felt the warmth of the small room. Suddenly, she was somewhere else and there was a cold damp wall next to her.

She was lost and wandering. On either side of her were walls curving in an elaborate labyrinth that didn't seem to end. There was something she needed desperately to find. She increased her step and heard echoed footsteps behind her. She picked up her pace and so did the person following her.

Then, she felt fingertips lovingly stroking her face. She knew that touch and a smile lit her face. Opening her eyes, she could just make out the shadow of Alex's face inches from hers.

"Hey, beautiful," he whispered. "Did I ever tell you how much I adore you?"

"Hey," she said sleepily.

"I'm sorry for all the drama earlier." He looked toward the door. "Lars told me how painful the trip down here was for you. But I just couldn't think of a better way to get you out of there and Doc insisted that you couldn't travel any further for several weeks. I guess it is all working out. Kristiana would never expect that you were still at Morgana."

"Can you stay for a while?" she asked.

"I can; Paolo seems to be down for the count." He snickered.

"Did you drug him?" she whispered.

"Not me specifically," he said, in a voice full of mischief. "Besides, I prefer to call it karma."

Valeria giggled and, this time, it didn't seem to hurt. "Karma?"

"Yes. You do know that he and Kristiana drugged me to near death many years ago."

"They did?"

Alex laughed softly and brushed her hair back. "Of course. I would have never chosen another woman, except when I awoke in her bed naked—"

"Naked?"

Alex lifted a brow and nodded. "As in buck..." He smiled and then continued, "In any case, it seemed like the right thing to do." He bit his lip. "Kristiana wants what she thinks she wants. I imagine that if I had ever loved her in return, she would have broken my heart as she did with so many others."

"Instead, she has spent her life in vengeance."

He pressed his lips together in thought. "I've had enough of Kristiana. Now I want to focus on my wife. Can I crawl in here with you?"

"Please!" she said, as Alex stripped down to his boxers and crawled under the covers with her. "Is Paolo going to be all right?"

"Oh, he will probably have one hell of a hangover." Alex pursed his lips again. "I'd say he earned it."

"What will happen in the morning when he wakes up and we aren't there?" she asked, and realized that her voice had no strength behind it.

"We've cleared out the room. In the morning, Lars will tell Paolo that you went to the hospital and were released. He'll assume that we went back into hiding. We thought about having an ambulance transport Ava, but without placing Paolo in the ambulance, we would be risking the lives of the ambulance workers." Alex stroked her hair.

"Daphne will have Paolo off Morgana by seven a.m.—earlier, if she can awaken him. We don't want him stumbling across Myrdd or the others."

Valeria tried to move toward him and realized that every muscle in her body ached. It had been more than twenty-four hours since the crash. She had justified that the pregnancy was some special alteration of her body chemistry, but now she was forced to acknowledge, as Alex obviously already had, that she was not immortal.

"Hopefully, the moaning from our friends will be gone, or quiet enough, that Paolo won't be able to hear it from the house. Daphne will be in the mood for '70s rock and roll—just in case. I must admit that the thought of Paolo's headache and the radio blasting does give me a sense of wicked pleasure."

"You've earned it," Valeria said sleepily, curling into Alex's arms. "Thank you for keeping us safe." She looked down and rubbed her belly.

Alex kissed her forehead, and then they heard the first of the moaning. It sounded like something from a zombie film.

His eyes lit up. "They're here!" Then he reached over and gently pulled the headphones over her ears.

CHAPTER 16

When Valeria woke, Alex was gone. Caleb was there with his bigger than life smile. "About time you woke up! We were afraid you were going to sleep right through your own birthday!"

"My birthday?" Valeria said feeling confused. "No, that's tomorrow."

"You slept all day and all night!" Caleb said. "Alex had to go get his clothes and stuff and he asked me to stay with you."

Her face lit with the smile of someone in love, while she felt the wonderful cool of the mountains in the fall.

The boy leaned his head back against the rail of the door. "Tavish let me go down to the moaning mud pile." Caleb laughed. "It's really cool," he added.

"Did they find Myrdd yet?" Valeria asked.

"I don't know. But I think there are a lot more oracles there than they thought. Alex is back," he said, glancing at the door. "I have to get more stuff."

He pulled open a door and lifted a stack of blankets and sheets. Then the front door flew open and Alex joined them.

"Good morning, beautiful!" Alex sat down next to Valeria. "We should celebrate today," he said, but she could tell there was tension behind his words.

It was her birthday. It had been just a year ago when she had first come here, still engaged to David. That was when she had found out the truth about herself and her history. It had been warmer last year, and they had enjoyed a Greek celebration on the back lawn to celebrate her special day. That was when she had fallen in love with their cottage, her new family, and Alex.

"Um, I'm not really up to celebrating today. Besides, everyone's busy, so from now on, I would like to celebrate a day later."

Alex nodded. "I'm going to make you an omelet and coffee."

"Don't you need to help the others?"

Alex's smile was not quite natural. "No. It's your birthday and I'm spending it with you."

She knew he was nervous about the anniversary of her curse. She was certain Doc was on call as well.

"Did they find Myrdd?" she asked, hiding the near constant ache in her ribs.

"Yes, but he isn't alert yet."

"It worked!" she shrieked, and then instantly regretted it as a sharp pain spread across her ribs.

"Yes..." Then she saw the spark return to his eyes. "I do have a gift...well, it is kind of a gift. Knowing how you hate surprises, I thought I would include you in this one. I'll show it to you later."

"If it has caffeine in it, and a bit of cream—by all means!" She laughed and, again, it hurt her ribs.

"Coffee! Well, let me see if we can handle that right away."

He exited into the main room of the house and then peeked his head around the corner and shrugged. "You know, I don't think you should be drinking coffee."

"Coffee. Now," she deadpanned.

"How about water-processed decaf?"

"It's my birthday and I want *real* coffee!" she whispered as loudly as she could, realizing that she sounded like a five-year-old having a temper tantrum. My God, what was happening to her? Married only months and turning into a demanding shrew. Fortunately, Alex just laughed.

She heard the blender and knew he was also bringing her a strawberry-kale shake. Moments later, he presented the tray.

"Thank you, Alex! I don't know what made me sound so...bossy."

He laughed again and it lit the room in a golden glow. "I know— you've been caffeine deprived for nearly a week!" he said in pretended shock.

She took a sip of coffee and moaned with pleasure. Alex went back to the kitchen, and a few minutes later, he returned with an omelet. Valeria realized that she had not eaten much since the accident, and before that, she'd been ill. She scarfed down the omelet even though she felt like she might explode. After she finished, and was happily sipping her coffee, he stood up.

"You're leaving?" she asked, disappointed.

"I had to leave you for a few minutes this morning, but I'm not leaving you the rest of today."

"Good!"

"So, uh…I have something. It's, well, kind of a birthday present." He walked into the living room and came back with a large cardboard tube. He pulled out something that looked like blueprints and spread it out on the bed in front of her.

"What is it?" she asked.

"It's for our new and improved cottage," he said. "I thought it might be good to include you in the plans since I know how much you love surprises," he teased, and then got serious. "But really, you should be involved in the plans. It's our home!"

She brushed the side of his face, "We don't need new plans—I loved it exactly as it was!" Just knowing they would rebuild their cottage gave her more energy; it just didn't reveal itself in her voice.

Alex lowered a single brow and looked at her for a moment. "Well, I was thinking that we needed another bedroom."

"For guests? They can stay up at the main house, can't they?" And then her eyes widened in understanding. "Oh!" she said. Her eyes lit up in sudden joy from her husband's seeming acceptance, and of the possibility of a life here at Morgana in their new and improved cottage, with their miracle child.

"Is that all right?" he asked, suddenly concerned as her eyes filled with tears. "I know it isn't like jewelry—"

"Are you kidding?" she interrupted and tears began flowing down her face. "This is the most precious…the most beautiful gift anyone—

even you—have ever given me!" By the time she spoke the words, she was sobbing uncontrollably.

"I had intended to get you something else. Something more romantic," he said apologetically. At that, she began to sob even harder and Alex looked concerned.

"Val?" he said as he sat down on the edge of the bed.

She tried to control the sobs as each one tore into her broken rib. "That is just the...the most...romantic thing I've ever...A home! Our home. With a room for our...for our baby!" she cried.

Alex wasn't quite sure whether to smile or comfort her. He bit his lip and watched his wife until he was fairly certain that she liked the gift. He rolled up the blueprints and placed them back in the tube and then he crawled onto the bed to hold her.

Once the sobbing stopped, he said, "I'm a bit nervous to ask, but is there anything else that you would like for your birthday? Anything you would like to do?"

Valeria smiled as she pulled out another tissue from the box on the bedside table and blew her nose. Her sweet Alex was terrified of making her cry again, and suddenly, she broke into laughter—and he did too.

"I love the plans!"

"You're sure? It didn't seem like you had a chance to really look. Do you want me to get them out again?" He started to rise and then, remembering her response, changed his mind. "No. Let's do that another time."

He was so nervous with her that it touched her heart.

"But, Val, is there anything you want that I can get you today...that won't make you cry?"

She had to laugh at that. She touched his face and kissed his lips. "Yes...I want a bath."

"A bath?" Alex repeated.

"Yes."

"Hmm, Mani only has a shower here, but let me see what I can do."

"Are you going to leave?"

He shook his head. "I had to shower and check on our project out there, but other than that, I am with you all day—"

"And all night?" she interrupted.

He smiled. "And all night. I am sorry to say that we will have to move you back to the main house soon."

"When?"

"When Melitta is revived. I gave them this home for a wedding gift. I expected that they would build another but they seemed to like it."

"I love this place," she said glancing around. "It's like your family—"

"*You* are my family," Alex interrupted, making Valeria smile sweetly.

"It's like they all moved on, but their hearts remained."

They curled together on the bed and read for an hour when an old-fashioned claw foot tub was delivered into the bedroom.

"That is the most beautiful tub I have ever seen!" she said in awe. It had a high area in the back to rest her neck and was the perfect size and depth.

"Don't get too excited about the tub. It's a birthday present for you today and a coming home gift for Lita."

There was a knock at the door and Tavish entered.

"So the lass wishes for a tub! I'm here to do yer plumbing." He winked at Valeria. "As you might have guessed, plumbing is my specialty," he said with a wicked glow in his eyes.

It took a little over an hour—as Valeria learned several new Scottish curse words—and finally, the banging of pipes and drilling was over.

"Your bath!" Tavish presented, and then nodded and left.

Alex went over and turned the brass handles, and in a moment, she saw the steam rising from the tub.

"I've checked with Mani and he has confirmed that you can have a bath as long as it isn't too hot."

He wrapped a trash bag around her broken leg and the soft cast. Then he helped her out of her hospital gown and wrapped a large towel around her. There were still traces of the mock blood from two nights before. It was the first time he had seen her naked since the accident and he noticed how many bruises and abrasions she had all over her body. He shook it off and unbuttoned his blue cotton shirt. Then he

245

lifted her off the bed and into his arms. This time, it only hurt her for a few seconds, and then his closeness stirred something inside her.

She brushed her fingers over his chest. "I like being here in your arms," she said.

"I like you here in my arms," he replied, his mood getting serious as he gazed into her eyes.

As Alex stepped toward the tub and lowered her into the lightly scented water, Valeria moaned.

"Did I hurt you?"

"No…it is heavenly!" she said.

Alex saw the goose bumps on her arm. He took a washcloth and poured her favorite soap onto it. "Here, can you lean forward just a bit?" She nodded and he moved the cloth over her neck and shoulders and back. She moaned again.

"Are you comfortable?" he asked and she nodded.

She drank in the feel of the delightful water with the golden fire in the fireplace beside them—her Alex beside her. It was more than glorious, it was also incredibly sensual.

"It would be perfect if you got in with me," she said with her eyes still closed. He laughed softly and brushed his lips over her neck.

"Doc says none of that until later," he whispered without looking her in the eye.

She took his hand and kissed it. "Well maybe you could just…sit in here with me."

He picked up a pitcher.

"Lean your head back," he said, his voice getting husky. He poured the warm water over her hair. "I don't think I can climb in there—or out—without hurting you." He picked up the bottle of shampoo and squeezed out a bit, rubbing it between his palms before massaging it into her hair. His hands moved up and down her scalp and neck in a way that sent her head spinning into thoughts best left until later.

"I think it would be all right if you got in." She gulped.

He poured a pitcher over her hair several times and then brought his mouth down on to hers with a passion she hadn't felt from him in some time. Her arms reached up for him forgetting their discomfort. He pulled himself back from her, breathing heavily, and then kissed her lightly one more time.

"I think..." he said, with his face barely hiding his amusement, "I had better get you out of this tub before you turn into a prune. Are you ready?"

She nodded, so he pulled the plug on the drain as they stared into each other's eyes. Alex gritted his jaw and turned to grab a towel. He wrapped it around her lovingly and then lifted her into his arms and carried her to the bed as if she were weightless. Then he took the other towel and rubbed it briskly through her long brown hair.

"Do you want to blow dry your hair? I can help," he said.

"No. I want you to lay down with me," she said, as she stared at him dreamily. Her beautiful husband...the man who just had a claw foot tub delivered so that she could bathe...the man who just shampooed her hair...the man standing next to her with the perfectly delicious, bare chest.

He crawled into bed and lay next to her.

"You know I am feeling better today," she said as she pressed her mouth to that chest. She felt that recently absent feeling of heat and moved her fingers over his chest and he leaned his head back and sighed in pleasure.

"Easy there," he murmured as his eyes rolled back as he moved away from her, but not so far that she couldn't continue. "You know, in some respects, I *am* only human."

Then the curves of his mouth turned up and he took her face in his hands. "You are driving me crazy, you know."

She kissed him passionately and then moved her lips to his neck as she ran her fingers over his stomach. This time he moaned lightly and took a quick breath.

"Beautiful, I don't think you're ready for this yet."

Valeria buried her face in his chest, hesitating, and then kissed his ribs lightly. "Well...I was thinking..." She bit her lip and stroked her hand along his side. "I thought maybe we could try...other things," she said, attempting to hide her embarrassment.

Alex closed his eyes for a moment and gently pulled her away, moving his face until he could look directly into her eyes.

His smile softened as he kissed her, but barely hid the amusement in his eyes. "I would love to try...other things...after you've healed a bit more. But right now, I think we need to cool it and allow you to recover."

She could feel the flames of deep crimson lashing against her cheeks and down her neck.

"What is it?" he asked, his eyes lit with love.

She buried her face in his chest again and swallowed. "I just...I know we're not on our honeymoon anymore, but I loved the way we were and it's probably naïve of me, but I guess I thought that we would be like that forever. And now, it feels like it's all changing and...I don't want that part of us to go away," she whispered as she buried her face in his chest.

His eyes glowed with love. "Do you think that's what *I need?*" he asked. Valeria shrugged and looked away, but he gently lifted her chin.

Still embarrassed, she pulled her chin from his hand and drew a deep breath. "No—I know you have extraordinary will power. I've never doubted that. But it's me...it's what I need." She looked into his eyes. "Alex, I need you!" She tried to catch her breath. She didn't want another hysterical sobbing scene like before.

Alex pulled her into him as he kissed her deeply, running his finger along the side of her face and down to her shoulder. Then he looked her in the eyes and said, "Beautiful, I promise you that as soon as you're healed," the corners of his mouth turned up, and this time, it was not from amusement, but desire, "the honeymoon will begin again and continue as long as you want."

"I don't want it to ever end," she said.

"It's decided then." He kissed her again and when he pulled away, she saw the spark of amusement back in his eyes. "And once you're healed, I would love to try...other things...if you still want to." He winked.

They curled together and the distance dissolved.

Alex's eyes closed in relaxation. He turned and murmured in her ear, "By the way, you might wish that you had allowed me to dry your hair."

"Why? Is it bothering you?"

"And you might also want to take a nap while you have the opportunity." His eyes lit with mischief.

"What's going on?" she asked.

"Hmm...let me just say that today is your birthday and you really don't believe that anyone here is going to let that slip by uncelebrated, do you?"

"I really don't like birthday parties—and especially not surprise parties," she said, brushing her hand over his chest.

"In that case, I am sorry to tell you that Camille hasn't had a party to plan in four whole months and she certainly wasn't going to permit this opportunity to slip away. Besides, it will be a wonderful way to get reacquainted with old friends."

She curled into his chest. "Well then, I'll tie my hair back. You will give me some notice so I can dress won't you?"

"Absolutely," he said as he stroked his fingers over her shoulder and up her neck. Within minutes, he felt her breathing slow, and he knew she was asleep.

CHAPTER 17

Awakening from the dream, Valeria lifted her head off Alex's chest and realized she was still wrapped in the towel. She lowered her brow. She was certain that she had heard something outside.

Suddenly, the front door flew open and a naked young man in his mid-twenties ran into the bedroom. He was extremely pale with light blond locks, a thin and hairless frame, and a face as guileless as a child's. Valeria released a small scream—which was a mistake with her injuries. The man froze in horror. Alex bolted straight up in bed, causing the intruder to cover his face in terror.

"Please do not harm me, sir!" the intruder said, as Alex covered Valeria with the sheet to shield her.

"Elliot!" Alex sighed in relief.

The intruder uncovered his eyes and then they widened. "Dear God! Is that you Alexander?"

Elliot seemed to come to life once more, and then realized that he was naked. He shrieked and covered his lower extremity with his hands and, seeing Valeria nearly naked, he shrieked again and moved his hands to his tightly clenched eyes.

"Oh, dear lord, I pray I shall wake from this nightmare fully dressed in my fine silks and lace."

Alex was out of bed in an instant. He grabbed the throw blanket at the foot of the bed and handed it to Elliot. "Elliot, let's get you some clothes."

Calmed by Alex's voice, Elliot opened his eyes again.

"Yes...please forgive me, madam, but somehow I have misplaced my clothing!" he said, holding the blanket, but not covering himself.

"Elliot!" Alex said and raised his eyebrows in a subtle attempt to remind the young man that he had again exposed himself. Elliot held the blanket in front of him but was completely distracted by the view of Valeria in bed. He leaned toward Alex and whispered loudly enough for her to hear.

"Alexander, pardon my question, but it appears that you have bedded the fair Cassandra!"

Valeria snickered as Alex grabbed him by the elbow and guided him out of the bedroom. She heard as he said, "I suggest we get you dressed first."

Elliot continued to hold the blanket in front of him as he walked with Alex to the main room—while exposing himself from the rear. He leaned to Alex and said in a loud whisper, "But you've *bedded* her? Please tell me what miracle allows you to bed such a woman."

"Elliot!" Alex warned.

"I only ask because I would like to—"

"Clothes now—answers, later," Alex said with slight irritation.

It was a few minutes later when Elliot said, "Alexander, what has happened to your fine clothing? Have you lost your fortune?" He continued, "Perhaps bedding the fair Cassandra cost you your fortune?"

Busy with searching for size-appropriate clothing for Elliot, Alex stopped at the young man's statement and lowered a brow. "Elliot, I am going to forgive that comment as I'm certain that this new world is a bit confusing. I'm certain that these sudden changes must be quite a shock to you. However, I will not tolerate inappropriate comments about *my wife*. Is that understood?"

Elliot lifted his arm and pointed toward the bedroom. "But she—"

"It would take me less than five seconds to turn you back out into the forest and then good luck finding more than a burlap sack."

"Alexander, I swear, I never meant a word of disrespect to Cassandra or to you!"

"Cover yourself with the blanket. I will return with some clothes."

Alex went back into the bedroom and rolled his eyes as Valeria continued to laugh—which continued to be painful. He grabbed a pair of jeans and a T-shirt from Mani's dresser and carried them into the main room.

"Here, these will be long, but they should fit."

Alex returned to the bedroom and flopped down onto the bed next to Valeria who still had a smile on her face.

"I would guess that's Elliot," she said.

"Yes, that would be Elliot."

Elliot's voice came from the other room. "I beg your pardon, Alexander, but these britches only have but one button. I'm unfamiliar with the gold metallic design, but I think it to be highly inappropriate."

Alex called out, "It's a zipper. Pull up on the—"

They heard a screech. "Have they not made safe clothing?" Elliot muttered to himself.

Valeria and Alex heard someone call out from far beyond the shack.

"ELLIOT! Where are you...you fool!" The low, irritated voice shouted through the woods.

"Maxi?" Elliot said. "I've not seen him in...I've not seen him since...Oh, dear, that was awful."

Alex glanced at his wife. "I suspect we should get you dressed. It appears we may have more company."

"That might be a good idea."

He picked up the hospital gown and Valeria scrunched her nose.

"Real clothes, please?"

The Louis Vuitton suitcase that Camille had packed was on a wooden chair and Alex opened it. He sorted through silk underwear and smiled.

"I don't believe I've seen most of these on you." His smile broadened as he held up a translucent silk g-string. "Something to look forward to." He bit his lip and then said, "All right, there are some yoga pants, a pair of jeans, and a T-shirt, or a sun dress?"

"I'd like to wear my jeans," Valeria said.

"Val..." he glanced at her stomach. "I don't believe you will be wearing your jeans for a while."

She frowned and quickly looked down at her belly. What had looked like mild bloating last week now definitely looked like a baby.

"I guess you're right."

"Considering what's to come this evening, how about this?" Alex brought a sundress and underwear to her and helped her dress. The movement while dressing was far less painful than earlier. In fact, she hardly noticed her rib.

"Ready to meet some of the others?"

"Yes, are they all...revived?" she asked.

Alex shook his head. "We're turning the pile every few hours and we keep finding more."

"I don't hear anymore moaning."

"No, the moaning mud pile, as Caleb calls it, is actually quite far from here. But we had nearly twenty oracles at last count."

"Twenty?" Her eyes widened in surprise."I thought you expected only ten."

"It was quite a shock to all of us. There must have been private executions—hard to imagine how Jeremiah pulled that off. Ready to meet Maxi?"

Valeria nodded and Alex opened the door. A tall thin man with a weary expression sat fully dressed in jeans and a button-down shirt. His hair was dark and wavy with traces of gray.

"Max!" Alex embraced him warmly. "Come and meet my wife."

Max rose and stepped into the room and Valeria realized that the expression was not weariness or disdain as it had first appeared, but sadness.

"Maxi, you'll never guess who it is!" Elliot said as he followed Alex into the bedroom.

"Why would I bother attempting a guess?" Maxi said gruffly. As soon as he saw Valeria, his temperament changed and he actually smiled. "Good Afternoon," he bowed.

"Max, this is my wife, Valeria."

"But she looks just like—" Elliot began.

Max turned toward him and gruffly snapped, "Of course we know who she resembles! I am quite certain—if provided an opportunity from your rambling—that Alex or the lady will fill us in on the details."

Max went over to Valeria, took her hand, and kissed it, causing her to blush; he continued to hold her hand as he smiled. Valeria realized that he had a very nice face when he wasn't scowling—some might even consider him handsome.

"Valeria is the reincarnation of Cassandra," Alex said, watching Max's expression and the fact that he was still holding her hand. He added with mild irritation, "Alright—enough of that Max."

"Forgive me, my lady...and Alexander. Beauty, such as your wife's, does take one's breath away." He released her hand and stepped away. "You have done well, Alex."

"Yes, I have undoubtedly married beyond my station." Alex winked at her.

"Now that is definitely not true! Max, please call me Valeria," she said.

"You may have noticed, things are far less formal now," Alex added.

"Please have a seat," Valeria said. "I'm afraid Doc has me bedridden for a few weeks."

Immediately, Elliot pulled his chair right up next to Valeria while Alex sat on the edge of her bed.

"I do have something of which I would like to request the dear lady's advice," Elliot said, glancing toward Alex for approval.

"What is it Elliot?" Valeria asked kindly.

"There is a lady," he said. "I am certain that she is my symbolon."

"Again?" Max said sharply.

Elliot ignored him, his eyes shined dreamily. "She is an angel on earth. I saw her for but a moment at...at the last council meeting. We have never spoken but she is here now!"

"Here?" Alex asked in surprise.

"She was my first vision in this new life—my angel was near me as I woke. She was sleeping," Elliot gulped, "as our grand artists may have painted her."

"You mean naked," Max said, rolling his eyes.

Elliot kept his eyes on Valeria. "Yes. I realized that I, too, was without clothing and I could not place her in such a compromising situation. That is why I ran."

"Do you know her name?" Valeria asked.

"No, my lady."

"Please, call me Valeria."

He lowered his brows as he gripped her hand with both of his in an expression of longing. "I'm not certain that my upbringing will permit that."

"Oh, for the love of God!" Max said. "Elliot, you are dressed now. Go speak to the girl!"

"But what do I say?" Elliot asked of Valeria.

"I recommend that you begin with hello," Valeria said.

Reaching into his shirt pocket, Elliot pulled out a piece of paper.

"As we have not been properly introduced, I thought a letter might be more appropriate," he said as he handed a rolled up piece of paper to Valeria. She glanced at the beautiful handwriting in large elegant swirls and her smile broadened.

"I was going to write it in Greek but then I realized that Latin is the language of love." Elliot cleared his throat and his eye twitched nervously. "I would like to arrange for delivery of this letter."

"I'm certain we can arrange that," Valeria said with a smile.

"Now that your most vital crisis is resolved, may I have a word with the lady?" Max said gruffly.

"Yes, yes…oh, of course, Maxi! Of course!" Elliot's face was still brilliant red with exuberance as he stepped away from Valeria and Max scooted his chair closer.

"Madam, are you ill?" Max asked in a voice that seemed a far cry from the tone he used with Elliot. "You look well."

"There was a car…a buggy accident," Alex said.

Max's eyes narrowed. "An accident?"

"Yes. I'm glad you're here Max—and Elliot." Alex turned to Valeria. "Max was one of the first oracles after Myrdd. He might be able to answer some of our questions about the evil eye."

"So what is the evil eye, exactly?" Valeria asked.

"The evil eye is associated with Envy's bite," Max said.

"Yes, but there is another aspect of it that we are particularly interested in; I've heard that, long ago, they associated it with the ability to see through other's eyes," Alex said.

Max lowered his brows as he sat quietly, contemplating. "You suspect it had something to do with the accident?"

"We have reason to believe so," Alex said.

"I cannot imagine that could be the case. Envy's bite can easily be spread; but as far as seeing through another's eyes..." He shook his head. "There were only two who could perform that magic, and they are both...long gone." Max steeled his face into a neutral expression.

"What do you know about it?" Valeria asked.

"It was called the evil eye of Hecate," Max said heavily, as if some hidden memory was attached to the words.

"Hecate?" Alex asked. "I didn't realize that she had anything to do with it."

"It was the gift that Hecate provided to Zeus during the War of the Titans and to one of his most trusted priestesses." He narrowed his eyes and then said quickly, "What do you wish to know about it?"

"How does it work?" Alex asked

Max's face took on a haunted expression. "Many years ago, before the War of the Titans, there was a mortal woman named Circe. She was beautiful and brilliant and far too ambitious for her own good," he said, shaking his head as if sad for the waste. "Circe befriended the Titan goddess Hecate."

"Excuse me, Max—" Alex interjected. Turning to Valeria, he said, "Beautiful, do you know about the War of the Titans?"

Valeria stared at Alex blankly. "No, I really don't."

"I am certain that Alex's explanation will be far better than mine," Max said.

Alex began, "Val, the Titans were a race of deities who were direct descendents of Gaia, mother earth and Uranus, the sky. They were the first Greek gods to gather together in one location. They were powerful—"

"And incredibly brutal," Max interjected, "particularly when it came to their young."

Alex continued, "Max is right. Cronus, fearing that one of his children would kill him, ate his first five offspring. Zeus, the sixth child, survived and forced Cronus to regurgitate the others. At the end of the war, three of the brothers divided up the earth. Zeus took control of the land and sky, Poscidon took control of the seas, and Hades, having drawn the short straw, took control of the underworld. The second generation were called Olympians, for their residence on Mt. Olympus." Alex nodded to Max.

"Hecate was a Titan," Max said. "However, during the War of the Titans, she assisted Zeus. She was known to be skilled with herbs and magic and developed an ability to see through another's eyes without them being aware of it—although that was not well known, as Zeus considered it his secret weapon.

"In order for Zeus to use this secret weapon, Hecate required a personal possession of the host. As Hecate's friendship with Zeus was too well known, she required someone that could infiltrate the home of the Titans.

"By Hecate's recommendation, and because of Circe's beauty and charms, she was selected. A week later, Circe returned triumphant with a lock of hair from Hyperion, Cronus' brother and a Titan.

"But Circe had taken the plans even further; when she was young, she had witnessed the madness and ill-effects of Envy's bite. So she lured Envy to the Titan's camp. As expected, Envy's bite created a rage that assisted the Olympians in winning their battle—but it also permanently infected Circe.

"At first, with Hecate's assistance, Circe was able to resist the madness. Hecate rewarded her by making her a priestess and teaching Circe the secrets of her magic. But it was as if Circe had stood too close to the flame. Soon, it seemed that she only desired what others possessed—Circe wanted immortality. She approached Zeus and demanded that he make her immortal. Zeus sensed her selfish intent and, instead, granted her a life of 1,000 years and promised to preserve her beauty.

"Not long after that, Hecate went to the underworld to serve as an attendant to Hade's wife. Before Hecate left, she gifted Circe with a magic kris."

"A kris?" Valeria asked.

"A kris is a sword-like dagger with a distinctive wavy blade," Alex said. "But besides being a weapon, it is considered a talisman with magical powers and a symbol of heroism. It was said to blind one's opponent with its sheen and heal any wounds during battle."

Max continued, "Many years later, Artemis, Apollo's twin sister, invited Circe to join a nation of female warriors known as the Amazons. Circe agreed but only under the name of Hecate. The story goes that she was killed during the Trojan War. And that is why Hecate is listed among the dead—and led to the historical confusion as to whether Hecate was a goddess or mortal."

"Circe was killed?" Valeria asked.

Max drew a deep breath. "I believed her to be dead for many years. Until I saw her."

"You…know Circe?"

"Yes," Max said as his jaw tensed. "She was my wife."

The stunned expression on Alex's face was mirrored on Elliot's.

Max turned his eyes away from Alex and Valeria. "It was long ago, and completely unimportant in this discussion." Pain pierced the cover of his gruff exterior and then morphed into a mask of mild interest—as if he were discussing a book he had read. "I can tell you that she was obsessed with immortality and would have willingly sold her soul to the devil in exchange for it. I know that she sought out Myrdd—believing that he could assist her in that purpose. I saw her many years later. By then, Envy's bite had taken its toll on her."

"I don't recall Myrdd ever mentioning Circe," Alex said.

"'Circe' was the name that Hecate had given her. Her birth name was Vivianna."

Alex's eyes widened. "Vivianna! Myrdd warned me of her repeatedly. But to my knowledge, I've never met her."

"Perhaps Myrdd meant that you would find her sometime in the future," Valeria wondered aloud.

"Zeus only gave her 1,000 years," Max said.

Brushing his hand along his jaw, Alex looked absorbed in thought and then asked, "Max, did Circe ever mention an immortal by the name of Kristiana?"

"No. I've never heard of a Kristiana. Of course, with that name, she would have come after the birth of Christianity."

"I knew her long before that," Alex said. "Do you know what became of Circe?"

Max shrugged. "The only thing I know of her, is that Circe was rumored to have been named the Sibyl of Cumae—I understand they now call the town Cuma. Other than that, all evidence of her existence was gone long before my last and only meeting with the Council."

Valeria narrowed her eyes. "Is that the sibyl who…" She turned toward Alex. "There was a story about her. What was it?"

Alex squeezed her hand. "There are several. Evidently she led Virgil's Aeneas on a tour of the underworld—"

"That sounds a bit more gracious than the Circe I knew. Perhaps it was more of a fantasy on Virgil's part. Though, Circe might have done it—if the reward was large enough," Max said.

"She also authored several books that were called *The Sibylline Books*," Alex added. "She took them to the king and offered him her written prophesies of Rome for a fortune. When the king refused, she burned the first volume and demanded the same price for the remaining books. He turned her down again and she burned another. Finally, the king paid. The books disappeared long ago. Although three different religions claim to possess them."

"Now that sounds more like the girl I knew," Max said. "Because of her access to the underworld, she would have also had continued access to Hecate. Circe may have been able to enlist the aid of the Fates or Hecate in causing an accident a few thousand years ago. But not today, as I am equally certain that neither the Fates nor Hecate would have gifted Circe with immortality."

"Could Circe or Hecate have taught others about the evil eye?"

"Hecate only taught Circe...and Circe was not one to share! If she had power, the last thing she would desire is for anyone else to possess it. Speaking of power, she did have an uncanny ability to find sources of power."

Max pressed his lips together and then narrowed his eyes in thought. "The last time I saw Myrdd, he was rambling with insanity, but there was something that he said that seemed to make sense. He said that I needed to use caution because 'she' could find the real power in any endeavor and use it to her advantage."

Stopping, Max glanced at Valeria, whose eyes were at half-mast. "I believe I have overstayed my welcome," he said.

"Not at all!" Valeria insisted.

Smiling at her, Alex said, "Beautiful, you've got about three minutes left until you're out."

"I look forward to seeing you later!" Max said and left with Elliot.

Once they were gone, Alex turned to Valeria and said, "I've been thinking about what Max said, and there is something odd about

Hecate's gift to Circe. The kris that was given to Circe is now known to be a weapon of the South Pacific."

"Yes? So, why is that important?"

"That is where Jeremiah resides."

CHAPTER 18

That night, Valeria could hear a considerable amount going on outside. After putting on a touch of makeup, Alex picked her up and carried her outdoors to a lounge chair where Valeria successfully pulled off being surprised.

The trees were strung with twinkling lights and there was a bonfire nearby. On the grass were tables and chairs for nearly thirty people. It was considerably cooler than the previous year, so heaters were set up by each of the tables and Valeria's lounge chair. Caleb brought out a blanket for her and handed it to Alex.

Ava and Camille brought Valeria a glass of liquid and Valeria raised her hand. "I can't have any champagne," she pouted.

Camille nodded. "We knew that—well, I knew that. So I brought you a sparkling cider instead."

The Three Musketeers toasted to another great year. As Valeria took in the crowd and the festivities, she noticed someone and tapped Alex.

"Who is that girl over there?"

"Who?" he asked, looking around. Then he spotted the young beauty dreamily sitting on a log alone. "Oh, that's Olivia."

The girl was perhaps seventeen with oracle blue eyes, perfectly pink pouty lips placed on her creamy complexion, and nearly white hair. Like the others, she wore a blanket as a poncho and a leather belt was wrapped twice around her waist. Even in that, she was stunning.

"I have something for her," Valeria said. Alex walked the short distance and tapped Olivia on the shoulder. She seemed shocked to be approached, but then she smiled sweetly and walked over to Valeria as Alex requested.

"Hello, Olivia, I'm—"

"Yes, yes, I know who you are. You are the Princess Cassandra." Her voice was as soft and sweet as Valeria had expected of such a delicate creature.

"I was Cassandra, but now I'm called Valeria."

"Oh," she said, as her eyebrows shot down in confusion.

"Olivia, I have a letter of introduction for you from—"

"A letter for me?" Olivia interrupted.

"Yes, it's from Elliot," Valeria said, as the girl's blush deepened. "The boy—"

"I know who he is," she said as her blush deepened. Valeria handed the letter to her and Olivia grasped it hungrily; without another word, she left to sit on the edge of the porch as she devoured every word.

After a few minutes, when it was clear that Olivia had read it at least a few times over, Valeria said, "Olivia, we can talk if you would like."

The girl sprang from her seat and threw her arms around Valeria, who suppressed a groan, as she was still quite tender after the crash. Then just as suddenly, Olivia returned to her seat on the edge of the porch and read the letter again.

Valeria felt Alex's smile as he pulled a chair up next to hers. "Young love," he said with a snicker.

"I would like to say a few words," Lars said as he stepped toward Alex and Valeria.

"Please," Alex replied.

Picking up a knife from the tray of a passing waiter, Lars clinked it against his champagne glass to silence the crowd. Then he said, "Welcome to the second annual celebration of Valeria's birthday! We've made a tradition of recognizing our Greek heritage and so, with that in mind, 'Opa' is a Greek statement for a celebration of life," he said. "It is an affirmation that all that really matters is health, family, and friends. It means," he glanced across all of the new faces, "that you are exactly where you are supposed to be. You are home! Alex has invited each and every one of you to make Morgana your home if you so desire!"

Alex leaned down and whispered into Valeria's ear, "I hope that was all right with you."

A tear escaped her eye. *"All right?* You have no idea the gift that you've given all of these people! I adore you!" She squeezed his hand. Morgana was home now and always would be.

Trays of food and drink started arriving by uniformed waiters coming from a trailer that was set up along the road to Mani's house. Another round of "Opa!" passed through the group.

Valeria sat watching the festivities and Alex said, "I'm going to chat with Doc for a minute. Is it all right if I leave you here?"

"Of course! I'm with family!"

Within a few minutes, Max approached.

"Hello, Max!" Valeria said.

"Good evening, Mistress Morgan!"

"Please, call me Val," she said.

"Val. That is a beautiful name," he said as he sat down next to her. "Forgive my ignorance. I've been absorbing the changes in language and customs. I'm not certain that casual communication is an asset. There is something to be said for a well-composed sentence and thought before speech. Still, I am enjoying the learning adventure."

"I agree! Still, it seems you are picking up the customs and language quite well," she said with a smile.

Max shrugged. "I have always had a way with language and hanging with the kid has been helpful."

Valeria raised her brows. "Caleb?"

"Yeah." Max smiled. "See, I am catching on! Incidentally, please tell your husband I said thank you. Evidently, he's established funds for all of us. Some ridiculous amount that I'm certain, with practice, I will be able to squander in a lifetime." Then his gruff mask reappeared as he saw Elliot approaching Olivia. "Oh, for the love of God! That man and his romance will drive me to drinking!"

Valeria watched Max for a moment and then raised a brow.

"What is it?" he asked.

"Sometimes it seems as if you despise Elliot, but I have an inkling that there is another emotion at play," she said.

"He's an imbecile!" Max said in defense. "He falls in love at the drop of a hat. He has these ideas about impropriety that drive me mad."

"But…" she said.

Max lowered his eyebrows and shook his head as if that was all there was to say. Valeria waited and finally Max sighed, and said, "But, I love him like a brother."

Valeria raised her eyebrow and the corners of her mouth turned up.

"I had some…issues. I guess that's what you call them now. Issues. And Elliot was there for me."

"Can I…can I intrude on your privacy to ask what kind of issues?" Valeria said, feeling quite self-conscious. As much as she respected other's privacy, for some reason, she felt compelled to ask.

"Love," Max said with a sardonically musical lilt. He shook his head as if he couldn't believe that he had been affected by Cupid's arrow. "Love…love left me sad and depressed and crying like a baby. It left me drinking too much, far too often, in an attempt to erase my unholy turn with immortality."

"Circe?"

The line on Max's mouth widened in a grimace. "Christ, that woman ruined me for life."

"What happened, Max?"

"Come now. I'm certain you have better things to do at your birthday celebration than to listen to my pitiful story."

Valeria tilted her head to let him know she was interested. Max rolled his eyes again and dropped his head as he pushed his fingers through his hair.

"Don't say I didn't warn you," he said with a side-glance. "I met her during the War of the Titans while she was Hecate's priestess and I couldn't take my eyes off her. Oh, I had my fair share of women…" Suddenly, Max realized that was a fairly indelicate matter to be discussing with a woman. He turned to study her reaction and saw that she didn't seem offended in the least. "Forgive me."

"It's all right, Max. Go on."

"I met with her on several occasions. Eventually, I found myself completely obsessed with her. I even asked her if she had cast a spell on me—to which she sobbed for hours and refused to see me for days. Women!" he said with a huff. "Finally, I begged her to marry me and she agreed. As a gift of our union, she wanted me to grant her immortality. When I told her that I would give her the world but that I did not have that gift to give her, she asked me to take her to Apollo so that we could be together forever.

"Finally, Zeus awarded her 1,000 years of life. I thought that would make her happy and we would be able to settle down. And for a while, she was satisfied. It was I who suddenly became obsessed with her immortality. As hundreds of years went by as if they were nothing, I began to feel terrified at the thought of losing her. I made the unforgivable error of accusing her of bewitching me."

Max looked down as if stricken with the repercussions, and when he spoke again, it was with great sadness. "She refused to ever see me again."

"You never saw her again?" Valeria asked, placing her hand on his arm. Max continued to stare at the ground.

"Years later, I heard that she had gone to Myrdd to seek his assistance in the matter. Myrdd admitted that a woman had gone to see him and that he had first given her visions of the future. My guess is that she used those visions to convince Aegemon that she was a sibyl. It was then that I realized that she had bewitched Myrdd with her herbs. Then, in order to destroy the evidence, she drugged him further.

"Several centuries later I was travelling in what is now Southern Italy. I stopped for the night and awoke to the feeling that I was being watched. When I opened my eyes, I saw her outline in the starlight. She was kneeling beside me in the darkness. I believed her to be visiting me from the underworld and I begged her to take me with her." Tears formed in his eyes and he swallowed them back. "That night I dreamed that we..." he sighed heavily as he picked up a stick and tossed it into the brush. When he spoke again, his voice was cold and indifferent. "In the morning she was gone and I was even more certain it was only a dream. Still, her sweet smell lingered on my bed."

"Four years later, I was drunk—as I was most of the time. She again came from the underworld into my dreams. This time, she was not so welcoming. I asked her how it was that she was permitted to leave the underworld and she blamed me for her plight. She said that she had decided to give me one last chance...because of our child."

"You had a child?" Valeria asked.

"According to...the apparition. As I said, I believe it to be only a dream. She went down the trail and returned a moment later with a beautiful dark-haired boy. I kept my distance, knowing that it was not possible for the child to be mine. Circe demanded that I take both her and the boy to the River Styx so that we could all be together forever. Perhaps it was all a dream, but it felt very real. I told her that I could not violate Apollo's sacred trust by bringing a mortal to Delos.

"She asked me if I truly wanted her to be gone. I was desperate, but I told her that there was nothing that I could do. I pleaded with her to take me with her to the underworld where we could stay together forever. Then she told me that, although it had taken many years, she now loved someone else."

He sighed heavily. "I made several attempts to end my sorry existence. Elliot decided that he was my nursemaid and nursed me back to health many times. Despite being an idiot...he's a good lad."

"And he loves you, too." Valeria said.

"Yeah—the imbecile should have better sense than to hook up with a cynic like me," he said.

Valeria smiled softly. "I think he has excellent taste in friends...and so do I."

Just then, Alex returned and slid onto a bench near Valeria. "Flirting with my wife again, Max?" he teased.

"Only mildly, but given the appropriate opportunity, you do know that I am completely without scruples," Max said with a smile.

Lowering an eyebrow Alex said, "Max, remember that I do know you."

Max shook his head. "Obviously you have manufactured evidence to the contrary. However, your dear wife has heard my tale of woe and can confirm my selfish nature."

"While I'm certain that you treasure your reputation as a rogue and a scoundrel, I do know the truth," Alex said as the corner of his mouth turned up. "Val, did Max tell you why he was executed?"

Taking Alex's hand in hers Valeria said, "I thought Max also signed the petition."

Max scoffed. "I have absolutely no interest in a council of immortals."

"Is that why you swore to Jeremiah that you were the one who had drafted the petition?" Alex teased.

Max huffed and rolled his eyes. "Elliot is the walking-talking poster child of naivety. He believes the best in everyone—including me. Damn fool! However, I assure you that my response was due to a brief moment of idiocy—of which I have been known for."

"Max insisted that Elliot had only signed the petition at his demand. As a result, Max was executed first," Alex said.

Max shrugged. "The boy hasn't even bedded a woman."

"You're a good man, Max," Valeria said with a smile.

Smiling kindly, Max said, "It has been my pleasure dominating your time. But I had better resume my role as chaperone or Elliot may find himself engaged to a woman with whom he has never even kissed! I've advised him to bed them and then you may never need to marry them."

"Spoken as a man with experience," Alex said with amusement.

"Yes, and it has been far too long." He pointed toward Ava. "So, is that one spoken for?" Max said eyeing Ava as she laughed in conversation with Tavish.

"Definitely," Alex said.

Max's eyes roamed and his eyes enlarged staring toward Camille. "That one?"

"Probably," Alex said.

"It would appear that I am cursed this evening to be only a chaperone." Max rambled over to Elliot and Olivia who were facing away from each other. He slipped into the seat between them and rolled his eyes.

As the clock ticked toward midnight without incident, Alex's mood soared. While they ate dinner, one waiter occasionally breathed out fire, causing the familiar "Opa!" shout. Then the dancing began.

Tavish danced while balancing one leg of a chair on his forehead. Two of the revived oracles formed a human pyramid and did amazing flips and jumps. Ava actually managed to balance the leg of a chair on her forehead for a number of seconds before it fell toward Max's plate. Of course, she caught it just seconds before it hit. Tavish gave her an approving nod as everyone applauded.

Ava laughed as she pointed to Tavish. "I told you I've been practicing!"

The crowd responded with, "Opa!" Glasses and a few bottles were clinked. Alex's eyes filled with joy as he began to speak to the crowd. "My father used to say that having been fed and quenched our thirst, and having enjoyed friendship and love, that we are filled with hope and confidence; that life abounds with all that we need and all we can say is…" Alex lifted an arm encouraging the oracles to answer.

"Opa!" the crowd responded.

"Well done!" Alex said with a laugh. "A year ago, I had the extraordinary good fortune to celebrate my wife's birthday here with our family. Tonight we celebrate not just the return of so many good friends, and not only my wife's twenty-eighth birthday…" A tear came to Alex's eyes. "Tonight, we also celebrate something that is as thrilling as it is a bit terrifying to me." Alex grimaced and several people chuckled. "In several months, I will become a father!"

Grabbing a plate from a passing waiter, Alex continued, "We break plates as a declaration of the hope that tomorrow there will be more." He squeezed Valeria's hand and kissed her hair. "Though this past year has been an extraordinary gift to me—I dare to dream of more! I dare to dream of a life lived here at Morgana with my beloved and," Alex sucked in a breath and then said in nearly a whisper, "our child."

He smiled with joy and threw the plate to the edge of the fireplace where it shattered to another round of, "Opa!"

Lars picked up his mandolin, while Tavish grabbed his fiddle. Various oracles joined in adding their voices or instruments to the mix until the music held a vivid richness that could be seen and heard and felt by all.

A team of waiters brought out trays of flaming deserts, followed by another round of, "Opa!"

Alex kissed Valeria as his eyes shimmered with candlelight. "I hope you are enjoying yourself," he said. She nodded, unable to speak of the joy she felt.

A few tables over, Olivia and Elliot sat blushing, still facing away from each other with a reluctant Max serving as a chaperone between them. Max looked disgusted and bored. Just then, Ava and Camille walked over arm in arm and sat on the bench next to Valeria.

"Hey, remember last year when Valeria thought we were fixing her up with Tavish?" Ava teased.

Alex's head rolled back as he released his beautiful, musical laughter that made Valeria certain that it must be near midnight, when Alex could finally be free from the dark fears of the curse.

"Please don't tell Tav! I don't need him getting any more ideas about my wife!" Alex quipped as Valeria pulled his face around and moved her lips to his.

When she glanced back, Ava had placed a stack of wrapped gifts next to her on the table. "You shouldn't have gotten me any presents!" Valeria said, and blushed.

"Oh, there are a lot more than this! This stack is from the family," Camille said. "Frankly, you don't have the ability or desire to shop and you are going to need a lot of things." Camille glanced at Valeria's belly and then at Ava. "Looks like we should have picked up some maternity clothes."

The first package contained a framed picture of Valeria, Ava, and Camille on her wedding day. Valeria's hair was in large rollers and they had their arms around each other in a beautiful and very cheesy shot—the Three Musketeers! She loved it.

"The rest are your wedding pictures. We couldn't replace the pictures that were destroyed in the fire, but we thought this might help make up for them," Camille said.

The next was a picture of Valeria in her wedding gown, hugging Tavish wearing his kilt. The soft look in his eyes touched her. Then there was a picture of Caleb nervously making the toast. The next was Lars pronouncing them husband and wife with Camille and Caleb standing on either side. She brushed her finger lovingly near the picture of Alex and choked. It was the beautiful expression of love in his eyes that would always be in her heart.

There was a picture of Weege and Kenny dancing, and a portrait of all of the guests surrounding Alex and Valeria taken from one of the bedrooms upstairs.

"We saved the best for last," Camille said as Valeria stared at a close-up of the bride and groom staring dreamily into each other's eyes.

"These are…just beautiful!" Valeria sobbed. She would have sobbed even without the hormones, but with them, all she could do was blubber. Alex kissed her neck.

The music started slowly with a mandolin and guitar. Alex rolled up his sleeves as he smiled seductively at her.

"Do you recall our first dance?"

"How could I forget?" she said. It had been the night that she realized she belonged here at Morgana—with her family and with Alex. It was the night he had proposed to her and presented her with the ring that he had created for her eons before.

"I believe that I am going to have to dance," he said. That made Valeria sob more. *Her Alex was so joyful that he needed to dance!*

Dancer's surrounded Valeria and began to step slowly to *Zorba the Greek's* sirtaki dance. As the musical energy built, over each round of the music more and more of the revived oracles joined in and the mood went from quiet conservatism and thoughtfulness about all of the years lost, to a spontaneous burst of enthusiasm.

Elliot found himself so euphoric that, without considering his actions, he sprung to his feet and dragged a shocked and elated Olivia to the festivities. Max rolled his eyes, but within minutes, he succumbed to the music and joined the rest. Valeria clapped and laughed.

As the music ended, Alex moved toward her with a glow of absolute pleasure, and everything but her husband became background noise and lights as the waiters and guests began to throw plates at the stones by the bonfire, yelling, "Opa!"

Alex lifted her from her seat and sat down on the bench with her in his lap. Taking her face in his hands, he kissed her with so much passion that her arms wound around him tightly, wishing he could carry her off somewhere more private. When they pulled apart, he stared at her for a moment—reminding her of the beautiful close-up picture of the two of them at their wedding.

"This past year has been the happiest, the most joyous time in all of my existence and it is because of you!" Alex said with such an exuberance that she immediately knew it was past midnight.

"It's been the best year of my life, too—and the best of every lifetime I can recall," Valeria choked. Her eyes widened and she smiled. "I want you to feel something."

She took his hand and moved it to her belly. He immediately became concerned.

"Is something wrong?"

"No. Shhhhh," she said, in an effort to calm him. Then she closed her eyes, concentrating. She felt the thump from the inside her belly and smiled. Alex knitted his brows in concern.

"What was that?"

"That was our daughter saying hello."

Alex's eyes lit with wonder as he wrapped his other arm around her and placed it on her belly. Suddenly he jumped. "She did it again!"

Valeria laughed softly. "Yes, she wanted to be very certain that her father heard her."

"Father! *I'm going to be a father!*" he said, as if he had just realized it. His eyes filled with tears of joy and he tried to swallow them back. She leaned her head against his chest and he stroked her hair.

After a few minutes, he said softly, "Doc says I need to take you back to bed."

"Good idea," she said and then craned her neck searching for Mani. She finally saw him alone under a tree looking off into the distance. "Where is Melitta?"

"I guess he's just not ready yet," Alex said cryptically.

"Alex what does that mean? Is she here?"

"Let's enjoy tonight." He shook off the darkness cast by the story of Melitta and smiled again. "We'll talk about that tomorrow."

"Okay."

"This isn't a story I would like to share with you tonight."

CHAPTER 19

The next few days, Doc insisted that Valeria stay in bed. However, she needed no insistence; she was exhausted from her minor travels but also exhilarated from the party and the pictures. They had given her a photo album. Most of the people she had known all of her life had photo albums, but until the past year, there had never been anyone she cared about enough to have pictures of. Now, she had a family…and a daughter who might wish to see how things were before she was born. That was one of the things Valeria had always been curious about. Had her mother been as joyously happy as Valeria was now? Somehow, she could never see her father loving anything as much as his beer.

Most everyone in the family was busy—including Alex. Now that Valeria had survived her birthday, he was helping out with the numerous tasks required so that the twenty new oracles could reestablish their lives.

It was a beautiful fall morning. Alex had been gone for hours. But now he returned, stoked the fire in the fireplace and opened the windows. The air was moist as if it had rained overnight. Just like at Camelot—it rained at night and the sky was its deepest blue by morning. Late fall never seemed as dismal here at Morgana.

"Max and I have decided to take matters into our own hands. Doc has kept himself busy, but I haven't seen him interested in reviving Melitta. Sometimes, I wonder if Myrdd's presence makes it more difficult for Doc."

"Why isn't Shinsu here?" Valeria asked. Then, placing her hand on Alex's, she said, "And tell me what happened with Melitta."

Alex sat down on the edge of her bed and a dark shadow fell across his face.

"Shinsu would be here. But these are dangerous times for all of us. Shinsu is intimately trusted in the council and by Jeremiah. She left with him to his island home after we resurrected the remains so that she could keep an eye on him."

Valeria shuddered. "She has paid a price! I will never understand how Shinsu could have ever married Jeremiah!"

"When Shinsu was brought back from the Elysian Fields, Myrdd refused to see her."

"Why? She was the love of his life, and he refused to see her?"

"Myrdd had been involved with a woman of ill-repute—perhaps this Vivianna. I believe that he was too ashamed to see Shinsu.

"Those days, I didn't attend council meetings. I was too absorbed in my art and searching for you. Still, I remember the horror when Doc and Lita returned to report that Myrdd had been executed." He shook his head in regret. "I should have been there with all of them."

Grabbing his hand, Valeria kissed it. "I am so grateful that you weren't executed! But I still don't understand why Lita isn't back with us."

"Before Jeremiah, the council was very democratic. What happened with Myrdd was a shock, but we couldn't help but believe that it was a one-time incident and that Myrdd had broken the rules of the immortals—though we still don't know the details of the crime. We heard that Jeremiah had 'proof' that Myrdd had violated the sanctity of Delos by bringing a mortal to the premises. Myrdd did not defend himself and was executed on the spot.

"At the next council meeting, Doc was in the Azores when Melitta presented the petition to remove Jeremiah. No one ever imagined..." Alex shook his head and drew a deep breath. "When they executed Lita, Maxi, and Elliot, it was a wake-up call for all of us.

"Doc was inconsolable when he returned from the Azores. Then he received Jeremiah's warning."

"His warning?" Valeria asked feeling the growing sense of horror. Alex nodded, his eyes growing wide as he remembered.

"Her head."

Valeria felt the wind sucked out of her lungs. Finally, she gulped and said, "Are her remains in the grave?"

Alex nodded.

"Well then, we'll have to take charge of this and dig them up." Valeria sat up and started to get out of bed. Alex took her shoulders in his hands and pressed her back down.

"No, love! You are staying here. Max and I have already planned to dig up her remains tonight as soon as Doc is distracted with patients. We thought we would try to revive her and if she doesn't...well, then we know." He sucked a deep breath. "We aren't sure how all of this works. We're just grateful that, so far, it has worked."

That night, Ava kept Valeria company. Lars was with Mani, while Alex, Elliot, and Max went to Lita's gravesite. Early the next morning, Valeria awoke in the bed alone. There was a hint of frost around the edges of the window and there was a fire roaring in the fireplace. When she glanced at the rocking chair, she was stunned to see Olivia sleeping, with a book in her lap. Instead of the blanket and belt from before, she wore a pretty pink turtleneck and long skirt. Olivia slept for a few more minutes, and then stirred and opened her eyes.

The girl jumped up and then offered an apologetic glance for having fallen asleep on the job. Valeria smiled and that seemed to calm Olivia.

"Olivia, did they find Melitta?" Valeria asked.

"Yes! Elliot said that he and Alex decided to take her to the other house so that they could surprise both Lita and Mani later. I thought that was very sweet," she said demurely, as her eyes fluttered and her cheeks turned pink. "Don't you think that was very sweet of Elliot— well, and Alex— to think of that?"

"Yes, they are pretty...sweet guys," Valeria said with a snicker. "Where's Camille?"

"Oh, she said she wanted to pick up a few things for Lita's homecoming." Olivia smiled, revealing her soft dimples.

"And how are things with Elliot?"

"Oh...good," she said with a blush.

Valeria tried to sit up and realized that she was larger today than just a few days before. She lay back down and then thoughts started coming together in her head.

"Olivia, I need a computer or a notepad."

"A computer?" Olivia asked puzzled.

"A notepad would be fine. There is one on Mani's desk."

A few minutes later, Olivia returned with a notepad.

"What do you do with that?" she asked.

"You write on it," Valeria said. She looked on the bedside table next to her and found a pen. She began writing names: Myrdd and Shinsu, Cassandra and Alex, Camille and Jonah, Ava and Lars, Tavish and…

She pursed her lips in thought, and then placed a question mark next to Tavish's name. She continued writing: Max, Elliot and Olivia. She continued writing until Alex arrived and slid onto the bed next to her—a sight which caused Olivia to blush a deep scarlet and look away as if she had witnessed an impropriety.

"Sorry, Olivia, but we do have a license," Alex said with a wink as he kissed his wife.

"A license for what?" Olivia asked.

He shook his head as if to say never mind. He shifted his attention to Valeria. "I hope you don't mind. You were sleeping and Melitta needed something to wear—"

"Of course, I don't mind!" Valeria felt a thrill. "She's alive? Oh, Alex!" She hugged him tightly. "Camille should pick up something new for her to wear—she would know what would look nice on her. But of course, she is welcome to whatever I have! We need to move out of here, too! Can I meet her?" She sat up and moved her leg.

"Whoa!" Alex said with a quick laugh, as he tossed an apple a few inches up and then caught it. "Oh! You'll be glad to know you can be a bit more mobile—Mani cleared you for crutches, as long as you don't overdo it. It seems you're healing well."

"Can I get up now?

He laughed. "Doc said occasionally!" Then he took a bite of his apple. "In the next few days, I'd like to take you out to meet Myrdd. We can't seem to coax him out of the woods and I suspect another familiar face might help." Alex narrowed his eyes and glanced at the notepad she was writing on. "What is this?"

She bit her lip and shrugged. "I was thinking about oracles and all of a sudden all of these names came to mind. I don't really know if they're even accurate."

Surveying the list, Alex began reading aloud, "Nicola, Anthony, Matthew, Dismas, Avaya," Alex said as he glanced up at her and lowered a brow. "Val, I don't remember telling you these names. I don't even know most of these names."

"Whose names?"

"These are the names of all of the oracles—at least I imagine this is all of the oracles."

Valeria shook her head, "It can't be. There's only ninety-nine of them. Not one hundred."

Alex's face lit up in surprise. "Who gave these names to you?"

"No one...oh, well, someone must have." Changing the subject, she ran a finger down Alex's chest and said, "You know, since we're going to give Lita and Mani back their home, and ours isn't ready yet, I wouldn't mind going back to St. John for a while."

He grabbed her finger and kissed it. "I wouldn't get your hopes up for that! Even if I agreed—and I don't—there is a large family of oracles who would bar the road out of here," Alex said. "Not until after this child is born and both of you are safe." Then he took another bite of his apple and stared at her for a few minutes and said, "Would you like to meet Lita? Because she would very much like to see you."

Valeria sprang up in bed as her eyes widened. "Well, what are we waiting for?"

∞

At the main house, in the room where Valeria had initially recovered from the car accident, Lita sat on the edge of the bed with her ankles neatly crossed. She rose rapidly when Valeria came in on her crutches—as if royalty had just entered. Lita smoothed the sides of her teal cotton dress that was significantly less feminine than Olivia's. But Lita's femininity needed no adornment. She had long, thick gray hair that sat below her shoulders. Her skin was darker than most, as if she had been in the sun. Her features were small and delicate but there was a strength in her eyes that defied the fragility of her appearance. Valeria remembered the angelic face over the tomb that Alex had carved, and realized that he had perfectly captured her essence.

"Please pardon me for requesting your presence! I was so anxious to see you again," Lita said in a voice that had a rich musical quality. Noticing Valeria staring at her, she fidgeted nervously and then glanced down at her dress and shoes and bit her lip.

"Will he like this?" Then she rolled her eyes, irritated with herself for being so silly. Valeria was still staring at her. Lita continued, "I don't know why I'm so nervous. I guess it's been such a long time, I wonder if he still..." She smiled apologetically.

"He never stopped," Valeria said softly. Lita let out a shaky breath, obviously relieved. Then she smiled as if a light switch had just been flipped on inside of her.

"I understand that they call you Valeria now. I so wished to meet you officially—I mean, this time." Lita swallowed. "We've known each other so long that it feels a bit strange to...of course, I don't expect you to—"

Suddenly overwhelmed with emotion, Valeria recalled the beautiful soul and embraced her as the sobs form. "I've missed you, my dear friend," were the words that sprang from Valeria's mouth before she could even evaluate them.

∞

The sun was setting when Valeria worked her way on the crutches toward Mani. He sat on a log by a bonfire with his fingers woven together. He was uncharacteristically unshaven and his clothes were a bit rumpled. He gave Valeria a weary smile. Then he suddenly looked with surprise at Valeria's belly.

"The child is growing!"

"Yes, she is. Doc, we've decided that you are taking a night off." Mani shrugged but Valeria persisted, "You need to shower and shave." Mani brushed his hand over his light stubble.

"Perhaps."

When he came out of the shower, Alex had left him a blue cotton shirt and tan slacks. Valeria handed him his razor and shaving cream. Mani seemed to be only following her instructions because he was too exhausted to argue.

Once he was finished shaving, Valeria said, "Mani, can you walk me back to your place?"

"Of course," he said. It was obvious he was lost in thought. She smiled, realizing that Mani hadn't asked her all of the questions she expected about why she was out alone or how long she had been on her crutches.

As they approached the house, Mani narrowed his eyes as if he felt a change but couldn't identify it. There were now flowers in the window and the shadows of flames from the fireplace. He turned toward Valeria wondering why she had stopped some distance from the door. The door opened and Alex stepped out, leaving it open as he walked toward Valeria.

"What is going on?" Mani asked as he glanced at Alex, who gestured toward the door. Mani turned back slowly as his breathing increased. Then, for the first time, Valeria saw something in his eyes other than the world-weariness he wore like a saddle bag. She saw hope.

Melitta stepped into the doorway and all Mani could do was stare, trying to focus his eyes on the shadow that looked like...

"Mani!" Came Melitta's desperate cry. Before he even registered her voice, his long legs had taken the steps, and the woman in the doorway was in his arms for the first time in centuries; and the man who never cried let out a joyful sob.

CHAPTER 20

"Myrdd isn't himself. I was hoping that seeing you would help," Alex said as he pushed Valeria in the wheelchair down the wooded trail.

They wove their way through the forest and came to a mass of vines and pine boughs that looked like some place a wild animal might inhabit. Alex stopped and called out, "Myrdd?" Valeria saw a sudden movement, like that of a frightened animal. "Myrdd, I'm going to bring Cassandra to see you. You remember Cassandra!" Alex spoke gently. He lifted Valeria from the wheelchair and moved to the front of the shelter, setting her on the ground. Alex sat protectively next to her, ready to move Valeria in an instant if necessary.

From the back of the shelter, she saw a flash of white, but her eyes had not yet adjusted.

"Don't be frightened," Alex said to her. Then he looked back at the shelter. "Myrdd? Can you come out? See, it's Cassandra." Valeria saw movement and, after more encouragement, saw an old man with a long, dirty white beard and flowing hair. He checked her out as if suspicious, and then calmed and curled into a ball near her.

"Myrdd? Do you remember me?" she said as she smiled softly. Myrdd didn't move. She glanced at Alex. "I'm going to try something."

Moving her body into as close of a ball as she could—considering her broken leg that was outstretched and her growing belly—she tried to mimic Myrdd's position. She sat there for nearly ten minutes. Then, Myrdd moved his head back and Valeria did the same. Myrdd looked at her suspiciously. She imitated his look. Myrdd looked up at her and leaned toward her. Valeria did the same. Finally, Myrdd seemed to relax a bit.

Valeria looked at Myrdd. "Can you do this?" She moved her hand in front of her, as if waving hello. Myrdd looked suspiciously at her and then duplicated her action. "Good!" she said.

"Can you do this?" She held up her hand and moved it in an arc and then turned it over. Myrdd thought for a moment and then duplicated the action quickly but without the grace that Valeria had demonstrated. Alex watched in astonishment. "Good."

Valeria sat for an hour and now had Myrdd duplicating her actions almost as well as she did them. She placed her hand on his and said, "Myrdd, now I want you to say what I say: hello."

Narrowing his eyes at her for a moment, he suddenly turned his head as if clearing the cobwebs. When he looked back at her, his eyes had cleared. He shook his head again and then smiled, his teeth covered in a dark film, and muttered, "Hello." Myrdd seemed surprised to hear his own voice. "Hello, Cassandra." He cleared his throat. "It has been some time."

Valeria laughed softly. "Yes it has, Myrdd. Do you remember Alex?"

Myrdd looked at Alex and pulled back his head. "Has it been this long?" Then Myrdd dropped his head and shook it. "It must be longer than it..." He looked up at Alex and then back at Valeria. "Alexander has found you...then it has been a very long time."

Alex smiled and spoke gently. "Yes, and we're married now. It's very good to see you again, Myrdd."

Myrdd reached toward Valeria and she noticed Alex lean forward as a defensive move, but he restrained himself from stopping Myrdd's actions. Valeria squeezed Alex's hand. Myrdd pointed to Valeria's stomach. "Are you…"

"Alex and I are having a baby."

"She is a good baby," Myrdd said, causing Alex and Valeria to exchange a curious glance.

"Myrdd, you need to clean up and get some food. And if you would like to, we would like for you to stay at the main house...I mean our home."

"I don't care to stay inside...too drafty. I prefer outside."

"Well, let's start with the food and shower and we can talk from there," Valeria said.

Myrdd came out of the shelter. Alex picked up Valeria and, suddenly, Myrdd noticed that she was wearing pants. "You dress like a man now?" he asked Valeria.

Valeria and Alex laughed. "Yes. Yes, I guess I do."

As Myrdd showered, Alex asked Valeria, "How did you know imitating Myrdd would help him?"

Valeria shrugged. "It's not like I figured out brain surgery. It was just...simple observation. I stayed in a foster home and the grandmother lived there and suffered from dementia. I noticed that when the other kids imitated her she seemed to do better. I guess I kind of thought that it was a way out of her fog. Eventually, she would actually talk to me."

Alex raised an eyebrow. "Hmm—that doesn't sound so simple to me!" Valeria smiled and leaned against Alex.

CHAPTER 21

By Christmas Eve, Valeria was finally walking. They had stayed at the main house for far too long with everyone watching her as if she had the fragility of a robin's egg...well, all except for Lita. With her gentle spirit and enthusiastic heart, Lita was a slave-driver and took charge of Valeria's physical therapy.

Valeria was now walking nearly five miles a day along the snow-covered back trails of Morgana with Lita and a guard. As packages arrived for the family, and were gathered under the tree at the main house, Valeria couldn't help but think how very different and thrilling the next year would be. She hoped that all was resolved and that they could live their lives as an ordinary family.

It was late afternoon and already, the sun was beginning to set. Valeria could smell the cinnamon, cloves and apple cider heating on the stove. It was typically spiced with rum, but this year, for Valeria, they made a virgin batch and the others added their own rum. Although Tavish kept a bottle of rum and added a bit of spiced cider to his.

Alex arrived with a sparkle in his eye and wrapped his arms around her. "Would you like to get some of your Christmas presents now?"

She nodded excitedly and he grabbed her coat. She zipped her down vest and pulled on her hat and boots as they walked down the trail. She hadn't been near the cottage since the night she had been carried to Mani's. As they got closer, she could see that the cottage had been rebuilt and a thrill ran through her.

"We'll replant the hydrangea next spring," he said as they rounded the side of the house. From the front it looked almost exactly the same as it did before the fire. She turned her head to look at the roof-line. It had always been beautiful, but now it seemed much higher and with two wide dormer windows.

"I added a room upstairs. I hope that's all right. Lita suggested we might want an extra room." Alex said. Valeria smiled as she hurried up the three steps and admired the wide porch she had always loved. It looked just the same and ran along the entire front of the house, with several sitting areas and an assortment of rattan furniture, including a porch swing. Even the river stone beams looked the same. She had always loved the mix of stone, gray-blue siding and white trim.

"Ready?" he asked as he held the wrought-iron door handle of the arched double doors. She nodded.

As the door swung open, Valeria's heart overflowed! It was their beautiful cottage but, somehow, it was even better. She looked to the right and there were a hundred classics—including a complete collection of the Bronte sisters and Jane Austin—all leather-bound with a red ribbon over them.

"That was one of your surprises," Alex said as he pulled the ribbon off. She scanned the titles, unable to move on until she had taken in the whole of the beautiful gift of books. There was *Moby Dick, The Scarlet Letter, The Count of Monte Cristo* and a complete set of Charles Dickens. She stared in awe and then she saw *Walden* right next to *Sense and Sensibility*—their two favorite books. She brushed her fingers over all of them and then turned and embraced her husband.

"Oh, thank you!" She swallowed back her tears.

Then she took a few steps and noticed that something was very different—there was a door on the bedroom.

"I thought that might be more appropriate," Alex said, and she smiled. In their bedroom, everything looked the same—except now, there was a rocking chair next to the bed. Again, her heart was filled with warmth and she swallowed back the tears. "Oh! Check in the bathroom," he said. Instead of the sunken tub from before, there was now a claw foot tub that humbled the one sent to Mani's house for Lita.

Alex led her back into the kitchen and then stood by a new room that was off from the kitchen and next to theirs. She opened the door and it was a beautiful pink and blue nursery. "Camille helped me decorate it. I hope it's all right," he said, suddenly uncertain of himself.

"It's gorgeous!" The first thing she saw was that it had a bay window, with seats that looked out on her ginkgo tree. There was a hand-carved crib and a mobile that hung over the crib with different types of planes. Valeria laughed as she saw a stuffed version of Alex's Helio in the mix. There was a matching rocker and a changing table and a closet full of tiny dresses. Her heart was about to overflow!

"Did you see the stairs?" Alex asked. Valeria sighed heavily, not wanting to leave the nursery, but forced herself out. She glanced up the winding staircase outside of the nursery and then took the stairs two at a time.

It was a play room that seemed to capture the light perfectly. Along one wall, was a collection of children's stories. She sighed at the complete *Anne of Green Gables* series, *Peter Pan* and then saw *The Secret Garden*—which held a special significance to her, as she had named her florist's shop after the story. By then, she couldn't withhold the tears if she tried. She hugged her husband and tried to get control of the sobs, when she saw something on a table in the corner covered with a white cloth.

What is that?" she asked as she brushed away a tear.

"It's...well, it's actually my Christmas present to you," he said as she approached it. It was about eighteen inches high, sitting in a lit alcove. She pulled on the cloth and there was a sculpture in white, Carrara marble of her, laughing as she joyously held a beautiful, baby girl in the air. At that point Valeria was lost in so much joy that she clung to Alex and sobbed.

Although it was a frequent occurrence, Alex still wasn't sure whether to smile or comfort her.

"Is it all right? Do you like it?" he asked, suddenly nervous.

"It's...I've never...Oh..." was the most she could seem to say.

Alex led her back down the stairs and into the bedroom. "I thought we might..." Before he could say another word, Valeria put her arms around him and kissed him with a passion that had been put on hold for far too long.

∞

That night they walked back up to the main house hand in hand along the magical trail lit by lanterns. Homer had been busy and, despite all the snow, the trails were shoveled. Christmas music was playing and they opened gifts of love with their family.

CHAPTER 22

Time seemed to pass quickly and it was already mid-January. Since they had been at Morgana for months without incident, Alex worked in his office where his studio used to be. There was still a studio, but it was now detached from the house.

The oracles were settling in to their new lives. Max was the first to leave Morgana to explore the new world. He was given a cell phone, a Europass for the trains, some cash, credit cards and a fake passport. He had even learned to text and considered it ideal. When Elliot would call, Max would push the call to voicemail. Then, after listening to Elliot's long voice mail messages, Max found it extremely satisfying to respond with a short, glib text.

One afternoon, while Valeria was reading in the cottage, Olivia entered, her eyes lit with excitement and a pretty package wrapped in ancient papyrus in her hands—a gift for Valeria. Valeria smiled hesitantly at Olivia, who sat in front of her, poised with her arms wrapped around her knees. Valeria carefully unwrapped it; inside was what appeared to be ancient, painted pot with a lid.

"Pretty!" Valeria said, looking at the pot in general. When she turned the it so that she could see the artwork in more detail, she noticed that there were four paintings, each was a scene of someone being brutally slain. Valeria lowered her eyebrows, smiling again at Olivia, this time with a hint of discomfort.

As she turned the pot to see the final painting, she felt something roll inside the vessel. Olivia's eyes widened and she giggled with excitement, as if some special treat were hidden within. Valeria pulled off the lid and, suddenly, the smell of death filled the room and she saw the bloody remains of a mutilated rat. She screamed instinctively and pushed the lid back on the pot as she fought the bile rising in her throat.

In an instant, Alex was by her side. Seeing Valeria's eyes on the pot, he picked it up and lifted the lid. Just as quickly, he shut it. Then he wrapped his arms around his very pregnant wife and held her for several minutes.

"She knows," he said.

∞

The family gathered at the main house—minus Daphne. They had called Elliot to come and comfort Olivia, as she was completely distraught. She had found the gift on the porch and expected it to be a late Christmas gift.

The remaining new oracles became guards, led by Tavish. It was decided that Myrdd's input was vital, so Alex and Valeria coaxed him to the main house where the rest of the family was gathered.

Myrdd sat on the floor in front of the fireplace in his dark brown robe, his arms wrapped around his legs. He rocked back and forth and refused to acknowledge anyone in the room.

Over the past few months, Camille had grown increasingly distant. Valeria was certain that it was difficult for her to be at Morgana with all of the joyful reunions among the oracles. Elliot and Olivia were engaged now, and Mani had Melitta back. Lars and Ava were living together for the first time in decades. And now, Alex and Valeria were there, not only happy, but expecting a baby. Tavish spent most of his time in Glasgow, and so Caleb was the only remaining unpaired mortal—who was merely twelve and was constantly beta testing his video game, rarely lifting his head from his computer screen. Despite Camille's recent despondency, when she entered the family room, her eyes widened as she stared at Valeria's expanded belly and exclaimed, "Good, God! I thought you were only a few months along!" Camille looked at Mani. "Doesn't it take, like...a year?" Valeria was pleased to see Camille so animated and interested.

Mani smiled calmly and affectionately patted Lita's leg. "Evidently, this is normal development."

"She's just moved into a more visible location," Valeria said as she gently rubbed her belly.

"She? *It's a girl?*" Camille asked with more excitement than Valeria had seen in some time. "We should have a party for the baby...an early party. Oh, yeah, a baby shower!"

"If it involves food and good wine, I'm in!"Ava said.

Lars raised a hand. "After today's surprise, I don't believe we'll be doing any celebrating at Morgana. We need to get Val out of here. Myrdd, would you like to join the discussion?"

Staring blankly down at the ground, Myrdd shook his head. "No. No, I..." he mumbled in a near-whisper, as though speaking to himself.

Valeria walked over to Myrdd and placed her hand on his shoulder.

"Myrdd?"

Feeling her touch, he glanced suspiciously at the hand on his shoulder and then up the arm. Abruptly, his eyes brightened. Alex noticed the change in Myrdd after Valeria's touch, and he glanced to Mani in question. Mani shook his head and shrugged.

"Cassandra! How are you child?" Myrdd asked.

"Not so much a child anymore," she said with a smile.

"No..." Myrdd drew his brows in and shook his head. "I knew child was the wrong word...what is the right word?"

"Cassandra is a woman now," Alex said gently.

"Yes...yes, that's it. She is a *woman*," he said, as if it was a new word for him. Then he glanced at Alex and batted his eyes as if stunned to see him. "Hello, Alexander!"

"Hello, Myrdd, it's good to see you!" Alex stared at Myrdd for a moment and then said, "Myrdd, what is it in Cassandra's touch that helps you?"

Myrdd lowered his brow and then said, "It's because it is the touch of the last oracle."

Lita's eyes lit. "Of course! The great healer!"

Valeria arched her brows. "*The great healer?*"

Lita continued, "We all have our gifts. You—well, actually, Cassandra—was known as the one who would reunite the oracles. It was said that the oracles were drawn to you and you were known as the great healer—greater than even Apollo's son, Asclepius!"

Lars leaned forward, taking charge. "Myrdd, someone sent Cassandra a warning message today. Do you know what actions we need to take?"

Myrdd pointed to Valeria and said, "Cassandra, the time has come."

"Yes, I know," Valeria responded.

Alex looked back and forth between the two. "Time for what?"

"There's something I must do," she said.

Then Myrdd narrowed his eyes at her. "Do you remember where you must go?"

Valeria thought for a moment, and then she widened her eyes. "I believe I am to seek out the Cumaen Sibyl."

Myrdd nodded.

"The Cumaen Sibyl?" Alex brushed his fingers through his hair, rose to stand, and then began to pace. "I'm sorry, love, but none of the temples are safe for you right now! A dead rat in a pot may mean that we need to go someplace else, but with the baby—and especially with how far along you are—I really think we need to lay low," Alex said. He didn't want to hear talk about fate or destiny. Right now, he believed that his destiny was with her, and any risk to that outcome was terrifying. "I believe the safest thing is to take Val to Puerto Rico with Mani and Melitta."

As Alex passed Valeria, she reached out and took his hand, pulling him down next to her. She brushed her hand along his face, attempting to remove some of his anxiety. "You're right," she said softly. Alex closed his eyes and sighed in relief as she turned to face the old man. "Myrdd, I have to think about the baby. I can't do anything right now that will endanger her."

Myrdd nodded without looking up.

"Myrdd?" she said, but he didn't respond. Valeria lowered her brows—something wasn't right. This was the first time that she had recalled any of the original plan and to change that felt wrong. She drew a deep breath and glanced nervously at Alex. "I'm sorry, but I think that we *have* to go to Cuma. After that, we can go on to Puerto Rico or anyplace else that seems safe," she said.

Alex's throat tightened as he gripped her hand. "Val, as you said earlier, we need to think of our child, and someone is determined to harm you." His mind frantically searched for solutions. "Perhaps Lars and I could go."

Her heart sank into the pit of her stomach. "No!" she said, fighting the memory of her life without him and the emptiness she had felt. "Alex, you promised you would never leave me again!"

"Maybe Lars and Ava could investigate this," Alex suggested, instead.

"Of course," Lars added.

"Sure, I'm up for a trip to Cuma!" Ava said as she took a chug of her water. "So...the famous Cumaen Sibyl?" Ava narrowed her eyes in skepticism. "Hasn't she been gone since before the time of Christ? My guess is that we can probably pay a few euros and get a nice tour."

"It must be Cassandra!" Myrdd's voice resonated throughout the room. Alex breathed out heavily and shook his head.

Valeria drew a deep breath in an effort to remain calm so that Alex might see that this was not necessarily a death sentence—although the whole thing felt ominous to her as well. "Like Ava said, she's probably not even there anymore. Maybe there's just some kind of clue at the temple." She released the breath and whispered, "Who was she anyway?"

Alex squeezed her hand and sighed. "The Sibyl of Cuma is arguably the most famous of the sibyls. According to Virgil, she had access to the underworld from her cave and guided Aeneid in and out— a feat that rarely occurred in all of history. In *The Divine Comedy*, Dante chose Virgil as a guide to the underworld because Virgil had been there. And I will not agree to take my pregnant wife to the very door to hell!" Alex said, determinedly.

Lars said, "Myrdd, why must Cassandra go to the temple in Cuma? Who is she supposed to meet there?"

Myrdd sat silently, refusing to speak.

Valeria lifted Alex's hand to her mouth and kissed it. She said, "Do you remember on my birthday—do you remember what you said?"

He shook his head. This was not a discussion he could even contemplate.

"You said, you dared to dream of more. Well, so do I. And *this* is our chance. I have to believe that we were meant for more than this blink of an eye that has been our lives together—that we were meant to live an extraordinary life."

Alex pulled back as if he had been punched.

"You don't think that our life together is...extraordinary?"

Seeing that she had hurt the man she adored—the man who had spent eternities creating a perfect life for her—she took his face in her hands as tears formed in her eyes.

"*Yes!* Yes, my love, it is the most extraordinary life I ever could have imagined! And it would be so easy to forget everyone and everything else and just get lost in the extraordinary pleasure of you and I. But when you think about the gifts we've been given—all of us," she said, as she glanced around to the other oracles in the room. "Don't you have to ask yourself: *Why did Apollo choose us?*" She leaned forward. "He gave us the gifts of time and money...and love. And I don't believe that it was so that we could simply hide here in our beautiful woods, living *careful* lives. I think that there is more for us to do—more for us to give—and a world full of pleasure if we refuse to allow others to determine our future."

Alex's face steeled itself against what he now knew was inevitable; after an eternity of waiting for the opportunity to protect her, she was insisting on placing herself at risk. He rose, narrowing his eyes and he asked, "*How can you even think of placing yourself at risk?*"

She turned on her knees and took his hand in hers. "We deserve more and I'm willing to fight for it!"

He took a deep breath, as he battled the pain of her words. He knew she was right, but how could he agree? "Beautiful, for me, the dream has always been about you—and now our child—and I just can't agree to this."

"She must," Myrdd said.

"Myrdd, I hope you understand, but under the circumstances, I can't accept your judgment of this situation." He took a deep breath and walked toward the door. "I'm going to...I'm going for a walk."

"Wait, I'll get my coat and go with you."

Valeria rose, but Alex was halfway out the door and avoided eye contact with her. "No. Stay here. I need some time to clear my head."

As he stepped out the door, he gave a side-glance toward his family. "Mani, will you keep an eye on her?"

"Of course."

"We all will," Lita added.

Valeria stood at the window and watched as Alex moved rapidly down the stairs and over the colorless field on the bleak winter day, disappearing into the forest. His words had stung. It was the first time he had ever been angry with her.

A tear rolled down her cheek. She desperately wanted to run after him, but there were answers that she needed. Lita walked over and patted her on the back.

"Alex knows things are changing and he's scared. But he also knows that you're right. Give him some time to cool off and then we'll walk you down."

The room was silent as Valeria wiped her cheeks and turned toward Myrdd, who was again curled into a ball. She walked over and knelt in front of him, placing her hand on his shoulder.

"Myrdd, Alex is concerned because of the baby," she said.

"Yes," he said without looking up. Valeria took Myrdd's hand and pressed it to her belly. "See? There's a baby in here." The baby kicked against Myrdd's hand and he jumped as though surprised, and then the clouds cleared from his eyes.

Suddenly, he spoke with clarity—as if the dead had been awakened. "Now is a tenuous time! There are things that must be done. Unless they are completed before the birth..." Myrdd lifted his hands and shook his head conveying the hopelessness of the situation.

Lars approached and knelt beside Valeria. "Tell us *exactly* what that means, Myrdd. What will happen if she doesn't go to Cuma?"

Sensing the tension in the room, Myrdd began to curl up in a ball. Valeria put her hand on his shoulder.

"Myrdd, do you know what will happen if I don't go to Cuma?" she asked.

The old man's faded eyes narrowed, and again the clouds cleared, but she sensed his reluctance to tell her and smiled to encourage him.

Finally he said, "Neither you nor the child will survive."

A shocking chill ran over Valeria, and she felt the effect it had on the rest of the family. She took a deep breath and let it out. "You're certain?"

"Alexander does not wait long before he succumbs—"

"Stop!" she said, wrapping her hands protectively around her belly as a sick wave of nausea crept over her. Immediately, Myrdd curled back into a ball.

Calming herself, Valeria ran her hand over her mouth. "Well, that isn't an option." Then she gave a side-glance toward her family. "Alex doesn't need to hear any of that." Then she drew another calming breath. "Myrdd, are we going there to see the sibyl?"

"She is waiting for you."

"Myrdd, can you show us where?"

Myrdd thought for a moment. "Yes. We will need the boy."

"Do you mean Caleb?" Valeria asked.

"Cool! Can I go?" Caleb asked, his eyes never leaving his computer screen.

"Not *that* boy," Myrdd said lifting a long thin finger toward Caleb. She saw the fog move back into Myrdd's eyes.

"Who then? Elliot?" When Myrdd didn't respond, Valeria stood and glanced toward Lars. "I guess we're going to Cuma."

∞

An hour later, Lita, Mani, and Valeria stepped into the brusque cold of winter in the mountains. In an otherwise colorless afternoon, Valeria could see a golden glow through the trees beyond the field covered with intermittent patches of snow.

As she opened the door to their cottage, she saw Alex on the couch staring blankly at the fire. She went to him and brushed her hand along the side of his face. He rapidly turned and pulled her into his arms as if he had already lost her again. She held him for a few minutes and then stood; taking his hand, she led him into their bedroom. There would be no more discussion of this tonight.

CHAPTER 23

Because of the progression of the pregnancy, Mani and Lita joined Alex, Valeria, and Myrdd on the private jet that headed to Naples.

Valeria had packed knowing that she would probably not return to her beautiful cottage in the woods. She hoped that someday her child might know it...if they survived. The plan was that after going to Cuma—provided that Myrdd had no further requirements of them—they would go to Mani's home in Puerto Rico and stay there, at least until the baby was born. She would again miss springtime at Morgana. But if that meant that they all lived, well, she could live with that.

Mountains surrounded Cuma, but as they neared the coast, it flattened to the sea. The crescent shaped coast of white sand and the deep blue Mediterranean led to the famous Mt. Vesuvius a few miles south. Alex, Valeria, and Myrdd drove to the Temple of the Cumaen Sibyl. Surrounding the area were olive orchards and bland, modern buildings that didn't fit with the ancient ruins. Alex had been unusually tense during the flight. And, although Valeria had not shared Myrdd's ominous words with Alex, he too seemed to feel the weight of hopelessness.

It was late afternoon when they arrived; due to the chill in the air, thankfully, tourists were absent. Valeria pulled her down jacket around her and realized that it could no longer zip up. Oh well, she thought, the baby was keeping her plenty warm. It was the uncertainty of these events that gave her a chill.

"Where do we go Myrdd?" Alex asked as he glanced around the park. They had convinced Myrdd to dress in slacks and a shirt but he pulled at the unwanted restraint of them, longing for his robe. When he refused to respond, Alex grabbed the flashlights that they had purchased and handed one to Valeria. "Here, take this, and let's get going so that we can be done with this before sunset."

They passed a dual arch made of brick and spoke of a better time for this temple. Finally, they saw the triangular entrance to the cave that bore into the mountainside; its granite slabs smoothed by time. They passed orange plastic barriers where excavation was still continuing, and then several marble slabs carved with quotations from Virgil's *Aeneid* that expressed what, according to the epic, Aeneas and the men accompanying him felt as they approached the cave of the prophetess.

For a moment, she felt the same fear mixed with respect as they stepped into the triangle-shaped entrance of the sanctuary. Inside the narrow space, she noticed how the hundred-yard cave seemed like a long birth canal.

Alongside the corridor, smaller triangular booths could be seen where it was assumed that people of antiquity waited behind brass rails, hoping for the Sibyl to prophesize for them.

At the end, where the slot widened, there was a tall, rotund rock cave with two alcoves alongside.

"Alex?" Valeria stepped into the sibyl's alcove and noticed that the echo was significantly increased within this location. She could imagine the sibyl sitting here—her voice sounding as if it came from God. "I pronounce this sibylline oracle in session," she said with a laugh that seemed to echo, and she giggled again. Hearing it echo, she began to laugh and had to get out of the echo chamber. Jeesh, she thought, she was getting giddy from all of the tension.

Myrdd furrowed his eyebrows as he walked from wall to wall looking confused. Sensing that he was getting upset, Valeria brushed her hand over his shoulder. Myrdd turned, his eyes wide with surprise as if he had woken from a deep sleep. He calmed and said, "This is not the place."

Then he walked out of the cave.

"Wonderful," Alex sighed with sarcasm.

The tension was definitely getting to him. When Valeria and Alex stepped outside, Myrdd was nowhere to be found. Valeria looked around and saw an ancient stone staircase that rose to the top of the hill above the cave. She scanned along the top of the hill until she spotted Myrdd walking rapidly.

"Alex," she said, pointing to Myrdd.

At the top of the stairs, they found Myrdd staring off toward the sea, his eyes searching intently over the numerous olive groves and vineyards.

"No, this isn't...no...no..." Myrdd said, lowering his brow as he shook his head.

"What are we looking for Myrdd? Perhaps Alex and I can help," Valeria said.

Myrdd continued to mumble.

"I think this trip was probably—" Alex began, sounding a bit relieved.

Myrdd looked up and said, "It was near water."

"The sea?"

"Not the sea," Myrdd mumbled. "It was round...from the fire...and a mountain."

Glancing along the horizon, she saw Mt. Vesuvius. "Do you mean a volcano?" Myrdd didn't answer and then she spotted a circular body of water that looked like it could be a crater. "Is that what you were looking for?" she asked.

Myrdd scratched his beard as he stared at the lake through his aged eyes and then nodded, as his breathing slowed. He climbed over the orange barricade and slowly scrambled down through the scrub brush and over the large boulders. Valeria turned to look at Alex and shrugged.

"Val, you're in no condition to be climbing down that," Alex said.

By then, Myrdd had already reached the bottom of the rocky hill.

"We can't leave him alone," she said sympathetically. "You can help me and we'll take it slow. It'll be all right."

Alex took a deep breath and glanced out at the miles to the sea where the sun was still a few inches off the horizon. "Val, I don't want to be that far away from the car."

By then, Myrdd's rapid pace was about to put him out of view. She could see that he was talking to himself and wondered what she had gotten herself—and her baby—into. She remembered the momentary glow on Alex's face when he saw the baby's heartbeat, and she was determined to make that dream a reality.

Pushing back her doubts, she climbed over the barricade. If she wasn't certain, how could she expect Alex to be all right with this?

"I'll be careful. We have to go!"

Alex reluctantly followed her and she was surprised how difficult it was climbing with her balance diminished by the pregnancy. At the bottom of the hill, she felt the angry kicks and ran her hand over her stomach as she looked down. "Sorry!"

They moved quickly through the olive grove. The cool air was a relief from the heat of their rapid pace, and the light clouds turned pink—an indicator that sunset was approaching.

Walking through a vineyard and a park, they caught up with Myrdd who kept pointing toward the lake. When the surrounding grounds turned to forest, they saw some signs, and indeed, the lake was from a crater. Myrdd followed a bike path, irritated with the modernization that had changed the forest he once knew. His feet began moving faster, and with more certainty. Finally, a cave opening appeared. Myrdd glanced at the entrance and then ignored it and began studying boulders in the vicinity.

As the sun began to sink behind a hill, they heard a noise from inside the cave. Alex grabbed Valeria and pulled her down behind him as they hid, while Myrdd continued to explore up the hill. Alex felt his heart rate climbing and prayed that it wasn't an enemy exiting the cave.

With her eyes widened in fear, Valeria heard footsteps as they exited the cave and turned toward their location. She gasped as the figure stood before them, completely shadowed by the remainder of the glow of gold behind him.

"*Alex?*" Came the familiar voice.

"*Max?*" Alex returned, incredulously. "What are you doing here?"

"Forgive me for frightening you."

"How did you know that we would be here?" Valeria asked, still winded from nerves.

"I had no idea that you would be here," he said.

Alex brushed his fingers through his hair trying to determine if this was another trap. "Then why are you here, Max?"

"Something that kid, Caleb, said a while back was troubling me." Max tilted his head and narrowed his eyes. "Actually, there's been several things that have been rattling around in my head. Last night, I finally put it together and decided to investigate."

"What?" Valeria asked.

"It has to do with that guy, Paolo, and his place in Carrara—Bella Vida."

"Bella Vida? Why would that trouble you?" Alex asked. "Kristiana named it."

"After you were married?" Max asked. Even in the twilight, Valeria noticed something in Max's eyes that she couldn't quite identify.

Alex nodded and then lowered his brows. They could hear Myrdd mumbling to himself as he fumbled around in the near-darkness.

"What is it Max?" Valeria asked.

"Valeria, you may not know this, but in our time, we were named for traits that our parents desired for us. Alexander, for instance means 'defender.' Your name, Cassandra, means 'to shine upon man'—how appropriate." He bit his lip. "My name, on the other hand, means, 'great one.' They certainly got that one wrong!"

"What does this have to do with the sibyl?"

"I'll get to that—and I assure you, it is relevant." Max pressed his lips together. "Circe's name was given to her by Hecate, but her birth name was Vivianna—meaning 'life.'"

"Okay," Valeria said.

"Are you coming?" Myrdd shouted.

"In a moment, Myrdd," Alex said.

"So Kristiana was named for..."

"The Greek derivation means 'Christian,'" Alex said. "Of course, she was named before the Christian movement."

"Right. And if she were an oracle—or perhaps had a friend who was an oracle—she would have known the validity that name would provide later, especially as the anti-pagan movements began." Max's eyes narrowed at Alex. "I assume you never provided Kristiana with a vision of the future?"

Alex shook his head. "No. Never."

"I'm still not following you, Max," Valeria said.

"Do you remember what Circe's prized possession was from the Titan, Hecate?"

"What did you call it? Some kind of dagger...oh, a kris?" Valeria said.

"Yes. A kris...that later became the symbol of spiritual strength in the south pacific."

Shaking her head as if trying to put it together, Valeria asked, "Are you saying that there is an association between Circe and Kristiana?"

"Circe's birth name, Vivianna, means 'life.' While the derivation of the weapon, kris, means 'beautiful.'"

"I'm sure there is a significance there that I'm just not seeing," Alex said.

"What did Kristiana name her home?"

"Bella Vida." Suddenly the color drained from Alex's face. "That translates to 'beautiful life.' Kristiana named her home after herself!"

"But Circe had a son," Valeria said.

"What's a girl to do? Her kid ages...and she doesn't."

Alex's eyes widened. "*Paolo!*"

"Myrdd said that Circe made demands of him. I suspect she was blackmailing Myrdd with the fact that he had fathered her son. But she also came to me," Max added. "So, Paolo may be my son, or Myrdd's. Of course, with Circe, who knows what the truth actually is," Max added.

"Except Kristiana is immortal and Circe was not?"

"That is true, and I haven't pieced that together yet," Max said.

Suddenly, Myrdd shouted down from the hill top, "The crystal." He frantically pointed to his neck. "Around her neck...the crystal. She lives because of the crystal!"

"The crystal?" Suddenly Alex recalled how Kristiana always wore the crystal—and how nervous she would became if he touched it. "Of course, it's the crystal!"

Rolling his eyes, Max said sarcastically, "Wonder what she exchanged for that piece of immortality?" Then he glanced up the hill and, again, Valeria could see his eyes tighten to mask his pain.

"Sorry, Max...I don't mean to be indelicate, but I see no way around it. I just can't believe that Myrdd would give Kristiana immortality in exchange for sex—especially when Apollo had promised the return of his symbolon."

Max shrugged nonchalantly. "My guess is that she worked her way into his world with seduction. From there, immortality must have had a higher price. I believe she would have easily traded anything for immortality—including her prized possession, the kris," Max said. "Round one of her blackmail probably provided her visions of the future. If she had drugged and seduced Myrdd, I'm sure that Myrdd would have thought nothing of giving her a transference. If he were drugged during the transference, who knows how much data she might have seen." Max's eyes narrowed at Alex, "That's probably how she first saw you, and where her obsession began—which I'm sure was long before you met her in Cararra."

"Why me?" Alex asked, as Valeria brushed his arm.

"Circe is a woman who needs to be loved completely. I believe that she dreamed of the kind of love that you have for your lovely wife. The kind of love she evidently found lacking in our relationship," Max said, matter-of-factly, as if that statement didn't just rip his heart out.

Valeria smiled sympathetically at Max. "I think you underestimate yourself, Max. You told me of her brush with Envy—followed by her constant exposure to hallucinogens."

Max tossed off the pain with the nearly imperceptible shake of his head. "In any case, I believe that Circe intended to use the visions from Myrdd to approach Aegemon so that she could become the Cumaen Sibyl. Those visions must have been what provided Aegemon with the locations of the oracles," Max added. "*And*...it explains her link to Jeremiah."

"How does Jeremiah fit in?" Valeria asked, as she pressed into Alex and his arm tightened around her.

"Circe had a fling with him, during the War of the Titans," Max said.

"*Jeremiah?*" Valeria said, completely appalled.

"Jeremiah—also known as Hyperion—the Titan who provided Circe a lock of his hair for Hecate's evil eye that gave Zeus a peek inside the Titan camp. After the war, Hyperion convinced Zeus that he and Circe worked together. Hyperion was the only other Titan who was not cast to the underworld.

"Of course, being the two-faced traitor that he was—Zeus eventually banned Hyperion from history."

"So, Jeremiah is Hyperion—Cronus's brother!" Alex said in surprise. "Kristiana and Jeremiah must have plotted Myrdd's demise...and Jeremiah's rise to power."

"Jeremiah eliminated anyone who might challenge his authority. But in order to gain power, he needed an army that could battle immortals! He needed—"

"Access to the underworld!" Alex said. "It was the dribs and Erebos who gave him the power."

Max's eyes widened. "Exactly! And he gained access to the underworld once Kristiana was made the Cumaen Sibyl!"

"You believe Kristiana has been hiding here?" Valeria asked.

"I do." Max looked up to the heavens. "Which means...she's alive." Valeria saw the relief that flooded his face. "My intention was to try to talk to her. Not that she would be willing to speak to me," Max said. Again, Valeria could see a slight twitch in Max's eye.

Alex turned to Valeria. "Val, you can't go in there. Kristiana may be waiting for you. Myrdd and Max can go, while I take you back to the car."

"No. Myrdd said that we have to see her."

Sensing a disagreement, Max edged away from the couple, but neither noticed. "I'll just be...over here," he said.

Alex continued, "Well then, I'll take you back to the plane and then I'll come back."

"I'm not leaving you!" Valeria said.

"Well then, it's decided. We'll disappear; we can just run away together," Alex said, relieved.

"Alex, if I don't go...we won't make it," she said in a near-whisper.

Feeling a hollow emptiness biting into his gut, Alex pulled her into his arms and kissed the top of her head. "Please don't say that," he whispered.

"I'm sorry."

"You know this?" he asked, as his voice took on a foreign sound.

"Yes."

Alex tightened his jaw, masking his emotions.

From up on the hill, with a tiny glow of gold along the purplish sunset, Myrdd's silhouette stood out. "We must go now."

Alex stared at Valeria, torn as his breathing increased. "You're certain?" he asked, as his eyes filled with pain.

"We have to do this." Alex nodded and took her hand.

Max lifted an arm to allow both Alex and Valeria to pass him on the path up the hill. "I'll follow from the rear and stay out of sight. You'll probably have better luck with her if she doesn't see me." He released a light chuckle that disguised his pain.

The three walked up the rocky hill following a stream of light from Alex's flashlight. As they neared the top of the hill, Myrdd pointed to a rock.

"This is the place that cost me my mind," Myrdd said. Alex moved Valeria back from the rock. "It is safe now," Myrdd assured them.

"How do you know that? If you had known before, surely you wouldn't have entered!" Alex said.

"It was the drink...it blinded me from the obvious."

"It's clean now. I would know if there were any more of the ethylene gasses," Max said.

Myrdd moved a six-inch rock from its place by the boulder; suddenly, there was a low rumble as the façade on the front of the boulder moved, revealing a narrow corridor.

"If we go in here, is there a way to get out?" Alex asked Myrdd.

"Yes," Myrdd answered as they entered. Alex, Max, and Valeria flipped on their flashlights. Myrdd placed his hand on the side of the wall and the door closed.

Myrdd whispered in the cramped hallway, "I must find the...oh, here it is," he said as he moved a stone and another door opened to a much smaller cave that was only a few feet high. Myrdd got down on his hands and knees and moved into the tunnel.

"Follow me," Alex said to Valeria, as he crawled into the cramped quarters.

Valeria hesitated. "It isn't that I'm at all claustrophobic," she huffed before getting down on her hands and knees, crawling into the darkness. She tried to focus on the thin stream of light ahead of her.

"Val, are you all right?" Alex whispered.

"Yes," she said, although she didn't feel all right. She was in a cave that felt too much like a tomb, about to meet the woman who had attempted to murder her several times and who would do anything to possess Alex.

Valeria heard a thump and a groan and then Myrdd whispered, "It ends here."

There was the sound of metal creaking on rusty hinges, and then they crawled into a larger hall. Alex helped Valeria up. All four of them crowded onto a landing. Ahead of them were ancient stone stairs with a seemingly endless decent.

"The stairway to hell," Max said with a chuckle.

"Watch the steps," Myrdd said. "I have rolled down these stairs more often than I care to admit," he whispered.

"Stay close to me," Alex whispered hesitantly, with an unsteady breath.

The going was slow as she shined her flashlight in the blackest of black, ensuring that she saw each step before committing to it. A few minutes later, Alex took her hand, indicating that they were at the bottom. Hearing breathing a few feet from them, Alex threw his arms around Valeria, ready to carry her back up the stairs if necessary.

They heard the smooth Italian accent, "Who is there?" A flashlight blinded them and Valeria moved her arm up to cover her eyes—but she most certainly recognized the voice.

Alex shined his flashlight back on Paolo and then released an anxious sigh. "What are you doing here?" Alex asked.

"I could ask the same of you!" Paolo whispered, and then realized that Valeria was with Alex. "Valeria, you are better now?" he asked as he stepped toward her.

"She's doing fine, pal," Alex said, with mild irritation. "So, why are you here?"

Paolo said, "I should have come here many years ago. I only had reason to return recently—I've come to stop her."

Turning to Myrdd, Alex's eyes widened and his voice constricted in panic. "Kristiana sees Paolo's thoughts. She will know that Val is here. It's far too dangerous to continue now."

Paolo narrowed his eyes. "Myrddin!" he said, with no effort to hide his antagonism. "I remember you." Turning back to Alex, Paolo nodded his chin toward Myrdd. "Why is *he* here?" Something in Valeria's appearance distracted him and he lowered his brows. He studied her face a moment, then his eyes critically moved down her body until Alex blocked his view.

"Do you mind?" Alex said, with a sharp edge. "That's my wife you're ogling."

Ignoring Alex, Paolo cocked his head to the side so that he could see around Alex. Then he lifted his flashlight so that the light moved up her body, locking on her enlarged belly. Paolo nodded to himself, as he realized the deception.

"Well, now you know, and so does Kristiana!" Alex said with growing antagonism.

Myrdd said to Paolo, "Boy, you must place a wall around your thoughts."

"I have not been a '*boy*' for a very long time," he said. Then, relaxing his tone, he said to Alex, "I realized how Kristiana was doing it, and I've already placed a wall around my thoughts. As an additional precaution, I have also taken moly."

"Moly?" Valeria asked Alex.

"Yes, bella, it is the herb that Hermes gave to Odysseus to protect him from," Paolo hesitated, "Circe, who had similar powers as my sister's."

"Well, holy moly*!* You're *sister*, huh?" Max said with a sardonic edge.

Paolo stared at Max, stunned, and then glanced at Myrdd.

"I see that, *for once*, I am not at a loss of paternal influence, although you are only a few eons too late."

"Good to see you aren't dust, yet," Max said.

"You should not be here either," Paolo said.

Sensing the growing tension, Valeria reached for Paolo's arm. "Paolo, Myrdd says I must confront the sibyl if we are to survive. Will you help us?"

Grasping her hand, Paolo said, "Bella, I have sworn to always protect you." Valeria pulled her hand back with irritation. "Please leave with Alex and the others."

DELIA J. COLVIN

"Fate determines who shall stay," Myrdd said, his deep voice resonating through the cave. He lifted a long spindly finger at Max. "You must wait here for now."

"Good!" Paolo said, giving Max an arrogant smile.

"As must you," Myrdd said, pointing at Paolo.

"I've heard that a little father-son time never hurt anyone," Max said, then he winced. "Well, except for Cronus—who ate his children and mutilated his father. And, of course, there's Zeus who banished his father to hell...and then, well, Oedipus and his father. Come to think of it, maybe you had better leave. But then, who knows who your father really is..."

Paolo's nostrils flared. "You really are an ass!"

Max's eye's narrowed as a shield. "So I've heard."

Suddenly, they heard footsteps that echoed from a distance. Alex held up a finger in front of his mouth to silent Paolo and Max. The intensity of the footsteps increased and they both nodded.

Alex, Valeria, and Myrdd continued down a stone hallway that descended at a steep angle. Again they came to a solid surface. Myrdd felt along the wall; finding a slight indentation, he pressed and a door opened. Valeria glanced around the enormous room—it was as if they had been transported to a medieval castle. It was lit by candelabras with worn tapestries that hung from stone walls. Ahead of them were heavy, once luxurious, red velvet draperies. Myrdd pushed back the drapery to reveal an equally enormous hall that lead to what appeared to be the main room.

They cautiously entered the hallway, following Myrdd, who seemed unperturbed by their surroundings. From one of the rooms ahead came the deep cough of a man, followed by slow footsteps on the stone floors from the main room ahead.

A moment later, they heard a cacophony of hacking, metal hitting a wall, and the shattering of china.

Then a man's voice yelled, "Damnit! I said Earl Grey—not English Breakfast!"

A pale, bald man with a skeletal face exited a chamber with a silver tray topped with broken china and Valeria recognized a drib from the underworld.

The drib disappeared around a corner—but left the curtain open to the room where the man was located. Alex stepped cautiously back into the hallway pulling Valeria behind him. They tried to get by the bedroom, but there was no way around it—the person in the room would see them. As they moved by, Valeria's eyes narrowed and she pulled Alex into the room where they had heard the man.

The room was barren of most furniture, except for a large bed, an armoire, and a desk. Valeria narrowed her eyes as she stepped toward the man on the bed, with Alex standing protectively near her.

The body in the bed rolled over and sat up fearfully. To Alex and Valeria's surprise, it was Aegemon. After the initial shock, Aegemon laid back down, indifferent to their presence. He was as pale as a drib and painfully thin, with deep purple and blue spheres protruding under his sunken orbs.

"If you've come here to kill me...again...you will have to take it up with the witch," he said.

"Aegemon?" Valeria said.

"She's decided to keep me alive." He looked away. "If you call this living." Then he wearily lifted a finger at Valeria. "Apollo warned me that if I attempted to harm you, I would lose. I mistook you for an innocent, but the way you infected me with pneumonic plague was brilliant. I never took you as a master of subterfuge." Aegemon laughed, which transgressed into a coughing fit.

As they began to back from the room, they heard the shrill voice of a woman.

"Guests!" Kristiana said, her voice full of venom. Alex and Valeria spun and realized that Myrdd was nowhere to be found. Kristiana's eyes were glazed with glee and machination, as they wandered down to Valeria's swollen belly.

"So, my Paolo has misinformed me." She lowered a brow as she brushed her fingers over the crystal on her neck. "Or perhaps you deceived him," she said to herself and then nodded as if she had determined that was the case. Her eyes rapidly shifted to Alex and widened for no more than an instant with an innocent joyfulness.

"Hello, Kristiana," Alex said softly, soothingly. Valeria noticed how his chest was rising and falling a bit too fast. "I would have liked to have settled things with you long ago. But that's all right. We can resolve everything now." Alex glanced subtly at Valeria, attempting to minimize Kristiana's attention on her. "You should go."

Valeria considered arguing, but Kristiana settled it.

"She stays," Kristiana said evenly as she walked to Alex, ignoring Valeria's presence. As she brushed her hand over his chest, Kristiana said, "Do you recall how sweetly we made love?" Alex drew a breath, uncertain of how to respond without antagonizing her.

"That was a long time ago," he said.

Kristiana continued to gaze lovingly at him. Valeria's eyes narrowed, repulsed, as Kristiana wrapped her arms around his neck and pressed against him. "I recall every moment of it. I think of it always. I know you must have enjoyed yourself." Then she lowered her brow for a moment. "You called me 'Circe' and you said you would do anything for me...*anything*." Then her eyes grew cold and her voice hardened. "Except the only thing that I wanted..."

"Kristiana...I didn't call you Circe," Alex said hesitantly, "I think you have me confused..."

"SILENCE!" she screeched as she pulled away from him and sulked, staring down at the ground. As she circled back to him, her voice became more reasonable and she drew a dagger from the belt of her ragged skirt.

Leaning into him again, she traced the point of the dagger along the edge of his face and he placed his hands on her arms trying to gain some control of the blade and her closeness. *"Remove your hands!"* she growled, smiling as he obeyed.

"You see, my sweet husband, I am the Cumaen Sibyl. You may not speak—and you may not touch me—unless I permit it. And you have been very, very bad. Now you should turn around." She pushed the point of the dagger into his right shoulder and forced him to turn. Once his back faced the entrance to Aegemon's room, she moved the dagger over his neck and down to his chest. Pushing the point near his heart, she forced him to walk backward into the main room, near her golden throne. Valeria followed at a distance.

"Do you recall how you used to love to touch me?" She ran the dagger down to Alex's stomach as she nodded toward Valeria. "Tell her. Tell her how you wanted me more than you could ever want her."

Seemingly unaware of Alex's turmoil, she smiled and said softly, "Did you know that we have a son?"

Narrowing his eyes for a split second, Alex said cautiously, "Paolo was a grown man when we..." Seeing the insanity beginning to cloud her eyes, he changed his approach. He had to get Valeria out of here. "Kristiana, you and I have things to discuss that should remain between just the two of us—"

"Alex, do you believe that child is yours?" Kristiana asked as she briefly pointed her dagger toward Valeria's stomach. "Did she tell you that she was sleeping with Aegemon while you pined away for her? Did she tell you that?"

Kristiana played with her crystal necklace, and then eyed Valeria suspiciously as she began to hum a lullaby. Valeria recognized it from her dream and shuddered from the haunting memory.

"Do you know how much misery you have caused me?" Kristiana asked—finally speaking to Valeria. "Why couldn't you remain dead?" She crossed her arms and seemed to be pondering a great truth. "I have learned not to depend on anyone but myself! Even the Fates lie. They promised me, but then they continued to bring you back. *Cowards!* Did they not know that Apollo was gone? I told them so." Then her voice sounded almost sane. "But now I've been promised that you will not return. It cost me dearly—but it is finally done. They have agreed."

Alex raised his arms, trying to calm her. "Kristiana, let's talk alone," he said.

"Conversation is overrated." Kristiana waived her hand dismissively.

Keeping his voice as calm as possible, he said, "Kristiana, you know that this has nothing to do with her. You and I should resolve this alone!" Seeing the rage building inside her, he played his trump card. "You know that if you harm her, I will never forgive you."

Suddenly, Kristiana thrust the dagger into Alex's stomach and Valeria screamed.

Kristiana leaned her face inches from Alex's, with the blade still in him. Seeing his stunned expression, she justified, "That was only a caress." Then she kissed him lightly, as he struggled to maintain consciousness; with an easy shove from Kristina, he fell to the ground.

She lowered her brows at his expression. "What?" She shrugged. "I did warn you that you must not speak unless permitted!"

Stepping over Alex, and dredging her skirt through the pool of blood now in front of him, Kristiana laughed lightly at Valeria's expression of horror. She swiped the bloody dagger over her skirt as she moved toward Valeria.

"I promised myself that you would watch me cut his heart out first, but I've changed my mind," she said in a seemingly rational tone that left icy chills on Valeria's spine. "Now I believe it would most please me if my husband watched you die."

Lunging forward, Kristiana anticipated Valeria's move and caught her arm with her free hand and twisted it behind Valeria's back. Then she moved the blade to Valeria's throat. "*Watch her die!*" she said rabidly.

"*Mother!*" Paolo said from the hallway. He caught the view of Alex in the corner, but didn't allow himself to look away from Kristiana. "Please!" he said, as he lifted his hands, attempting to calm her.

Kristiana's face lit up and her eyes brightened. "My Paolo!" She smiled with pride. "Still so handsome!" She glanced down at Valeria and her eyes lit up like a child's, as she said conspiratorially, "Paolo...see what I have for you? A new toy! Do you like her?" She smiled and began petting Valeria's hair with the blade of the dagger. "I could take her to the underworld for you and I could keep her alive for a short while...not long. You could play down there, like you did many years ago—remember your friends? Would that please you?"

Paolo narrowed his eyes and tightened his jaw. No one had known the secrets of his upbringing. He never discussed the playground that would've been any other child's nightmare—or the friendships that others would consider hellish.

"Mother, you must release..." Paolo thought for a moment as he took a cautious step forward and then decided, he said, "You must release Isabella." Paolo took another step. "Do you recall that she is my wife? My Isabella? Do you remember?" He took another step. "Please release her, and then I can take you to our home—our Bella Vida. It's a beautiful home and I have waited for you to join me there," he said, reaching for Kristiana. Still holding Valeria, Kristiana jerked back, away from Paolo, nearly breaking Valeria's arm.

"Mother, we could be happy at Bella Vida—please!" he said as he reached for her again. Kristiana swung the dagger and slashed Paolo across his hand.

Aegemon's voice came from his bed in the other room. "Grab her necklace! That'll kill the witch."

Hearing Aegemon's suggestion, Kristiana glared toward the dying man's room and then back to Paolo. A low growl worked its way to her lips. "Have you betrayed me, Paolo?" Kristiana glared at him before turning her rage toward Valeria. Yanking Valeria's head back, Kristiana growled, "Look what you have done—*you have turned everyone against me!*"

"Not everyone," Max said calmly as he stepped into the room. Kristiana was stunned into near silence.

"Max?" she murmured, as her eyes widened in confusion and affection.

"Circe, you really are alive!" Max smiled softly and, suddenly, the anguish and pain in his eyes melted. "I've missed you. I didn't believe I would ever see you again," he said in nearly a whisper as he held out his arms to her. He took another step toward her, as Kristiana tightened her grip possessively on Valeria.

"Do you love her, too?"

He locked his gaze on Kristiana's as his head turned slowly. "There is no one in this world who I will ever love, as much as I love you," he said, keeping eye contact with her while taking another step forward. Her eyes softened as they filled with love.

"My...Max," she said, closing her eyes to take in the pleasure of the moment. When she opened them, she seemed confused. Squinting, she bit her lip and her eyes began to move back and forth slowly, increasing in speed as if a rapid crossfire was occurring in her mind. Then her face began to twitch as it contorted in agony.

"Circe?" Max said, reaching for her.

She held up the dagger, defensively, and then yanked Valeria's head back further, as though she would either break her neck or slice it in an instant. Max lifted his arms calmly and then Kristiana screamed, *"All of you betrayed me!"* She moved backward to a heavy metal door.

With each step, Valeria was thrown off balance due to Kristiana's unpredictable steps. Kristiana's eyes darted to Paolo. "Even my beautiful boy...Do you know that I am the only one who will ever love you?" She began to sob like a child, and yanked Valeria's head back with her. Paolo's eye twitched as he shook off her words that had haunted him for an eternity.

Lifting his arms, Max stepped back. "Circe, the kid is right, we could go to Bella Vida—you, me, and...Paolo. We could have the life you've always dreamed of," he said.

Shifting her weight nervously, from foot to foot, Kristiana glanced at Valeria. As she stared at her swollen belly, and as if she had just noticed it, Kristiana's eyes widened in shock. Glaring angrily back and forth between Max and Valeria, her face reddened in rage. *"Have you been sleeping with my husband?"* She jerked Valeria back toward the door. Kristiana lowered her brows and she began to whisper the words she had just said as if she had just heard them. "Max...did you do that to her?" Kristiana asked with so much pain that all Max could do was turn his head as she stared at him, desperate to find some sanity in her eyes.

Alex tried to rise to his feet, but he couldn't find the strength. He watched in horror, unable to do anything to stop what appeared to be inevitable.

For the first time, Valeria spoke in a voice that was tense, but determined. "Kristiana—Circe—I really don't want to hurt you."

This caused Kristiana to laugh hysterically as she jerked Valeria around to face her. Placing one hand on her neck, and raised the dagger. "I was a great warrior! You were just a princess—who do you expect will win?"

Before Max and Paolo could move, Valeria raised both of her arms up and slammed her locked fists over Kristiana's elbow, forcing it to bend and automatically diverting the knife from her throat. Then she said, "I didn't survive New York by being fragile!"

Clinging to Kristiana's hand with the dagger, Valeria threw a two knuckle punch to Kristiana's larynx. Paolo lunged at Kristiana's arm that was holding the dagger. When Valeria pulled her hand back, her fingers caught on the cord that held the crystal. Just then, Kristiana swung around Paolo to kick at Valeria's stomach. Valeria turned to avoid the impact and felt the snap of Kristiana's cord and the dagger dropped to the ground.

The shriek stopped all action as Kristiana's eyes widened in shock. Her left hand clutched the crystal and her other hand flew up to cover her face—horror replacing the mix of her other emotions. In an instant, the smell of stagnant air was replaced with the smell of rotting flesh. Kristiana glanced at Max as her horror turned to grief. He reached for her, but she shook away from him as tears filled her eyes.

Then Kristiana's rage returned and she grabbed the dagger from the ground and lunged with fury at Valeria. As the dagger approached her chest, Valeria found herself suddenly airborne and then recognized the comfort of Alex's arms that were now around her. They careened into the wall and rolled onto the cold stone.

There was the sound of old hinges giving way and an eerie breeze moved through the room, accompanied by a feeling of deep despair from the lost souls.

Kristiana stood at an ancient metal door as her fingers moved over her newly disfigured face; she stared at Max and said, "Now, no one will want me."

"Circe!" Max said stepping toward her. She held her hand up as if to stop him and stepped back toward the threshold to hell. But this time Max refused to back-off. "Please, come to me."

Shaking her head as she mourned her beauty. "I know you could never love me now," she cried as her foot hit the edge of her throne and she lost her balance. Kristiana grasped the air as she disappeared into the blackness of the underworld.

Paolo pushed the metal door closed and it groaned as it clanked shut.

Alex's hands were shaking as he held Valeria tightly; they wrapped their arms around each other, grateful for the moment as both of their hearts raced.

"Are you all right?" he whispered in her hair. She nodded.

Taking a deep breath, Valeria pulled back and looked at the bloody hole in his shirt. "Are you okay?"

"I'll be fine in just a few minutes," Alex said. They sat there holding each other while Alex recovered. Then he stood and helped

Valeria up. "Is there a way out of there, Paolo? I should probably go after her."

Aegemon cackled from his bed. "You oracles are supposed to know so much!" he hacked. "You go and you'll be lost forever in her world—just as she has always desired!" He laughed and hacked again.

"No, Alex!" Valeria said in a near cry.

"Don't worry, I could never leave you!" he said, as he rubbed his hands along her back. Then he brushed her belly and felt the baby kick. "I'll just wait for her to return."

Paolo's face was unusually pale as he wiped a trembling hand across his brow. He drew a deep breath and let it out slowly. "Time is different in the underworld," he said, nearly breathless as he stared at the ground. His voice gained strength, and when he looked back up, his color had returned and he seemed nearly recovered. "If Kristiana believes that she is in danger, she will bring an army—certainly an army of dribs, but perhaps even Erebos." He pursed his lips for a moment and said, "I do not believe she will harm me. I will go for her."

Suddenly, they heard the screech of metal and noticed the same eerie breeze move through the room. All eyes turned toward the door to the underworld, as Max stood at its entrance.

Alex lowered his brow. "Max, if you step through there, you may never return."

Max smiled wistfully at Valeria. "For once in this cursed life, I dare to dream for more...and I'm willing to fight for it. I'll spend the rest of my days convincing her of that, whether in this world—or that one."

Alex shook Max's hand and Valeria hugged him. Rubbing his arm she said, "Take care of yourself, Max! You've been a good friend in the little time I've known you." Then she kissed his cheek and Alex and Valeria stepped away from the door.

"Wait," Paolo said. "I need to know...are you...?"

Max narrowed his eyes and shrugged casually. "So she says..." Then as Max began to walk through the entrance to the underworld, he stopped and turned back to Paolo. "But if that were true, that would make me...a very happy man." Max almost smiled and then he stepped into the other world and was gone.

"We must leave this place at once!" Myrdd said, having appeared out of nowhere and now standing in the hallway in front of Aegemon's room.

Aegemon sneered at Myrdd from his bed. "I should have known that *you* would come back!"

As Alex and Valeria passed his room, Aegemon lifted an arm. "Cassandra, please...one moment of your time."

"What is it Aegemon?" Stopping in the hallway, Valeria eyed him cynically. The fact was, she felt weak from everything that had just occurred and had no patience for Aegemon or his tricks.

"Please...please come," he pleaded. She glanced at Alex and then shrugged as they stepped into his room. As they neared his bed, Aegemon grasped her hand. She felt his pasty grip and jerked her hand back, fighting to keep the revulsion from her face.

"I know that you have a good heart—not like the rest of them. And I know that you will understand. One...very small favor?"

"Not likely," she said and then had a moment of conscience for the dying man. "What is it that you want?"

"Will you leave me a coin...for Charon?"

"You are headed to Tartarus!" Paolo huffed. "What difference will a coin make?"

A drib returned with a tray of tea and startled by the newcomers, he dropped the tray and ran from the room. Aegemon eyes widened as he whispered, "Please don't let me end up like him!"

Valeria glanced at Alex who reached into his pocket and flipped a coin that landed on Aegemon's bedding. Aegemon greedily grasped it and held it as the greatest of gifts. He closed his eyes. "Thank you, Alexander! Thank you! I shall never forget your kindness!"

Alex and Valeria exited the cave without another word.

.

CHAPTER 24

In the small jet, Mani and Lita immediately examined Valeria and confirmed that both she and the baby were fine. Still Alex insisted that Valeria rest during the flight and she had no problem agreeing. She was exhausted.

As Alex pulled Valeria into the bedroom, Lita approached with a blush in her cheeks.

"Alex, Mani, and I were thinking that instead of heading right to Puerto Rico...Valeria's favorite place," she teased, "we might stop in Sao Miguel."

"Sao Miguel?" Valeria asked.

"Of course!" Alex smiled and then turned to Valeria. "The Azores—it's where Lita and Mani were married." Lita's blush widened and Mani came back and wrapped his arms around Lita.

"Sao Miguel is small enough that we would know if there was any danger. It would give us a chance to ensure Valeria's recovery from the stress over the past few days," Mani said.

"And, it would be a second honeymoon for the two of you!" Valeria gushed, causing even Mani to blush.

∞

It was a magical holiday for the two couples in Sao Miguel. They stayed several days in an elegant B&B on the coast.

During the day, they strolled like tourists without a care, down ancient streets and long rocky beaches, eating the most incredible seafood and shopping. On the tiny island, they felt free from concern—certain that Kristiana would be gone for some time; and with Max in the underworld searching for her, perhaps there was hope that she was out of their lives forever.

Lita suggested that Valeria might want to purchase some things for the baby, as well as new maternity clothes. It was the first time Valeria had shopped for anything for the baby and it somehow made their future seem more likely.

While Alex and Mani perused an aviation store, Lita and Valeria sat outside, enjoying the warmth from the sun.

"I'm glad to see your ankle has recovered so well," Lita said.

"Thanks to your magical touch and hellacious physical therapy!" Valeria laughed as she brushed her hair back from her face.

Lita raised her brow. "*My* magical touch? Well, that's awfully funny coming from you!"

"What do you mean?" Valeria asked, as she wrapped a rubber band around her ponytail a third time and then released it.

Lita stared out to sea and shrugged. "The legend of the last oracle."

Valeria's eyes grew wide and then she laughed. "Yes, well I'm afraid *that* is all it is—a legend!"

Lita smiled. "You know, you have always been humble; even when you were one of the most powerful and respected women in the world. Of course, I never had the opportunity to meet you as Cassandra...but I wish I had."

Valeria blushed and looked down. Biting her lip, she said, "Lita? I've noticed things...changing." Lita glanced at Valeria's belly in concern. "No...nothing like that. More like...I seem to know things now, like the names of oracles whom I've never met. Names that Alex says I probably never even knew as Cassandra. And then there was the vision of the crash." Valeria stared out to the sea. "I did have something like that happen before when I had the plague, except it seemed more like a memory then. I guess I assumed that it was from the fever. But when Myrdd said that we needed to go to Cuma to the temple...well, I already knew that."

Brushing Valeria's shoulder, Lita smiled softly. "I don't know. It does seem as though you were able to heal Myrdd's memory by your touch alone. Perhaps you are healing yourself as well?" Lita suggested. "Or perhaps it's from the love of Alex and your new family."

Valeria wanted to tell Lita of her increasing concern that they had more threats to face. But the conversation ended abruptly when they saw the men returning.

As they window shopped, Alex's face lit up. He guided her into a small store that smelled of freshly cut wood and featured hand-made furniture. They headed toward the window where Valeria saw a hand-carved cradle. The wood work was breathtaking. All Valeria could do was cry—she did a lot of that lately—as Alex insisted that it be sent to their cottage. Seeing Alex so animated and enthusiastic, she could actually envision their life together without the dark cloud that constantly seemed to haunt them.

Later, they stopped at an outdoor café and had lunch. Valeria watched as Mani laughed joyfully at something Lita said. The glow in his eyes and his laughter made Valeria realize that love had transformed Mani. When she thought of Camille, she suddenly understood why her moods had shifted. How difficult it must be for her to see so many reminders of a happiness that she would never again know. Valeria pushed that thought away as she quietly ached for her best friend.

She wondered what would happen after she had the baby. Would they go to St. John? Somehow, she couldn't envision a life with a baby in their open-walled, Caribbean love nest. In fact, she couldn't see that life at Mani's in Puerto Rico either, or even here in the Azores. She loved Manhattan and missed her brownstone. But the only place that felt like *home* was their cottage! She tried not to think about it and convinced herself that it would all sort itself out.

As they walked along the rocky beach, they passed a house. It was a beautiful two story beach house with sand-worn shingles and a steep roof-line. The base was mostly windows and a wrap-around porch. Valeria was instantly attracted to it. Then she saw a picture in her mind of what it would be like to stay there.

She saw Alex and a two-year-old little girl playing on the beach, while Charlie, the dog, rolled in the sand. There was Lita and Mani holding hands and relaxing on lounge chairs with Lars and Ava. She saw Camille with an attractive black man—who looked exactly as she had imagined Jonah to look. The man was tall and slim with oracle blue eyes that were enhanced by his dark skin and charismatic smile. Camille was wearing a white, blue, and green sarong when Jonah pulled her onto his lap and they laughed joyfully. Then Camille wrapped her arms around his neck and Valeria saw something she had never seen in Camille's eyes...the true happiness that could only be found between symbolons!

On the drive back to the airport, Valeria couldn't get the picture of Camille and Jonah out of her head. There was something so real about it.

They climbed the stairs to the plane when Alex noticed that Valeria stopped and clung to the rails. "Val, are you all right?"

"No...I just—" Suddenly, the kaleidoscope effect started and she felt nauseous and dizzy. Luckily, she fell right into Alex's arms and he carried her onto the jet. She lay down on the bed and Mani came back to examine her; but by then, she was fine—and she had a purpose.

"Camille needs to meet us here," Valeria said.

"Sure, maybe next year, after the baby," Alex said.

"No, I think she needs to meet us now. Can you call her?"

"What's going on?" Alex asked, lowering his brows with concern.

"I know this sounds ridiculous, but I think...." She took a deep breath, feeling foolish. "Jonah is here."

Alex's eyes widened. *"Here?* Why would Jonah be on Sao Miguel?"

Valeria pushed herself up on her elbows. "I can't tell you why...I just...I just know it." She blushed, thinking how awful she would feel if she was wrong and how disappointed Camille would be. But she had such certainty that she had to try.

Lita sat down on the bed behind Alex and brushed her hand over Valeria's ankle that was swollen from overuse and pregnancy.

"Valeria, perhaps we should see if we can find him before telling Camille?"

"Probably—but I think she has to be here," Valeria said.

Mani strolled back and pressed his lips together. "Valeria may be right. Jonah was here."

All three heads spun to Mani.

Mani continued. "Jonah had seen a vision of other oracles here in Sao Miguel. That's how I met him." Lita raised her brows in surprise, and Mani looked away for a moment before he drew in a deep breath. Releasing it, he said, "It was during a council meeting...one I should have been at." Lita squeezed his hand and he continued, "Until then, Camille and Jonah did not know any other oracles."

"How long ago was that?" Valeria asked.

"At least two hundred years before Jonah disappeared. The other oracles seemed certain that he had been off the Caribbean and I had no reason to doubt it—until you just mentioned it," Mani said.

This time, they rented a beach house and, the next day, Camille arrived.

"Let me guess, it's a surprise baby shower and I'm the one surprised!" Camille said as she hugged Valeria and Lita at the airport.

They went down to the beach and Valeria suggested that she and Camille walk while Mani, Lita, and Alex relax on a bench on a small bluff above the beach. The sky was a misty blue as the white-capped waves rolled in, crashing on the sand.

"Camille, I know that this sounds absurd—"

"Absurd? You? Never!" Camille interrupted. "What's going on?"

"We were walking here yesterday and I saw a vision of you and Jonah...I've never met Jonah, have I?"

"No," Camille said and Valeria could see her pushing back her hope.

"Let me try to give you a transference. I want you to tell me if this is Jonah. If not, then please, let's just have a wonderful holiday and you can stay with us in Puerto Rico until the baby comes," Valeria said, suddenly feeling apprehensive.

"Okay," Camille said with a hesitancy in her voice that Valeria had never heard.

They sat on a large piece of driftwood with the cool breeze coming off the sea and the soft white sand at their ankles.

"Now remember—I'm not very good at this," Valeria said, offering her hands to Camille.

"I've got time," Camille said. They looked into each other's eyes and felt the affinity of their wonderful friendship, when suddenly

Camille's eyes grew wide in amazement. She jumped to her feet with tears in her eyes.

"That's...him!" Camille choked. "Where is that house?" she said searching up and down the beach as Alex, Mani, and Lita joined them.

"It's down here a ways," Valeria said.

They walked with purpose a half mile down the beach and then stared at the house.

"He was here?" Camille said and Valeria nodded.

They walked up the wooden stairs that lay in the sandy dunes, and then stepped onto the porch of the wind and sand-weathered home. Camille rapped on the glass pane of the front door. Finally, an older woman answered.

Mani asked the woman in Portuguese about the history of the property but, evidently, the woman was new to the island and had no idea. Mani explained that they believed that their ancestors had owned the land. She suggested a neighbor whose family had been with the original Spaniards who had occupied the islands. As they left, Camille saw an ancient sign near a barn that read, "Kali House." Camille raised her hand to her chest as tears filled her eyes.

"What's the matter, Camille?" Valeria asked. "Are you all right?"

Camille just nodded and then took Valeria's hands in hers. "Jonah was here!"

"Why do you say that?"

"Kali House! He called it Kali House!" she said, talking so fast that Valeria could barely follow. "That was his nickname for me—well, it was to poke fun at me."

"Kali?"

"We were in South Africa when a group of women began calling me Kali. Jonah thought it was hysterical. It's Swahili for 'fierce.' He saw it as kind of a badge of honor. I saw it as an insult. Still, it stuck." Camille drew a deep breath. "He's near here! We're going to find him!"

"Yes we are!" Valeria said, relieved that her intuition had paid off.

The elderly neighbor invited them in, speaking Oxford English. He offered them tea, and they sat politely while he described the entire history of the island.

After nearly twenty minutes, Camille interrupted the old man. "I'm sorry, but we're wondering specifically about the history of the blue house down the road."

The old man thought and said, "Yes, they used to call it Kali House when I was young—but not so much anymore. It has quite a history. Of course, it has been restored many times. I recall it being restored twice in my lifetime; once in my youth and then just a few years ago."

"Could there have ever been a black man who owned it?" Valeria asked.

"Oh, yes! A Negro man most certainly lived there! You do know that we are not a racist country as other European cities and the world at large are. Is he related to you?" the old man asked.

"When? I'm sorry, when did the man live there?" Camille asked, almost interrupting the man.

"I would have to say, around the 1960s. He was an older gentleman, perhaps in his fifties. He and his wife moved here. Let's see, I believe that the man was transferred to the orient. He was a mathematician as I recall. Was he your grandfather?"

Valeria bit her lip and squeezed Camille's arm. She could see that Camille was losing patience with this discussion.

"Senor Batista, we're wondering more about the history from the 1700-1800s," Alex said.

The old man's eyes widened and he turned to Camille.

"Were you aware that the Portuguese began the Atlantic slave trade in the 1500s? We took Gibraltar and there we encountered the Negro for the first time."

"Yes," Camille said, not making eye contact as the old man seemed proud of that heritage.

"Although the Negro was brought here to assist in the planting of sugar cane, most were sent to Brazil or the Caribbean. Despite that, here on the Azores, there were Negro landowners even in the 1500s."

The old man looked troubled and then rose and left the room without a word. Valeria glanced at Alex who lifted his eyebrows and shrugged. They waited over five minutes before the old man returned with a large tome.

"I thought so! See, my memory is not as poor as my children seem to believe. Yes, right around 1750 a black man...I can't seem to find his name here," he said as he scoured the pages slowly.

Finally, Camille had enough and jumped up. "Let me see that!" she said, pulling the book from the man. Realizing how rude she had just been, she said, "I'm so sorry—I don't mean to be rude. May I look at your book?"

The man, shaken by Camille's actions, nodded wide-eyed and sat back down. In a weak voice, he said, "Yes...yes, of course."

Camille brought the book over and sat it on the coffee table where she and Valeria could study it. They read the article, "...when in 1751, a recently freed, young Negro, made an offer to purchase the property and the sale was approved," Camille read with excitement. "Okay...and then..." her eyes scanned the page and rapidly flipped to the next page. "The *blue-eyed Negro!*" she announced and continued.

"Oh! Blue eyes. Then you *must* be related," the old man said, recovering from Camille's actions.

Lita smiled softly at the old man. "Yes. We are all related."

"Well, that is interesting—isn't it. But not so very different from—"

Camille interrupted excitedly, "He rebuilt the house and then..." she flipped the page several times. "Is there another book? This seems to only go to 1752."

"I believe so. Would you like the next volume?"

"Yes, please," Camille said as she and Valeria followed the old man down a long hallway and into his well-stocked library. He pointed to where the next thick tome was on the far wall. Camille grabbed it hungrily and sat down on the brown leather sofa as Valeria slid in next to her.

"She has an interest in history, I see," the old man said to Valeria, a little put-off by Camille's lack of manners—which was an oddity for Camille.

Valeria smiled softly. "It's an important subject matter to her."

"Oh, yes. I recall when I was preparing my doctoral thesis..." But by then, both Camille and Valeria were scanning the text.

Camille released a gasp. "Did you read this about the pirates?" she asked Valeria.

"Oh, yes, we did have our share of pirates! They were not only in the Caribbean!" The old man chuckled as if exhausted by the encounter.

Camille shook her head in frustration. "I know he would have come for me if he could have. He must have come here believing it to be free of slave trading—then there would be only one enemy. He probably believed that Mani would still be here and be able to help him find me."

"You must be Buddhists. I have seen Buddhists here," he said.

"Buddhists?" Valeria asked, feigning interest.

"Yes. Reincarnation and all that. Myself, I have a more practical approach."

"Oh," Valeria said, praying that she was not going to get an education in the gentleman's "more practical approach." She turned her attention to Camille. "Something must have occurred not long after 1752," she said as they continued to scan the book.

"Absolutely, something occurred." The old man chuckled again. "One of the deadliest earthquakes in history!" Senor Batista said.

"An earthquake?" Camille asked.

"Yes...why, yes," he said, now flustered with the attention. "The Great Lisbon earthquake. Let's see, if my memory serves it was on All Saints' Day in 1755."

"So, what happened to the people here? Probably buried?" Camille asked. "If they were buried, then he's still here!"

"Yes, or they were swept away by the tsunami," the old man added.

"*Tsunami?*" Camille's face turned nearly white. "No...don't tell me there was a tsunami!" Then she grabbed Valeria's arms and in a voice two octaves higher she said, "If it was a tsunami he could be anywhere by now!"

"Archeology—how interesting! Funny, you don't look like an archeologist."

"I'm certain he's here, Camille," Valeria said, as the old man continued.

"You might be interested to know that this was the first earthquake studied scientifically for its effects over a large area and it led to the birth of modern seismology and earthquake engineering."

Before Camille could tell him that she had absolutely no interest in that, Valeria lifted a hand to silence her and looked at the old man and said, "Thank you, Senor Batista. That is interesting, and most helpful." Then she looked back to the book, but finding no other information, she took a deep breath. "Senor, do you know where the victims of the earthquake—"

"Oh, the tsunami killed as many as the earthquake here on Sao Miguel."

"Okay, or the tsunami—do you know where they were buried?"

"Of course!" he said confidently.

Camille shook her head, ready to ring the old man's neck. "*Where? Where are they buried?*"

"Most were buried at sea."

Jumping from her seat she approached the old man and, reluctantly, Valeria stood in front of Camille.

"Senor Batista, if someone were buried on the island where would it have been?"

The old man narrowed his eyes, completely unaware of Camille's pending physical assault.

"Well, some would have been buried in the island cemetery—"

"Great! Thank you!" Camille said as she walked rapidly to the door and then turned, anxiously waiting for Valeria.

"All right, the island cemetery," Valeria said, patiently waiting for the rest of the answer.

"You are having a child soon aren't you?" he said. Camille's eyes widened as a signal of her growing impatience.

"Yes, I am." She smiled and drew another breath. "So the island cemetery or..."

"Well, they might be buried in a family plot—I'm certain you thought of that."

"*Family plot!* Why didn't we think of that?" Camille said, rolling her eyes.

"Yes. But after great disasters, like the 1755 Great Lisbon quake and tsunami, as well as the volcanic eruptions a few years later—"

Camille interrupted as she narrowed her eyes and stalked back into the room. "Are you telling me that he expected us to live someplace with tsunamis and volcanic eruptions? *What was he thinking?*"

Valeria said, "What happened after the disasters?"

"Some archeological excavations have shown that the grave diggers buried multiple people in one gravesite."

"Oh, just great!" Camille said exasperated.

Patting the man's arm, Valeria smiled sweetly at him. "Thank you, Senor Batista, you've been of great assistance!" She stood and then put her arm on Camille's and led her out past the main parlor where Alex, Mani, and Lita patiently waited.

As they crossed back to the dirt road, they followed it along the property line to Kali House with its overgrown fields and searched until they finally discovered the family plot; but there was no gravestone for Jonah.

"Let's just dig them all up and then wait to see if he comes to," Camille insisted. Alex grimaced.

"I have a better idea," Valeria said. "Let's check the local cemetery first."

They drove to the nearest cemetery and found it bordered by a four-foot white adobe fence. Carved crosses sprung from numerous locations.

Without saying a word they got out and began roaming the graveyard. Finally, Camille said, "Jeesh! You would think I would know where he is!" Her eyes filled with tears. "I'm sorry Jonah!"

"We'll find him," Valeria assured her friend, willing the words into truth.

The five of them each took a section of the graveyard. When they returned to the middle— without seeing his name—Camille said, "All right," as she gulped back her tears. "We'll go back to the family plot and just...dig it all up!" She huffed. "Maybe we should rent a bulldozer or whatever you call those things."

Valeria narrowed her eyes and said, "Something isn't right." She looked from left to right.

"All right, maybe not a bulldozer, maybe...maybe we can get one of those drill things that they use to break up the road and just take the bones out," Camille added, as her hope began to plummet.

Glancing up the hill, away from the sea, Valeria began walking toward the edge of the graveyard but her focus was further up the hill at an unkempt vineyard.

"What is it, Val?" Alex asked as he glanced up the hill.

"I don't know," she said. "Something..."

She evaluated the landscape and walked out of the graveyard, around the fence, and up the hill to the vineyard. She continued to glance around the area thoughtfully. Then she spotted an old man walking down the dirt road toward her, followed by a sheep dog. She waved an arm to call to him. Alex followed Valeria while Camille continued to plot the destruction of the family cemetery. The man stopped and adjusted his beret.

"Excuse me," Valeria said, but the man responded in Portuguese.

"Mani?" Alex yelled.

Mani walked over to join them.

"Mani, will you ask him when they moved the graveyard from up on that hill to its present location."

A moment later the man was gesturing up the hill and then to the cemetery in a long story. Mani responded several times and then thanked the man, waving to him as he continued down the road with his dog.

Mani raised his eyebrows and said, "He says that there was a mudslide in the fall of 1987 that removed most of the original gravestones. A local farmer wished to plant a vineyard here, but he did not wish to build below the cemetery. So after the mudslide occurred, he agreed to move all of the caskets to the current location of the cemetery—despite the possible curse from the spirits of the dead."

"He didn't move them," Valeria said, as her eyes lit.

"The man said that these vines refused to produce fruit for the farmer because of the lies to the dead. Finally, the farmer abandoned the vineyard. "

"I'll risk it!" Camille said with a smile. "Where do we dig?"

Valeria walked back up to the vineyard. She walked around for a few minutes and then she said, "I think right here."

They drove to town and picked up two shovels, a canvas tarp, and several flashlights. After several hours of digging—with Mani claiming to be an official of the state who was conducting an investigation into the activities of the previous owner, to anyone who stopped—Alex hit a casket and they opened the lid.

Camille stared at the remains. "Is that you, Jonah?" she lowered her brows and shook her head. "I...I just don't know."

Valeria brushed Camille's back. Mani looked at the body and tilted his head for a moment and then walked all around the grave and said, "I do not believe this is him. This man is not tall enough— Camille, I recall that Jonah was over six feet and very thin boned," he said.

Camille nodded and was about to cry. Alex placed the lid back on the casket and was about to bury it again when Valeria said, "Alex, wait. I'm sorry, but there's just something..."

"What is it, love? Do you believe that this is Jonah?" he asked as he leaned the shovel against the crook of his shoulder and stretched the fingers of his blistered hands.

"I don't think that's Jonah, but I do think he is near...very near." She glanced around the vineyard. "I think that he's somewhere here— maybe like Senor Batista said, maybe he's under this casket. Can you pull this one out?"

Alex glanced at Mani. "Alright!"

It was near sunset when they were finally able to remove the casket. Underneath was just more dirt. But they kept digging. Finally, Camille and Valeria had to run to a hardware store to pick up a ladder. When Alex and Mani needed a break from digging in the cramped quarters, Lita or Camille replaced them. Of course, everyone laughed when Valeria volunteered to give one of them a break.

The sun was setting and the hole was nearly eight feet deep. They were all pondering how deep they would dig before giving up when Alex hit the boards of another box. It took over twenty minutes to break just a couple of the boards in the lid of the casket. Valeria shined the light on parts of the body. The other casket had been rich wood, lined with silk. But this did not appear to be a man that was a landowner. This body had been thrown into a cheap wooden casket with no accoutrements.

"Maybe after the earthquake and tsunami they ran out of caskets— or maybe they didn't know who he was," Lita offered.

"Or maybe this was just a wild goose chase," Camille said. "I'm sorry, Val—I don't mean to be ungrateful. I just really hoped we would find him this time."

"I'm so sorry for getting your hopes up!" Valeria choked.

After a few minutes, Alex climbed out of the grave and said, "Well, this man was definitely not a pauper."

Turning toward Alex, Camille narrowed her eyes as he held out a gold chain and a small coin-like medallion. Camille sucked in a breath and, with her trembling hands, she ran her thumb over the medallion.

"It's him," Valeria whispered.

Camille's eyes filled with tears as she held out the medallion with the seven circles. Then she reached around her neck and pulled out a chain with the same medallion. Valeria sighed with relief and then embraced her closest friend who would no longer be lonely.

∞

That night, Camille sat with Jonah in the far-bedroom. Valeria insisted that Myrdd leave the plane, where he had created a comfortable cubby under a dining table. Myrdd wasn't pleased, but he came without much of a fight. It was not the quietest of evenings, but it was thrilling to know that Jonah would be back with them the next day.

Myrdd wandered into the room where Jonah's remains were. He stared for a moment at Camille who was sitting next to the bed with her head on the mattress asleep. Then he stared at the medallions on the bedside table. Without a word, he picked them both up and went into the living room where Alex was sleeping with his head on Valeria's lap.

"Do you remember?" the old man whispered.

"Remember what, Myrdd?" Valeria responded.

He took the two medallions and held them next to each other. Then he turned them, pressing their rough bottom edges together to show that they had once been one. Valeria thought for a moment—there was something so familiar about his actions. There were words she wanted to say, but she couldn't find the right ones.

"There was a game that you taught me when I was young," she said in surprise, as she stroked her hand over Alex's head.

"Cassandra, it is time for you to remember that game for our trip to the North Country," he said.

Valeria whispered so that she wouldn't wake Alex. "Myrdd we aren't going to the North Country. We're going south." She didn't want to tell him the name of their location as she wasn't certain that he could discern friend from foe.

Myrdd walked over to the fire without responding and sat on the floor, pulling his legs up to his body as he rocked.

"Myrdd?"

He didn't respond.

"Myrdd are we supposed to go to the North Country?"

She noticed his subtle nod.

"Where is it that we are supposed to go?"

"The boy knows," he said, still staring into the fire.

"The boy? Is that Caleb, or maybe Paolo?" She thought for a minute and then remembered a vision that Alex had given her of Myrdd calling him 'boy.' "Myrdd do you mean Alex?" Again, Myrdd nodded. "Alright, I'll talk to Alex tomorrow," she said in a whisper.

∞

The next morning they were awakened by a loud cry from Camille's room. Alex and Valeria sprang from their bed, ran down the three steps, and raced to the end of the hallway. Mani and Melitta were there in their robes and pajamas. Camille was standing with her hand over her mouth, staring at the bed in stunned silence.

"Camille?" Valeria said, running toward her and wrapping her arms around her. Then Valeria turned to see what she was looking at. In the bed was the man who Valeria had seen in her vision—Jonah! He was dark-complexioned, with an angular face. Something about his presence, even now, spoke of intelligence and gentleness, while still courageous.

Mani was checking his vitals. "He is breathing."

A choke came from Camille's throat and Valeria brushed her back, attempting unsuccessfully to push back her own tears. Mani smiled and then said, "He is healing faster than most."

Mani stepped away and Camille pressed her head to Jonah's chest and then lifted his hand and kissed it.

"I'll make breakfast," Alex said.

∞

The day was uneventful as they all waited for Jonah's full recovery. Myrdd occasionally glanced at Valeria as if she needed to talk to Alex about their change in plans, but she just couldn't bring herself to break the mood.

Jonah actually opened his eyes by late afternoon, and by evening, he and Camille sat side by side on the couch. The glow of love in their eyes reminded her of newlyweds forced to attend their own reception.

Finally, Alex smiled mischievously and said, "Jonah, you look like you could use some more rest."

"I *am* kind of tired," he said with a wink as he stretched his arm around Camille.

"Perhaps you should walk—some exercise may help you regain your energy. There is a treadmill here," Mani said, oblivious to what Jonah really needed.

"Treadmill?" Jonah asked, looking at Camille for a definition. She rolled her eyes and shook her head as if he didn't need to know about it.

Lita brushed her hand along Mani's chest. There were many things she loved about her husband, but sometimes his scientific mind got in the way.

"Jonah, in my humble opinion, it does appear that you could use a bit more *bed rest*," she said with a knowing smile. "My husband has obviously forgotten how...*tired*...he was when I returned." Everyone laughed, including Mani.

"I feel I owe you an explanation of what happened and why I required your rescue," Jonah said.

"Jonah—later!" Camille said as she jumped up and grabbed his hand. "They can wait, but I've waited long enough!"

∞

The next morning Alex, Valeria, Myrdd, Mani, and Lita packed and made breakfast for Camille and Jonah, delivered it on a tray, and then said their goodbyes to the reunited lovers. Myrdd continued to glare at

Valeria and she knew that she had to tell Alex. Jonah, dressed in jeans and pulling on a T-shirt, stopped them.

"I apologize if this dress is too informal," Jonah said, and then noticed that the rest of the family were dressed the same. "Alex and Valeria, I do have some vital information for you. Please come inside. This won't take long."

Everyone returned to the living room and sat down. Myrdd narrowed his eyes.

Glaring at Jonah, Myrdd said, "Tell him about the North Country."

"I've not forgotten, Myrdd."

Alex glanced at Myrdd and Jonah in confusion. "You two know each other?"

Jonah nodded as he sat down. Camille came out of the bedroom in a nightgown and robe; she sat on the back of the couch behind Jonah and brushed her hands over his back, her eyes full of love.

"Myrdd came to find me in Africa before I was taken. He gave me the two coins and told me that they were vital to our future. And to the future of other oracles," he said.

"What do the symbols mean, Myrdd?" Lita asked.

"They are the Walls of Troy," Myrdd responded.

"The Walls of Troy? I remember the symbol," Valeria said.

"May I see the coins?" Alex asked.

Camille went into the bedroom and retrieved the two medallions and handed them to Alex.

Alex lowered his brows and Valeria felt the burning glare of Myrdd.

"All right, Myrdd," she huffed. She turned to Alex and already saw the concern in his eyes. She smiled softly. "Something in this symbol fixes things. I don't know how, but it does." She took the two medallions. "See how they fit together?" she asked, and Alex nodded. "There was a game that Myrdd played with me when I was a child. Give me your hands," she said.

He turned to face her and narrowed his eyes. Valeria had never before offered to give him a transference. He took her hands and felt the energy.

He saw the hands of a child. She was perhaps five. She had some sort of puzzle in one of her hands with a large flat circle a foot across with seven rings, like that of a maze. The circle opened at the bottom and there was a compartment in the middle. It was open like a garden labyrinth and there was pink sand that filled the one inch deep walls. Myrdd held another identical puzzle filled with blue sand.

"Child, what happens if we turn these upside down?"

Myrdd pushed his long beard over his shoulder as he lifted Cassandra's puzzle so that the opening was at the bottom and all the sand began to flow onto the floor.

"You upset Lord Apollo with the mess!" Cassandra giggled, her brown curls bouncing with her joyful laughter. Myrdd frowned and she patted his cheek. "I understand you can't smile right now. But I will remember! When the puzzles are turned too far, they become empty and you get nothing." Her brilliant blue eyes sparkled as she smiled and her dimples deepened. "But if you turn them sideways," she said with a thrill as she turned the two puzzles so that the openings faced each other, "then you get the snake that eats its own tail!" Cassandra giggled at the image. "It goes on forever!" She drew an infinity symbol of a sideways eight in the pink sand.

Myrdd nodded. "And how many circles are there?"

Cassandra smiled, but was serious as she noted Myrdd's concern. "I will remember...it is seven."

Myrdd narrowed his eyes. "And what must you do?"

"When the time is right, I must recover the contents!"

Myrdd nodded.

Alex smiled at his wife proudly. She had mastered the art of transference! Then he saw her serious mood.

"I'm also familiar with this symbol," Alex said.

"As you should be," Myrdd responded, now standing near them.

"Alex," Valeria said, hesitantly. She grabbed his hands and, sensing her seriousness, he turned toward her. "Myrdd says that we need to go to the North Country."

"While there may be merit to going there, all of this will have to wait until after the baby," Alex said as he brushed the side of her face affectionately.

Valeria drew a deep breath and glanced at Myrdd.

"I think it has to be now," she said softly.

Alex stood up frustrated. "It was only a few days ago when you had a dagger come inches from killing both you and the baby. *Please*, let's just go on to Mani's."

He drew in a deep breath and kneeled in front of her. Taking her hands in his, he said, "Val, I feel like I've been holding my breath each and every day since I found you, praying that I could hang on to this dream for just...even one more day; one more day when I have you in my arms. Just *one more day* when I can wake with you next to me," Alex said as he swallowed back his tears. "After you survived the curse and the pneumonic plague, I was able to start dreaming again. Then there was the council, and the fire and the baby. Once you survived your last birthday, I felt like I had more than I have been promised in this lifetime. Please, all I want is a little more time..." He laid his head against her stomach and she stroked his head.

"We...we have to go. I'm sorry," she said.

"Is it Myrdd who's insisting?" Alex turned to Myrdd. "Where were you when Kristiana was waving the dagger at my wife and daughter?"

"I was where I was meant to be," Myrdd said with confidence. "I have my own difficulties to resolve. This one is yours."

"And you...you take no responsibility for this?"

Myrdd shook his head. "I take responsibility for what I must. My crimes have already cost me dearly. My purpose now is to set things right."

"I'm sorry to intrude, Alex. But Myrdd is right," Jonah said. "I've seen it in my visions. You must go to the North Country now."

Alex let his head fall back as he felt an old sadness overtake him.

"Where is the North Country?" Valeria asked.

"Cornwall, England," Alex said.

"You will need assistance," Myrdd said.

"Who?" Alex huffed.

"The boy," Myrdd said. Involuntarily, Alex rolled his eyes; this time, he was certain that Myrdd meant Paolo.

"Great!"

∞

Jonah and Camille remained in the Azores. It was such a gift for Valeria to see Camille so happy. She only hoped that she would have eternity with her symbolon. Alex refused to give Paolo any specifics about where they were going. He suggested that Paolo fly into Heathrow and that Alex would have a plane waiting for him in London to take him to their destination.

As the Gulfstream headed north from the Azores, Alex pulled Valeria onto his lap. "At least Aegemon isn't a threat anymore."

Mani and Lita sat happily across from Alex and Valeria. Mani pulled out a medical journal, while Lita had just discovered eReaders and the myriad of books available to her in an instant.

CHAPTER 25

They landed along the southern coast of England with its dramatic cliffs, and were transferred by limo to a nearby inn. That night, Valeria slept soundly in their Victorian-styled bedroom, dreaming of springtime at Morgana.

The next morning, she sat in the lobby, sipping her herbal tea and longing for coffee. The windows around the grand hotel permitted a view of the English garden and countryside. She was warmed by the golden glow of the magnificent fireplace that was wide enough for a five-foot log. She needed that bit of warmth as it was still mid-winter in this part of the world and a light snow had fallen during the night. The snow created a mystical quality as the white of the ground kissed the misty curling wisps of white and gray over the sea.

Despite this new excursion, Valeria could finally envision their perfect world—without fear or death or loneliness. Having just moved into her third trimester, she was having fun tickling the baby's feet and knees as they pushed out from the now cramped quarters of her belly. Valeria would grab whatever protruded and could feel the baby squirm, imagining her laugh, feeling so joyful and loved.

There was something special about being here—the place where Alex had spent most of his adolescence learning from the wise Myrdd. Valeria hoped that they would find the answers and freedom they so desired. Then she heard the familiar voice from behind her and sighed as her wonderful fantasy ended.

"Alex, you are going to listen to this crazy old man when he tells you that you must again place Valeria in danger?" Paolo spat, angrily.

She sipped her warm tea and tried to concentrate on the fire so that she didn't have to listen. But, by then, Paolo had sat down on the leather sofa facing her, forcing her into their discussion. Alex slid onto the couch next to her and she turned into him and put her arm over his shoulder.

Alex smiled briefly and lifted a hand toward Myrdd. "I do see Paolo's point—although we don't know that there is any danger in this journey." He patted Valeria's leg.

"What is the purpose of this? What was the purpose of the last fiasco? If not for my intervention, Kristiana would have killed Valeria," Paolo continued crossing his legs and sitting back, confident that he'd made his point.

Suddenly, Alex was distracted by a strong kick against his arm that came from Valeria's stomach. He smiled before returning his attention to the intense conversation. Alex wanted to point out that, although it had been Paolo who stopped the initial attack, Max had played a major role in saving Valeria. But Myrdd had said that Paolo was necessary and Alex would not antagonize him by presenting what he saw as fact.

"All that was required was accomplished," Myrdd said with his booming voice.

Mani and Lita joined them and so Alex looked to Mani for support.

"There is something Cassandra must do," Myrdd said calmly.

Exploding with impatience, Paolo leaned forward and nearly yelled, "What do you mean with your cryptic messages, old man? You expect us to perceive *that* as wisdom and then I should be willing to risk *her* life. You must give us some reason to believe you."

Myrdd nodded patiently. "It is not for you to believe or understand. It is all for the protection of the last oracle."

"And yet, you continue to endanger her!" Paolo raged.

"Yes, it is her path," Myrdd said.

Valeria looked at Paolo and Myrdd and suddenly thought that she might find some resemblance, but then she changed her mind. Paolo did look quite a lot like Max. The issue with Paolo and Kristiana

342

presented an interesting conundrum. If Myrdd or Max—both oracles—and Kristiana—a mortal, albeit a sorceress—could produce an immortal child, then perhaps Alex and Valeria's child could be immortal, too. If Valeria remained mortal and her child was immortal, then Valeria would be the only one to age.

But if Valeria somehow became immortal, and her child was mortal, it would be difficult to watch her own child age past her. Perhaps, Valeria thought—just perhaps—she was asking too much to have them both be immortal like Alex. After a life of living disconnected and feeling alone, she finally had a family she loved and would fight for. She had a love that ran to the core of her being and defined her. And now, they were going to have a child—which had been an impossibility in the world of oracles. For her and Alex to live with their child was certainly so much more than she had ever dreamed her life might be.

"Where are we going?" Valeria asked.

Myrdd's face clouded as he stared at Alex. "The face in the stone…"

"Now they call it Tintagel," Alex said.

∞

Their limo wound along the narrow, wintry road following the English cliffs; periodically, they would see older homes with their quaint thatched roofs. Myrdd sat quietly and then he turned to Valeria and said, "You must waste no time. When you find it—you must open it immediately! You must remove it—do you understand?"

Valeria glanced at Alex and then said, "Myrdd, what is it that I'm supposed to remove?"

Myrdd's eyes clouded. "I…I'm not certain…"

"And *this* is the man who we are entrusting with Valeria's life?" Paolo said to no one in particular.

"You said that I mustn't waste time," Valeria said.

Myrdd nodded. "Yes…that is correct…there is no time to lose…" Myrdd looked around and mumbled to himself, "I must keep my wits about me." He took a deep breath. "What was it that you asked?"

"You said that there was something that I needed to remove," Valeria said laying her head on Alex's shoulder and then lacing her fingers with his, wondering if this excursion was a mistake.

"Oh, yes…oh, yes." He thought for a moment. "You will know… But do not waste time! You must remove it at once…that is vital. Do you understand Cassandra?"

"I think so," Valeria answered.

They arrived at the ruins of Tintagel castle and walked along the tourist trails. Myrdd took no interest in the tourist phenomena and hurried along a trail that was at first the main path into the castle, but then diverted his direction toward a coastal trail that was not commonly followed during the winter.

Undeterred by large waves that lapped at them, or signs that advised of falling hazards, Myrdd continued quickly along the trail. The land jutted out to the sea, giving them a spectacular view of the ruins.

"See the face in the stone?" Alex said as he pointed at the cliff below the ruins; it had a distinct face carved in it over the years by wind and salt and sea. The cliffs reminded Valeria of an old movie called, *Widows' Peak* where the women plunged themselves off the rocky cliffs and into the violent sea in an effort to reunite with their lost loves. She shivered.

"We don't have to do this," he said, taking her into his arms.

"I'm…fine," she said and nodded toward Myrdd.

Paolo followed along the trail occasionally complaining as if his considerations were of the utmost importance. As they made their way around a sharp inlet, the trail rose at a steep pitch. Valeria glanced down and watched the violent throws of the waves as they at first crashed and then snarled around the rocky inlet. Below them was a cave at the base of the cliff that was partially filled with water. Finally, Myrdd stopped and Valeria saw two ancient carvings on the cliffs.

Myrdd ran his fingers over one of the carvings of the labyrinth with its seven circles to the center. "The Walls of Troy!" he said with finality.

"It hasn't changed much in 3,000 years," Alex said.

Valeria was taken aback by Alex's statement. "You know about this?"

He nodded as he appreciatively brushed his fingers along the carving on the right. "I created this one." Then he pointed to the one on the left. "That one was already here when I arrived—I assume Myrdd carved it."

"Not I...Apollo."

"Apollo?" Valeria asked.

Suddenly, Myrdd looked out toward the sea and his lips pressed together in a thin line. His eyes gazed dreamily at the water. "If I live, I would like to see her again," he said softly. Then the clouds returned to his eyes and he sank to his feet, wrapping his arms around his legs.

Instantly, Valeria felt a shadow cast over them. In a moment of sudden clarity, she felt the hopelessness of the situation, yet she knew that her path had already been chosen. Myrdd appeared completely disconnected, as if he had used every ounce of focus he could muster and now had to await the outcome.

"Val?" Alex asked, concern lacing his voice.

Turning away from Alex, she ran her finger around the carving. "It's seven circles to the center. If we do this right, we get the snake that eats its tail." Her finger traced the infinity symbol in the middle of the carving. "We get an eternity!" She forced a smile to her face. "Only seven circles to an eternity with you!" Then she wrapped her arms around Alex—suddenly afraid to let go. It would all be different soon.

She shivered as a cold wind whipped over the coast and Alex said, "At least it isn't as cold inside the cave." Before releasing him, she brushed her hands over the side of his face and then through his hair, savoring the moment and creating a memory.

"You know I adore you," she said, as tears flooded her eyes.

"We'll be on our way to Puerto Rico in no time!" he said. But she could tell by the look in his eyes that he didn't believe it either. A tear streaked down her face and he brushed it away.

"We can turn around," he whispered. "It's not too late."

She bit her lip and closed her eyes for a moment. "This...this is our path," she sighed.

There were steps carved into the sandstone. Alex turned to Paolo. "You go first. I'll help Val. But if you could, please give her a hand up."

Paolo lowered his eyebrows in irritation. "Of course I would help Valeria!" Then he climbed up the six steps.

"I don't need any help," Valeria said to Paolo, as she climbed up the stairs. But the fact was that she was grateful that Alex stood behind her and Paolo was at the top. Her balance wasn't what it used to be.

Once Alex reached the top, he pulled Valeria into his arms and kissed her. "Gorgeous view here," he said, standing on the narrow ledge.

Paolo grumbled, "Let's get this over with so that we can return to some semblance of sanity."

Alex pulled three flashlights out of his backpack and handed one to Paolo, who headed off into the cave; he handed another one to Valeria.

"Sometimes, there are bats in the cave's entrance. Paolo's probably already scared them off, but why don't we give him a minute." Alex held her behind him. Satisfied that the bats weren't an issue, he stepped inside the cave. She took a moment and, instantly, the musky moisture of the cave filled her senses as the dark absorbed them. She saw Alex's light move rapidly up as he disappeared from sight. Then she heard struggling.

"Alex?"

"*Val, run!*" he shouted. But she was frozen. She held her flashlight up, but the movement was so rapid she couldn't determine what was happening. Then she heard the unmistakable sound of a woman's growling and grunting—*Kristiana!*

"I'm not leaving you!" Valeria said as she tried to shine a light on Alex and Kristiana. Where was Paolo? She backed away from the struggle, uncertain whether to move back toward the entrance, or further inside the cave. She raised her flashlight to use as a weapon, but as soon as she did, she could no longer see them.

"*Alex!*" Valeria cried.

In the darkness, she could only see an occasional flash of what she was certain was Kristiana's dagger, captured by the sunlight that was filtering into the cave. Valeria tried to determine what exactly was happening and how to help, but with the few inches of coverage from her flashlight, and their rapid movement, she couldn't determine what to do. Then she saw that Alex had Kristiana pinned against the wall. He turned to Valeria as Kristiana fought him like a wild animal.

"Run, Val! Please!" he pleaded.

"I'm not leaving you," she said.

"Please!"

Valeria began to move toward the entrance and nearly tripped. She shined the flashlight behind her and saw Paolo lying against the wall with a bloody hole in his chest.

Suddenly there was something obscuring the light at the cave's entrance and Valeria recognized Myrdd standing tall. "Run, Cassandra!" He pointed into the cave.

Kristiana struggled away from Alex and ran with the dagger toward Valeria and Myrdd.

"No!" Alex yelled, as he grabbed Kristiana, but her forward movement was too fast and instantly, Alex, Myrdd, and Kristiana went over the ledge outside the cave. She could hear the thuds of bodies, and the distinct sound of a body slamming against the rocks that jutted from the cliff, falling over a hundred feet to the sea below.

Stunned and terrified, Valeria moved toward the entrance. Well below them, she saw Myrdd's body on a rock as the waves crashed over him. Valeria glanced around the water for Alex, but didn't see him.

She stepped outside the cave, onto the narrow ledge and there Valeria saw Alex face down and unconscious on the ledge below. She glanced around nervously. *Where was Kristiana?*

A hand grabbed at her foot and she stomped on it just as the dagger swung, barely brushing the flesh of her ankle. She felt a frantic kick of her child, and she turned and ran back into the cave. Instantly, she was cast into total darkness, except for the small stream of light coming from her flashlight.

Keeping one hand on the inner wall to guide her, she wondered if Alex was alive. Would he recover? Suddenly, the vision of Myrdd in the sea filled Valeria's vision. She wondered if Alex would survive only to be killed, with her and their child. *No!* She forced the thought away.

She continued through the labyrinth, wishing that Alex was beside her. What if she never saw him again? She choked back a cry. Then she heard Kristiana, singing the haunting lullaby from her nightmare.

"Kame nana na kimithis...Kame nana na kimithis..." The contrast of the sweet lullaby of a mother calming her child's fears in a slightly off-key rendition, as she came to murder another mother and child, was terrifying.

Valeria picked up her pace and wondered how many circles she had run. She desperately wanted to cry out for Alex, but she didn't want Kristiana to hear her. She moved faster, feeling the terror building within her.

Her foot hit a rock and she tripped. Valeria caught herself on her hands, but her small cry alerted Kristiana, who released a mad cackle. Then Kristiana continued her song—as it transformed into a battle march.

Picking up her pace, Valeria realized that she had felt an occasional knob on the side the cave. She had passed two of them. They must identify the circles. That would leave five circles remaining. She felt herself moving deeper and deeper into the mountain; as her claustrophobia began to take control, she forced it away. She thought about Alex, but now it wasn't just their love and their lives that mattered anymore. There was only one thing that mattered and that was keeping their child safe!

Valeria's hands were covered in sweat and the flashlight slipped out of her grasp. As it hit the ground, the light went out and she fumbled around desperately searching for it. When her foot kicked it, she followed the sound until she found it. Rubbing her belly, she whispered, "I won't let her harm you!"

She passed another bump in the wall—three more circles—as she listened to the sound of Kristiana's lullaby. Over the sound of her heart pounding it seemed as if she had increased the distance between her and Kristiana. Then she wondered if it was just the change in acoustics with the increased number of turns in the wall.

She thought of Alex again and prayed that somehow she might see him again. Already the emptiness was nearly overwhelming. She wondered how she would keep her promise to her child.

The memory of the bloody hole in Paolo made her nauseous and she wondered if he would recover. Despite everything, he had become a friend. Then she thought of Myrdd and how easily Kristiana had slaughtered him. Suddenly she had a near-paralyzing thought—if Kristiana had thrown Alex over the cliff, he would drown and that would be the end of him. A pain hit her chest. She couldn't think that! She had to believe that Alex was safe—that they would all be safe.

Valeria counted, one more circle. The distances were shorter and shorter around each turn now. At last, the cave opened to a circular chamber the size of the large living room. There was nothing in there except for a large metal crate with intricate symbols carved into it. Valeria recognized some of the symbols, including the triquetra and another three-pronged symbol. The crate stood waist high and a light shined down from the roof of the cave on two carvings of labyrinths, just as she had seen at the cave's entrance. Kristiana's voice was even closer now. Myrdd had told Valeria to remove something. She remembered the rules, she had to turn the labyrinths, but not too far, or she would have nothing. As she rotated the knobs on the box, they slipped through her fingers—her hands were too sweaty.

Using the bottom edge of her shirt, she wrapped it over the knobs. Turning them with all of her might, she felt them give, and then she heard a latch release. She lifted the lid of the box and inside was a large book with an infinity symbol painted in gold on the cover.

"You must remove it!" She remembered Myrdd's words—was this what he was referring to? She could still hear Kristiana and knew she would be there in less than a minute. She began reading the pages as quickly as she could. There had to be some clue that would tell her how to protect herself and her child against Kristiana.

"Val!" She heard Alex's frantic cry through the tunnels and she felt immediate relief; he was alive, even though, he was too far away to help her now. She shook the thought off and continued to read. Flipping back several hundred pages she read as quickly as she could. Just then, the volume of Kristiana's song increased.

Valeria read a line and lowered her brows. "A blinding sword?" She lifted the tome, but there was no sword to be found. She set it back down. Valeria knew that she would not attack Kristiana with a sword, but perhaps she could somehow defend herself and her child.

DELIA J. COLVIN

The speed of Kristiana's song increased with the volume, "Na meroni na ksupna, na megaloni o..."

Suddenly, Valeria was keenly aware that the singing had ended and she felt the hairs on the back of her neck rise at Kristiana's presence. She needed something to protect herself from the dagger she knew Kristiana still had, and so she lifted the tome. When Valeria turned she was stunned to see that Kristiana's once beautiful face had withered, with black patches marring its surface from her brief moment without the crystal.

"In all of these years, I have only had the pleasure of killing you myself but twice. The first time you returned, my husband saw the vision of you in the river. Fortunately, he told me how and where I would kill you before I had even decided. His mistake was that he took the time to pack...I did not!" Kristiana sighed happily. "I would like for him to know that he caused your death this last time." She tapped her foot impatiently and growled, "Call to him!"

"Alex!"

His voice was a cry of desperation. *"Val!* Are you okay...is she..." Kristiana laughed hysterically and it echoed throughout the tunnels.

Valeria could hear his struggled breathing as he raced to her and it broke her heart to know that he would see the inevitable.

"I'm bored." The corners of Kristiana's face rose in a macabre smile as she grabbed her dagger and hurled it toward Valeria. Lifting the book, Valeria successfully blocked the blade from her chest.

The room filled with an enraged battle cry as Kristiana ran at Valeria and knocked her to the ground. Then, pulling her dagger from the tome, Kristiana thrust it at Valeria in rapid-fire succession, while Valeria tried to block the blows.

The thrusts stopped and Valeria felt extraordinary and immediate relief when she saw Alex and Paolo grab Kristiana and pull her away.

Alex took the dagger and Paolo locked Kristiana's arms behind her, as Alex ran to his wife. Valeria sat up slowly. She had lived!

"Alex?" she said wrapping her arms around his neck. He held her close and she could feel the pounding of his pulse.

Kristiana craned her neck back to look at Paolo. "Paolo, my sweet boy...you live!"

His voice came as a whisper. "Yes..." Then his eyes filled with tears. "I am sorry, Mother." He reached to her neck and, suddenly, Kristiana acquiesced and leaned her head against Paolo's chest.

"My beautiful boy!" Kristiana said softly as Paolo yanked off the leather cord that held her lifeline.

In that instant, her eyes filled with horror. Her skin began to wither, turning green and brown and then, finally, black. Kristina's voice was almost like an echo, as she hummed her haunting lullaby that eerily continued a moment after her body turned to dust.

They stared at her remains in a mix of shock and relief. Alex's expression went from relief to sudden horror as he stared at Valeria. She saw Paolo staring at her with the same expression.

"We're safe now," she said. But she didn't feel safe. She felt a strange feeling as if the world was moving away from her. She glanced down and saw blood gushing from dozens of wounds in her chest.

Gathering every bit of strength she had in her, she brushed her hand over Alex's face. "I'm sorry," she whispered before losing consciousness.

Alex picked her up. "Hang on, Val! Hang on! We're going to get you out of here!" A sob caught in his throat and then he said, "Doc's going to fix you up! Paolo! Let's go, Paolo!"

Paolo seemed in shock, but then picked up Valeria's flashlight and ran back into the labyrinth. Alex followed carrying Valeria in his arms.

"She's still breathing! Hurry, Paolo!"

The circles seemed endless, but finally they saw the light. Mani and Lita, having received the silent communication from Alex, were at the entrance to the cave with supplies and a blanket to act as a stretcher. Mani wrapped gauze tightly around Valeria's wounds and then they carried her along the rugged trail.

By the time they got her to the car, she was drenched in blood and had stopped breathing. Alex began CPR, while Mani tried to stop the massive hemorrhaging.

On the jet, Lita hooked Valeria up to equipment that kept her heart and lungs working as they took off toward home. Alex sat helplessly by, clinging to Valeria's hand and refusing to believe anything except that his love would survive.

A few hours later, they arrived in Innsbruck and a medical helicopter transported them to Morgana.

CHAPTER 26

The romantic bedroom where Alex had first proposed to his beloved no longer looked quite so romantic—as it continued to fill with even more hospital equipment that Mani ordered. Still, Alex consoled himself knowing that it was better than the hospital where he had been barred from entering her room due to the quarantine.

Alex listened as Mani performed an ultrasound; he closed his eyes, praying for the familiar, reassuring sound. A moment later, Alex heard that rapid heartbeat. He opened his eyes and stared at Mani. He couldn't bring himself to ask him if the baby was all right.

"The baby appears to be unharmed," Mani said flatly.

Caleb and Tavish sat in the great room by the fire, lost in their pain. Paolo sat by himself until an hour later when Daphne arrived and held him tightly.

Alex didn't ask Mani how his wife was—he knew. He had watched her die too many times before. It was late in the evening when Camille and Jonah arrived. Most of the family had not met Jonah, but there were no hugs or introductions—only a shared grief.

Finally, Alex felt Mani's hand on his shoulder. "Alex…"

Shaking his head, Alex covered his face. "Don't, Doc!" Alex tried to stop the trembling in his chest.

Mani rubbed Alex's arm.

"I am sorry, my friend. These are just not injuries that will heal."

It was a few minutes later when Camille came in, sobbing, and hugged Alex, who didn't want to be hugged. He didn't want anything except for his wife to open her eyes and smile at him. After all the centuries of waiting for her and despite all of their enemies now being conquered, he had failed her.

Mani cleared his throat. "She is breathing on her own for now. She may even regain consciousness briefly and rally. But at this point, my only goal is to keep Valeria's heart going for at least another week to improve the chance of the baby's survival."

Alex held on to his sobs. "I can't talk about that now."

Later that evening, Lita came in and rubbed Alex's back. "I thought you would like to know that Myrdd has recovered. Ava and Lars are bringing him back."

Alex nodded and then crawled into bed next to Valeria. He brushed her hair back from her face. Her eyes were still open, but he could see no life that was Valeria in those beautiful oracle blue eyes. He brushed his hands over her lids to close them.

Camille tried to find something to say. "You don't think about it now...but," Camille swallowed, "let's just pray that...well, you know..." Alex tried to distance himself from the emotion—unwilling to accept that this was the end.

∞

The next morning, most of the family waited on the porch or in lawn chairs under the newly blossoming trees. The grass was green and Homer and his wife brought baskets of pansies to hang from the porch.

Alex had fallen asleep and when he woke, he saw a faint light back in Valeria's eyes.

"Thank, God!" he choked as he brushed her hair back and swallowed. She tried to speak from under the oxygen mask and he pulled it from her face.

"Is it spring yet?" she whispered.

When Alex nodded, she closed her eyes and smiled.

"Can I..."

"What beautiful? Anything you want—anything."

"I...I want to lay under our tree."

"I think you should take it easy right now! Let's get you recovered first!" Alex said.

Mani approached Valeria's bed as Camille went to the door, relieved.

Mani smiled kindly at Valeria and said, "Alex, I think if we all help, we can take Valeria outside. The weather is quite pleasant." Alex looked at Mani as if he were insane.

"But, Doc—shouldn't she..."

"Sometimes the needs of the soul outweigh the needs of the body," Mani said.

Lita touched Camille's shoulder and whispered, "Camille, she's rallying."

Stepping into the great room, Camille asked, "What does that mean? That's a good thing, right? I mean...she's conscious!" Camille said quietly, so that Alex couldn't hear. But when Lita shook her head softly, Camille repeated, "She's...conscious, though!"

"She needs to say goodbye," Lita whispered softly. Camille began to sob as Lita held her.

Mani, Alex, Paolo, and Tavish, gently lifted Valeria onto a stretcher and then carefully carried her out the front door, down the steps, and then around the side of the house to her ginkgo tree where a million diamond shaped leaves had recently sprouted on nearly every inch of the branches. Valeria kept her eyes closed until she was there. She looked up and smiled at her ginkgo tree and the blue sky beyond, as she held Alex's hand.

Mani patted Paolo and Tavish on the back. "Let's give Alex and Valeria some time alone." Reluctantly, Paolo went back to the porch where he could continue to see her, his face frozen in a mask of despair. Caleb and Elliot returned to their game of chess, while Daphne and Tavish competed in archery.

"See how it's thrived here? I always knew it would," she whispered.

"How could it not? When it's surrounded by so much love," he said.

"Promise me..." she said, as a tear escaped. "You won't be so sad that you forget...her." Valeria ran her hand over her stomach.

"*You and I* will take good care of her! You and I will," he said as he battled his emotions.

Her eyes closed for a moment.

"*Val?*" Alex cried out.

She nodded and opened her eyes as a tear rolled down her cheek. Then she looked at him with wonder. "Do you know how beautiful you have made my life?" she said brushing her fingers over his face. Alex kissed her palm. Then she lowered her brows and tightened her jaw, battling the tears. "I'm so...sorry for this. I know this won't be easy."

"You're going to be fine, now," Alex choked. "That, my love, is our destiny."

She closed her eyes again and nodded. He wasn't ready for the reality.

"Will you come for me?"

"Please don't go!" Alex cried.

"Promise you'll come for me," she whispered.

"Please don't die!"

"My love..." She opened her eyes and they were crystal clear as she smiled. "We never really die."

He kissed her once more as she released her last breath.

∞

The family gathered around Alex as he lifted his wife—his symbolon—and carried her back into the bedroom in the cottage he had built for her. Then he stepped back as Mani and Melitta tied down her limbs and inserted a tube down her throat to automate her breathing, while hooking up another machine to compress her heart and keep her alive long enough to safely deliver the baby.

CHAPTER 27

It surprised Alex when he woke the next morning to the sounds of birds singing. How could nature go on as if nothing had changed? He sat inconsolable, next to his beloved wife's body. He couldn't think of eating. He didn't want to talk...he didn't deserve to sleep...he didn't deserve life. He had failed her—again.

Always before, he could cling to the vision of their marriage—his vision from 3,000 years before. He had always imagined that vision was a promise of their happily forever after, but now he knew that vision had been trickery.

Still, he couldn't regret an instant of his time with her. That was his dream—he only wanted more of it—he wanted an eternity with her and anything less was just not enough. He could see how the others felt; their need to say words that might somehow make a difference...but words could never change the reality, nor ease his pain.

The only thing he seemed able to do was watch as her chest mechanically rose and fell to artificially keep her and the fetus—that was never quite real to him—alive. He knew what was to follow...that terrible time of watching her body disintegrate or when they tried to take her from him. The agony of those moments had tormented Alex during most of his existence, and now he would have an even more painful memory to add to those—the loss of his wife, having almost survived this time. And now, there were no visions of the future to cling to.

∞

A few days later, Mani ran another ultrasound. He thought that perhaps the baby might be ready to survive outside of the womb. But he decided to delay the cesarean section until absolutely necessary. He didn't believe that Alex was ready to see the equipment turned off. Frankly, Mani wasn't certain he was ready to confront that.

That afternoon, a delivery truck arrived. Alex's eyes moved to the window and he saw Camille sobbing as she asked the delivery man to take the package up to the main house. Alex saw that it was the cradle that he and Valeria had purchased in the Azores, but he felt no emotion over seeing it He shook back his thoughts again—it was better not to think.

"Alex?" he heard Daphne say. He opened his eyes and saw her enter the room hesitantly. She stood nervously angled between the door and the bed, as if posing for escape, her hands balled into fists.

His face was gray and he could not speak.

"I…uh…I have two things. One is…well, I brought…" Daphne swallowed and then raised a coin. "She'll need this." Alex turned away and so Daphne sat the coin on the table by Valeria. "It's for Charon," she said in almost a whisper. Alex shook his head and closed his eyes as he pressed back the emotion. "She'll need it to go to the Elysian Fields and uh…" Daphne's voice faded.

Alex didn't acknowledge her comment. He couldn't bear to think of waiting 500 years—or even 50—to see her again. But even more, he couldn't bear to think of her being gone forever; and the coin represented finality. It was better not to think about that.

Daphne stepped away from the bed and toward the door as her chest rose and dipped a bit too fast. "Alex, I have something I must tell you." Her voice sounded strange, causing Alex to awaken from his fog. He blinked and then tried to focus on her, but the vision of his wife obscured most of his world. Then he noticed the tears in Daphne's eyes. In the eons that he had known her, he had never seen her nervous and had certainly never seen her cry.

"I really don't want to tell you this…but I must," she said, as if convincing herself.

"What is it Daph?" he said, forcing the words out.

"It...it's a secret that I've kept for 3,000 years." She looked up nervously and then choked. "I do hope you can forgive me." She clamped her eyes shut for a moment. Then, in a brief moment of bravery, she blurted, "I am the reason for so much unhappiness in your life." She opened her eyes, knowing it was cowardly and a tear escaped. She quickly dismissed it with her hand.

"What are you...talking about, Daph?"

She fidgeted and then said, "Did you ever wonder how it was that you were the only oracle to survive the drowning by Aegemon that day?"

He wasn't in the mood for this. "You were there when Aegemon threw me in. I'm grateful to you for that." He brushed his fingers through his hair. He was really too exhausted to care about some minor infraction that happened 3,000 years ago.

She drew a deep breath and quickly brushed away another tear. "I knew you would be there. I merely waited for you."

"You knew?" He gazed up through the haze with this sudden revelation.

"Yes."

He waited for her to continue but she just stood there, hanging to the doorframe like a life preserver. "A vision?" he guessed.

"No."

"Daph, just tell me," he said, exhausted.

"Before Apollo went on to the Elysian Fields, he came to me and gave me a task of great importance. I was to save you from drowning and then take you to Cassandra...in Troy," Daphne said, nodding toward Valeria. Alex lowered his brows, it didn't make any sense.

"See? Apollo *did* try to protect you—he just never imagined that I would...." She glanced at the floor unable to make eye contact with him. "I have always had a penchant for competition...well, you know that. So when a woman I knew—we all know her now—Circe, well, Kristiana, began to speak of a man and how she would steal his heart, I challenged her to a contest. It was harmless at first. Both of us believed that if you chose us over Cassandra, who was said to be the most beautiful woman in the world, then that would mean that the winner was...well, you get the idea. Still, I always planned on following through on Apollo's request, until..."

"Until when?" Alex asked, his heart rate now climbing.

"Until I saw you." Her chest moved heavily with fear.

Alex began to feel the shock of his and Valeria's 3,000 years of agony. If Daphne had followed through, Cassandra would not have been so hopeless, and would not have ingested Aegemon's poisoned drink. She would not have drowned. And, perhaps, Troy would have survived and the two of them could have been together all of these years. "I don't...understand how this... Why, Daph?"

In a brief moment of courage, she looked him straight in the eye. "You know why." Alex nodded slowly.

"I had never cared about anyone else before." She glanced up for a moment, admitting, "Well, except for myself." She looked down again. "I kept thinking just a little more time...surely, there could be no fault with a few more years. Of course, I always planned on assisting Cassandra. But I thought if we waited a little longer then you might," she gulped, "care for me."

"Oh, Daph!" Alex whispered in a sudden moment of realization. All the years of pain his beloved had suffered—all the loneliness—it all could have been avoided. Suddenly, the anger began to boil within him.

"Alex, I truly did not intend any harm to come to her...or to you. I truly did not. I knew that if you did not come for her, Cassandra would take matters into her own hands—*and she did!* And when you found her drowned, and I realized that she had been cursed by Circe..." She shook her head in denial. "I knew that I could never tell you. But...see? I've...grown and here we are. And now you know. I am so very sorry."

Laying his head in his hands, he sat quietly, wanting to shout and blame Daphne for it all. Instead, he worked to control the rage that welled inside him like a wild cat trapped and seeking its escape.

Daphne took a few steps toward Alex and started to move her hand to his shoulder in an attempt to comfort him.

"Please, don't touch me right now," Alex said flatly, battling the pain of her confession.

"Alex, please tell me that you can forgive me someday," she said, holding her ground.

"I'm going to go for a walk and when I return, it would be best if you weren't here."

Pressing her lips together, she restrained her sobs. As she started to step out of the bedroom, she stopped and clung to the door frame for a moment. "I always loved my blue eyes. I thought they were beautiful with my hair—everyone said so. But after Cassandra...drowned...the first time, I knew that my eyes should have always been green for the wicked creature that I had become. I didn't have the courage to actually change them. That's why I wore the contacts. Not really to be different, but to remember what my envy did to your life. I am so sorry."

Daphne broke down, sobbing as she exited the room. Lita went to her and held her. Immediately, Alex stood and walked past them both, and out the front door without speaking.

As Daphne watched him leave, Lita said, "He'll forgive you. He's just in pain right now."

"I don't think he ever will," Daphne said as she brushed a tissue under her eyes. Camille came in.

"Lita, can you help me?" Camille asked. "I want to put the cradle back in the nursery before Alex returns."

"Of course, Camille!" Lita said and stepped outside.

Daphne glanced outside and, with no one else in the great room, she returned to the bedroom and picked up the coin and placed it in Valeria's hand and closed her fingers around it. Then she went back to the great room and glanced at the place where she had spent so much time with the man she adored—who would never love her—and she left.

Outside, Alex saw the flowerpots and lattice covered with Bougainvillea—Valeria's favorite. Homer was evidently unaware that the reason for the flowers was gone forever. Alex wondered what he would do with the cottage now. He wondered if he could bear to be here and then he wondered if he could bear to leave.

CHAPTER 28

"Alex," she said, as she brushed the side of his face. Feeling her touch, he opened his eyes to the miracle of his symbolon, alive once again.

"You're back!" he cried joyously.

She smiled and took his hands in hers. "For now...but, this is a lousy substitute."

Alex lowered his brows. "What do you mean... You're...back!" Then he began to wonder if it was a dream. Something felt...different. "Beautiful, tell me you're back."

Valeria continued to smile, but it faded into sadness. "We have things to do...and they must be done now." She looked up and drew a quick breath. "We haven't even discussed a name for our daughter."

"I was thinking, Jenni—that was your name the first time that I kissed you," Alex said.

Valeria smiled. "How about Genesis—for our new beginning. We could call her Genni for short."

Alex nodded as he held her hands and glanced out the window. He saw the tulips that broke through the ground by the ginkgo. Eventually, the hydrangea would climb back to its original height just above the porch railing. Alex drew a deep breath.

Suddenly it occurred to him that his love had been wearing a blue print, hospital gown—not the white flowing gown she now wore. The wounds around her chest were no longer there. He brushed his hand along her mouth and there was no warmth...no breath. Then he moved his hand, hesitantly down to her heart and there was no beat. Valeria's expression turned sad and concerned.

"It's a lousy substitute," she said again.

"Please promise you won't leave me," he pleaded.

"Genni will need your love. Please don't forget that."

"Val?" Alex cried frantically.

Her eyes shined with love. "You are always in my heart." She leaned forward and kissed him and then she was gone.

∞

"Val!" Alex cried as his head bolted straight up from the mattress. But his wife was in bed, still covered with equipment, breathing the mechanical breaths of the machinery.

It had been three weeks since he had been told that she was gone...and in his dreams, she still came to him every night. But the harsh reality was right in front of him. Mani came in and pulled up a chair next to Alex.

"My friend, I have been monitoring Valeria and she is in labor."

Alex sucked in a deep breath wondering if this time his dream was real.

"Could she be—"

"No, Alex. Valeria is gone. We will do a cesarean section. You may stay if you wish."

"But what if she isn't...gone? What if you're wrong?" Alex brushed the tears from his face—he couldn't seem to get a hold of his emotions this time.

Considering Alex's question, Mani said thoughtfully, "After the cesarean, we will turn off the equipment. If she is alive, she will continue to breathe."

Alex nodded in defeat. It had been just a dream. "I'm going to go for a walk."

He left their bedroom and passed his family. He needed someplace where he felt her with him; someplace where he didn't need to tell anyone that he was "fine." He couldn't be there when they turned off the equipment and he felt that there was something wrong with him because he didn't particularly care about their child. He should care! She was his child...their child! But he battled his emotions and wished he had something other than his grief to offer the baby.

He found himself walking down toward Mani's house. From there, he couldn't decide where to go. The last thing he wanted was to see or talk to anyone. He found himself walking near the cemetery and then he noticed the activity. Homer, the ancient caregiver, was working. Alex stopped in his tracks as his heart began to pound furiously. Efficient Homer was already digging her grave!

"What are you doing? She isn't even gone yet!" Alex cried. Homer looked up, concerned that he had upset Alex.

As the rage built in him, Alex marched to Homer and ripped the shovel out of the old man's hands. "We're not burying her! Not until...not until..." Alex began shoveling the soil back into the hole and then, in a moment of fury, he took the shovel and swung it against a boulder. It felt good to hit something. He swung it again and again.

Ingrid, Homer's wife, saw his actions and ran back to the cottage for help, for once concerned about her husband. Alex continued to swing it against the rock over and over until the shovel broke in half. Then he dropped to his knees and used his hands to continue refilling the grave. "No one is burying my wife! Do you understand, old man?"

Alex glanced up and saw fear in Homer's eyes. The kindly old man who had been there with him for so many years—generations of his family had served at Morgana—was now afraid *of him.* Seeing what he had done to Homer, Alex felt ashamed. He stopped refilling the hole as the sobs overtook him and he dropped into the soil. *Would Homer and Ingrid leave now? Probably.*

In an instant, the sadly familiar pain hit his heart. He grasped at his chest and struggled to breathe...knowing that she was gone. Moments later, it stopped with a finality that tore at his soul, as he lay in the dirt, sobbing. He felt a hand on his shoulder and when he turned, he saw Homer looking concerned.

Alex sobbed, "Please, forgive me."

The old man nodded his head sadly and then shuffled off. It was nearing sunset when he heard Lita's soft voice and realized that he had been asleep.

"Ava and Lars found Myrddin and he's now fully recovered," Lita said. Alex lifted his face from the dirt as she passed him, walking into the cemetery. "Homer and Ingrid felt terrible to have upset you," she said gently.

He brushed the side of his face and felt the dirt crumble to the ground. Lita was holding something and he tried to focus...finally seeing a pink bundle that she held with one arm, but there was no crying from the bundle.

It was early evening and cool. Still, Lita wore no coat as she stood near her former gravestone with the statue of the angel that was in her likeness. It was odd to see her standing next to the angel that Alex had carved nearly 500 years earlier. Alex thought of how appropriate the selection had been.

"You did a beautiful job on this sculpture. I think we'll have to do something different with it now."

Finally, Alex found his voice. "Isn't it too cold for her...out here?" he asked.

Lita bounced the pink bundle just a bit and looked adoringly into her face. "I think she's just fine. Although, she would like to meet her papa. Isn't that right, beautiful girl?"

Alex shook his head. "I'm...filthy...and I...I..." He swallowed, terrified of the flood of emotions that he was barely holding back. "I'm not ready for that," he said.

Lita smiled at the infant and said, "It's just a little dirt. In a few years, she'll be eating mud pies and..." she sighed happily and glanced at Alex with tears in her eyes. Then she knelt down by him and turned the tiny pink bundle to face him. She had a pink cap and a few brown curls escaped from the edges. What amazed Alex was the expression on the baby's face, as if she understood his agony. He took in her milky white complexion and the long, dark eyelashes that framed her oracle blue eyes.

Alex was too mesmerized to care about dirt or tears as he gazed at his daughter. "She's...beautiful," he said in hushed reverence.

"Yes. She is truly one of the most beautiful babies I have ever seen." Lita turned her slightly to look at her face. "And look at her watching you. You know what she's wondering?"

He shook his head.

"She's wondering when you are going to hold her." Alex was taken aback by this but he couldn't seem to take his eyes off his daughter. Lita passed the baby to Alex. "So you're going to support her neck and her bum—like this." Lita moved Alex's hands on the tiny bundle.

He laughed and although tears fell from his eyes—he no longer noticed. "She's...so light!" he said holding her inches away from him so that she wouldn't get dirty.

"You can hold her closer. She prefers that."

"Isn't this blanket too tight around her?"

"No. It's called swaddling. It helps new babies feel safe." Lita glanced around. "But she probably needs to go back inside now. Let's take her back up to the cottage."

Alex stood up and cautiously carried his daughter back to the cottage.

"What's her name?" Lita asked.

"We're going to call her Genesis—Genni."

CHAPTER 29

Valeria stood on the back of Charon's ferry as it moved down the river causing her white gown to flow behind her. On the edge of the dark cave was a ledge where three women worked with a spinning wheel. One woman sat at the spinning wheel although it was covered with cobwebs and no longer seemed operational. Another woman held a ball of yarn and she was locked in the motion of wrapping and rewrapping the same thread. The youngest of the women walked to the edge of the river. Leering at Valeria, she reached out to the string leading to the ball of yarn, and snipped the thread.

Time passed, but it was only a consequence of motion. As they came to a fork in the river, an ominous figure stood as if passing judgment. The figure nodded at Charon and they proceeded toward the light. Then, from the darkness of the cave, she noticed they were moving up a stream and it seemed to be getting lighter.

The surroundings were transformed and it was as if the River Styx was a gentle creek moving through a beautiful, golden countryside. The boat pulled up along the field and Valeria stepped off the ferry as Charon nodded to her with the coin still in his hand.

Valeria began to walk through the field. The sky was a brilliant blue and, in the distance, she saw a beautiful oak. She watched as it transformed into a ginkgo tree that was even more magnificent than her tree at Morgana. There was a tug at her heart, but soon it was gone.

There was an odd ruffled movement up the hill as if someone had cut a video and hastily taped it back together. Valeria noticed that the shape—or lack of shape—seemed to be moving toward her, and then it morphed into nearly a mirror image of herself.

"Cassandra!" The woman said as she ran through the field with her brown hair flowing behind her in a light breeze. Valeria took in the startling resemblance of this woman.

Suddenly, Valeria felt the most joyous of feelings and held out her arms for the woman. "Coronis!"

The two women hugged each other and, if tears had been possible, they would have been on both of their faces. Valeria noticed that Coronis's eyes were a far lighter blue than her own. That must have been how others could tell them apart.

Coronis took Valeria's hand to lead her near the ginkgo tree. Lifting a brow, Valeria said, "So, tell me cousin. Is it possible for a mere mortal princess to truly find love with a god?"

With a glow, Coronis looked up dreamily as a spark brushed her eyes. "I can tell you that the mere mortal princess has been in a beautiful dream for...ever." Turning playfully to Valeria, Coronis asked, "And so?"

"Yes, I found Alexander. We have a child!" Then her smile faded and she again felt the tugging of her heart. "Is your child...Asclepius...is he here? How does that work?"

"*No, cousin!*" she said, as if that were an absurdity. Then her smile widened. "He was left to live his life...with my closest and most trusted of friends."

"Where?" Valeria asked, but Coronis's attention was diverted by a magnificent figure on the hill. Immediately, Valeria recognized Apollo. "That must be the god who is now my cousin!" she giggled.

Taking her hand, Coronis gushed, "He will not admit this to you, but he is so grateful for your matchmaking. Otherwise, he may have continued to chase those silly and unattainable maidens...and I might have ended up the object of some lesser god's affection...or worse—a prince!" They laughed, but as Apollo drew nearer, Valeria became more serious and reverent. "I will see you again, cousin!" Coronis whispered as she blew Valeria a kiss and then faded and, in an instant, was gone.

Apollo looked as though he had inspired Michelangelo's David. He was over six feet tall with light brown hair and soft blue eyes.

"Cassandra!"

Valeria bowed. "My, lord!"

"I have something for you! But now, come, let us walk," Apollo said as he took her arm and led her up a hill. Somehow, despite Apollo's stride, Valeria had no difficulty keeping up. "I am pleased to see you here."

"I am pleased to see you, my lord. The sky is not so blue without your presence."

Apollo offered her a knowing smile as he said, "But I am not your symbolon."

Glancing away, Valeria said, "No."

Apollo lowered his brow and slowed his pace. "You are not happy here?"

"As happy as one might be...without one's symbolon," she said.

"Of all the symbolons, you and Alexander have always been special." He stopped and turned to her. "I've come to realize that the oracles will require the power of the gods to fight the gods."

"My, lord, I am concerned about this battle...and I wonder if there will ever be a time when I am again with my symbolon."

Smiling gently, he took her arm as they continued their walk.

CHAPTER 30

That night Alex sat in the bedroom and rocked his daughter—with his wife's lifeless body on the bed next to him. His anguish over Valeria was still devastating, but now he had something to cling to and something else to occupy his mind. He had returned to the cottage with Genni and then passed the infant to Lita. Once he had Lita's assurance that she would hold Genni until he returned, he showered and cleaned up.

Now sitting in the darkness, he heard a discussion outside the cottage. Lita returned with a bottle. "Would you like me to feed her this time?" she asked.

"Yes, please." He narrowed his eyes as he glanced out the window. "What's going on out there?" he asked.

"I'm not sure. It's been going on for hours."

"I think I'll go see for myself," Alex said.

As he opened the door and saw Lars, Ava, Myrdd, and Paolo.

"Lexi!" Lars said. Alex quickly placed a finger over his mouth to quiet him.

"Genni will probably be asleep any minute. Lita's feeding her," he explained. Although his world had crumbled, there was a light in the darkness that was Genni, and he pledged to battle the darkness that threatened to swallow him. Lars and Ava smiled and nodded.

"She is a good baby," Myrdd said.

"I'm glad you're back, Myrdd," Alex said, his eyes betraying the bittersweetness of the moment.

Alex sat down and said, "You don't need to stop your discussion on my account."

Ava brushed a hand over his shoulder. "Honey, we should have been discussing this at the main house but..." Ava said and glanced at Myrdd. "Evidently, Myrdd wants to be here." She shrugged, indicating that they had no control of Myrdd's actions.

With a fire in his eyes, Myrrdd pointed to Alex. "You must go to her!"

Alex turned his head to peer into the bedroom window with sudden hope and anticipation, but Myrdd shook his head. "She is no longer there."

"Where then, Myrdd?" Alex asked, as he felt his heart beginning to pound again.

"The Elysian Fields," Paolo said. "Daphne says that is where she is now."

Alex shook his head cynically. "I no longer believe anything Daphne says!"

Paolo looked down and pressed his hands together.

"Alex, Myrdd said the same thing as soon as he recovered," Ava added, as Lars nodded in agreement.

Alex glanced in through the bedroom window where Lita was smiling as she rocked the pink bundle.

"What about Genni?" he said, feeling torn. "Val's father deserted her—although that was mostly an emotional desertion. But how can I do that to her daughter?"

Myrdd spoke, "It is part of his plan."

"Whose plan, Myrdd?" Lars asked, but Myrdd was lost again. "Myrdd?"

Paolo drew a deep breath and said, "Alex, I believe that you must go to Valeria now if you are ever to see her again."

"No offense, pal, but you aren't high on my list of trusted sources either," Alex said lowering his brow.

Paolo continued, "It makes sense though, does it not? That is why Myrdd insisted that Valeria go to Cuma—"

"Please!" Alex said raising an arm and gulping back the tears. He couldn't have this conversation with Paolo right now.

Standing to return to his daughter, Alex felt a delicate hand on his shoulder and turned. It was little, blond Olivia.

"Hello, Alexander!" she said as her face turned beat red—reminding him of his beloved. She cleared her throat. "I apologize for the intrusion." Alex narrowed an eye and saw Elliot standing at the base of the porch. "I had a dream—"

"Despite your hardships at this time, I told Olivia that she must share this with you!" Elliot interrupted.

Alex nodded, and Olivia continued, "I had a dream that you were wandering your way through a labyrinth," she said.

"That's hardly news," Alex said, and then instantly regretted it as Olivia's blush increased and she stared at her feet.

"I am so sorry to be intruding at such a time. Perhaps Elliot was wrong and I should come back later," she said in almost a whisper; then, with a small curtsy, she turned.

Realizing what he had done, Alex put his hand on Olivia's shoulder to stop her from running. Instantly, Elliot was on the porch and physically removing Alex's hand.

"Unhand her!" he said. The first word came out bravely. The 'her' came out in a screech. But Alex removed his hand.

"I am so sorry, Olivia," Alex said. Then he glanced at the red-faced young man, and added, "And Elliot! I just have not been myself. Please forgive me!"

Elliot looked down and, even through his light hair, his scalp was red. He looked up and his eyes were big and terrified.

"Olivia, please have a seat and tell me about your dream," Alex said gesturing to a rattan loveseat.

Nodding to Elliot, Olivia took his hand and they sat next to each other as Olivia pressed her ankles together.

"Well," Olivia started, "you were walking through a labyrinth. Only there was...I think it was more like a...like a maze. There were different ways that you could turn. You were guided by—"

Ava interrupted, "I hope it was Virgil, because we've probably burned bridges with the Cumaen Sibyl." Olivia and Elliot glanced at her accusingly. "I'm just saying," Ava said as she shrugged in apology.

"Go on, Olivia, please," Alex urged.

Elliot nodded at her and she gathered her courage again. "Well," Olivia said in an embarrassed whisper, "actually, I don't know who the guide was...because he was in a shadow..." Olivia narrowed her eyes for a moment before continuing, "But it felt like there was...I suppose it was like, an angel who was guiding you."

"Olivia, have you been reading Dante recently?" Alex asked.

She shook her head innocently, and Elliot spoke on her behalf. "I asked her the same question when she told me of her dream. But Olivia has never read or studied Virgil's *Aenied* nor Dante's *Divine Comedy*," Elliot said. "That is why I determined that we should approach you with her dream."

Lars drew a breath. "Olivia, as an oracle, what visions have you had?"

Her pink mouth turned into a perfect pout as her brows dropped to ponder the question. "What do you mean?"

"Olivia, we all have visions or gifts that focus on a particular area. Have you ever had visions or dreams of Val—Cassandra—or Alex?" Lars pressed.

She looked down and said softly, "I don't believe so." Then she turned to Elliot. "I thought perhaps it was only a dream." She took his hand. "Elliot, we should leave this poor, grieving man to his peace."

They stood, and Olivia released a light sigh as they walked down the steps and around the surviving hydrangeas. Suddenly she stopped and, without turning to face them, she said, "I come from there, where I would gladly return—if not for your absence. And now, love has moved me and compels me to speak."

All eyes turned toward Olivia. "Those were the angel's words to you."

Alex's eyes grew wide.

"Those were the words of Beatrice," Paolo said in a ghostly whisper.

Olivia's face was blank. "I do not know a Beatrice." Alex sat speechless.

Elliot's face filled with understanding, "Dearest, Beatrice was Dante's lifelong love from afar. In his *Divine Comedy*, Beatrice, who is in Paradiso, requests that Virgil go to Dante's aid and escort him through the underworld."

Olivia's face was still blank. "Elliot, I have never heard of Dante or Beatrice."

Elliot smiled joyfully at the girl, as if she had just uttered the most extraordinary words. "My Olivia has no interest in literature or theater," he informed Lars and Alex.

Paolo narrowed his eyes. "I believe the interpreted line is 'I come from there, where I would gladly return.' Beatrice did not say, '—*if not for your absence.*'"

Alex's eyes rimmed with tears. "You're right Paolo. Beatrice didn't say that—Val did!" he said as hope again filled his heart. Alex stepped down the stairs to Olivia. "Thank you, Olivia! Thank you!"

She blushed and glanced down at the ground, but seemed to be standing taller—as was Elliot.

Lars stood. "Lexi, I think we should consider a family meeting. And despite your upset with Daphne, she should be present. We need to determine if something can be done."

CHAPTER 31

Lita was rocking Genni as they sat in the living room at the main house.

"I am absolutely certain that was a message from Val. She wants me to bring her back!" Alex said. "And I know that if there were not a way for us to leave the underworld, she would never call me away from Genni!"

Lars lifted a hand. "It isn't that simple, Lexi—"

"Why not?" Paolo interrupted, as he gestured emphatically. "We have confirmed an entrance via the temple of the Cumaen Sibyl. Alex must bring her back to us. There is no time to waste!"

"Paolo, honey, we all want the same thing," Ava said sympathetically. Paolo looked away and then took Daphne's hand. She sat next to him with her eyes downcast to avoid an meeting Alex's gaze.

"But is it the right thing to do?" Camille asked. "Alex, you know that Val grew up alone...how could you leave this child?"

The room was silent and Alex thought for a moment. "I've thought a lot about that, Camille. If it weren't for Genni, I would have been gone this morning." He lifted his arms helplessly. "I...don't have experience in this new realm of parenthood. So, I had to think of what my father might have done. And what I do know, without a shadow of a doubt, is that Ian would have gone to hell and back for my mother. And that is what I intend to do—bring back Genni's mother!"

Lars sighed and went to the whiteboard near the fireplace. "All right. Let's see if we can figure this out then. We know that Alex can enter the underworld. What we don't know..." he wrote as he spoke, "Can he find Val? Can they find their way out? And is it possible for either of them to leave the underworld? There is enough opposition to make extraction seem nearly impossible."

"Yes, but we have conquered the impossible before!" Tavish said.

"Let's list the possible adversaries, as this may be our show stopper," Lars said.

"Cerberus," Camille said. "Always hated dogs, but a giant three headed dog—"

"Who is Cerberus?" Olivia asked innocently.

"Dearest, he is 'the Hellhound from Hades' and guards the gates of the underworld, to prevent those who have forged the River Styx from ever escaping. It is said that he has only an appetite for live meat."

"All right, Cerberus," Lars said as he wrote it down.

"What if we exited from the temple? We might be able to get by Cerberus that way," Alex said.

"Impossible," Paolo said.

"Why?" Alex asked.

Paolo shrugged and looked away and so Lars said, "We'll come back to that. What other obstacles?"

"Hades—he isn't going to give up a soul or a body!" Ava said.

Lars wrote down 'Hades' on the whiteboard. "Any others?"

Caleb was absorbed in his computer game as usual.

"If we can find a way to get by those two issues, I believe Alex and Val can escape," Jonah said.

Suddenly, Caleb's eyes lit up. "Hey! What if Alex used the motor from before and swam out? Then he could get by Cerberus."

"Might work," Lars wrote that down as a possible solution. "But then, how would they get out of Delos? They have to exit at either the temple or Delos. It seems like the Cumaen temple is a more likely extraction point."

"My sister—I mean, my mother—told me that an exit through the temple could only be completed with the assistance of Hecate. As Hecate was a friend of my mother's, I do not believe she will assist you."

"Good point," Lars said. "There may be other exits but the only two that we know will lead to a desirable destination are through the temple or Delos. If the temple isn't an option, how can we get Alex and Val beyond Delos and the adamantine gates?"

Ava offered, "Looks like we'll have to bring Shinsu in on this."

"After our last trip into Delos, I think it's too risky to have Shinsu open the gates for us," Camille said.

Jonah leaned forward. "I have a thought..."

"Yes?" Camille said as she brushed her hand across his back.

"Don't we have another issue that is just as pressing as bringing Val back? I mean, what happens after we bring her back? We'll still have Jeremiah and his army working to destroy us," Jonah said.

"What's your point, Jonah?" Ava asked.

"My point is that resolving both of those issues at the same time might cause enough distraction that we may be able to get rid of Jeremiah *and* get Alex and Val out."

Lars rubbed the crease between his brows. "How do you see that working?"

"I haven't thought it through yet, but perhaps Shinsu could help us. There would have to be an innocuous reason for the meeting. I believe that with all of the revived oracles, we might have a chance to get Jeremiah removed."

"Perhaps Daphne and I could announce our engagement," Paolo said without looking at Daphne, whose mouth dropped open in shock.

"Yes! That might work!" Tavish exclaimed.

"You might ask me if I'm interested," Daphne said coldly.

Paolo turned to meet her disapproving eye. "It is only for the sake of Valeria. If I wished to marry you I would propose properly. Perhaps I should do that."

Daphne turned her head away from his in irritation. "*No...you should not.* Not now. Not while you are continuing your love affair with another woman and constantly willing to risk your life for her."

Ava rolled her eyes. "Aww, come on, Daph—you're hardly one to talk!"

Paolo brushed her leg and she pushed his hand away. "Perhaps that is what makes us perfect for each other."

"Or perhaps not so perfect," Ava said with a laugh and then her voice grew serious. "Why don't you two take your lover's spat outside unless you have something constructive to add to this discussion?"

Daphne turned her head away from Paolo.

"Paolo, I don't believe the council would be interested in flying in for another one of your engagements anytime soon. I think we need to talk to Shinsu," Lars said.

"Sue..." Myrdd said absently.

"Next question is how will you find Val?" Lars asked.

"That is not an easy one to solve. There are no known maps of the underworld from the temple—other than Dante's or Virgil's descriptions."

"Alex, you're planning a walk through hell, but what if you never even find Val?" Daphne said.

With his eyes darting around the room, Paolo lifted his hand to his mouth, tapping his foot nervously. He crossed his legs and sat back and then leaned forward and crossed his legs the other way. Finally, he said, "I will go for Valeria."

The others in the room stared at him in disbelief—except Daphne whose green eyes took on a woeful expression.

"You?" Alex said. "What's in it for you?" He glared at Paolo.

"Alex, Paolo did save Val several times. I think it is worth thinking about," Lars said.

Slapping his hand down on the arm of the chair, Alex said, "Absolutely not!"

"Alex, I only wish to help! I do not wish to see Genesis alone...that is all," Paolo said. With that, both men glanced to Lita who had turned Genni on her knee and was gently bouncing her and tapping on her back.

Staring longingly at his daughter, Alex immediately cooled down. "Sorry, pal. Didn't mean to...well, you know," he said, watching as Lita laid Genni in the cradle.

"Alexander must go!" Myrdd said, and Alex shrugged as if it was settled.

"Why, old man? You offer us these absurd statements of what must be—but, so far, your advice has cost us Valeria!" Paolo spat.

"Alright...alright. Alex, it's up to you," Lars said.

"I believe that Val means for me to come for her. That's what she said, and that was what was in Olivia's vision. I can't imagine that we were ever meant to be apart."

"All right—it's settled. Alex will go to the underworld. Next, is how will you find your way to the Elysian Fields, and then back out? There is no map. Everyone who has ever gone there and come back out was guided. We have no trusted guides. If only we could somehow conjure someone—well, an ally—to help us navigate it."

"I can help you," Paolo said as he fidgeted nervously.

"How? Kristiana may have given you a tour of the underworld— but she would have never taken you from the underworld to Delos! She's technically a mortal and would not have had access. As an immortal you would've had access to Delos. But there is no way you went from the temple to Delos!" Lars eyes narrowed and then he stared at Myrdd. "Unless..."

Camille's eyes widened as she stared at Paolo and then Myrdd. "Paolo, did Myrdd take Kristiana into Delos? Was she the mortal who cost him his life?" she asked

"Not exactly," Paolo said as he stared at his tightly clenched fingers. "Though, I have gone from the temple to Delos."

The rest of the oracles stared at Paolo suspiciously except Myrdd and Daphne, who were totally absorbed in their own worlds.

"Honey, we all appreciate your desire to help, but right now we need the truth. And I hate to be brutal, but why would you or Kristiana violate the rules to go from the underworld to Delos? It's not like there was anything to gain from it! You were already a freak of nature with your mother as a mortal and your father probably—" Suddenly, Ava realized what she said and winced as she glanced at Alex and Genni and said, "Sorry...I'm better with boats!" Turning back to Paolo she continued, "Let me rephrase—You were already immortal and Kristiana obviously had nothing to gain from it. Seems like a helluva risk for a kick!"

Alex added, "Further, there are no oracles whom have ever made that trek. The only mortal visitors to the underworld who ever returned had guides, and were most likely fictional!"

Paolo swallowed as he glanced up for a moment and then down at the floor. "As you have already surmised, I am not a god—or even a poor relation," Paolo huffed, as he dipped his head and winced at the confession. "I do not know if my father was an oracle."

"He had to be—you're immortal!" Camille said. "So your father must be either an immortal, a god, or an oracle."

"My father was not a god. And I am not certain that my father was immortal. I..." He swallowed again. "I swam in the River Styx as a child—that is why I am immortal."

"You're not..." Alex began, and then he understood. "You were born mortal?" he asked.

"Yes," Paolo said, humiliated by the admission. Daphne stared at him as if he had suddenly grown horns.

"So you and Kristiana were the mortals who Myrdd brought to Delos," Tavish said.

Myrdd looked up from his position by the fireplace. "Yes, I betrayed my oath. That is why I had to be punished."

Alex shook his head. "Wait a minute—that doesn't make any sense! Myrdd would have had no reason to go through the underworld to Delos," Alex challenged.

"Myrdd did not take me to Delos," Paolo said.

"Paolo, wasn't that why Myrdd was executed—for bringing you into Delos?" Alex asked, feeling frustrated.

Standing, Paolo began to pace without making eye contact with anyone. "That is what... Kristiana told Jeremiah," Paolo said. Camille rolled her eyes. "But that is not what occurred," Paolo finished. "Myrdd did not take us."

"Myrdd confessed to taking a mortal to Delos—I was there!" Tavish said.

"He...was confused." Paolo faced the fireplace. "Mother counted on his confusion. She fed him the lie and threatened him for 2,000 years until he believed it."

Suddenly, Camille stood and said, "You were a grown man when those charges were brought! You permitted his execution?"

"Yes, my mother and Jeremiah lied and I did not step forward," Paolo said, and Myrdd looked up in surprise. "Myrdd refused to violate the agreements, and so mother went to Hecate and asked for her help. She agreed to distract Hades so that Kristiana could bring me to Delos, where she tied a rope around my ankle, connected it to a post and then she permitted me to swim. The only condition was that my mother could not enter the river herself and violate the requirements of the Fates. Hecate had already requested favors on my mother's behalf."

"Cassandra's curse?" Lars asked.

"Yes. Mother used Envy's poison to anger the Fates...and Zeus. But the Fates and Zeus refused to violate Apollo's immortal creation— the oracle, Cassandra. Instead, they modified her immortality with the curse."

"If you knew that—why didn't you tell us?" Alex demanded.

Paolo shook his head. "I would have if the information had been necessary."

"It's been necessary, pal! All those years I've spent wondering who or what was responsible...and you knew!" Alex's eyes widened in disbelief. "*You knew she would die when you married her!* All my warnings..." he shook his head in anguish.

"No!" Paolo's eyes widened. "I did not expect that they would take her from me. My mother knew that I would marry Isabella. I expected that she would allow her to live." Then Paolo looked away, unable to meet Alex's angry gaze and muttered, "Besides, there was nothing that information could have done to protect Valeria."

"We sat here—all of us—discussing the curse and pondering its origin, and all the while, you had the answers," Alex said, his entire body shaking with anger.

"Alex, that information would have only precipitated the current tragedy. At the time of our discussions, it appeared that the curse had been eliminated—and it has been! If it had not been eliminated, then there was nothing for any of us to do."

Tightening his jaw Alex got up and paced. "Paolo, just tell us the truth!"

"I am telling you the truth now," he said quietly.

"Is this your way of being the hero?"

"No. I will abide by your decision about what should be done. However, I can accompany you into the underworld and provide you details about how we were able to get by Cerberus."

"Tranquilizers," Alex said. "I did read Virgil's *Aenied*."

"That would work." Paolo nodded.

"Valerian root?" Ava asked.

"Poppy extract," Paolo said.

"An opiate," Alex added.

Lars nodded to Mani. "Alright—we need a monster-sized tranquilizer."

"I can help you with that," Mani said.

"Good! Now we need to discover some way to summon an immediate council meeting."

Jonah lifted a finger. "I have a thought," he said, glancing at Alex. "What was it that Jeremiah charged you with?"

"A frivolous abuse of council," Alex said. "Why?"

"I believe I know how we can summon a council meeting." Jonah turned toward Paolo. "We'll need your help!"

"But I must guide Alex to Valeria and then into Delos," Paolo said.

"Can you draw a map?" Jonah asked.

"Perhaps," Paolo responded.

"Jonah, can you develop that plan," Lars asked.

"Yes," Jonah said with a nod.

Lars paused, momentarily stretching his arms. "Okay, so let's assume that Alex can find his way through the underworld to Valeria, and then into Delos without harm. And, let's say we find a way to hold a council meeting. Our only other obstacle is Hades! Any ideas on how to distract Hades without any of us becoming victims of his rage?" Lars asked.

"Impossible!" Paolo said. "We don't have Hecate to help us!"

Genni stirred in her cradle and Lita picked her up.

Caleb glanced up from his computer briefly and said, distractedly, "Genni wants Myrdd to hold her." Then he lowered his head again, concentrating on his laptop.

Lita glanced at Myrdd who was crouched in a ball on the floor and rocking. Lita made eye contact with Alex and then glanced at Myrdd. Alex narrowed an eye and then, with a doubtful glance, shook his head.

"The child," Myrdd muttered. "She...she..."

"Caleb, I don't think Myrdd is quite ready to hold Genni—she's awfully small right now. Perhaps Myrdd would like to *see* Genni, while I hold her." Lita knelt by Myrdd. "Myrdd, would you like to see the baby?" she asked.

Myrdd stopped rocking as his eyes began to dart toward the child and then away. Alex and Lars leaned forward in their seats, ready to spring on Myrdd should the need arise. Myrdd drew a deep breath and then noticed Genni's tiny hand reaching out for him. He chuckled softly. When he held out his finger, she wrapped her hand around it. Myrdd's smile widened.

"I do not repel her," he said.

"Of course not," Lita said in a sweet motherly voice.

"Still, I do believe she would prefer her father," Myrdd said, still smiling at the tiny infant.

Lita stood and handed Genni to Alex, whose face lit as he wrapped her in his arms and stared adoringly into her face.

"Where were we?" Myrdd asked.

"When?" Ava asked.

Myrdd stood and glanced at Alex. "Oh, yes—Hades! It will not be necessary to distract Hades."

Alex narrowed his eyes. "Why not, Myrdd?"

"He will only require an exchange."

Paolo stood again and rolled his eyes. "*Only* an exchange! Who did you have in mind? Any mortal could be substituted for me. But Alex is an oracle. That would require another oracle. And Valeria... Who would Hades consider a fair exchange for the last oracle? Shall we kidnap some potential prospects?" Paolo asked sarcastically.

Turning slowly to Paolo, Myrdd lifted a finger, narrowed his eyes, and in a booming voice said, "*You*...you shall set things right." Then Myrdd glanced around the room and his eyes focused on Alex. "Cassandra knows those whose fate it is to go in your place."

CHAPTER 32

It was the next morning when the family gathered inside the temple of the Cumaen Sibyl—this time with no concern of an attack. The plan was that Alex had all day and into the evening to get himself and Valeria to Delos. Then, the rest of the family would fly to Corfu and meet that night at the emergency council meeting.

Alex stood at the entrance to the underworld and stared at the door.

"Are you frightened?" Camille asked.

"How could I ever be frightened knowing that she's there?" Tears rimmed his eyes. "I only pray that this works."

Mani patted Alex's shoulder, "Once you give Cerberus the tranquilizers it will take about twenty minutes for him to sleep. But remember that he will only be out for a short while. Paolo estimates fifteen to twenty minutes."

Paolo nodded and then said, "Alex, Daphne would like to speak to you before...I told her that I would ask you first."

Alex shrugged grudgingly, and Daphne approached him.

"Alex, I want—"

"Daph, I'm sure that someday, after all of this is resolved..." He winced, hoping that there would be such a day. "I want to be able to trust you again. Until then...we will pretend this never—"

"Alex, I'm not asking for your forgiveness. I know that's...not possible. But please, remember what happened to Orpheus." She bit her lip and said, "You know that even if Orpheus had looked back...he wouldn't have seen her."

He remembered the story of Orpheus who was permitted to enter the underworld to retrieve his bride as long as he didn't look back. After exiting the underworld, Orpheus felt so relieved that he turned to hold his wife and she vanished forever.

"What do you mean?" Alex asked.

"You will be able to see and communicate with Valeria while she is still in the Elysian Fields. But once she leaves for Delos, she will have only limited opportunities to speak or be seen. Don't question her presence—trust your instincts! You do know that she will need to testify for the Council."

"My guess is that she will want to testify."

"Other than while she's testifying or while on Charon's ferry—"

Alex interrupted, "*Charon's ferry?* Why would she be there?"

"She will wait on Charon's ferry while you negotiate with Hades." Daphne said. "Just remember that other than those instances I've just mentioned, you won't be able to see her until she is free from the underworld."

Alex nodded.

"One more thing—be cautious of your agreements with Hades. If he permits you to take Valeria, remember to abide by his rules—and don't look back." Her eyes softened and he almost pitied her. "And... someday, when this is all over with, please don't hate me," she said, touching his arm.

"I don't hate you, Daph," he said, uncomfortable with her tone.

She removed her hand and then turned and left.

"Your daughter would like to tell you that she shall see you soon." Lita looked adoringly at the infant and then handed her to Alex.

He held her tightly and walked a few steps, facing away from the others. "Genni, it might seem that I am deserting you. I hope you don't ever believe that. Some might even tell you that's true. What is true, is that I am heart-broken without your mother," Alex began to choke and Lita put her hand on his shoulder. "A life without her is near unbearable." He swallowed and bit his lip to regain control. "Still...*I adore you!* Seeing you is like seeing a mirror to my beloved...*you* are a symbol of our love."

He kissed her forehead while the infant stared at him, as if she understood every word. Alex turned to Lita. "So, Genni, I am going to leave you with," he drew a rough breath, "Lita and Mani," he said, tears forming in his eyes again. "If I never come back, I know that they will love you as their own." Lita nodded as tears spilled from her eyes. "I pray that both your mother and I see you on the other side," he said. He squeezed the child, kissed her forehead, and then handed her to Lita. Without another word, he opened the door and in less than a moment, he was in a cold cave with no entrance or exit.

∞

Alex could feel the helplessness of his surroundings and its effects on the souls. He prayed that his beloved had not been banished to any place so cold and gray. He walked along the path for what could have been minutes, hours, or days—he had no sense of time here. When he approached a tunnel, a cloaked figure appeared and his heart began pounding nervously.

The figure moved closer and, suddenly, Alex worried that he would not reach Valeria. He was about to turn and run when the figure raised his arms and said in a ghostly tone, "Abandon all hope, ye who enter here!"

Involuntarily, Alex sucked in a breath. Then he realized that he recognized the voice, but, in this environment, he couldn't quite place it. He narrowed his eyes.

"Max?" he said, peering into the darkness.

"I'd prefer it if you called me Virgil," Max said, pulling the hood off his head. "Great, get-up, huh? Got it from a drib."

With sudden relief, Alex hugged Max, and although Max gladly accepted the affection, he followed it with, "Come on...let's not get all mushy here. After all, we are currently trapped in hell. Not exactly a cause for celebration."

"Val is..."

"I know," Max said, the compassion returning to his voice.

"Is she in the Elysian Fields?"

Max nodded.

Alex lowered his brows. "Have you found Kristiana?"

Scratching his face, Max said, "Yes...she's not in good shape."

"I'm sorry, Max,"

He smiled wistfully. "I wouldn't be any place else...even if it is hell."

Alex nodded, "I understand."

"All right," Max said, taking a deep breath. "I am playing Virgil to your Dante and your Beatrice is awaiting your arrival in Paradiso! Shall we go?"

CHAPTER 33

Shinsu sat in her garden. She longed to see Myrddin—it had been far too long. Perhaps years and distance had changed him, but her heart belonged to him always. Still, the ruse had to continue for a bit longer.

A boat pulled up to the dock and Shinsu watched as Jeremiah walked up her stone path between rose bushes, leaning heavily on his cane. He kissed the side of her face. She turned away from his as if something had just distracted her.

"Jeremiah, it would be appropriate to call before you appear! Good heavens, it's as if you believe I have nothing better to do than await your arrival! I deserted that notion long ago," she said as she rose to go inside her white adobe home. "Tea?" she asked as she glanced over her shoulder.

"We need to discuss the emergency meeting taking place this evening. The other council members should arrive on the island shortly." Shinsu nodded as she filled the bright red tea pot with water— nearly drowning the sound of his voice. Tolerating him was something that she had no interest in doing anymore, especially knowing that Myrddin was alive. At least Jeremiah had enough interest in his young wives that he didn't bother her anymore.

"Sit outside. I'll be there in a moment," she said tersely. Jeremiah nodded and, leaning on his cane, he hobbled outside to an Adirondack chair.

A few minutes later, Shinsu arrived with a tray of apples and cheddar, and two cups of tea, along with an elegant teapot.

"Shinsu, you know I despise apples and cheddar."

She tilted her head ignoring the comment. "I must have forgotten!" She poured them both tea and, before he could say more, she turned away and sat down in her chair.

"Shinsu, may I have sugar in my tea?"

She turned on him with her eyes tense. "Jeremiah—I believe that you have confused me for the servant children who you take for your wives," she said with mock sweetness. "If you wish to have sugar in your tea, you can purchase it at the store in town."

Jeremiah sighed and set down his delicate china cup. "Shinsu, what has upset you? Does this have anything to do with the meeting this evening?"

Pull it together. "Let's get down to business, shall we?" she said.

"Yes! Let's do!" Jeremiah responded sarcastically as he turned his face from hers. "So, what is this all about?"

"I received this by personal messenger yesterday. I felt it deserved our immediate attention."

Jeremiah took the message from Shinsu and read it. He moved his lips while reading it rapidly and he suddenly stopped—in shock—and then read the remainder. And then he read it over again. Shinsu knew she should look away, but something in her needed to see Jeremiah squirm. She set her tea cup down on the table between them.

"Well? Certainly you have assimilated the finer points of the note!" Shinsu said.

Jeremiah continued to stare at it and then finding his voice said, "You should have..." He cleared his throat. "Protocol requires that you permit me to call the emergency meeting. I don't know that this couldn't have been investigated outside of Delos. I've spent so much time here in the past six months, I almost wonder if it's worth it to go back and forth!"

"But then who would you bed? You know there are laws about that kind of thing here," Shinsu said, as she rose and took his tea cup. "As far as notifying you, I did inform...what is her name? Your fourteenth wife...oh yes, Ruth, And Ruth informed me that you were busy with your twenty-third wife." She waited for Jeremiah to nod and then took the cups inside.

"Shinsu, is that what this is about? I thought our time together these past few months had remedied your insecurities." Shinsu cringed. "But I assure you that if that is what you wish for, I shall attempt to find more time for you."

"When would that be Jeremiah?"

Jeremiah smiled coolly. "Have no worries, if that is what you desire—that is what you shall have."

She glared at him for an instant which he chose to interpret as a demand for a schedule.

"Shinsu, I'm pleased to see your interest! Let me assure you that we shall work this out all in good time, my dear! Of course, back to the subject at hand...from now on, I prefer that you—"

"Jeremiah, after 500 years, I *am* aware of your preferences!" she said calmly. "However, as you can see, this letter claims that there was a 'frivolous abuse of council' and I *do* know how you feel about that! Certainly, if an engagement would be cause for an immediate council meeting, such an accusation as this must also be addressed immediately!"

Tapping his cane, Jeremiah held the note up toward her. "Shinsu, is there any indication of whom this note came from?" Shinsu swooped it from his hand and glanced at it and then filed it in her bag.

"Why would that be pertinent?"

"Well, I've been thinking that perhaps we've had too much of a show of power. Perhaps it would be better if we handled this...privately."

Shinsu rolled her head back and laughed. "Privately? My goodness, Jeremiah, I almost believe the accusation is about you!" She patted his cheek as if she was teasing, and then said, "Don't worry, we will simply address it tonight. If no one steps forward, then we will drop it. But my guess is that we'll have all the details we need this evening," she said with a cold glare, watching Jeremiah squirm.

"It's just that with all of the trouble with the damned oracles..." Realizing his words, he glanced up at Shinsu, who nodded in irritation. "Sorry, my dear...sometimes I forget."

"Yes, I know." Shinsu walked to her gardening table and picked up her hedge clippers. Then stepping to her hedge, she began chopping as Jeremiah rose to follow her.

"I do hope you know that I hold you in very high regard."

"Of course..." Shinsu slammed the hedge clippers together in a violent action, causing Jeremiah to jump back. A branch flew up in the air and landed on Jeremiah.

"Shinsu, what in the devil has gotten into you?"

Drawing a deep breath, she kept both hands on the hedge clippers but lowered them...a bit too closely to an area that Jeremiah held near and dear. He pushed the clippers aside. "Is this about Rose?"

"No, Jeremiah, I've lost count of your wives and I no longer see it as a personal affront. Now, I just perceive it as the efforts of an over-sexed man to regain his youth by touting falsities."

Jeremiah began to erupt and she held up her hand to stop him. "I have tolerated the humiliation for 500 years and I do assure you that I am quite over it. I am also aware that I was a key component in your ability to take control of the council. No one would dare challenge you while I was at your side—at least while Myrddin was gone—"

"I have asked you repeatedly not to discuss your former...husband."

"It is a fact that Myrddin was my former spouse—my symbolon. I was made an oracle and brought back from the Elysium Fields *for him*."

"And he cheated on you!"

Shinsu's voice became vicious as she seethed, "I do not intend to discuss Myrddin's possible sexual misconduct *with you!*"

He held his hand up as if he would slap her. Then, seeing the challenge in her eyes, he calmed himself and backed down. "Shinsu, what has come over you?"

Taking the hedge clippers back to her bench, she pulled off her gloves. "Not a thing, Jeremiah. Why?"

He wiped a few droplets of perspiration from his lip. "Because of the recent trouble with the Trento family, I do have some concerns."

"Yes, well, we shall discover the source of the letter this evening—that I am certain." She turned to him. "Now then, run along! I have business to attend to."

"I'll come by at ten tonight."

She shook her head. "No, thank you, Jeremiah," she said. "I've got...errands. I'll get my own ride."

CHAPTER 34

Paolo sat on the trog, the boat specially designed to travel into the hidden caves along the cliffs of Gaios. A storm was brewing to the west and already he could see that the water was choppier than usual. Still, he saw the stars. By the time he would leave—if he left—it would be storming overhead.

The driver glanced back at him and he reclined his seat but remained upright. He loved this part. It reminded him of a roller coaster ride, dangerous and thrilling. He sipped his champagne and then set it in the holder. He remembered that the last time he had taken this excursion into Delos, Valeria had been with him, and they were engaged. He remembered the way the moonlight played on her eyes and the white gown that was so exquisitely fitted just for her. Now, he only prayed that he might see her again.

The trog throttled the engine to perfectly position the boat. Paolo saw the lights of other trogs approaching and knew the driver would be in a hurry to catch a fare from another immortal. Paolo stared out at the angry waves crashing on the cliffs and boulders ahead of him, and again felt that thrill. The trog headed full speed into the cliff. Paolo used to believe that the speed was to titillate the guests. After having kayaked into the cave, Paolo now knew that it was in order to gain momentum before the driver killed the engine in the cave. Otherwise, they would have to battle the tides for hours and use the rope that ran along the edge of the cave to get to the ledge, where they crossed the bridge into Delos. Paolo had pulled himself along those ropes—they were covered in algae and provided very little traction.

For some reason, this event triggered memories of his first time in Delos—perhaps because this trip into Delos was most certainly his last. This time, he was not thinking of the time as a boy when he had swam in the forbidden and dangerous waters, but the time when he had finally been acknowledged as an immortal. Of course, it was after Myrdd had been executed and Jeremiah had validated his membership into the exclusive club.

To hear his name announced as an immortal had been the dream of a lifetime—for him and Kristiana. It had been her insistence that, somehow, her son would be recognized, even though she never could be.

He remembered hearing whispers as he entered the council that he was a direct descendent of the god, Adonis. The corners of his mouth turned up at that suggestion. Few remembered that Adonis was the product of a relationship between incestuous mortals. Still, he understood the reference was neither to the incestuous relationship nor to the question of his mortality. It was a reference to his dark good looks and he had learned to play them to his advantage.

Just then, the trog entered the narrow cave and cut off its engine. Paolo remembered that on his first trip, if he hadn't been so intrigued with getting into Delos, he would have asked the driver to take him out and do it again.

But this was a different trip, and the results would forever close this door to him. As he stepped onto the ledge and lit the torch, he waited for the trog to disappear around the corner as it exited the cave. The waves rolled in ferociously and Paolo glanced down the cave, for the first time seeing the real danger. The ledge was wet and one false step at the wrong moment—as the waves were rolling in—and he would probably never escape.

The bridge was lowered and he crossed to the adamantine gates. There, he waited for the drib to arrive with the gondola. Most immortals joked of how frightened they had been with their first view of the poor, dead souls—but Paolo knew them well from his childhood in the temple of Cuma and the underworld.

By the time Kristiana had taken him to the temple, there were only remnants of the ethylene vapors. And because he was not an oracle, the hallucinations didn't last nearly long enough for his liking, but that was in his youth and he was past all of that now.

As Paolo stepped off the gondola and onto the island of Delos, dressed in his tux, he subconsciously ran his finger along the neck of his shirt.

He glanced at the table of food and saw a young immortal woman winking at him. He offered her his most seductive smile as she approached, and then he lightly brushed his lips along the key points of her neck that would ensure a physical response.

"You look lovely this evening, Martina."

"Paolo, you haven't called me in decades!" she said with a pout.

"I have been...otherwise engaged. However, perhaps I should find some time."

He needed all the friends he could get tonight. He smiled at her seductively and then glanced around at the group of immortals. He realized that although he called them friends, there was not one whom he could depend on to stand up for him if it were required.

Straight ahead was a wall of heavy silk that housed the extraordinary kitchen facilities. The River Styx circled on either side, with its brilliant shade of oracle blue—although the immortals would never acknowledge the color as such because they perceived the oracles to be of a lesser breed. They had a strict social order with gods and their immortal descendants at the top, oracles in the middle, and mortals nearly inconsequential.

He scrutinized the group and then permitted his eyes to briefly wander to the edge of Delos, where a narrow walkway led down to Jeremiah's prison cells and then—if one made it past Cerberus, the flesh eating mutt—they would find themselves in hell. It took a nod from Minos to veer to the light and the Elysian Fields.

As he studied the eight thrones of red and gold velvet, placed for each head of the council, he noticed the candles lit from crystal chandeliers that hung dramatically off the fifty-foot ceilings. One hung right over Jeremiah's chair. He smiled; it would take so little to loosen the rope to it. But Shinsu's seat was next to Jeremiah's and Shinsu was a friend. In fact, it seemed that it was only the oracles who he could ever count on—despite their differences!

He took a glass of champagne from a passing drib and worked the room socially until he reached the far left wall. Glancing around he saw that no one was watching, and his eyes darted beyond the wall and down the River Styx. *Where were they?* As he coolly brought his glance back to Delos, he sensed someone watching him, and his eyes met Shinsu's. They nodded casually and then both wandered toward the grand buffet.

Sliced beef wellington, trout almandine, lobster, and a myriad of other luxuries covered the table. A drib tossed custom made salads for guests. Paolo took a gulp of his champagne. He had no interest in food at the moment. His stomach tightened as he thought about the plan. It would require split second timing for it to all work out—and there was much at risk for many if they failed—which they likely would.

Eyeing a woman in the distance, he smiled, lifted his champagne glass toward her, and slid his hand into his pocket in a perfect GQ pose—a move that had won him the attentions of almost every woman. But tonight, he was not interested. The woman's eyes lit in invitation. As soon as she turned to speak to someone else, Paolo's eyes darted around the room again and, without facing Shinsu, he said, "They are not here yet. We will need to stall." His eyes darted to the cave wall to where he expected them to emerge. As the woman turned back to him, he returned to his role as the son of Adonis—and offered her a lascivious grin.

"I have business that will keep us occupied for a short while. If it goes beyond that...we're in trouble. Where is Daphne?" Shinsu asked, attempting to hide her concern.

"She should be here," he glanced at his Rolex, "now." They turned to see Daphne stepping off from the gondola, wearing a loose one-shoulder gown that shimmered green and blue with silver beading. Her red hair danced from her shoulders.

"And the rest?" Shinsu asked.

"In position," he said, as the rich smells of the food filled the air.

"You know that Jeremiah's eyes will be on Daphne—as a member of the family," Shinsu said casually, with an underlying tension.

"Yes, we are counting on Daphne being a distraction," he said. Then, seeing Jeremiah glaring at him, he whispered, "We're being watched—laugh," Paolo said and they turned to each other and laughed without a hint of amusement in their eyes. Once Jeremiah turned to speak to another young woman, Paolo continued. "Lars suspected that having Daphne here would put Jeremiah on edge. If he is nervous, he might make mistakes."

"Jeremiah is most certainly on edge." She looked away. "I'm going to mingle before the meeting is called to order. I don't want Jeremiah to suspect you in this. Of course, he already does."

"In that case, he won't have long to wait for his suspicions to be confirmed."

Paolo wandered off and chatted with the other immortals about meaningless topics. Then he went to the bar and ordered a twenty-one-year-old scotch and tossed it down as he glanced at his watch. It had been over fourteen hours since Alex had left. He wished that he could have some confirmation about their status. He was nervous...and he was rarely nervous.

"Make that two," Daphne said to the drib bartender who grunted and poured her a double. Paolo took her hand and lifted it to his lips.

"You look lovely," he said, but without his typical charm.

"Is Jeremiah watching?" Daphne asked.

Paolo's eyes scrutinized the crowd. "Yes, he is coming to see you. Join me by the wall when you are done with him." Then Paolo disappeared into the crowd as Daphne chatted briefly with Jeremiah.

It was only a few minutes later when Daphne met Paolo by the cave entrance to the underworld.

"Any sign of them?" she asked, as she peeked beyond the wall.

Paolo shook his head as the gong sounded, indicating the beginning of the meeting.

"Ready?" Daphne asked.

"No."

Jeremiah sat in the first of the ornate red and gold chairs with Shinsu next to him. He placed his hand over Shinsu's. Paolo had known both of them most of his life and found Jeremiah's act of affection humorous. Shinsu's eyes narrowed in repulsion, although she left her hand in place.

"Shinsu has received a letter that states that there has been a frivolous abuse of this council." Jeremiah sighed. "My dear, would you like to present the letter to me so that I might share only the significant portions of the letter with this council?"

Shinsu glared at Jeremiah for a moment and then her eyes drifted to Paolo—who offered a slight shake of his head to indicate that Alex and Valeria had not yet arrived. Shinsu had hoped to be able to remain a voice of reason within the council, as she had done so many times before with varying degrees of success. She had intended to calmly vote—based on the evidence—to remove her spouse from the council.

After all of that business was handled an annulment would be automatically approved. But unfortunately that was not an option tonight. She would have to separate herself from Jeremiah and the council before the evidence against him was presented. This was dangerous for Paolo—who had always inspired a sort of motherly affection in her—and all of the oracles involved, but it was their only option now.

Drawing a deep breath, and with marked disgust, Shinsu pulled her hand back from under Jeremiah's. "Actually, there is another matter that I believe takes precedence over these accusations."

"What's she doing?" Daphne whispered.

Paolo clung tightly to Daphne's hand. "Stalling."

"As there are times when romance and love determines the immediacy of a meeting—there are also times when the opposite should also constitute immediacy," Shinsu said.

Jeremiah looked a bit lost. "This was not on the agenda! May I ask what this is about, my dear?"

"All in good time, *my dear,*" she said, venomously. Even from the distance, Shinsu's unexpected disrespect took Jeremiah and the rest of the immortals by surprise. His eyes widened and, for once, he was speechless. Shinsu gave Jeremiah a cold glare. "As I am certain you have suspected, Jeremiah, the accusations involve you."

"Me?" Jeremiah said sanctimoniously.

"Someone has sent me a letter that accuses you of filing false reports for your own promotion. The letter states that he or she has evidence that Myrddin did not violate the laws of Apollo—and that you were aware of this," she said ominously, as a hush fell over the crowd.

"This is not the letter you presented to me, as the head of this council, just hours ago!" Jeremiah said as he pounded his cane against the stone floors.

Smiling sweetly, Shinsu turned to Jeremiah. "I'm certain that the council understands. I could not relinquish information which might incriminate you—and it certainly does!"

Despite his black, leathery skin, Jeremiah nearly turned white.

"This is absurd!" he declared. "I am the head of this council—the son of a god—and I will not be ordered about by...by," his face filled with loathing, "an oracle!" Jeremiah spit. "I call Erebos!" The masked henchman appeared from the shadows with his double-sided axe.

Shinsu eyes turned arctic blue as she smiled. "At least we all know how you feel now." He scowled. "And I assure you that the feeling is mutual!" She glanced at Jeremiah. "I have filed the appropriate forms for the investigation of this...accusation."

"I demand that my accuser step forward!" Jeremiah bellowed.

"And I am certain that your accuser will be most happy to oblige your demand. However, as I stated earlier, there is a more pressing matter at hand...for now," she said, turning to the council. "Due to the evidence that Jeremiah murdered my husband with the intention of using my association to gain power with the council, he most certainly married me under false pretenses. His statements regarding the oracles at this meeting support that charge. Therefore, I request an immediate end to this ruse of a marriage. I have filed for an annulment, effective immediately."

"You cannot do this! It requires my—"

"Au contraire, Jeremiah, you are currently under criminal investigation."

"Shinsu?" he said stunned.

"You will find the paperwork, along with a copy of the original letter in your packets." She grimaced. "Gentlemen, please open your packets as I wish to dissolve this unholy union immediately."

"Shinsu!" he said again.

"Jeremiah, you are repeating yourself!" she said, glaring at him, as he sunk into his seat.

Luther, a council member stood, and stated, "Shinsu, none of the council wish to interfere with your...marital affairs. But it does seem that we should first evaluate the data and take testimony on the charges against Jeremiah, try him, if appropriate, *and then* address the marriage."

"Council, you know me to never be frivolous. We can spend an hour arguing which issue should be addressed first, or you can simply open your packets and end this portion of the meeting. However, I do assure you that my request—and its timing—is critical to this entire case, and will save us the embarrassment of what is potentially a very awkward situation!"

"Shinsu, did you write that letter? Do you have knowledge as to Jeremiah's misconduct?" Luther asked.

She shook her head. "If I had ever suspected that Jeremiah had been involved, I would have presented it to this council then and there!"

"I don't believe that we can force Jeremiah to testify with an anonymous note," Marco, another council member, said as he pulled on his bushy brows.

"I have reasonable confidence that the accuser will step forward when the time is right," Shinsu said. "Now then, may I have your signatures so that I might end this mockery of a marriage?"

Jeremiah rolled his eyes and pulled his knee up in his chair as he turned to the side.

"You needn't have gone through the formalities of a council meeting. If you wished to be rid of me—as with all of my wives—all you needed to do was ask."

"Ask you? Why bother?" Shinsu's eyes steeled on him.

"There is an obvious irreconcilable break in affinity between husband and wife. And the prejudicial statements by Jeremiah support the claims made by Shinsu. Therefore, this council sees fit to annul this marriage," Luther announced.

With a satisfied smile, Shinsu brushed her hands together as if done with a nasty task. Jeremiah slumped in his chair, fuming.

"All of that was completely unnecessary and a waste of our precious time," Jeremiah muttered. Shinsu approached him with a cold gleam in her eyes.

"Oh, it was completely necessary. And I'm pleased to see Erebos. I find it extraordinarily satisfying to watch you squirm under the pressures that you have inflicted upon so many." She stood up straight and now calm, said, "You are extremely fortunate that I do not condone your brand of punishment."

"I demand that you identify my accuser!" he said, suddenly enraged. "Or I will show you my brand of justice! You and your oracle friends will all be gone if I have my say!"

Shinsu laughed as if he had just told a joke. "This council was formed by Apollo *for* the oracles."

"Only one of them is here—it must be her!" Jeremiah shouted as he pointed to Daphne.

Paolo's eyes narrowed as he wrapped his arm protectively around Daphne and whispered, "Trust me, it will not go that far!" Daphne smiled icily at Jeremiah as she nodded to Paolo.

"Did you forget that I, too, am 'one of them'?" Shinsu asked.

"I demand that the oracle, Daphne, testify!" Jeremiah said.

Paolo squeezed Daphne's arm. "We are out of time," he said as he brushed his lips along her cheek and then walked slowly toward the council.

Raising his voice, Paolo said, "The source of the letter was not from Daphne." Paolo took a sip from his champagne glass. He looked calm and collected, even a tad bit arrogant. But the action was strictly to give him a moment to gather his wits and calm his pounding heart.

"You? After all I have done for you?" Jeremiah shrieked. "Others told me you were nothing but a self-centered...gigolo—I should have listened!"

Luther lifted a hand to stop Jeremiah's ranting. "Paolo, did you write this letter?"

"I am not the author, but I am familiar with the contents of the letter." Approaching the front of the room, Paolo continued, "If I may, there is some history that I believe is vital to the charges against Jeremiah."

"Go ahead," Luther said.

"I will have your head for this!" Jeremiah raged.

Luther raised his brows, "Paolo, I must warn you, your testimony must be pertinent or Jeremiah is correct, you will most certainly be charged with at the very least, a frivolous abuse of council and you will be punished."

Paolo drew a deep breath and started to run his finger along his collar, but stopped himself. *Where are they?* His mind began to wander down the path of the evening's most likely outcome—he and the rest of the oracles would certainly be slaughtered. He felt a pang in his heart when he thought of Valeria and Shinsu, Daphne and Alex. In fact, there was not one of the oracles that he now didn't consider a friend of sorts, even Tavish. Still he would delay the inevitable as long as possible.

"During the War of the Titans, a naïve, mortal girl served as an informant for Zeus against the Titans and formed a friendship with one of them." Paolo glanced up at Jeremiah and lifted a finger. "You, Jeremiah!"

"This is you're charge? Luther, haven't we heard enough of this?" Jeremiah grumbled.

"Paolo, get to the point" Luther said barely concealing the threat.

"Council, I assure you that this is all pertinent. Please permit me to continue." He took a few steps forward and felt all of the eyes of the immortals on him. In a few minutes, they would stop looking at him as if he were the son of Adonis. The whisperings and flirtations would end...as would the invitations. He sighed. "That girl formed a friendship with you and Aegemon."

"Members of this council enjoy a certain advantage of friendships. If you have a point here, then by all means, get on with it!" Luther said.

Paolo sighed again. He was stepping through a minefield. "That triad plotted against their perceived enemy—the oracles."

"Plots! Is that what you offer us as proof against Jeremiah? Paolo, please tell us what does this fairy tale have to do with our business here?" Marco asked, as he offered a sympathetic glance to Jeremiah.

"It has to do with returning Delos to the oracles," Paolo stated.

"I should have known when you started chasing that oracle, Cassandra!" Jeremiah bellowed.

Paolo shook his head with a sardonic smile. "There are very few who know this history and I'm certain the Council will find it interesting—Hyperion."

"Is that the accusation? That I changed my name?" Jeremiah narrowed his eyes in a threatening glare. "Remember Paolo, that if there are any actual charges made, all of those that had knowledge of this possible illegal misconduct will also be charged."

"Hyperion, it was you who assisted the mortal girl and her illegitimate child to gain entry to Delos, so that the child might swim in the River Styx."

"I have no idea what you are talking about!" Jeremiah blasted with a side-glance to Paolo, trying to assess his intentions.

"You are wondering if I will speak the truth. I see it in your eyes. You believe that everyone is as cowardly as you," Paolo said.

"Paolo, be cautious of your tone! Until we have seen proof of any misconduct, Jeremiah is the head of this council!" Luther said.

Nodding, Paolo paced in a circle in a manner that suggested that he was trying to calm himself. As he faced away from the council, he shot a brief, nervous glance to Daphne who offered a slight shake of her head. They weren't here, yet. This was about to end very badly.

"I apologize, council. However, I do know this to be the truth...because I was that mortal child. Hyperion—Jeremiah—brought my mother and I here. Years later, you introduced me as the son of a god."

Jeremiah's eyes widened with terror. "I do recall an immortal child who wished to swim here," Jeremiah stuttered. "If you admit that was you, and that you were not an immortal, then you have misrepresented yourself to this council and I will have you executed on the spot!" Jeremiah raged, as his face swelled with anger.

Shinsu said, "Come now! You introduced someone as an immortal without evidence? I don't believe anyone in this council would believe that."

"Jeremiah, there is no question that you knew I was a mortal. In fact, my mother often spoke with disdain about the price she was forced to pay for your involvement—and my introduction."

"Take him, Erebos! I've heard enough of his lies!" Jeremiah demanded.

Erebos stepped toward Paolo and the dribs took his arms and pulled him forward. "Shall I produce witnesses?" Paolo asked, raising his voice.

"According to you there were no witnesses! How dare you accuse me of such a vile act!"

As Paolo was brought forward, Shinsu raised a hand. "Paolo states that he has witnesses. If this is a false accusation, we shall know soon enough."

The dribs held their position as Paolo took a close look at Erebos's double-edged axe and felt a tightening in his throat. But he held his head high as he glanced around the room at those who had admired him and flirted with him for centuries. Only a few words later and now they sneered at him with disdain, seeing him as a mere mortal who had violated the sanctity of Delos.

"Council, as Jeremiah is under investigation in this situation, I believe that we should permit Paolo to bring forth his witnesses. Certainly, none of you could refuse that," Shinsu said.

Luther nodded. "Paolo, call your witnesses; but be warned that if this is a trick, you will be executed on the spot!"

The dribs released Paolo and, again, he ran his finger along the neck of his shirt. Then he lifted a finger. "I call my witnesses!" Paolo announced but no one stepped forward. He turned around to face the rest of the immortals. "Come now, none of you will step forward?"

They turned their faces in disgust.

"Erebos—I order you to remove Paolo from this meeting!" Jeremiah declared. The dribs reached for Paolo, but he yanked his arms free.

"Please allow me a few moments to convince my witnesses to speak."

"You have one minute Paolo," Marco said. "You have accused Jeremiah of crimes that must be corroborated by witnesses. Either present your witnesses, or your charges against Jeremiah will be dropped and you will be punished."

Drawing a breath, Paolo glanced around the room. "Perhaps my witnesses are concerned that they will be met with Jeremiah's form of justice should they attempt to speak the truth."

The remainder of the council members conversed and then Luther said, "Yes, Paolo, we do see your point. The council has agreed to guarantee the safety of any immortal who speaks the truth on your behalf."

Raising an eyebrow, Paolo said in a further attempt to stall, "To clarify for my witnesses, anyone who speaks the truth on my behalf will not be executed because of their testimony—is that correct?"

"Yes, Paolo," Luther said, losing patience.

"In that case, I call my witnesses!"

There was an awkward silence. Paolo shrugged smugly to the council as his heart pounded, but otherwise, the room remained quiet.

"Will no one speak?" Paolo said working to keep his voice strong. He would not give Jeremiah or the immortals the pleasure of seeing his fear. He would keep his cool even as the axe fell on his neck.

Luther nodded to Erebos and the dribs pulled Paolo back to the stone. Paolo yanked his arms free and then straightened his tie as he lowered himself to his knees. He avoided eye contact with Daphne and Shinsu. He didn't want to see the regret in their eyes. Instead he winked seductively at Martina, who turned, repulsed by his advances, and then he laid his head on the stone.

"I will speak as your witness!" Alex said, as he stepped from the trail by the River Styx. Paolo sighed and rolled his eyes at Alex in relief.

"Oh, thank God!" Daphne sighed in a near whisper as Alex passed her.

"Things getting a little tense?" Alex said, as he brushed his hand over her shoulder.

"Val?" Daphne asked quietly, and Alex nodded as he walked toward Paolo, his jeans and polo shirt seeming out of place in Delos.

With the dribs distracted Paolo stood and walked toward Alex. "You took long enough!" Paolo said quietly.

Alex shrugged. "Sorry, pal."

"Valeria?"

"I believe so," he whispered. Then turning to the council, Alex said, "Paolo didn't write the letter. I did!"

"Alexander! I might have suspected! Council, Alexander is a criminal. Any letter he has written is certain to be full of lies. Erebos!" Jeremiah said and then turned to Shinsu. "If you knew of this, I will have your head as well!"

"Jeremiah, if Alex is not considered an appropriate witness, I have others," Paolo said. He turned toward the entrance as a host of boats entered Delos with Lars, Ava, Camille, Mani, and Caleb. Jeremiah's eyes widened and his jaw dropped as he saw the previously exterminated oracles, including Lita, who clung tightly to Genesis—and Myrddin.

Jeremiah's eyes darted around the room and then he hobbled to several of the other council members and began whispering commands. Getting nowhere with the council, Jeremiah said, "Myrddin! I might have known you were behind this!"

"You see, I assured you that it would have been extraordinarily awkward for a council member to have two spouses—well, except for you, Jeremiah," Shinsu said.

Shinsu stepped in front of the council. "I suggest that we permit all of these witnesses to speak before making any judgments!"

Luther nodded his agreement.

"I demand that Alexander Morgan be removed from these proceedings!" Jeremiah choked again. The dribs took Alex's arms and moved him toward Erebos.

"Just one moment, Jeremiah," Shinsu said, and then her eyes narrowed. "Alexander, I did not see you arrive by gondola. How is it that you find yourself here in Delos?"

Alex smiled coldly at Jeremiah. "I came from the underworld."

"Impossible!" Jeremiah said.

"But true, none the less," Alex said calmly.

"Jeremiah, in that case, I am afraid that you have no jurisdiction over Alexander. He has come from the underworld and is now under Hades' jurisdiction."

"My nephew, the lord of the underworld, is to make a decision even in my small kingdom of Delos?" Jeremiah asked.

Paolo lifted a hand. "I do not believe that you may call it '*your kingdom,*'. Delos is the home of the oracles."

"Hades may take Alexander back for all I care!"

Suddenly the council members looked unsure of themselves, Luther said, "Jeremiah, Shinsu, I'm not sure what's going on here. But I believe that before we make any further judgments here we, as a council need to investigate the initial charter—"

Shinsu lifted a hand, "You need only wish to see the truth. Delos was established for the oracles. The truth is that this current council has no power here." She glanced at Alex, "Please continue."

"I did not come alone," Alex said. "The soul that I have brought with me wishes to testify."

"How?" Luther asked.

"Through the stone of truth."

Suddenly, the rose and gold quartz plate lit with the form of a hand and there was a vision of Valeria on the screen overhead. Alex sighed heavily with relief. He had trusted his intuition, as Daphne had recommended, as she was right.

"What is this?" Jeremiah asked. "Another criminal is now going to speak?"

Valeria narrowed her eyes at the council head. "Jeremiah—I do not require your approval to speak! This council was presented to three. Those three, or their representatives—as approved by Apollo and Zeus—are the only ones permitted to hold council here!"

Caleb wandered toward Alex. "That's the third triumvirate," he said to Alex proudly. Alex shook his head subtly to silence the boy.

"Young woman! We are all aware of your history and this is a council that is present in *this* world. As you, evidently, are no longer of this world, you may not testify."

Valeria's voice had a power behind it that caught Jeremiah by surprise. "You have no authority here. By the laws of Apollo, this council shall now be returned to its rightful leadership and therefore Jeremiah, you are excused."

The noise from the crowd rose, as Jeremiah stepped toward the oracles. "Erebos, I order you to execute these intruders!"

Erebos stomped toward Alex, as Valeria said calmly, "Erebos, your domain is in Tartarus—not here. I suggest you return to the hole you crawled out of. Your services will no longer be required. Further, Jeremiah, I remind you that the laws of the third triumvirate state that you must allow at least one designee of each of the positions!"

Erebos seemed confused as he glanced up at the image of Valeria on the screen and then back toward Jeremiah.

Jeremiah's eyes sparked with outrage. He glared from Valeria and then back at Erebos. "Erebos, *I* am the head of this council and I will inform you of when you may leave."

"Jeremiah, you were given no power in any of the worlds—as it was a well-known fact that you are not to be trusted."

Suddenly, in a fit of rage, Jeremiah hobbled on his cane to the quartz stone of truth, pulled it from its pedestal. Immediately Valeria's image disappeared from the screen. Jeremiah threw it with the strength of a young Olympian. The stone hit the wall of the cave, broke into two halves, and then dropped into the river.

Seeing his wife silenced and her image erased was the last straw for Alex. It was as if Jeremiah had actually assaulted her. His face reddened as he moved toward the former council head in a fit of rage. "I've had enough of you!" Alex said with all of the pain of the past few years and the realization of Jeremiah's role in his agony. He grabbed the ancient man by the neck and dragged him to the edge of Delos and then held him out over the River Styx—ready to drop him in and allow Cerberus, the three-headed dog, to have his way with him.

"Alexander," Jeremiah choked. "You are not a murderer," he said as his eyes bulged. "You don't want to spend an eternity in Tartarus. That is not a place that you—"

"Drop the bastard!" Paolo yelled. "Just drop him!"

There was an extraordinary silence within the cavern that was suddenly broken by Genni's coo. In an instant, Alex was reminded of who he was. He was a husband—a symbolon—and now a father.

Slowly, he released his shaking hands from Jeremiah's throat. Jeremiah immediately collapsed forward as he coughed and sputtered. Then Alex drew a deep breath as he returned to his daughter.

A moment later, Caleb said, "Alex, Val's soul is still here."

"How do you know that, Caleb?" Alex asked, with his heart still pounding.

Shrugging, Caleb said, "I don't know how...I just know."

"What does she want?" Camille asked.

Tavish laughed and folded his arms. "She wants us to drown that stinking rat, Jeremiah."

Caleb laughed and he turned to Lita and scrunched his nose. "She says she wants Myrdd to hold Genni."

Lita glanced at Caleb and then at Alex. Myrdd was still staring at the ground. Finally, Lita said, "All right, my friend."

Glancing toward Shinsu, Lita had a moment of inspiration. "Shinsu, perhaps you could help."

Shinsu nodded as Lita handed her the tiny pink bundle. "She is a beautiful child, isn't she!" Shinsu said with a glow.

"I thought you might be able to help Myrdd hold Genni," Lita said.

Shinsu continued smiling at the infant. "There is something very special about you, isn't there?" she said to the baby, as she bounced her in her arms and stepped slowly toward Myrdd.

Then she glanced at Myrdd, who barely made eye contact with her. And, while keeping her eyes on the child, she said, "Myrddin, you have become quite a recluse. Cassandra has requested that you hold her child. But I don't believe I am quite ready to give you up yet," she said to Genesis.

Myrdd held out an open palm and Shinsu lowered her brows and shook her head. "Oh, no, no!" she said in mild irritation. "Myrddin, that will simply not do at all—don't you recall holding a child?"

"I...I've forgotten." He looked to the ground, confused and upset with himself.

"Well, Myrddin," she huffed, "infants never were your forte. Give me your hand!" she said as she took his hand and wrapped it around her and the infant. Then, with her face lowered to observe the child, she felt the arms of her symbolon moving around her. She closed her eyes as his arms moved snugly around her and the child. Then he peered over her shoulder and the fog cleared from his eyes.

Speaking to the infant, Shinsu said, "Myrddin and I never had children. We were too old by the time he got his nerve up to propose." Her face glowed, although she hated to admit that she was thrilled by his touch. "Of course, those days were so very many years ago—nearly an eternity," she said musically, as if she were telling a fairy tale.

Then Myrdd's hand reached up to brush her cheek and, shocked by the action, Shinsu jumped and turned. She saw the soft glow of love in his eyes and her heart filled with love for her symbolon.

"Hello, Sue!" he said as the color returned to his face.

Her face lit with a playful smile. "Hello, you old, cheating goat!" But her eyes sparkled and her skin flushed.

"I've missed you!" he said.

She winked and whispered, "We'll talk more later." Then she turned to Lita. "Perhaps you had better hold this precious child." Shinsu passed Genni back to Lita. Then Shinsu returned to Myrdd and he wrapped his arms around his wife.

Within an instant, there was an eerie feeling in the cavern. An odd breeze picked up that seemed to come from the underworld. The room dulled as if the source were absorbing the available light. There was a presence in the tunnel and the immortals subconsciously backed away from it—even the dribs.

The presence continued to move down the cave from the underworld. Suddenly, there was a ripple on the river and then Charon's boat appeared with a ghostly vision of Valeria wearing a white gown.

Behind Charon's boat, a giant of nearly eight feet rounded the corner, walking on top of the river and stepped onto Delos. There was a hushed whisper among the immortals.

Hades brushed his fingers along his dark beard and then lifted a finger at Jeremiah. "Uncle, it has been too long since we have visited." He turned up the corners of his mouth and the glacial chill of his smile matched the color of his eyes. With mock sincerity he added, "You never come to visit anymore." Then Hades released a loud laugh. "Hyperion—or is it Jeremiah now? You have what belongs to me, and I want him back," Hades said, narrowing an eye at Alex.

"It has been too long," Jeremiah said hesitantly, as his eyes darted back and forth nervously. "And, as far as I am concerned, he is yours to take and good riddance!"

Alex bravely stepped forward. "Hades, I was in your land, but it was only to right a wrong. The Fates and Jeremiah interfered with the destiny of my symbolon, as was laid down by the laws of Apollo, and she was wrongfully taken."

Raising a single eyebrow, Hades twisted his mustache and lifted his mouth in a calculating smile. "Now then, Alexander, mistakes are unfortunate—but they do happen. Be a good boy and step onto

Charon's ferry. Be with your symbolon. You must know that once you have entered my kingdom, you may never leave. That *is* the rule!"

"Hades, I would not have been forced to enter your kingdom without this deception." Alex lifted his hands. "How can we resolve this?"

Licking his lips, Hades responded, "Alexander, I am a simple god. I have simple needs. I do not interfere in the business of others. I only know that you have come into my land and so you must return. I have already recovered Cassandra. Come, be with her! I will attempt to make arrangements with Minos, as he is the judge of souls, so that you might join her in the Elysian Fields."

Alex felt the pull to be with his love and he could feel her yearning as well. But he hesitated and Hades added, "Bring the child if you wish." Then Hades glanced hungrily at Genni for just a moment. "You would enjoy the Elysian Fields—Cassandra enjoyed her stay there!"

"Genni is not an option!" Alex said with finality. "But we do have an exchange."

"Whom do you offer?" Hades asked, as he eyed the oracles hungrily.

"Aegemon has offered to go in my place," Alex said. "There is another. If you allow Cassandra to speak, I'm certain this could all be resolved to your satisfaction."

Hades dipped a brow. "Ah, yes, Apollo's not so humble servant, Aegemon," he said. "Bring him to Charon's ferry."

Alex and Tavish walked to the Gondola and lifted the stretcher carrying Aegemon. As they crossed the island, Aegemon looked up weakly and said, "Thank you...Alexander."

They stood just short of Charon's ferry and Hades motioned them to proceed. "Once Aegemon has boarded, we shall barter."

Tavish stood his ground. "We will not load Aegemon until we have received confirmation from you that Alex and the lass are released." Then Tavish added under his breath, "You lying, cheatin' bastard."

Hades glowered at Tavish, but then smiled and said, "Come now. Set Aegemon down in the ferry and we can discuss it."

"I cinnot!" Tavish said, as he glared at Hades.

415

"Hades, Aegemon must be an exchange for me. Do you agree?" Alex asked.

Shaking his head in sympathy Hades said, "As much as I would like to make that exchange, Aegemon was already mine; therefore, I cannot make that agreement."

"You can and you shall!" Tavish said as he sat Aegemon's stretcher down, just short of Charon's ferry. Tavish posed for a moment with his hands on his hips as he glared at Hades and then swaggered back to the oracles.

Charon reached a long gangly hand from his robe and pulled Aegemon by the collar onboard his ferry. Aegemon stood up as if fully recovered.

"Perhaps I can give you some credit for transporting him a portion of the distance." Hades glanced around and then lifted a long finger at Caleb. "However...I believe that boy could make up the difference. I might be willing to take Aegemon and the boy in exchange for you," Hades said.

"My wife had a plan. I'm certain that if you permit her to speak we could resolve this!"

Hades glanced at Valeria's image and then he shook his head. "I prefer to work one on one." Hades glanced at Caleb again. "It would take quite a lot to release the last oracle! Perhaps that boy—I might take him."

Caleb let out a half-laugh and Alex shook his head at Caleb to silence him.

"It's cool...it's just like my game...you know, the third triumvirate," Caleb said in a near-whisper.

"The third triumvirate?" Alex asked.

"Yeah, you know...the game I made."

Alex huffed in confusion. "Caleb, I'm not following. *This* is about your game?" he said with doubt, certain that Caleb was mistaken.

"Yeah...pretty cool, huh?" Then Caleb stepped toward Hades. "Sweet! I always wanted to see the underworld."

Alex shook his head in frantic concern. "Caleb—you aren't going! Neither Val nor I want that!" he said.

Caleb whispered to Alex with a playful smile, "Don't worry—I'm pretty good at this!" Then turning back to Hades, he said, "So, like I was saying, Val's not the last oracle and I think she should be able to talk."

"You can't fool me! I know these things!" Hades said.

"What is the third triumvirate?" Alex asked.

Caleb turned his back on Hades. "It's like this: the first triumvirate is the first thing you have to conquer. Okay?" Alex nodded as Caleb continued, "They're the Moira."

"The Fates?"

"Yeah...it's like they have control of the game and until you beat them you still have play by all their rules. And you have this cool bag of tools and you have to use the right ones in the right order. Otherwise, you have to wait for another chance!"

"Alright..." Alex said, not at all certain that he understood what was going on.

"Once you break their control, you have to go to the next level, and beat the second triumvirate. That's harder because there's three of them, and you have to get past Aegemon, Hyperion, AND... What was that witch's name?" Caleb asked.

"Uh...Kristiana?" Alex asked, now completely confused, and amazed that Hades had permitted this discussion. "You...you knew this?"

Caleb nodded. "Lastly, you have to put the third triumvirate back in power."

"Who is the third triumvirate?" Alex asked.

"Ha! That's the group that has the power over the council."

Alex stared at Caleb in confusion and suddenly wondered if he were in a dream.

Caleb continued, "So the third triumvirate...well, it's the first oracle, the last oracle, and Apollo...but their designees can speak for them."

"Alright...." Alex released a small laugh and then whispered to himself, *"Who are you Caleb?"*

Continuing, Caleb said, "And, like I said, Hades has to leave the third triumvirate—or their designees—here to run the council...that's the rules on this level!"

"And I need a suitable replacement for the last oracle!" Hades growled.

"Val isn't the last oracle, but she is a designee."

"I don't believe you!" Hades eyes filled with doubt. "Don't you lie to me!"

Caleb got back in Hades' face and narrowed his eyes. "I just realized something. You're a lying cheating goon, just like Dagoth Ur."

"Who?" Ava asked to no one in particular.

"Dagoth Ur, he's a villain in Elder Scrolls," Caleb said, happily.

"In what?" Ava asked.

"Elder Scrolls—a video game." Caleb rolled his eyes as if everyone knew. Then he whispered to Alex, "I got a 500 point bonus for standing up to Hades—as long as he doesn't fry me!"

Certain that Caleb's outburst was a death sentence, Alex prepared to defend the boy. Instead, Hades responded as he might to his own child and said patiently, "It is my responsibility."

Alex's eyes narrowed and this time his voice had more volume, "Who are you Caleb?"

Shrugging nonchalantly, Caleb smiled and then turned back to Hades. "If you don't believe me that Val isn't the last oracle—ask Myrdd."

Hades cast his eyes toward Myrdd. "You are a part of the third triumvirate of Delos. It consists of the first oracle, the last oracle, and Apollo! Is that not true?"

Myrdd's eyes narrowed as if trying to remember. Then he cleared his throat. "Yes, that is true."

"And Cassandra is a part of the third triumvirate," Hades stated, losing patience.

"Cassandra is most certainly an integral part of the third triumvirate."

"As I stated earlier!" Hades voice escalated.

Myrdd began mumbling, "Yes, she is...I mean, she is a part of the triumvirate, per se."

Losing his temper, Hades said, "Is she—or is she not—the last oracle?"

"No. She is not."

With his eyes widening in sudden realization, Alex looked at Caleb and said, "It's...you?"

Caleb ignored the question as Myrdd cleared his throat again. "Cassandra is...a very gifted oracle...Apollo's favorite. But, no, she most certainly is not the *last* oracle."

"Who is then, you fool?" demanded Hades.

Myrdd lifted a hand. "If you must have a member of the third triumvirate, there is only one possible exchange—me."

"No, Myrddin!" Shinsu said.

Myrdd turned to Shinsu. "I am the only possible replacement."

Shinsu stepped forward. "Then I will go with you!"

Myrdd brushed his hand over her face and then smiled at Shinsu. "Forgive me, Sue, but I have lived too long in the quagmire of this mind and I long for the golden fields of Elysian. I am the first oracle. There is one designee for the first oracle...and that is you, my wife. That is why Jeremiah required your union!"

"Myrddin, how long am I to stay here without you?" Shinsu said, with sudden panic in her voice. After all of these years, she finally had him with her and now he would be gone.

"Until the council is no more," he said sadly. With a tear in her eye, Shinsu threw her arms around Myrdd's waist, as his arms encircled her with a yearning older than Delos. He pressed his lips to her forehead and she moved her mouth to his. Then he suddenly jerked away, knowing that if he didn't, he would never leave and without turning back, he stepped onto Charon's boat. Once onboard, he turned to face Shinsu, his eyes filled with longing.

"Hades, will you release Cassandra now?" Alex asked, feeling the desperation in his chest.

"If that was what was intended, you should have had my agreement first! Myrddin is no bargain—he has not had his wits about him for many years. However, I am a fair man and I shall accept Myrddin and Aegemon for you, Alexander." Then he pursed his lips and said, "I believe that the boy has been attempting to trick me! It is known throughout the land that this council was formed by Myrddin, Cassandra, and Apollo! And so the third triumvirate was dissolved only months after its inception when Apollo left for the Elysian Fields."

"Well it wasn't. And Val—I mean, Cassandra—was there because the last oracle hadn't been born yet. So Val was standing in...it was kind of an emergency," Caleb explained.

"What are you talking about, boy?" Hades demanded, his patience diminishing.

"Well, Val was what you call...um...a vessel for the last oracle."

"Genni?" Alex said, stunned.

"Yeah, cool, huh!" Caleb laughed. "And Genni would have to agree to go with you, but she can't talk yet."

"Cassandra, I give you your voice, and demand an answer once and for all. Are you, or are you not, the last oracle?"

The specter of Valeria stepped toward Hades.

"No, I am not. I am, however, a designee for the last oracle."

"This is ridiculous! This council was dissolved as soon as there was no designee for Apollo!"

"Apollo did not leave this council without a qualified designee." Valeria lifted a hand. "Apollo and Coronis produced a son, Asclepius and the legend does not do him justice. The son was imprisoned in an electrical cocoon for over a thousand years, but was finally set free by Myrdd."

"The child did not live! He was killed by Zeus's lightning bolt!" Jeremiah grumbled.

"It was not from Zeus. It was from you, Hyperion. And Asclepius was not killed. From that incident, Zeus banished you from history," Valeria said.

"That child is dead!" Jeremiah insisted.

Valeria shook her head and smiled. "The third triumvirate is alive and is in control of this council. As a result, Hades, you must ensure that it still exists."

"I will take the boy as an exchange!"

"The boy cannot go. He is Apollo's designee."

"Caleb?" Alex asked.

"I am willing to resolve this. But I must have an exchange!" Hades said.

"There is someone who wishes to go." Valeria looked toward the oracles and said, "Your brother, Apollo, and his wife, Coronis, are awaiting your arrival with open arms."

The oracles began looking at one another in confusion. Hades spotted the subject of Valeria' communication and nodded to Valeria, approving the exchange.

Daphne covered her mouth as a sob escaped. Paolo stared as she whispered in awe, *"My brother forgives me?"*

Valeria smiled softly and nodded.

Paolo said, "You aren't...Daphne?"

Daphne put her hand on Paolo's arm. "My name was Artemis Daphnaia. If I had gone to Alex with my given name, he never would have..." Then she brushed her hand across Paolo's face. "I am sorry. It seems that I have done nothing but cause pain. Forgive me, Paolo. You have been such a...sweet distraction."

Paolo lowered his brow and swallowed as she started to walk away. He reached for her hand and pulled it to his mouth. "I will miss you!"

As Daphne headed toward Charon's Ferry, Valeria's image stepped off and the two women took hands. Daphne smiled softly and said, "Please take care of Alex...and Paolo. They are very special to me."

Then Daphne stepped onto Charon's ferry as Valeria's image faded from Delos.

"My business is done here," Hades said with a gleam in his eyes that cast a frightening glow through Delos. Then he turned and walked down the River Styx.

Caleb turned around to face the immortals. "I think everyone had better leave." Then he added, "Well, except for Alex."

Jeremiah lifted his hands. "*No one* is leaving here now! I alone announce the ending of a council meeting and I have not done so," he said.

Ignoring Jeremiah's remark, Caleb said to the immortals, "If you don't leave now, you'll probably be trapped here forever."

Shinsu nodded with tears in her eyes.

"Caleb—what's going on?" Alex asked.

"It's the next thing...and it's pretty cool! You'll like it! I figured we needed something even cooler than just fighting off the bad guys. So, I got this idea from Jonah. You only get to do it after you finished battling the bad guys though...and we've still got two more to go."

Suddenly, the gondolas began to fill with immortals, frantically escaping Delos.

Alex was still in stunned silence as Lita came to him with Genni. Alex kissed his daughter's head and he said to Lita, "You had better take her out of here." He drew a short nervous breath. "Hopefully, we'll see you soon."

A moment later, Paolo joined Alex and Caleb.

"You aren't leaving?" Alex asked, and Paolo shook his head. Then Shinsu came to stand by them. There was a roar of thunder from outside the cave.

"Caleb, do we have time to wait for the trogs?" Lars asked.

"Um...I don't think so," Caleb said. The immortals, listening to Caleb's words, began to throw the dribs into the river as more of them clamored aboard each gondola.

The immortals had left and the oracles were filing into the last of the gondolas. Mani helped Lita into the gondola with Genni, when a frightening howl filled Delos.

With a battle cry, Jeremiah stomped confidently toward the gondolas without the use of his cane.

"Do you think I am going to permit all of this? Who do you think I am?" he bellowed. In an instant, he appeared to be nearly seven feet tall.

"I AM THE SON OF GAI AND URANUS!" His voice filled Delos, causing the crystal chandeliers to clink together from the reverberation of his voice. He reached into the gondola as it was leaving Delos and tried to yank Genesis from Lita's arms.

"No, Jeremiah! You can't have her!" Lita said. Jeremiah leveled his arm against Lita's face and her head cracked on the edge of the gondola.

Typically calm, a dangerous expression filled Mani's eyes as he leveled the oar like a baseball bat. As Jeremiah began to laugh, Mani lifted the oar and swung it at Jeremiah hitting him in the chest with the force of a professional baseball player. Jeremiah flew across the room, hit the back wall and sunk to the ground. He shook his head trying to regain focus and charged at the gondola that was now exiting Delos, plucking the child from Lita's arms.

"Leave now or the child will be gone!" Jeremiah said as he hung Genni by her blanket over the river.

Nodding at Mani, Alex said, "It's all right Doc, you had better go. "Get Lita and the rest of the oracles out of here."

Mani glanced at his wife as she recovered and then led the other oracle-filled gondolas out of Delos.

Caleb, Alex, and Paolo all started to move in slowly on Jeremiah, who took a few more steps toward the river. "You think I will not release this child? I am the brother of Cronus—the father who swallowed his children. Believe me, I have no sentimentality when it comes to offspring!"

Alex glanced at his daughter and her tiny pink hat fell into the river. He heard Cerberus begin to growl and then Genni turned to look at Alex. The expression of love in the infant's eyes took his breath away and he knew he would die to save her.

Alex, Paolo, and Caleb surrounded Jeremiah.

"There is no reason to harm Genni," Alex pleaded. "Please, I'll do whatever you want. Please don't harm her!"

"You and that foolish girl." Jeremiah narrowed his eyes in disgust.

Alex took a step toward him. "All right, Jeremiah. What do you want?"

"I want to hear Cerberus tear your limbs off. I want to know that the rest of your days will be spent in Tarturus!"

Nodding, Alex said, "All right. Just hand Genni to Shinsu."

Jeremiah dropped the infant for an instant and then caught her by a piece of blanket.

"Alright! Alright! I'll get on Charon's boat. Okay?" Alex walked toward the ferry.

"No! In the water!"

Alex raised his arms. "Alright, Jeremiah," he said as he crawled into the river and held on to the edge. "I'm here...now, give Genni to Shinsu."

"Shinsu—we'll wait for you!" Camille called from the last gondola.

With a ravenous look, Jeremiah suddenly tossed Genni down the river toward Cerberus as he began to laugh.

The cries of the oracles could be heard as the infant flew through the air and then landed downstream in the river. Alex had already released the river's edge and was swimming with all of his might to reach the child. Finally he reached her and pulled her out from under the water. She drew a breath, calmly as he held her in his arms. Alex's face flooded with relief, although the current was swiftly carrying them both toward hell and into the darkness.

As Jeremiah watched with glee, Caleb said, "I have something I've been waiting a long time to give back to you!"

Suddenly, out of the River Styx, came a wailing sound and a wavy dagger flew out of the river and into Caleb's hands. As it landed, it lit with Caleb's electricity into a brilliant blazing white.

Erebos approached from the shadows and swung his double-sided axe at Caleb. Caleb ducked and jumped and then the dagger and the double-sided axe struck. There was a sizzling sound and Erebos dropped his axe. His eyes widened as he glanced at his scorched hands and then down at his double-sided axe.

"You'd better leave or I'll slice you in two!" Caleb said.

Erebos began to back toward the river as Paolo stepped in. "Not so fast!" Paolo swung at Erebos, knocking him down with every punch.

Caleb swung the blade above his head, like a samurai, as his eyes focused on Jeremiah.

Jeremiah's eyes filled with disdain. "I am immortal—as is Erebos! Do you honestly believe you can threaten me with that?"

"I may not be able to kill you. But I can send you to Hades and I doubt he'll release you this time," Caleb lowered the dagger and plunged it into Jeremiah's chest, causing Jeremiah to glow with the electrical jolt.

Charon's ferry began moving down the river. Alex continued to kick toward the edge but he was being pulled too fast toward Cerberus. He prayed that he could get Genni onto the ledge before they were in complete darkness. As the ferry passed Alex, Daphne watched sadly.

The wake from the boat pushed Alex to the opposite side of the river. He grabbed onto the slick edge as Shinsu arrived.

Shinsu unwound her long, silk scarf and tossed it to Alex. He grabbed it and pushed off, hearing the threats of Cerberus's growls.

Clinging to Genni and the scarf, Alex slowly worked his way across the river. Finally Shinsu put the wrap under her foot and reached for the child. As she secured Genni in her arms, Alex moved his free hand to the slick limestone.

"Get Genni out of here! Caleb says something is about to happen. I don't know what it's about but..."

Nodding, Shinsu hurried to the waiting gondola on the other side of the island.

Paolo had beaten Erebos to a pulp and finally Erebos frantically dove into the river and swam past Alex.

Just then, the dagger began to lose its glow and Caleb pulled it from Jeremiah and flung it deep into the cave past Charon. There was the sound of a yelp from Cerberus and Caleb laughed.

As Jeremiah stood on the edge of the river, dazed and confused, Paolo moved toward him and smiled coldly. "Now, it is my turn!"

Raising his arms in defense, Jeremiah said, "I have always tried to protect you! That woman, Cassandra—" Before Jeremiah could finish, Paolo's fist slammed into his jaw, knocking him powerfully along the edge of the river. Jeremiah groaned and too weak from the shock he laid there. Paolo went to him, and lifted him again.

"That one was for Genni and this one is for Valeria..she goes by Valeria now!" The force of the hit launched Jeremiah into the river.

Paolo shook his head, enraged. "You don't get off that easily!" Paolo dove into the river, continuing to beat a now terrified Jeremiah.

Cerberus's growls grew louder as Jeremiah and Paolo drifted past Alex.

"Paolo!" Alex yelled, in an attempt to alert the man that had been his brother and his friend to the impending doom. Cerberus growled hungrily as Paolo disappeared into the darkness and Alex was stunned at the sudden loss that he felt.

Strolling casually down the ledge, Caleb looked quite pleased with himself and seemed completely unaware of the tragedies that were unfolding.

"Caleb, you need to go with Shinsu and Camille!" Alex shouted.

With a casual glance back at the gondola, Caleb said, "Shinsu doesn't want to go."

"What?"

"Well, we were talking and we decided that it would be best if this place wasn't here anymore. Seems like it's causing more problems than it's helping and Val agrees. Besides, Shinsu wants to be with Myrdd and if she leaves then there really isn't a third triumvirate anymore."

Alex's fingers slipped on the limestone.

"Caleb...I can't hang on. You need to leave, now!"

"We all gotta leave."

Down the river they could hear the sounds of Cerberus and the crunching of bones and cries of men being eaten alive. Alex couldn't stand it and yet he knew that was his fate.

"What happens next, Caleb?" Alex said as he treaded water and clung to the slick wall.

The boy's eyes widened with excitement. "Um...well, the next thing is a really cool flood...more like a giant wave—you know, a tsunami! The first one's kind of like a warning. The second one—"

"*Camille*—get Genni out of here!" Alex shouted and with that he lost his grip on the limestone and began to flow down the river. "Caleb! You need to go with Camille!"

"Don't worry, I made sure Genni's safe!" Caleb shouted.

Suddenly, he was surrounded by blackness with the warm current and the frightening sound of flesh being torn. He thought of Paolo and the thought made him sick. Soon enough he would be there. He heard Cerberus distracted by the scent of him and gave into the inevitable. The womb-like sensation calmed him as he plummeted toward hell and he wondered momentarily if the river had been designed to lull one into a false sense of security. It would all be over in a moment, he thought...all of his dreams of a life with his love. After 3,000 years this was how it would end. He only prayed that someday he might be with his love in the Elysian Fields.

Then he heard a loud rumbling from the bowels of the earth. Alex heard Cerberus whine and then Caleb shouted excitedly, "Here it comes!"

There was a shuddering of the land and then he felt the strength of the current stop and suddenly he was headed the opposite direction, back toward Delos. With the new current, Alex fought to keep his head above water. Shinsu stood in the middle of the island as walls of water moved around her and somehow avoided her. Then Alex felt himself pulled back toward the underworld and was again cast into darkness. This time he was moving much faster than before. Alex struggled for breaths and to find something to hold on to, but he was roughly bounced against the cave edges and then he felt something near him.

He heard the woman's familiar British accent in the darkness. "Alex! I see you! Reach to your right. My arm is there..."

"Daph?" Alex said in shock.

"I'm right here—I can pull you in. I'm strong enough. Trust me!" she said.

And in a moment he was on the ledge in the dark as Daphne's arms went around his chest. He relaxed for a moment in relief, catching his breath. Alex knew he should move out of her arms. But emotional exhaustion took over and he couldn't seem to budge.

Finally he said, "I'm...sorry about Paolo." Although he couldn't see her, he felt her nod as she brushed her hand over his chest and kissed the side of his neck.

"Daph," he said softly. "Please don't..."

"Just once I just wanted to feel you in my arms," she said. "I'll...behave now."

Her hands took his and he was surprised how small they were. He squeezed them gently. "Thanks. Other than...well, you know—you've been a good friend."

"Have I?" she asked and then swallowed. "There's another wave coming. This one's much larger."

He heard the deep rumbling from the bowels of the earth and this time Cerberus began to howl. Quickly, the rumbling escalated and the cave began to shudder.

"Will I see you again?" he asked.

Daphne shrugged. "I don't know," she said.

In an instant, the shuddering became a thundering roar. Alex felt himself pulled back into the water and away from Daphne and then the wave hit.

He felt his body pummeled along rocks—uncertain if it was the top, base, or side of the caves. Then in the darkness, he prayed for those moments of cool air on his face when he could catch his breath and work to shield his head from the rocks.

Suddenly, the temperature of the water dropped from bathwater warm to chilling cold. At that moment, he knew that he was no longer in Delos but in the cave that might take him out to the sea...or trap him deep inside the earth forever.

As he slammed against a rock he felt the slimy algae of the rope and grasped frantically for it. He worked against the current that yanked his body around and finally wrapped his arms around it. Then he waited for a change in current and wrapped his legs around the rope, although by doing so he was underwater. He wondered if the tunnel had filled completely with water or if there might be a moment when he could breathe. His prayers were answered and the tide rolled out.

He breathed and his arms and legs shook uncontrollably. Then he saw a flickering of light and saw Shinsu's tiny frame at the entrance to Delos. She had a peaceful expression on her face as she lifted her hand as if to say goodbye and then he heard the low rumble and knew that the adamantine gates were closing forever and again he was cast into blackness.

As he inched himself along on the rope occasionally rising to search for air pockets on the outflow of water he could hear the thunder exploding outside the cave. The louder the thunder was, the closer he knew he was to the exit. As the water came back in he clung to the rope with his arms and legs and prayed that Caleb had gotten free. Then he thought of his love and he wondered where they would be reunited. Would she be at Morgana waiting for him? The dreaded image of her lifeless body on their bed came back to him and he shook his head, refusing that image.

Suddenly he heard Hades warning, "Don't look back." He wouldn't! He would wait until he was safely ashore...then he remembered the image of Shinsu closing the adamantine gate for the last time. With horror, Alex realized that he had looked back into Delos and suddenly a sick dread crept over him. *That didn't count!* That wasn't looking back—that was only because he was disoriented, he justified. But the thought refused to leave him.

After nearly an hour of working his way through the powerful currents and clinging to the rope during the ingress of water, Alex finally saw the reflection of a flash of lightning followed by earth-shattering thunder and briefly saw the white foam—he was at the entrance. The water had been warmed by the River Styx, preventing hypothermia.. Out in the sea, it would most certainly would be a problem.

He remembered swimming out with Valeria nearly a year before and the feeling of her alive and in his arms was nearly an overwhelming thought. He waited for the outflow of water and dove down near the bottom of the cave and prayed that he was still heading in the right direction—remembering that the waves could wash him to the center of the earth and he would never find his way out again. Without the night vision goggles that he had used the previous attempt, he had no way of knowing if he was headed in the right direction. He prayed that his friends, his family and his daughter had survived somehow. Then he wondered if all of this had been for nothing? If he didn't make it, no one in the family would come looking for him as they would assume he was permanently locked in the underworld.

His face broke the surface and he heard thunder as he gasped for air and then heard another wave and dove. *Don't look back!*

The rain began pounding down in large drops as the winds picked up. At least the lightning occasionally lit his surroundings. He surfaced and now finally free of the rough inbound currents, he searched for a sandy beach that he could safely swim to.

There was another flash of lightning and he saw something in the water. He stared and tried to get his eyes to focus and then he heard the voice.

"Alex!"

It was Caleb. Alex swam the short distance and found the boy clinging to a log. He grabbed at the log and tried to avoid touching Caleb. But the rough current made it impossible and soon he rammed into Caleb and noticed—*there was no electrical shock!*

"Caleb!" Alex cried in desperation. "Did you see Genni?"

"Genni is safe. I made sure Camille got out before I..."

Alex's eyes narrowed, "Caleb did you," He sucked in part of a wave and coughed it out. "Did you...make that wave?"

"Umm, yeah," he said a bit sheepishly. "I told you that you didn't have to worry! I've been waiting here a long time for you! Everyone else just rode it out."

"Everyone else?"

"Yeah."

"Oh," Alex said unable to comprehend the events of the last few hours as he kicked his legs heading toward a sandy shore.

"Caleb?" It was time to ask the question and, although he was terrified to hear the answer, he had to know. He gulped back a tear. "Caleb...do you know? Did she...did Val..." He couldn't finish the question.

Lightning struck and the rain began to pound even harder. In an instant, Alex found himself pleading, *"Do you know? Did she make it?"* Sobs began to overtake him.

Suddenly, there was a light moving toward them from the sky and Alex thought he heard the sound of an engine. But with the loud whistle of the wind and the crashing of waves, he thought it might be his imagination. A moment later, he heard a splash in the water near them. Then he saw the diver.

"They said you speak English," The diver said.

"Yes," Alex said, confused.

"Good! I am going to take the boy up first and then we'll get you."

Alex tried to think of how to avoid killing this diver with Caleb's touch. But then the diver wrapped a harness around Caleb without any zapping sound or cries of pain, and in a moment, the boy was being pulled up into the helicopter.

"You're next!" the diver said as the cable lowered for Alex.

A few minutes later, Alex was airlifted out of the water. He wondered what turn of fate had him being rescued from the sea during a storm such as this. As he was hoisted up into the helicopter, a hand reached out for him and Alex took it and was pulled into the darkness inside the helicopter. He busied himself with unfastening the harness when the lightning flashed and he saw the person responsible for the rescue—*it was Paolo!*

As if out of his control, Alex wrapped his arms around Paolo and held him with relief, as if he was his long-lost brother. After some time, Alex shouted over the engines, "How?"

Paolo shrugged and yelled, "Evidently, I am an acquired taste."

Alex wiped the water from his face and then stared at Paolo in disbelief.

"Cerberus and I played when I was a child." When Alex's eyes widened, Paolo shrugged. "All boys should have a pet, no?"

After a few minutes of taking in the situation, Alex said, "I don't know about Val..." Then he noticed that they were heading northwest toward Venice. The rain and the wind shoved the chopper around until a few hours later they touched down on the front lawn of the main house at Morgana.

Alex shed the blanket, jumped from the helicopter, and ran through the marshy grass to the trail that led to the cottage. The rain poured down on him as he arrived at the ginkgo tree. He felt the trembling deep within him as he realized that the light was on in the master bedroom. He rounded the porch and flew up the steps. He couldn't bring himself to look in the bedroom window. Instead, he took three breaths and then pushed open the large wooden door—praying he would see her.

The great room was empty. He brushed his fingers through his soaked hair as he wiped the rain from his face.

"Val?" He closed his eyes willing her to answer.

There was no response. As his hope began to fade, he glanced around the great room, searching for signs of her presence. Then he worried—what if she had floated out of Delos? What if she was stuck behind the adamantine gate, now barred forever? What if Hades took her because of his error of looking back at Shinsu?

With a clap of thunder, he willed those fears away and moved toward the bedroom. He couldn't bear it if she was still there...dead. Bracing himself on the doorframe, he felt his heart pounding as he stepped around the corner and forced himself to look.

His breath caught when he saw that it was empty. Alex searched the house and then recalled the hole in the ground that Homer had dug, and a sick panic rose within him. He couldn't bear to think of that. No! She was alive...she was up at the main house or perhaps she had gone somewhere else because of the storm. He walked back out onto the porch and stood there trembling. *Where was she?* Suddenly, the pain of the past few days overtook him and he fought back the tears that threatened to cloud his vision. He couldn't believe she was gone from him forever. He couldn't think that! His feet began to move on their own cognizance down the road and toward the family plot. With each step, his hope plummeted further.

Within minutes, he found that he was running. His speed increased as he passed the new homes for the oracles and beyond Mani's house and then he slowed unable to take in the reality.

The hole had been filled and he sunk to his knees and clawed at the soil as he cried, "Oh, Val..."

He lay there for minutes and then he heard a voice, as if from a dream, "Alex!"

Turning his head slowly, willing it to be real, he saw her, still in the white gown as she had been on Charon's boat. His heart pounded—needing her to be real. She took a step to him but his limbs seemed frozen...afraid that he might discover that she was still only an apparition. He noticed that she was soaked and then he glanced to her feet and saw she was barefoot.

She wiped the rain from her face. "I woke and you weren't there...so I—"

Alex was on his feet. But he couldn't bring himself to reach for her—terrified that the very real vision of her would disappear. He swallowed.

"Are you...real?" he choked. Tears filled her eyes and she nodded.

He released a short sob and still unconvinced he asked, "This isn't a dream?"

She took a step toward him and took his hand in hers. She lifted it to her lips and caressed his hand. "Feel my breath?" she asked.

Alex nodded, feeling mesmerized by her touch, but still too uncertain to respond. Then she took his hand to her heart that was pounding as heavily as his.

"Feel my heart?" she asked?

He stood in stunned silence as the tears flooded his eyes and then he asked, "Are you..."

Valeria smiled softly"My love," she said, smiling softly, "we are as we once were, immortal symbolons with our eternity ahead of us."

Alex pulled her into his arms and brought his mouth down on hers with an avalanche of joy and love and passion.

CHAPTER 35

It was spring and the dogwoods and tulips were in bloom. Spring at Morgana was as beautiful as Valeria had always dreamed it would be. The family pictures hung on the walls and now there were more...considerably more. Alex had replaced most of her belongings, including her china, from museums and other collections.

But the most beautiful thing in the world was in front of her...it was her beloved husband—her symbolon—playing with their daughter, Genesis. Alex released his beautiful musical laughter, followed by Genni's exquisite childlike giggles and Valeria decided that the combination had to be the most beautiful sound in the world.

Caleb and Tavish sat on the porch in front of a chessboard that they had been concentrating on for nearly an hour. Caleb reached down and brushed Charlie's floppy ears. Charlie leaned his head into Caleb's hand, grateful for the touch. When Genni cooed, Caleb rose and went to Alex. As he approached, Genni reached out her arms for Caleb.

"I guess she wants you!" Alex said as he patted Caleb's back. He handed Genni to the boy who had previously been barred from most human touch, and tears sprang to Valeria's eyes. "Use both hands, please," Alex warned and Caleb complied.

"Hi, Genni! I'm going to teach you how to play really cool video games when you get older. Some people call me Raiden. But you don't have to...you can just call me Caleb."

Paolo sat alone on the porch still brooding...he had been brooding for weeks. Valeria walked out the door and sat down next to him. He glanced over briefly and nodded.

"I owe you an apology...and a thank you, again," she said.

"Be happy and live a very long life. That is all the thanks I need," Paolo said with a wistful smile.

"I intend to." Glancing at Caleb who was making faces at Genni—who would then giggle—and Alex, who had picked up his copy of *Walden*, Valeria smiled, perfectly content. "I am so sorry about Daphne."

Paolo stared into the distance so that he could say the words without completely feeling them. "I had decided it was time to marry. She was not interested—I did not expect that. And now, she is gone." His eyes flashed intensely, and with a sigh, Valeria watched as Paolo continued to battle his emotions.

"She wanted to go," she said. Paolo shrugged and tightened his jaw. "Paolo, Daph wasn't for you."

The discomfort on his face was evident. "She was a good woman."

"She *is* a good woman...but you don't love her," Valeria said.

Paolo swallowed and said, "I will never love anyone as I have loved you." He glanced away and then, seeing Alex approaching, he instantly regretted his words.

She reached for his hand and squeezed it. "Yes, you will." He looked at her in pain and then turned his head. "You *will* find love." She leaned forward and he turned toward her. "You will love her far more than you ever believed possible." Paolo tried to look away but her intensity pulled him back in. "She's waiting for you."

"Do not tell me that..."

"She is lost...like I was...like you are. And when you see her, your life will be transformed, as mine has been. She is waiting for *you*, Paolo. Don't give up."

He closed his eyes and clenched his fists as Alex sat down next to Valeria.

Paolo rose, unable to meet their eyes, and mumbled, "I am going for a walk."

Watching Paolo's sudden exit, Alex said with a hint of concern. "Everything all right?"

"Paolo needed a bit of direction."

"What's new?" Alex said with a laugh, as he pulled his wife into his arms and kissed her temple.

EPILOGUE

Walking through Central Park, Valeria wrapped her camelhair coat tightly around her waist and then linked her arm around Alex's. He walked beside her, pushing the stroller where Genni was fast asleep. The leaves were brilliant shades of gold and reds.

Valeria no longer had "birthdays." She had stopped aging and healed immediately from any malady—as they had discovered one afternoon when she sliced her finger with a knife and the cut healed within seconds. But today, they were walking from Alex's birthday surprise for her—he had purchased the apartments on either side of Valeria's former brownstone on 95th and Columbus and converted it into a home large enough for the entire family.

The crispness in the air, the brilliantly covered trees, and the view of the architecture over the reservoir never failed to thrill Valeria. She brushed a gloved hand over Alex's. As they turned on to 5th Avenue, Rosendo was working his booth and selling his brother's paintings.

"Hey, Rosendo!" Alex said with a friendly wave. Rosendo was helping a slew of customers, but stopped and stared as he recognized Valeria from two years before.

"Holy..." he said, and then a customer demanded his attention, New York style, and he went back to taking her money.

A few blocks over, they turned into the restaurant with the green awning. Valeria picked up a sleepy-eyed Genni as Alex folded up the stroller.

Inside Sarabeth's, they went to the table in the middle of the crowded restaurant and joined Weege, Kenny, and their little boy, Morgan. Lars and Ava, Mani and Lita, Tavish, Paolo, and Caleb were all there, too, and there were still a few empty seats.

Valeria gave Alex her coat and then sat Genesis in the high chair. On the other side of the table, Kenny held Morgan, who seemed entranced with baby Genni.

"Whadaya say?" Kenny said, wearing plaid ill-fitting pants and a polka dot shirt.

Morgan raised his hands and said, "Hubabuba!"

Kenny shined with pride as he said, "He's a chip off the old block!"

Alex pulled the wool scarf from around his neck and handed that and their coats to Katie, the waitress who *still* couldn't seem to keep her hands off Alex.

Noticing this, and Valeria's near-irritation, Alex kissed his daughter's forehead, and then pulled his wife into his arms followed by a lingering kiss that made Valeria's knees weak and brought a blush to her cheeks. He pulled away a few inches and offered her a playful wink. Valeria noted that his timing had been spot on as the waitress— now with her jaw hanging open—stood directly in front of them with two pots of coffee.

"Sorry, just can't keep my hands off my wife!" Alex said, as the corners of his mouth turned up in the delicious smile that Valeria so loved.

With a smug grin, Valeria said, "Is that coffee for us?"

The waitress mumbled a polite, "Yes."

Valeria pointed to the pot and said, "Caffeinated, please—and make it a large one!"

Camille and Jonah entered and joined in on the festivities. Katie returned and took their orders and then disappeared into the kitchen.

Valeria noticed that Caleb suddenly looked more like a young man than the boy from before. He had sold the rights to *The Third Triumvirate* and was wealthy in his own right. She stared at him for a minute and realized that he had a few whiskers.

"Better teach Caleb how to shave," Valeria said to Alex, loudly enough for Caleb to hear.

Brushing his hand along his jaw, he nodded, and then lifted his arm in a victory fist. "Shaving! *Yes!*"

Glancing around the table, Valeria took Alex's hand as she thought about how deeply connected she was to this beautiful life.

Genni said, "Mama" and Valeria pulled her daughter from the high chair.

"Hello, beautiful girl!" Valeria said. Genni's face lit with a marvelous smile—which Valeria was certain came from Alex. Then Genni pressed her face to Valeria's leaving a slobbery kiss. Valeria laughed and then said, "I love you too! Are you hungry?"

"No," Genni responded, but nodded her head as her eyes got wide. Alex laughed his musical laugh and then reached for the diaper bag.

"I'll feed her," he said, pulling out a small mason jar of blended kale and strawberries from the diaper bag. Valeria put Genni back into her high chair. Genni pounded the tray excitedly waiting for her food.

Paolo was sitting between Tavish and Caleb when he glanced up, his eyes widened as they followed a young waitress across the room. She had jet-black hair pulled into a ponytail and the tiny body of a dancer. She gracefully moved from table to table with a sparkle in her eyes. Valeria recognized her immediately.

"Oh, my gosh! Weege, didn't that girl work for us?"

Before Weege could answer, Paolo was out of his seat and approaching the waitress.

"What do you need? Out of coffee?" the dark-haired waitress asked.

Paolo glanced at Valeria and she saw that he had the strangest look on his face—as if Cupid's arrow had finally struck. He leaned down and whispered in the girl's ear and the waitress jerked her head back in amused irritation.

"I've heard a lot of lines, buddy, but that one takes the cake! You have my tattoo do you?" she said, and then raised a delicate brow as her eyes sparkled with playful mischievousness. "So, is that your best attempt to hit on me?"

"No. No, I..." Paolo shook his head, feeling a bit confused by her response. Women didn't respond this way to him, except for Valeria. "Have we met before?"

"Nope," she said, and then took a deep breath. "And it takes way more than a pretty face and a cheesy line. But, look—I've got a job to do, so why don't you sit down, Romeo, and I'll bring out your breakfast while you think of something interesting to say—and preferably not a pick-up line!" Paolo just stared at her and she released a joyful giggle, shook her head, and veered back toward the kitchen.

Valeria glanced to see if her husband had caught the exchange, but he was completely absorbed in running airplanes filled with strawberry and kale into his daughter's open mouth.

When Paolo returned to the table, his face was lit with a silly grin. "Bellisima..." he muttered under his breath.

"I guess that's better than bella," Valeria joked.

Alex glanced at Paolo's face and his love-struck smile, and then to the back of the waitress as she headed into the kitchen. Then he said, "Sorry, beautiful. By that look, I would guess that Paolo's over his crush on you."

Suddenly, Weege said, "Nicky! That's her name!"

Valeria nodded. "That's right! She was a runner for me a few years ago. I really liked her." Valeria smiled playfully. "Paolo, trust me, Nicky will give you a run for your money!"

"Which one was she?" Alex asked.

"Right over there," Valeria said as she pointed to the corner. Suddenly, Alex's jaw dropped and the color drained from his face.

"What professor? A student? Is there something you want to tell me?" Valeria teased, as Genesis reached for her. "Just a minute, baby girl."

Valeria took a wet wipe and began to clean Genni's face and hands.

"Can I hold her now?" Caleb asked. When Valeria turned back, she noticed that Alex seemed frozen as he watched the waitress, Nicky, pour coffee and move from table to table.

"You know that I was just teasing you." When Alex didn't respond, she asked, "What is it?"

Nicky smiled pleasantly when she reached their table. "More coffee?"

Alex bit his lip. "It can't be," he said under his breath, and then he stood. *"Antonia!"*

"I'm sorry?" Nicky said, clearly confused. "Do I know you?"

Alex lowered his brows and continued to stare at the girl. "It's me...Alex."

Valeria's eyes widened and she smiled at Camille.

Nicky's bright blue and green eyes lit with humor. "Sorry, my name is Nicky," she said, and then she noticed Valeria. "*Val,* hi!" Nicky hugged Valeria warmly.

"Weege is here, too," Valeria said.

"Weege! Did Valeria ever find out that you were reading her journals?" Nicky teased. "I never told!" she laughed as Weege began to defend herself.

"She left 'em there! What was I supposed to do?"

All Valeria could do was laugh. She laughed a lot lately. She noticed Alex was still staring at Nicky. "So...Antonia? You don't mean...*your sister?*"

Alex raised his eyebrows and nodded. As their food arrived, Alex watched the lovesick expression that washed over Paolo's face and laughed at the irony that they might just be brothers again, after all. There were questions that would need to be answered. Had all the lost oracles been reincarnated? Could they recover their immortality as they had with Valeria's?

There would be some more explaining to do, to help Antonia remember, but with his symbolon, and Genni next to him, all he could feel was a deep joy that permeated every fiber of his being. Alex wrapped his arm around Valeria in contentment. His family had never felt so complete.

∞

PERSONAL MESSAGE FROM DELIA COLVIN

I hope you enjoyed The Last Oracle! As much as I enjoy writing, I enjoy hearing from readers. If you enjoyed this or any of my other books, it would mean the world to me if you would send me a short email to introduce yourself and say hi. I always personally respond to my readers.

I would also love to add you to my mailing list to receive notifications about future books, updates, and contests.

Please email me at deliajcolvin@gmail.com so I can personally thank you for trying my books.

Delia

Titles by Delia J. Colvin

THE SIBYLLINE TRILOGY

The Sibylline Oracle

The Symbolon

The Last Oracle

Firefly Nights

Acknowledgements

A huge thanks to my wonderful cheerleaders and loves: my very own symbolon, Randy Colvin who has enthusiastically marketed my books to anyone that even nearly looked like they might read this genre...or not. To my daughter Jennifer, whose love and support has always been phenomenal and to Jen and Dan for bringing into my life that beautiful little red-head, Aubrey.

A special thanks to the phenomenal friends that have made significant contributions, either through their support and/or for braving the rough drafts of the book: Al Hatman, Dave Khanoyan, Irene Enriquez, Joyce Wallace, Marv Halbakken Pamela Marta, Sherry Skym and the sisters of my heart, Dr. Mary Jo Palmer and Pauline Lagana.

The wonderful people who have shined their bright light of friendship on the dull days when nothing seemed right: Aly Camacho, Amanda Elliot, Anna Gregory, Annissa Blankinship, April Morales-Santiago, Arletta Stewart, Ashley Linton, Christy Huber, Cindy Roenigk, Dawn Gillespie, Dewitt Wilcox, Dianna Baker, Diggy Modesti, Donna Marshalek, Donna Krigler, Emily Kubat, Heather Bagwell, Jackie Hague, Jackie Sultan, Janet Campbell, Jean Gilbert, Jennifer Giuliany, Jenni Schillizzi, Jessica Carrera (no relation to Paolo—I did check, lol), Jo Anthony, Joanna Mylin (thanks for your beautiful Pinterest site), Joned, Josie Cruz, Joy Grams, Judy Winston, Karen Ang, Karin Manis, Katelynn Streets, Katherine Cheeks, Kathy Mccadden, Kelly Benigno, Kristin Genso, Krissy Wright, Kris Martin, Laura Delk, Laura Sitcler, Laurie Brown, Dr. Lesli Smith, Lilly Nolta, Linda Moore, Lisa Urueta, Lisette Brodey, Marling Hardman, Marsha Marker, Mary Kutsch, Mindi Blake, Misti Prewett, Natasha Deschatelets, Nicky Pray, Nicola Thompson, Rachel Caplinger, Rorie Doty, Rosanne Eskenazi, Saima Caverly, Sarah Pruitt, Shannon Johnson, Shannon Smith, Sharon Stover, Sharon Chalk, Sheila Blanco, Sherri Goodner, Shruti Rajagopal, Sherry Christenson, Tara Massey, Tara Clayton, Toni Prince, Trisha Rodriguez, Vanessa Branch and Virginia Hughes,

Also, very special friends and family; Carol Ostrander, Camille Baker, Weege Anderson, Mona DesJarlais, and the beautiful Maelyn DesJarlais.

In any endeavor you are only as good as the people that surround you. In that I have been fortunate to have stumbled upon these fantastic seasoned professionals. Many thanks to my wonderful editor, Colleen Albert, cover designer, Natasha Brown and Rachelle Ayala for her beautiful formatting. I'm also grateful for the extraordinary talents of Nick Coppola, Kyle Culver and Jaylan Aburto for the video book trailer for the trilogy. And last, but definitely not least, the amazing Melissa Foster—bestselling and award-winning author, queen of pay-it-forward and friend to authors around the world! I owe so very much to you for your wisdom, your never-ending generosity of spirit, and your down-to-earth and up-to-date understanding of the publishing world.

About the Author

DELIA J. COLVIN

Delia has lived all over the country from Fairbanks, AK, to Huntington Beach, CA to Knoxville, TN. but considers Danville, CA home. She currently resides in Prescott, Arizona, with her husband, Randy and their two Cavalier King Charles dogs.

She has worked as an Entrepreneur, Sales, Advertising, Air Traffic Control and as a Russian Interpreter.

For more information and contact information go to: www.DeliaColvin.Com or email DeliaColvin@gmail.com

Made in the USA
Charleston, SC
21 September 2013